D0211165

IN

OUR

MIDST

IN OUR MIDST

—a novel—

NANCY JENSEN

DZANC
BOOKS

DZANC BOOKS

5220 Dexter Ann Arbor Rd.
Ann Arbor, MI 48103
www.dzancbooks.org

This is a work of fiction. Names, characters, businesses, places, events, locales, and incidents are either the products of the author's imagination or used in a fictitious manner. Many of the historical details referenced are true, but the central characters are invented; any resemblance to real persons, living or dead, is coincidental and not the author's intent.

First US edition: April 2020
Interior design by Michelle Dotter
Cover design by Matthew Revert

Printed in the United States of America

10   9   8   7   6   5   4   3   2   1

For Mia, who remembered

and for Lisa, who believed

1941

I

NINA'S FAVORITE MOMENT WAS THE HUSH, just before she pushed through the swinging door from the kitchen into the dining room of the restaurant, holding out her best Dresden platter, filled to its gold-laced edges with thin slices of fruit-pocked *Christollen*, chocolate *Lebkuchen*, and hand-pressed *Springerle* in a dozen designs, fragrant with aniseed. Following close behind would be her husband Otto, bearing the large serving bowl brimming with *Pfeffernüsse*, crisp and brown—each spicy nugget no larger than a hazelnut—ready to dip them up with a silver ladle and pour them into their guests' cupped and eager hands. Next would come the boys, Kurt first, with two silver pitchers—one of hot strong coffee, the other of tea—and then Gerhard, carrying the porcelain chocolate pot, still the purest white and so abloom with flowers in pink, yellow, and blue that it seemed ever a promise of spring. Nina's mother had passed it on to her in 1925, a farewell gift when she, Otto, and the boys—Kurt a wide-eyed three and Gerhard just learning to walk—had left Koblenz for the Port of Hamburg, bound for America.

Today marked the tenth anniversary of the Aust Family Restaurant's St. Nikolas Day celebration, its hallmark the Austs' offering of ample holiday sweets for everyone, free of charge. Their little festival had begun in another troubled time—the lean winter of 1931—but this year, with so much anxious talk of Roosevelt's mounting arsenal, of Japanese emissaries and the Panama Canal, Nina had wanted to do more to welcome the people of Newman, their adopted home, as cherished friends. Working through the night and into the early hours of this morning, she had prepared St. Nikolas cookies, eight dozen of them—dark and buttery, formed one by one with the intricate wooden mold carved by her grandfather. The gingery saints waited now, standing in neat rows, in an immense shallow basket beside the restaurant door, ready for each guest to carry home.

Pressing the door open with her back, Nina twirled into the dining room, her platter held at a slight tilt for all to see. The hush exploded into a cheer. At the piano, seventeen-year-old Hugh Sloan, Gerhard's best friend, sounded the first notes of "Masters in This Hall," and his twin sister, Bess, sitting on the bench beside him, called out for all to sing. Not everyone knew the words—not until the chorus, when suddenly the crowd, even the children, rang out in a fellowship of goodwill, singing,

Nowell, nowell, nowell, nowell, nowell sing we loud!
God today hath poor folk raised and cast a-down the proud.

Hugh and Bess sang the verses, and with each rise of the refrain, the singing grew more joyous. All the while, Nina offered the platter, speaking close to each person's ear, saying, "Try this" and, "Oh, please…as many as you like," while her husband and sons poured out hot drinks all around.

Beyond the wide windows looking onto Elm Street glittered a bright, wet snowfall, and against the ashy light of midday, great fat flakes lent a cozy charm to the frame houses and brick storefronts, all neat but plain, in this southern Indiana town. To Nina's eyes, Newman would never be as beautiful as even the most ordinary places she knew in Germany, and certainly not as beautiful as Koblenz, with bounties of lovely warm stone, spires and cupolas, half-timbering and turrets—but then, one ought not to compare a town of more than a thousand years to one of less than a hundred.

When they left Koblenz, she and Otto had worn leather purses under their clothing, strapped tightly about their waists. Divided equally between the purses, as precaution against theft or separation, was the money given them at great sacrifice by Otto's family to buy farmland in Indiana. A ridiculous plan—conceived by Otto's father, Ernst, on the strength of a letter from a cousin who had emigrated thirty years before and had taught himself the trade.

"Franz learned, and so can you learn," Otto's father had said to him. "Look what our cousin has made of himself. Do as Franz tells you, and you will make your way faster still."

Otto had agreed, but only Nina could see he did so because he felt he had no choice.

In those years, after the war, the French army controlled everything in Koblenz, and there was almost no work—no profession a man could take up that would do more than feed his family, nothing that would allow him to claim his true place in the world according to his gifts. Each time Otto's father spoke of farming, in that romantic way of men who have soothed their eyes gazing at well-planted fields without ever having put a hand to the plough, Nina could see her husband's great strong shoulders sinking another degree.

They had not been false when they took the money—they had intended to buy the land—and through the first month they lived in Franz's house, they began to think they might make a difficult but satisfying life for themselves as farmers. Little Kurt waved his arms and roared with delight when he was lifted into the hay wagon by one of Franz's grown sons, and the rolling fields backed by forested hills sloping gradually toward the river reminded them a little of home. After many weeks, Franz drove them into Newman to speak to a lawyer about buying the land, and they stopped for a meal at a restaurant, one of only three in town, a charming place on a principal street, occupying the downstairs of a two-story family house. A house, Nina silently noted, that was for sale.

She said nothing that day, nor for many days—not until she was sure. Not until she had watched Otto carefully and understood that, while he was clever enough and strong enough and dedicated enough to make a good life for her and the boys out of this land, his spirit, in the doing, would wither and die.

When Nina looked at her husband now, a robust man of forty-five serving up handfuls of tiny cookies, directing his boys where chocolate or coffee was wanted, she saw him again in his youth, before the war, happily tapping a keg at *Königsbacher*, filling glass after glass perfectly to the rim with lovely golden beer, handing out each one with his sincere blessing. After the war, while he again filled the glasses of the brewery's surviving patrons, Otto's miraculous laugh and rollicking song could tear away the shroud woven out of their great and many losses.

Once again, she was glad she had spoken all those years ago, on a clear night with an orange moon, the mixed sugar and straw scent of the grain-corn harvest settling over them. Otto had stared past the barn and across the fields at that serene land and she thought perhaps he had begun to see it as Franz did, but when he turned to her in the light of that strange moon, he looked at her as a man must look at the one who wields the ax that splits the prison door.

Nothing about the years since had been easy, except for Otto's joy. After signing the final papers on the mortgage, he to set to work, spading up patches of grass in front of the house, reseeding the ground with lilies and wild poppies, painting over the greyed-white siding with blue-tinged green, suggestive of ancient forests.

An embittered Franz refused their invitation to the grand opening, and Otto's family in Germany answered their letters coolly, offering little more than acknowledgment of the small sums Nina wired each month in repayment of the loan. Not until the summer of 1933 was there even a tinge of warmth, when Otto's mother wrote with obvious relief that she and Ernst were moving to Hamburg with Otto's sister Elke and her young husband. *The new Chancellor has sworn to break the wicked Treaty*, she wrote, *to make Germany free and whole again*. In letters that followed, Nina's mother-in-law hinted they should return to Germany, as they had no land to hold them in America.

But they were held, Nina tried to explain in her replies, held by what they had built—their restaurant, their small sweet Germany, a community of spirit birthed in this new land. Otto was its heart, vibrant and bright, beating at the center. "What does it matter?" he would say. "Where there is good food and good welcome—and good music, too—there will be good friendship."

Indeed, today, there was good music, thanks to Hugh's sprightly playing, and the energetic singing it inspired had driven out, at least for this short time, all talk of war.

Nina had not really noticed the change as it was happening, but suddenly a few weeks ago—as one startles at realizing the long summer day has gone dark—she recognized the mood had turned. Her customers' voices, once open and warm, became clipped and nervous when she passed near. They spoke of war as a certainty, agreeing with each other that America's alignment with Britain and France was not only a duty, but a moral obligation, the only hope against Nazi tyranny—the same customers who, well into autumn, had sat at her tables cutting sausages, spreading butter thickly on bread, proclaiming that President Roosevelt would not let the Europeans trick the country into fighting another of their wars. Then last week, just as she had turned toward the kitchen to prepare the order for a family who had been coming to the restaurant for fifteen years, she heard the man, in a tone floating between earnestness and jest, quip to his wife and children, "There's another dime for Adolf."

And that humiliating day at the post office, more than a year ago, when she had felt so many of their neighbors' eyes turning coldly toward them. Upon receiving notice that they were required to register as aliens—aliens of an enemy nation—the four of them had stepped up to the window together to ask for the forms. The postmaster, Mr. Jackson, spoke angrily, as if they had played him a trick. "You're not citizens? You should have filed your papers years ago. Why haven't you?" Everyone in the post office, customers and clerks alike, stopped what they were doing and stared at the Austs, waiting for their answer.

What were they to say? It was no small matter to reject one's homeland.

In the summer before Kurt entered the senior high school, they had nearly decided to file first papers, but then Otto asked for a copy of the oath they would have to swear. On their back porch, the single overhead bulb drawing a thick flutter of moths, he had read it aloud to them, shocking them into silence with the vow to "absolutely and entirely renounce and abjure all allegiance and fidelity" to the country that had given them life, to respect no other bond but their bond to America.

After reading the paper again, slowly, as if this time the words might say something else, Otto said, "A man chooses his wife and pledges his faithfulness to her and to their children, but in doing so, he does not turn and spit on his father and say, 'You have no claim on me.' I cannot swear this oath."

In the restaurant now, having finished the first tune, the assembled company was singing "Joy to the World." Her platter nearly empty, Nina threaded back through the tables toward the kitchen, trying to avoid knocking into Otto and the boys, who were refilling cups a little too hurriedly, eager to set down their trays and gather at the piano, where they would fill the afternoon with German carols.

When she reached the kitchen door, Nina held the platter high and called out, "More to come, dear friends!"

Many laughed, raising their cups. Others whistled and lifted their hands.

But instead of applause—a great pounding, loud and urgent. A thunder of wood and rattling glass.

A rush of cold as the door flung open.

A shout: "The radio! Turn on the radio! War!"

In the doorway now stood a man stamping his feet, his black coat pocked with snow.

"You have a radio here? Turn it on!"

Behind him, the sidewalk had filled with people—where had they all come from?—and some of those on the sidewalk stepped into the street to flag down cars, motioning for the drivers to lower their windows. Others pushed into the restaurant, wedging past the man in the black coat, sitting down uninvited in the empty seats at the dining tables. Everyone turned toward Otto, who had drawn aside the curtain concealing the little nook where he did his bookkeeping. He was reaching up to the radio on the shelf above the desk.

"I'll do that," said the man in the black coat, his bulk and determination forcing Otto aside. Still more people came in, shoving each other, crowding at the windows and between the tables, standing wherever they could make space. Someone thought to close the door, and the chaos of chatter stopped on the instant.

For a few moments, it was quiet, as if the snow had fallen inside the restaurant, covering everything in deep drifts, absorbing even the sound of their breath.

Into this silence leapt a broadcaster's voice, clear but seeming to tremble in a cloud of static.

A dawn sky thick with rising suns. A harbor on fire. Untold dead.

When they had all heard the report twice through, the man in the black coat turned off the radio and left. Most of those who had come after him followed, not a word passing among them. Everyone else was still, frozen.

Out of the corner of her eye, Nina saw Hugh shift on the piano bench, arching his fingers. She waved, signaling *No,* but the warning was not needed. Hugh had not been on the point of playing again; he had moved only to close the lid over the keys.

When he did so, the piano uttered a low thrum, enough to break the silence. Now all the words came in whispers—whispers that prompted women to smooth their dresses and wipe their children's faces and men to reach for their billfolds for money they laid noiselessly on the tables. People began to leave as if by assigned turn, everyone else waiting while one family gathered coats and purses, hats and Bibles. Some of the men nodded as they passed Nina, who had moved to the front door to pick up the basket of St. Nikolas cookies. A few of the women gave brief, tight smiles before looking away.

Though Nina held the basket out to everyone, no one reached in to accept a gift—no one but a small boy who wrapped his fat fingers around the saint's waist, grinning up at Nina and saying, "Thank you, Mrs. Aust." At those words, his mother yanked the boy roughly onto the sidewalk, slapping the cookie out of his hand. The boy wailed as he was dragged away, mourning St. Nikolas, now shattered across the snow.

II

DOWNSTAIRS IN THE RESTAURANT, GERHARD was singing. In the low light of the vanity lamp, Nina picked up two more hairpins and shoved them into her tightly wound braid. She held her breath, straining to catch the soft chords of Hugh's playing. *Yes.*

Here at least was one fragment of their sweet world, untouched for the moment by yesterday's news—but only for the moment. Perhaps that was why the boys had gone on in their usual pattern. Every day, all the year round, even when it meant wrapping themselves in wool and oilskin against the weather, these two met at 5 a.m., walked together down to the river and back again. They would let themselves into the restaurant, and while Hugh warmed up his fingers playing scales, Gerhard made coffee in the kitchen, vocalizing as it brewed. While they drank their coffee, they would decide on the morning's repertoire, and then, for an hour or more, they would play and sing, stopping only when Bess tapped at the door, signaling it was time to go to school, or do the Saturday marketing, or, on Sundays, for Hugh to walk with her to church.

Behind Nina, Otto stirred in the bed and sat up. "What *Lied* does he sing?" he asked. "Can you hear?"

Nina stepped to the door and opened it, leaning out to listen. "'*Du bist die Ruh,*'" she said. *You are the calm, the restful peace*—the tone softly worshipful. It was a love song that might also have been a prayer, with words as easily addressed to a loving god as to a beloved girl, a pledge of gratitude to one who was at once his longing and the satisfaction of his longing. When her son sang this piece, Nina had to struggle against weeping, yearning to know to whom he was singing, imagining how he might bid farewell to his love if he were called to war.

In a voice that was pure, not bold and round like his father's, Gerhard's phrasing was driven by such intelligence of heart, as subtly and intricately layered as a tapestry, that even listeners who understood no German at all felt the poetry.

How different from Otto and Kurt, who both loved to sing, but who, even more, loved to be heard singing. With Hugh at the piano, they met with half a dozen others every Thursday evening just before closing time, inviting anyone who wished to linger over coffee to listen as they wandered from folk song to Wagnerian aria, visiting all that lay between those musical poles. They favored the drinking songs, meant to be sung by a chorus of men booming together, their arms thrown about one another's shoulders.

Though Gerhard cheerfully swung his voice in among the rest, his particular gift was lost in these performances, as was Hugh's. Hugh played the chorus songs with crisp confidence, but when it came to *Lieder*—Schubert or Brahms or Wolf—he played not so much *for* Gerhard as *with* Gerhard. It was something divine, the music they created together, as if these two had been the ones born twins, instead of Hugh and Bess.

Standing beside the bed, Otto stretched up his arms, as if to touch the ceiling, then brought them down, slow and controlled, to press his palms to the floor, stirring his blood to waken his body. "So," he said, stretching again to the ceiling. "Are we to open?"

Nina shrugged, shaking her head. They had talked it over late into the night and had come to no decision. Like Otto, she had felt they should not open, but not for the same reason. He had suggested that to do so might seem disrespectful—a flagrant pursuit of commerce at a difficult time, like selling cakes at a funeral—and when

Nina agreed, Otto went on: "I think many of the shops will close. But some people must come to their offices, and they will want their lunch—so perhaps for them, we should open."

"No," Nina said. "No one will want to miss hearing the president speak. Everyone will stay in to listen to their radios."

"We have a radio."

Nina had not known how to reply. They should not open the restaurant—of this, she felt certain—but she could not find a way to explain her reason to Otto.

There had been a moment yesterday—after everyone had listened to the news about Pearl Harbor and the strangers who had come in from the street had left—when the guests in the restaurant sat suspended, as if keeping still would teach them what to do next. At first, Nina had thought this was what every person in the dining room, as one, must be feeling.

Then, the thrum of the piano, changing all.

When the talk began, it came hesitatingly and hushed, slowly smoothing to a stream of whispers, almost soothing until Nina noticed the sharp glances—at her, at Otto, at Kurt and Gerhard. Furtive little darts, and all the time, *whisper whisper whisper*. Nina listened, trying to locate a thread she might follow toward understanding, but she could hear only the stream of sound, moving faster now, rhythmically. Like a chant—*Hitler, Hirohito, Hitler, Hirohito, Hirohito—Hitler Hirohito. Hitler. Hitler. Hitler.*

Like snakes, hissing.

She knew it had not actually happened, the hissing, but she had felt it then and felt it now: a relentless simmer under her skin. For all his depth of feeling, Otto was a man of logic, and she could think of no way to make him understand.

"Whether we open or not," Nina now said, "we need bread, so I am going down."

As Otto stretched again toward the ceiling, she stepped in front of him, and when his arms descended, he wrapped her in them.

She hugged him tightly about the waist, pressing her cheek into his breastbone, still bedazzled, after more than twenty-five years, at how perfectly her cheek fit there. "I'll make the bread and start a stew," Nina said, squeezing her husband with all her strength so that he would answer by holding her tighter still. "And then after the sun comes up, you can watch to see who opens their shops. The druggist must, I think, but maybe no one else."

Coming down the steps, Nina stepped squarely on each stair tread, not wanting to disrupt the boys' rhythm with the clack of her heels. She waited until the song ended before she opened the door that shielded the staircase from the restaurant dining room. To her surprise, Bess was there too, standing beside the piano, sipping from a teacup.

"Is it so late?" Nina lifted the edge of one of the window shades, suddenly alarmed that she might have overslept.

Bess shook her head. "Hugh said I could walk with them this morning."

"I like to see you in the morning," Nina said, kissing the girl's cheek. "All of you. My treasures."

"I haven't seen Kurt come down," Bess said. "He hasn't left yet?" Her skin pinked a little along her cheekbones.

Ah—there it was. Another happy clue. Over the last few months, Kurt's manner toward Bess had sweetened. Years ago, he'd made up a pet name for her, *Bess the Blest*, always speaking it teasingly, like the squawk of a jay. But lately when he said it, his tone had been more as the purr of a cat, and Nina had noticed Bess responding shyly, but in kind.

Almost from the moment when Gerhard returned from his first day of school, gleefully dragging Hugh by one hand and Bess by the other, Nina had hoped that, one day, one of her sons would settle his heart on Bess—for if Bess were to wed either of them, Nina would become to her *Mutti* instead of *Tante Nina*. A marriage would tie them all together, as true family.

"Kurt's just getting up." Nina said, taking Bess's hand. "Come. You will help me with the bread, yes?" She nodded to the boys. "And play us something cheerful." Hugh struck out bright notes in a skipping rhythm, beginning a silly tune their music master, Herr Vogel, had taught them years ago about a man boisterously proud of his enormous nose.

In the kitchen, Nina handed Bess the bowl of eggs and a whisk. "You can do the whites for the *Brötchen* and I will finish the rye loaves."

While Bess separated the eggs, Nina lit the oven and then carried the bowls with the sourdough sponges to the work table, quickly mixing in flour, salt, and caraway seed. "How is your mother?" she asked.

"All right, I think. I hardly see her. When she's not at work, she spends most of her time with Mr. Beale."

Nina had hoped for a less familiar answer, but she had not really expected it. She had never known Iris Sloan to spend more than a few months without a gentleman friend, perpetually anticipating a marriage proposal that never came.

The children's father had walked away the summer they were seven. While Iris was at work, he'd borrowed a car—he said he'd borrowed it—and had driven Hugh and Bess to a park a dozen miles outside of Newman. He'd packed a hamper with more food than they had ever seen—bread, ham, cheese, cold roast beef, fruit, and small cakes—and told them they were to have an all-day picnic. He set the hamper on the ground between them, telling them each to take a handle, and while they giggled and stumbled and worked to match their steps, he walked away. Left the car—which, along with the food, turned out to be stolen—and walked away.

To keep her children dressed and fed and in school, Iris had worked as a maid, a store clerk, a factory seamstress, and now as an aide in a convalescent home. Despite their long years of acquaintance, Iris would not accept directly from Nina's hand even the smallest gesture of help, no matter how much she needed it. Every gift passed through the children—a roasted chicken, a loaf of bread, a half-dozen potatoes, a length of cotton or a skein of wool—as well as Iris's simple notes of thanks. Mrs. Sloan was proud—and deservedly so, Nina thought—for despite all, she had brought up a pair of bright and healthy children in times so trying that many other women in her place would have surrendered their little ones to the county home. And no doubt she had been lonely—Nina could not imagine living without Otto any more than she could imagine living without her head or her heart—but year after year, Iris was drawn to flashy young men with film star charm, men who disappeared as quickly as they came, leaving her gloomy and snappish with the children. So Nina worried for Hugh and Bess, bruised along with their mother each time she fell.

Turning the dough onto the counter, Nina drove her fists in deeply—pushing, lifting, twisting. "And what do you think of him? Of Mr. Beale?" She knew he made his living as a jeweler—some years ago, she had taken Otto's watch to him, to replace a broken crystal. He seemed to her different from Iris's other men, but what could one tell about a person, really, from a single visit to his shop?

"He's all right, I guess." Bess whipped the egg whites in such a frenzy Nina had to press two fingers into the girl's wrist to calm her strokes.

"Gently," Nina said. "Whip in time—like a waltz." She opened the kitchen door and called out to Hugh, "Your sister needs a bit of Strauss, for the beating of eggs." He struck up "The Blue Danube" and Gerhard sang, "*Donau so blau, so schön und blau....*" Nina hummed along until Bess caught the tempo.

"Your mother is happy with this gentleman, I think. Is it so?"

Bess nodded.

"Do you believe he wants to marry her?"

"Maybe," said Bess. Her whipping slowed. "He's crazy about Hugh."

Nina drizzled water over the dough to make it easier to work. "Hugh only?"

"Oh, he's nice enough to me. Very kind, really. But it's a son he wants." She tilted the bowl so Nina could judge whether the egg whites were ready.

"Another minute," Nina said, and Bess started beating again. She watched the girl a moment longer before gently adding, "Darling, you must not persuade yourself there will be no room in his heart for you. Natural it is for a man to see his younger self in a boy—like a second future. If your Mr. Beale wanted only a wife, he could find a woman without children. And if he wanted only a son, he would bring a young man into his business and not bother to court your mother. I believe this is a man who wants a family. And he could dream for none finer than yours."

Bess shrugged.

"You must invite them here, your mother and Mr. Beale. For tonight, as my guests." She rapped the edge of the bowl so Bess would stop beating the eggs and look at her. "And I promise when Mr. Beale comes, I will make him see you are dearer than rubies. I will make them both see."

A smile nudged at Bess's cheeks. "I'll ask." She set aside the whipped whites and began separating more eggs into a clean bowl.

Nina had taught her that to make the best *Brötchen,* she must not whip more whites at one time than were needed for a single batch. From the beginning, Bess had been able to feel under her fingers when the dough was right for its purpose. With time and attention, and good instruction, she could become an excellent baker and a fine cook. "Come back after school," Nina said, "and I will teach you to make *Sauerbraten.* We start with how to choose the cut—you can go with me to the butcher. And the spices are different for beef than for pork. The meat must rest in the brine all week for the best flavor and tenderness, so this will be for our next Sunday lunch."

In the dining room, the music was pierced with a jeer, "Stop the Danube, brother!" Kurt had come down. Often he jokingly challenged Gerhard to a singing competition by bellowing out a phrase from one of his own favorites, but there was none of that this morning. Instead, Nina heard Otto's voice, too. He and Kurt seemed to be quarrelling.

Nina opened the kitchen door halfway and leaned out. "What's all this?"

Otto was holding a small American flag, like a child's toy—something one of the boys had gotten once at an Independence Day parade.

Kurt's jaw was tight with anger. "Everyone will think you're mocking." He looked at Nina, gesturing at the little flag. "He wants to put it up. Outside the door. It's ridiculous!"

Otto pressed the flag's small stick against the doorframe, judging its mounting height. "I can get a larger one. But this will do, I think, for today."

"*Vati*, it's not our place. Do you want to ask for trouble?" Kurt moved nearer the piano, as if he thought doing so would bring Gerhard and Hugh into a triangle of solidarity. The younger boys looked down at their music.

Otto stepped toward her. "Nina, what do you think?"

She believed Kurt was right—putting up the flag might bring trouble—but she would not say so in Kurt's hearing. She would not let her son believe he had gained the upper hand over his father. "Let me see it, please," she said, and Otto gave her the flag. She tested its weight, rubbed the cloth between her fingers, examined the slender dowel on which the flag had been fixed. "This is not sturdy enough for the weather, Otto. It would be a shame to spoil it. And I think there is nowhere we can hang it inside that will seem to have enough importance."

Otto took the flag back and rolled it onto its dowel. "Yes," he said. "I can get one meant for outdoors."

Kurt smacked his fist into his open palm and started to speak, but Nina checked him with a glance.

Otto went on. "I must get a mount for the pole at the hardware store. Surely someone there can tell me where I might buy a flag." He looked around at all of them, in turn—even Bess, who had come to stand beside Nina. Letting his gaze rest finally on Kurt, Otto said, "But your mother is right. This is not good weather. The wind is too harsh. In the spring, perhaps."

Nina held the door fully open and gestured for the men to come into the kitchen. "Now, all hands to work if you want your breakfast. Otto, you slice the meats. Kurt can do the cheese. Gerhard and Hugh—find what bread remains from yesterday and get out the mustard and the jams. I will make more coffee." She put her arm around Bess's waist. "And you will finish today's *Brötchen*."

Hugh and Gerhard slid past her to search for bread, but Kurt stopped his father with a hand on his shoulder. Otto turned to face him, and they stood looking at one another for a moment—eye to eye, now that Kurt had grown so tall.

"My son," Otto said, with three gentle taps on Kurt's cheek. "Time to eat."

III

WHEN SHE WAS ALONE, THE smell of bread baking made Nina miss her little boys. She glowed over the young men they had become, confident and clever, but she had cherished their smallness, the nuisance of their nearness, always getting in her way, upsetting the flour bin, tugging at her apron and asking, *How much longer, Mutti? How many more minutes for the bread?* And then other questions would come tumbling toward her, faster than a line of falling dominoes—questions about what made the oven so hot, how many stalks of wheat it took to make one loaf of bread, why their father was so much taller than she was, where they had been born, how many rivers there were in Germany and where the rivers went.

This morning at breakfast, the shadow of Otto and Kurt's quarrel had hung over everyone's talk as they sidestepped any mention of what had happened yesterday—in Hawaii and in the restaurant. Kurt's outburst about the flag had shown Nina that, like herself, he had felt a troubling shift in the way people looked at them, spoke to them—people they had known for years. And Otto had given way so easily that he too must have begun to realize they would now have to test each step with great care, until they were sure of where they stood. The four of them would have to face all this together—and soon—but over breakfast the boys had seemed to be asking for a temporary delay, choosing to talk of ordinary things: Gerhard confessed to procrastinating over a paper for his economics class, trying to persuade the more punctual Bess to help him. Kurt extolled the virtues of a car that had come into the shop for repair—one its owner now wanted to sell and that Kurt wanted Otto to buy.

By the time Gerhard left for school with Bess and Hugh, the darkness had lifted and their eyes were bright. Otto gathered a handful of letters to post and told Kurt he would walk with him to the repair shop to look at the car. When Kurt had gone back upstairs to get his overcoat, Otto said to Nina, "Don't worry, I am not going to buy this car." He pulled her to him, kissing the top of her head. "I will look at it first, for Kurt—then to the post office, and on the way back I'll stop in the drugstore for the newspaper."

"And a chat," Nina said. Otto was, after all, Otto.

He grinned like a child caught reading a book under the covers. "Perhaps a small one," he said. "I promise to be back in time to set the tables for lunch."

She wished now that she had asked him to wait to look at the car tomorrow—just to post the letters, get the newspaper, and come back straightaway. This morning, with everyone gone, the kitchen, the restaurant, the whole house had seemed to grow larger, into a great echoing hollow. She disliked the emptiness.

Nina switched on the radio, turning it up loud so she could hear it in the kitchen. There was a news report—Britain had declared war on Japan—and she was about to turn the radio off again when regular programming resumed, flinging dance music across the dining room.

She went back to the kitchen. Bess's *Brötchen* had risen nicely— four dozen perfect, plump rolls lined up on two baking trays. Taking the rye loaves from the oven, she changed the position of the racks and slid in the rolls. She checked the clock to mark down the time. In ten minutes, she would rotate the trays so the little breads would bake evenly.

Though the dance music played on, she thought she heard someone at the front door, trying the handle. It wasn't like Otto to forget his key. Nina came out of the kitchen and turned off the radio. The door rattled as someone outside tried to force the latch. Then—five pounding knocks.

The window shades hadn't been raised yet, so Nina called out, "Otto? Is that you?"

"Open the door." It was a man's voice, but not Otto's.

Nina raised the shade that covered the glass. There were three men outside—a police officer and two others, wearing winter coats and dark felt hats. All of them strangers.

She pointed to the notice of serving hours etched onto the glass and called out, "We open at eleven thirty."

One of the men said more forcefully, "Open the door."

The police officer knocked on the glass and pointed at the handle.

Nina unlocked the door, ready to repeat that the restaurant was not yet open, but all three pushed past her.

The officer said, "You are Mrs. Otto Aust? Nina Aust?"

She nodded. "What is wrong? My husband?"

"FBI." The man who had spoken turned back the lapel of his coat and showed her a badge. "You need to come with us."

"Where? What is this about? Is my husband all right? My sons?"

"Order of the President." The man snapped open a piece of paper, typed and signed, but he pulled it away again before she could see what was written there.

"What is it you want?" Nina said. "Who are you?"

"FBI," the man said again. He reached inside his coat and brought out a slim wallet. He held it open long enough only for her to catch a glimpse of a seal and a name: *Parks*.

"Let's go," Parks said.

Nina clasped her hands tightly together to still her trembling. "But why? I don't understand. My family."

The policeman stepped closer. "Your family is fine." He nodded toward the other men. "They just want to ask you a few questions."

"Certainly," Nina said to the officer. *Careful steps,* she said to herself. She pulled a chair out from the nearest dining table. "We can talk here. I can get you some coffee?"

Parks grasped her elbow. "You are coming with us."

Nina tried to shake away, but his grip was firm. "My husband will be back soon. Can we not wait for him? Or we can walk to the drugstore. If he's not there, he soon will be."

"Right now, Mrs. Aust."

"But I have bread in the oven. For the restaurant lunch. I must not let it burn."

Still holding tightly to her elbow, Parks said to his companion, "Go in there and turn off the oven." He pushed Nina toward the front door.

"May I leave a note for my husband? To tell him where I have gone?"

"No need. You'll be back soon."

The other man came out of the kitchen. There was flour on his coat sleeve.

The police officer blocked the door, and for an instant Nina thought he was going to stop the men from taking her. "Do you have a coat and handbag you want?" he asked.

Nina nodded. "Upstairs. In the flat."

"Let's go up, then." The officer took her arm.

"Please," she whispered when they reached the landing. "Can you not tell me what is the trouble? Can you persuade them at least to wait until my husband returns?"

He shook his head. "I'm sorry. Just get your things. We have to go now."

In another moment, they were on the sidewalk. Nina's hands shook so badly that twice she dropped her keys in the snow when she tried to lock the door. The second time, Parks snatched them up and turned the lock. He put the keys in his own pocket.

Two women coming down the sidewalk stopped, stared, and then quickly crossed the street.

A police car—a state police car—had been left running at the curb. The officer took the driver's seat. The other FBI man got in the backseat, and Parks directed Nina to get in the back as well, quickly shoving in beside her so she was pinned between them.

The policeman switched on the siren and pulled away from the restaurant with a sharp U-turn, pointing the car up Elm—in the direction Otto had walked. All along the street, people hurried out of shops to see what was going on. Wedged between the two men, Nina craned her neck, straining to glimpse Otto as they passed the drugstore, but the car was moving too fast for her to see anything clearly.

IV

ON AND ON THEY DROVE. Out of Newman, through the country where Franz's farm lay somewhere out of sight to the east, past signs naming towns Nina had only heard of, and then past other signs for towns she had never heard of. The land became flatter. The winter sun climbed higher. No one spoke. Mile by mile, the car seemed smaller, the air thicker, and the combination of heavy air and silence threatened to drive her mad. She longed for a glass of water, for a bit of air. Even to take a deep breath might relieve her, but she feared the effort would break the dam she was holding with all her strength against hysterical sobs.

In her mind she saw Otto coming back to the restaurant—not worried at first, thinking she had only stepped out for a moment. Unless he had heard the siren. And he must have heard the siren. How much time would pass before he realized something was terribly wrong? Many people had watched the men put her into the police car. Would they fear to get involved? Would one of them tell Otto what had happened? And then what would he do? He would think *police* meant the local police, and he would beg someone with a car to drive him across town to the station—but then what would happen when he did not find her there?

And Kurt and Gerhard? Already the hour must have passed for them to return home for lunch, expecting to eat a little stew and fresh bread before helping serve the customers. They would find the restaurant dark, the tables unset, trays of under-baked *Brötchen* gone cold in the oven, both their parents missing.

She could bear it no longer. She clutched at her throat to steady her words. "Please," she said. "Where are you taking me?"

On her left, Parks said, "Indianapolis."

So far! A hundred miles at least from Newman. All for a few questions—or so the officer had told her. "My husband," she said. "My children. How will they know where I have gone?"

"We'll get a message to your husband."

She could not know if Parks was speaking the truth. This was the same man who had said that she would be home again soon—but what was soon? His tone was angry and impatient. He would tolerate no more questions from her. She was helpless.

More silence. Many miles. More signs naming unfamiliar towns. After another great long while, a sign for Indianapolis.

And then everything moved quickly again, as it had in the restaurant. The police officer stopped the car abruptly at a curb before a tall building the color of damp sand. Parks jumped out of the car and pulled at Nina while the other FBI man shoved her from behind. She had barely set her feet on the sidewalk before the men took her arms again and hustled her through a door and down steps to a basement.

They took her into a brightly lit room where a stone-faced woman in a stone-colored dress sat behind a desk. Immediately, the woman rose and told Nina to stand against the back wall, facing front for a photograph and then to the side. From here, the woman led her to a high counter where she took her fingerprints, and then she pointed to a chair facing the desk and told Nina to sit and wait. Not to speak.

The woman sat again at the desk, moving some papers about until she found a small white card. On the card, she wrote a series of numbers in heavy black ink, and then she reached beneath the desk and brought up a wooden crate. She tossed the card into it and looked at Nina. "Okay, let's have it," she said. "Coat, handbag, jewelry."

Nina stood to take off her coat, glad to be free of its weight, and handed it over with her purse. The woman rolled the coat into a fat bundle, shoved it down in the crate, and laid the purse on top.

"That apron, too," the woman said, and Nina looked down, confused at seeing herself wrapped still in the blue floral print. She'd forgotten she had it on. Small puffs of flour rose from it when the woman dropped the apron into the crate.

"C'mon. Jewelry, too."

"I wear only my wedding ring," Nina said. "I would like to keep it on."

"Regulations." The woman held out her hand. "Everything will be kept safe." The way she said the words made it clear she did not mean for them to offer comfort.

The ring was tight. Her finger had grown plump around it. When she had tugged the ring free and watched the stone woman let it fall on top of the apron, Nina stared at the crate. Suddenly it seemed to contain everything that was left to her. These few small things, now thrown carelessly aside. A wail welled up inside her and she pressed both hands across her mouth, trying to hold back the cry.

"She's ready," the woman said, directing her words to the two FBI men—Parks and his companion—who stood in the doorway.

They each grabbed one of her arms and took her to another room, smaller and windowless. There was only one chair, and they dropped her onto it. The men stood in separate corners, facing her.

"Where were you born?" The question came from Parks. The other man, she noticed, had a notepad in his hand.

"In Germany," she said. "In Koblenz. On the Rhine."

"Date?"

"1898. The seventh day of March."

"You entered the United States in 1925, is that correct?"

"Yes."

"With your husband and two children?"

Nina nodded.

"Answer out loud," Parks said.

"Yes. With my husband and sons."

"Both your children were also born in Germany?"

"Yes."

"As was your husband?"

Yes, Yes, Yes she wanted to scream. Clearly he knew the answers to all the questions he was asking, so why was he asking? "Yes," she said. "My husband was born in Germany."

"Do you still have family living in Germany?"

"Yes."

"And you have sometimes sent them money?"

An icy spear plunged into her stomach, and then a great flame seemed to burst through her whole body. "Please," she said. "May I have a glass of water?"

"It's not very warm in here, Mrs. Aust. Are you feeling hot?"

"I am very thirsty," she said. The other man, she noticed, wrote even this down on his pad.

Parks went to the door and opened it. He spoke to someone, but she could not hear what he said. He returned to his corner. "Now," he pressed. "About the money?"

Someone had been watching her. These men from the FBI, or anyone else, might have guessed that she wrote letters to family in Germany—but how could Parks know about the money wired to Otto's father? Probably Otto was being watched as well—perhaps even the boys. But why? And for how long?

"My husband's family shared money so we could come to America," she said. "We have been paying it back from the time we opened our restaurant."

"The restaurant." Parks let the word hang in the air while he looked at his partner. Something passed between them, something they must have agreed upon in private, but Nina could not guess what.

"When you registered as aliens last year, both you and your husband wrote on your forms that the reason you had come to the United States was to buy farmland."

Nina imagined herself a mouse, sensing the spring of the trap. "That is what we wrote, yes."

Parks' face twitched in agitation. "Do you own a farm?"

"No."

"What did you do with the money?"

"We opened our restaurant."

"And why did you change your plans? Did you think you would be too isolated on a farm?"

Nina closed her eyes, trying to send herself back sixteen years to the harvest moon night on Franz's porch. This man Parks wanted to trick her into saying something she did not mean. Something that wasn't true. "The farm," Nina began, "was a plan made by my husband's father."

"So you just took the money? You lied."

Now Nina felt a rush of anger, and it made her braver. "We did not lie. We expected to buy the land. But after living on our cousin's farm for a time, we knew we could not make a success of it as he has done."

"But you thought you could make a success in a restaurant? Just like that?"

"Not just like that," she said. She told him about Otto's work at the brewery in Koblenz. "And my father," she went on, "was a butcher and sausage maker. Myself, I studied cookery for two years when I was a girl, from fourteen. Before the war." She looked down to her lap and added quietly, "Before the last war."

"You've paid it all off, then? The money you say you borrowed?"

"Not all," Nina said. "Not yet."

"But you stopped the payments? Why?"

"Stopped?"

"You heard me. The last wire of funds to Ernst Aust was May 1940—on the tenth. You say you still owe money, so why did you stop?"

"It had been a long while since we had heard from any of our family," Nina said. "Three times before we sent payments but did not receive acknowledgment. We could not know if the money had reached them, so we have been keeping it at the bank until we hear from them again."

"And how long is it since you've had a letter from Germany? Any letter?"

Nina did not answer. Why should she give him the satisfaction of parroting what he already knew?

"Nothing from family since September 1939—isn't that right? Not since your *Führer* started gobbling up Europe?"

"He is not my *Führer*," Nina said.

Silence stretched across the room. A minute. More.

Her interrogator paced, crossing close in front of her, nearly brushing her knees. She tucked her feet against the lower rail of the chair. For a moment Parks stopped and stood with his partner. Together they looked over the notes on the pad, exchanging a few whispered words.

At last, Parks returned to his corner. "We're nearly finished, Mrs. Aust. Just a few more questions." He leaned comfortably against the wall, settling in. "Your younger son is planning to return to Germany, isn't that right?"

Her anger vanished behind a new, wider fear. She looked at her hands, clenched into fists, and tried to will them to relax. "No," she said. "There are no plans."

"You are telling me your son has never expressed a wish to go to university in Germany?"

Nina looked up. Here was a new trap—but what was the way out? "I did not say that. No plans are in place."

"But your son does want to go to Germany to university?"

"Not university," Nina said. "The conservatory. To study music."

"Music?"

"My son is a gifted singer. A beautiful voice."

"There are music schools right here," Parks said. "Why go back to Germany? What can he learn there—what specifically—that he can't learn in the United States?"

A heaviness had settled in her chest, and she felt a little faint. She tried to draw a full breath, but could manage only shallow sips. "It is true that there are many fine schools of music in America." She felt foolish at being forced to pander this way. "My son wishes to make a study of *Lieder*—the art song."

"German music?"

"Classical music," Nina said.

"Classical German music."

This was not a question, so she did not respond.

"And your son has tried to persuade an American classmate to go to Germany with him for this—study?"

Hugh. The man must mean Hugh. What could he know of the boys' dreams? How could he know? And how could she straighten out the tangle he was making of innocent hopes? Parks was waiting for an answer, and Nina's mind could not race ahead fast enough to work out all he might be trying to imply—something wrong, something devious.

"My son has a friend," she said, choosing each word carefully. "He plays the piano very well. Since they were boys they have talked of becoming a duet. To make their living by performing *Lieder*." She looked at Parks directly, hoping he would try at least to see the truth in her eyes. "It is a dream only. There are no plans. His friend could not possibly pay the expense of study."

"But you could? You could pay for your son to go?"

"Not now, of course," she said. "Not now, because of the war. But yes. My husband and I have saved many years for our sons' advanced studies—whatever they might choose."

"You seem to have a great deal of money, Mrs. Aust. How is that?"

"I don't know what you mean. We do not have much money. We are not wealthy."

"You certainly seem to have a lot more than most people in New-man," he said. "Money for education. Money to start a business. Money to send to Germany. Money to go there. Where has all that money come from?"

What was he suggesting? "Our restaurant has been most success-ful," she said. "My husband is an intelligent man, very sensible about business. And we are frugal people."

"Right." Parks said the word under his breath, but the tone of contempt cracked like a slap. He paced again. "*Frugal people*," he said, turning the phrase into a curse. "So frugal. So successfully planted in our soil, this sweet little Germany of yours. Or was *birthed* the word you used? In a letter to your mother-in-law?" He snapped his fingers and his companion flipped his notepad to another page and held it out. Parks nodded once. "April 1938."

Parks drew a long breath. Then another. Nina could see he was pleased with himself, enjoying the way her anxiety filled in the air left by his great pauses. "Out of this frugality you claim—how much did you pay to Vogel?"

Vogel? Herr Vogel? "I do not understand the question," said Nina.

"You aren't going to pretend you don't know Wilhelm Vogel?"

"Of course I know him," Nina said. "I knew him. He is dead—two years last autumn. I do not understand your question of pay-ment. Never did I give Herr Vogel any money."

"For three years of work? Nothing?"

"No money. Only food. I engaged Herr Vogel to instruct my son in music. In exchange, he took as many meals in our restaurant as he liked."

"An average of five times a week," Parks said.

Nina stared at Parks, waiting to answer until he looked straight at her. "I made no accounting. Our exchange was based on friendship."

"So you admit Wilhelm Vogel was a personal friend."

"Of course he was a friend. Why should I say not?"

"And what about his friends? All those friends he sometimes brought to your restaurant for meetings? Friends of the New Germany? Or would you prefer I say *Amerikadeutscher Volksbund*? Fritz Kuhn's outfit. Vogel was the local representative."

Her heart pounded so fiercely she could feel it in her spine. She pressed her shoulder blades into the hard back of the chair, forcing herself to sit straighter. "What is the question you wish me to answer?"

"What was your involvement—your family's involvement—with the Bund?"

"None."

"You admit to a relationship with Vogel. You knew he was a member."

"I did not," Nina said. Her heart calmed a little. A trap sidestepped. "My husband and I do not require guests to declare their political beliefs before dining in our restaurant. Everyone who comes to enjoy a good meal is welcome there." *Even you*, she considered adding. "Always Herr Vogel paid the bill when he came with others. And we showed him the same respect we show to all our guests. We did not listen to his conversation."

Parks watched her, his eyes narrowed to needles, his mouth a vile smirk. "How many accounts in Germany?"

"Accounts?"

"Bank accounts. One for every Aust? How much money—in *Reichsmark*, if you like. Or dollars?"

"None," Nina said. "We left no money behind. We keep no bank account in Germany."

"How much in *Rückwanderer Marks*?"

"Resettlement marks?" Her heart speeded again. "We did not buy. Why should we?"

"We'll see," Parks said, taking a step out of his corner. He crossed to the corner where his partner stood holding the notepad. He crossed back. Seven times he did this—seven times there, seven times back, before he turned abruptly to face Nina. "Tell me about your other son. The eldest."

"Tell you what of him?" The words lodged in her throat, choking her. This would not stop. When Parks had asked a thousand questions, he would call for a replacement, who would ask the same thousand questions. If only she could have a glass of water—even just a swallow, but she dared not ask again.

"He's a mechanic, isn't he?"

"Not a qualified mechanic, no. He assists at an auto repair shop."

"Learning, then? To become a mechanic?"

"He learns, yes," Nina said. The knot in her throat thickened. "But not for his profession."

"Your son isn't satisfied to be a mechanic? Not good enough for him?" Parks could make any choice sound like a crime.

"It is honest work," she said. *Honest*? Was that the right word? Would Parks think she was condescending? She tried again. "It is respectable work. But it is not my son's wish for his life."

"So what is this wish of his?"

"Kurt will be an engineer. Already he has been accepted into university—Purdue University—for his study. He is to begin his course in September."

"Engineering? Likes to build things, does he? Likes to know how things work? Roads? Bridges? Dams? Or does he care more for the machinery?"

Nina said nothing.

Parks returned to his partner in the other corner, turning his back to her, and the two men conferred as before, in whispers. After a few moments, Parks twisted his head and said over his shoulder, "That will do for now, Mrs. Aust."

She started to stand.

"You stay right there," Parks said. "We may have other questions for you later."

How much later? Hours? Days? "I would like to telephone my husband," she said. "Please. To tell him I am all right."

Parks did not answer. He went to the door and opened it. The stone woman came in, a glass of water in her hand. Nina wanted to reach for the glass, to snatch it away and gulp down every drop, but she gripped the edges of the chair seat to gather her control.

The woman set the glass on the floor. "Do you need the toilet?"

Suddenly she did—so painfully she feared she could not even stand without wetting herself. She stood up slowly, stiffly. The woman laid a hand in the middle of her back and the weight and warmth of that hand felt oddly comforting. They walked down a short hallway. "It's this door on the right," the woman said, and as Nina grasped the knob, she turned to offer her thanks, but the woman reached past her, opened the door, and almost forced Nina inside, stepping in behind her and closing the door.

"Go ahead," the woman said.

The interrogation had been worse than the long, silent journey. The journey had been worse than the moments in the restaurant. But this was worse still. The room was tiny, with only a toilet and, on the facing wall, a sink with a filthy mirror—barely enough room for one human body, much less two. The woman turned her back to Nina, facing the sink—a mockery of even the illusion of privacy. Nina had no choice. She was forced to pull up her dress, to wrestle her pants down from beneath her girdle, and to squat over the toilet—observed by a stranger who watched every moment of her humiliation reflected in smeared glass.

V

A FTER NINA HAD RIGHTED HER clothing and washed her
hands, the woman returned her to the interrogation room
and locked her in alone with her single glass of water.

Hours passed—or at least what seemed like hours, for she had
lost all sense of time. There was nothing to look at, nothing to
count—not even separate bricks in a wall, only smooth plaster all
around and plain concrete under her feet. Nothing to drive out
the sights and sounds, like a film screening inside her head, of her
arrest, of being crushed in the car between Parks and his silent
partner, of Parks' irritable and haphazard questions and her fearful
answers.

Sometimes she tried to edit the film—she refused to open the
restaurant door, insisting on waiting for Otto; she fought against being put into the police car, shouting for help, screaming out that
she was being kidnapped; she sat stoically, refusing to answer any
of Parks' questions—but no matter how she diverted the path, she
could never find her way to a different outcome. This was what had
happened. She could not imagine what might come next, and so she
could not prepare herself to meet it.

The door opened. The stone woman was there, holding the crate
with Nina's things. The woman set the crate on the chair. "You need
to verify that everything is here," she said. "Then get your coat on."

"I'm going home?" Tears of relief streamed down her face.

"Oh, no," the woman said. "They're taking you over to the Home of the Good Shepherd."

Nina took her apron from the crate and put it on. She picked up her purse and set it on the floor beside the chair, then dug down into the folds of her coat to find her wedding ring. Not caring if the stone woman thought her foolish, she held the ring to her lips and kissed it, because she could not kiss Otto. "Someone will notify my husband?" With a tiny push, the ring slipped securely into place, and she felt less frightened, less alone. "So he knows where to find me?"

"I don't know anything about that," the woman said. "Just check your things."

Nina picked up her purse, opened it, looked inside. Everything was there—even her keys.

She shook out her coat and put it on. "What is this Good Shepherd house?" she asked, fastening the buttons.

"Run by nuns," the woman said crisply, "for wayward girls, thieves, prostitutes."

"Why am I going there?"

The woman sneered. "It was either there or the city jail—and they're not set up to hold you Nazis. Not the women."

So this is what they thought.

How long did it take, Nina wondered, for a person to stop hoping for nonsense to be turned into sense? How long before one stopped asking for explanations and simply responded like a radio to its dial? "Who calls me Nazi? Who says this?"

"You have all your belongings? Everything you came in with?"

Nina met the woman's glare of hatred with one of her own. "I have them," she said.

"Let's go, then."

Two men were waiting for her in the bright room where she had been fingerprinted. A police officer and a man wearing an overcoat and a hat—like Parks, but he was not Parks. Another FBI man, most likely, though he did not bother to identify himself.

This time, the woman held Nina's arm to lead her outside while the men followed. Up the steps, out the door, and into the night they went. More snow had fallen. The blaze of the streetlights against the black sky scalded Nina's eyes, and she felt exposed, as if thousands watched her being hurried to a police car and pushed into the backseat.

The officer got behind the wheel and the man in the coat took the passenger side, leaving her alone in the back. "I am not a Nazi," she said, loudly and firmly, but neither of the men responded.

The drive wasn't long. In a few minutes, they had moved out of what Nina supposed must be the city center, away from the streetlamps and traffic signals, onto residential streets, the houses made visible only by the occasional rectangle of light suggesting a window beyond which someone might be writing a letter or sewing on a button or telling stories to a child.

They stopped before a three-story house from which no lights shone. Once again, Nina was pulled roughly from the car, trapped between a pair of strangers who squeezed her arms painfully. She had forgotten until now that she was wearing her indoor shoes. The walk had not yet been cleared, and with every step, snow swept over her feet in small drifts.

When they reached the entry porch, the door swung open. An elderly nun in a white habit appeared—immaculately white, it seemed, in the glow of her candle. She moved aside to let them pass.

Another nun, considerably younger, also holding a candle, stood a little beyond the door, beside a staircase. She held out her hand to Nina—offering, beckoning, but not demanding—and when Nina grasped it, the men's hands fell away from her like the angel-loosed chains from Saint Peter's wrists. Behind her, the two men spoke in low voices to the nun who had opened the door, but Nina made no effort to hear what they said. The hand that held hers now was firm with kindness, and she was willing to follow wherever this sister might lead her.

They moved through a sitting room into a hallway, passing several closed doors, and came to a kitchen where two oil lamps had been left burning. In the center, three tables of varying shape had been pushed together to create a single long one. A gas cook stove sat catty-corner to a sink, both of which seemed much too small to manage the kitchen tasks for the number of people implied by the chairs around the makeshift dining table. To the right of the sink stood a glass-fronted dish cupboard, next to it a few open shelves that appeared to serve as an ill-stocked pantry, and beside the shelves, a telephone fixed to the wall. On the other side of the kitchen, opposite the cupboard—a painful flash of home in the form of an oak desk like the one in Otto's little office, its surface so covered with neat stacks of letters and bills and account books that the top could never be rolled down. Otto often worked at his desk late at night, preferring the golden arc of light thrown by the oil lamp to the blinding flood from the electric bulb.

Still holding Nina's hand, the nun pulled out one of the chairs and invited her to sit. "I don't suppose they've given you anything to eat?"

Nina shook her head. "Only a glass of water. Quite long ago."

The nun brought a glass and a pitcher to the table. She poured out water nearly to the rim and when Nina had gulped it down, the nun filled the glass again and set the pitcher beside it. "We have a bit of soup left from our dinner," said the nun. "It's not much, I'm afraid, but when we got the call that you were coming, Mother Philomena asked me to put it back on the stove. That was she who opened the door. I am Sister St. John." The sister went to the stove and poured the contents of an enamel saucepan into a bowl and then brought the bowl and a plate of sliced bread to the table. She sat down across from Nina. "There are two other sisters here—Sister Mary Joseph and Sister Visitation. And five other women staying with us at present."

The soup was a watery brown broth with a few shavings of cabbage and small chunks of gristly meat, and the bread was pale and dense, with floury lines running through it. "I am very grateful, Sister." Nina dipped the edge of the bread into the broth. She wondered if Otto had been able to save Bess's *Brötchen*, getting it back into the oven before it cooled and fell. "Will you tell me, what is this place? Is it a prison?"

"Not a prison, no," said Sister St. John. "A mission."

"Then I am free to go?"

The sister picked up the pitcher again and refilled Nina's glass. "I'm sorry," she said. "You are not."

"It is a prison, then. With nuns for jailers." She laid her spoon on the table and pushed away the bowl of soup, still nearly full. "I am not a Nazi."

Sister St. John nudged the bowl back toward her. "Would you like to tell me who you are? While you eat?"

Nina's head throbbed with the fear and fury, confusion and grief that had all gathered there. Was the sister really only Parks' replacement, someone seemingly kind, the better to trick her and wear her down? And would there be others after this, whose shared purpose was to split her into fragments, collecting and rearranging only the pieces that suited them?

"I am Aust," she said. "Mrs. Otto Aust. I have lived in the town of Newman, with my husband and sons, since 1925. We own a restaurant."

Sister St. John leaned across the table. "Your family—do they know where you are?"

The sobs she been holding back since morning burst forth.

The sister rose from her chair. "Do you have a telephone at home?" She knelt beside Nina and, very gently, took her hand, turned up her palm, and laid a handkerchief in it.

"Yes," Nina said, the word itself a sob. "In the restaurant, we have a telephone."

"I'll ask Mother if we may call your husband. It's very expensive—but I think she will allow a few minutes." Sister St. John went to the desk and brought back a pencil and a used envelope. The letter had been removed and the envelope had been opened carefully along its seams to expose the clean writing surface inside. "Only Mother may place a call," she said, tearing free a thin strip from the envelope, "so write down the number here."

Nina pressed at her eyes with the handkerchief, already wet through. "My husband is Otto," she said. She wrote his name beside the number. "My sons are Kurt and Gerhard." She looked into the sister's eyes as she held out the slip of paper. "And I am Nina."

"Finish your soup," said Sister St. John. "I'll go ask Mother about the call."

The soup had gone cold. An oily film floated across the surface, but Nina ate it as if it were the food of the gods, tipping the bowl to let the last drops flow into her spoon. To speak to Otto, if only for a moment—for now, that would be enough. She could tell him nothing about why she had been taken away, why she had been questioned, why she was here now with the sisters. But at least he would know where she was, and if Sister St. John would give him the address, he could find a way to come for her—tomorrow or the day after.

Sister St. John returned. "Mother will be here in a moment." She picked up the empty bowl and said, "That was the last of the soup, but would you like more bread?" Without waiting for Nina's answer, she brought the loaf to the table and cut two fat slices. She passed the bread to Nina, a hint of girlish mischief in her smile. "So, you and your husband have a restaurant? Perhaps God has sent you to help us with our cooking?"

For the first time since early this morning—when she was still so far from here, in her own kitchen—Nina smiled. "I would like to help." She unbuttoned her coat and held it open. "Look—already I am wearing my apron."

Sister St. John laughed—a bright, bubbling laugh—and she clutched Nina's hands as if they were old friends, and this made Nina laugh, too. The knots of her fear and outrage loosened.

They were still laughing when Mother Philomena came in with her candle, her head bent forward, as if heavily burdened by the short black veil over her white habit. She snuffed the candle, set it on the table, and took the chair next to Sister St. John. "Mrs. Aust, do you understand why you have been brought here?"

"I understand nothing," Nina said. "So many times I have asked, but no one will answer. Please, Mother, do you know?"

"Not in any particulars," the old nun said. "The man from the government, the one who brought you here, showed me a warrant. It identifies you by name and address and describes you as an alien enemy, considered to be dangerous. Potentially dangerous. The warrant orders your confinement."

"Confinement? Here? For how long?"

"Until there is another order."

"But how is there to be such an order? How can I make possible such an order? To whom must I speak?"

"I wish I could answer your questions, Mrs. Aust, but I can't."

Nina felt as if an iron yoke had been dropped over her head, onto her shoulders, and it was all she could do to hold herself upright in the chair. "I understand," she said. "You cannot tell me what you yourself have not been told."

She looked toward the cluttered desk against the wall, and then to the opposite wall, to the pantry shelves, the telephone. At least there was still that hope of comfort, offered by Sister St. John. A few moments with Otto's voice. "May I telephone my husband now? I know it can be a short talk only."

She looked to the young nun for a supporting word, but Sister St. John turned her eyes toward the floor.

"Mother?" Nina said. "It is very late, I know—but my Otto, he will be waiting beside the telephone, or if he has had to go out, one of my sons will be there in his place."

"I myself can call your husband, Mrs. Aust," said Mother Philomena, "to tell him you are here, that you're safe. But you cannot be allowed to speak to him. This is one of the many restrictions we have no choice but to observe while you are with us." Her tone was indeed like a mother's—sad at what she must say, but immovable.

"May he come here? To see me?"

"I'm sorry, no. Not at this time. He can apply to the FBI for permission to visit—and I will tell him when I call—but it's a long process and the request may be denied. A guard is required, you see, and no provision has been made for one—not here. You can write and receive letters, but they all have to pass through a censor. I am told the delay will be shorter if you both write in English—but still, it will take weeks for each letter, and any one of them can be stopped entirely."

Nina rubbed at her eyes, aching and burning with dryness, her tears spent. Otto—and her boys, too—would not rest until they had corrected this terrible mistake. They would find out to whom they must speak and what they must do to prove that she was an ordinary woman, no danger to anyone. Until then, she would have to wait.

She wanted to show Mother Philomena that she would give no trouble—that seemed important, and perhaps it would be to her favor, if someone questioned the nuns about her, so she said, "Sister St. John has asked me to help with the cooking. I would like to begin in the morning, with the bread."

Mother Philomena closed her eyes and bowed her head, as if in prayer. When she opened her eyes again, she looked at Nina. "Your offer is very kind—but I'm afraid you won't be allowed to mix with the other women here." She stood up. "You'll be confined to your room. Sister St. John will show you there now. The third floor." The younger nun came around the table to Nina's chair and reached again for her hand.

Mother Philomena went on, "You're free to talk with any of the sisters—one of us will bring your meals—but we are not often at leisure."

She would break under this weight. Even the sturdiness of Sister St. John's arm, now wound about her waist, lifting her, guiding her out of the kitchen and toward the stairs, could not shore her up.

Somewhere, in an office in a city she would likely never see, some man who had never met her had signed a paper ordering her to be snatched from her life, deciding she was too corrupt even to teach women of the streets how to bake bread.

VI

O N THE SECOND DAY, NINA slept, rousing only twice to walk with Sister St. John down one flight of steps to the shared washroom while the other women were having their meals. Both times, the sister waited for her outside the closed door.

On the third day, Nina couldn't sleep for hunger, so she forced herself to eat the food brought to her on trays—thin oatmeal; some soup beans and tinned fruit; a gluey, tasteless stew.

On the fourth day, the nun called Sister Visitation brought her a housedress, faded and gone at the seams, but clean. The sister apologized for having no fresh underclothing to offer, but she told Nina she could take half an hour to bathe and wash out her things. Anticipating that Nina might be cold while waiting for her clothes to dry, Sister Visitation had brought her a sweater and an extra blanket, also old and worn.

Though it felt good to be scrubbed clean, the cold water had chilled her deeply. Back in her room, she pulled on the sweater, wrapped herself in the blanket, and set the little wooden chair by the window so she could sit on it while resting her feet on the cot, tucking her bare feet beneath the bedclothes. Straining against the silence, she listened for sounds of women working on the floors below, women permitted to be useful. She stared out the window at the roof of a shed and with her fingernail she etched flowers in the frost on the inside glass.

On the fifth day, Sister St. John brought her a jigsaw puzzle she'd found in a donation box, and she stayed for an hour before dinner, urging Nina to talk while they worked the puzzle together. Nina said little. It was not that she distrusted Sister St. John, but she feared the nuns might be forced to repeat everything she said, and Parks had shown her how easily the most innocent details could be twisted into evidence of guilt—though guilt of what, she still could not comprehend.

"Your husband calls every day," said the sister. "Sometimes three and four times. Mother Philomena asked me to tell you he will be seeing a lawyer tomorrow morning—an appointment arranged by a friend."

"Did he say what friend?"

"The name was Beale, I think."

It took a moment for Nina to remember that Mr. Beale was the jeweler, the man who had recently begun keeping company with Bess and Hugh's mother, Iris. The children must have asked for his help. Accepting this aid would be difficult for Otto, for he was a proud man, but she knew, too, that he loved her far more than his pride.

She wanted to ask Sister St. John if Otto had said anything of the restaurant, of how they were managing without her—besides *Brötchen*, Bess could bake a simple farmer's bread; Kurt could stir up a passable onion stew, and his cabbage rolls and meatballs were nearly as good as her own; Gerhard and Hugh would set, serve, and clear the tables, entertaining in between—but because the sister had offered no word about any of this, Nina felt afraid to speak. If the news had been good, the sister would have shared it.

The next day and the day after that, Sister St. John did not come. Instead, Sister Mary Joseph and Sister Visitation brought her meals. She asked if her husband had called again, if he had said anything of his visit with the lawyer, but both of them told her they knew nothing of any phone calls.

After everyone else in the house had gone to bed, Sister Visitation came one last time to walk with her to the washroom. When they reached the second floor, Nina stopped before the washroom door and looked down the darkened hallway, hoping to catch a glimpse of her friend. "Might Sister St. John bring the breakfast tray tomorrow?" she asked.

"Mother makes our daily assignments," replied Sister Visitation.

Nina lay awake all night, sifting her memory for every word that had passed between her and the sisters, searching for any clue that might explain why Mother Philomena was punishing her this way, separating her from the only person here whose eyes revealed a generous heart. A moment later, she would chide herself for unreasoning suspicion. Why imagine this was punishment at all? Perhaps Sister St. John's absence came of nothing more than an ordinary rotation of duties. Or, what if this had nothing whatever to do with the sisters themselves, but instead was something Parks and his lot had ordered Mother Philomena to do?

To know nothing. To be able to learn nothing. To be deprived even of the smallest assurance—this was what torture meant. She never doubted Otto, but at times she could not help doubting that he had ever been told where she was. How could she be sure that Mother Philomena had telephoned him that first night? And if she hadn't, then all the calls Otto was said to have made, the appointment with the lawyer, were only invention. Still—had not Sister St. John particularly named Mr. Beale? Or was her memory of that but a dream?

On the eighth day, the fifteenth of December, Nina took the puzzle she and Sister St. John had worked together, broke it into pieces, and put it together again.

She tried to remember, one by one, all the *Lieder* Gerhard sang. If she could do this, and then imagine herself in the dining room with him, seated two tables away from the piano for the best sound, she could fill one idle day to its corners, but when finally she was able to hear the opening notes of the first piece, truly hear them, the dream was broken by her own agonized cry. What if, without knowing it, the last time had already come, and she would never again be saddened or cheered, wounded or healed, by her son's perfect voice?

On the eleventh day, one week before Christmas, during the tiresome hours that stretched between the arrival of her lunch and dinner trays, there came a brisk knock followed by Sister St. John's voice: "Mrs. Aust, come quickly!"

Before Nina had even risen from her chair, Sister St. John was inside the room. "I don't know what's happening exactly," said the sister, reaching into the narrow closet. "Two police officers have come for you."

Dozens of questions crowded into Nina's mouth, but tears overtook them. She had no strength to stop this flood of fear, and she was ashamed of her weakness.

"Better put on your coat," said Sister St. John, holding it open for her.

Nina slid her arms into the sleeves and fastened the top button. When she turned to pick up her purse, she was surprised by the glint of tears in the sister's eyes. A small swell of something Nina recognized as herself filled her chest, enough to give her the power to take her friend's hands in her own and say, "Thank you, Sister. For all your kindness to me."

Mother Philomena waited with the police in the foyer. The old nun acknowledged her with a nod before slipping, ghostlike, around the staircase and out of sight. One of the officers said, "This way, ma'am," and opened the door, revealing a bright, cold winter afternoon. She stopped and turned around, meaning to say goodbye to Sister St. John, but she too had vanished.

The officer who had opened the door walked ahead of her, the other walked behind, but neither of them touched her. The first officer opened the back door of the police car and allowed her to settle herself in as if she were a passenger in a taxi.

As the first officer started the car, the second asked him something about his family's plans for Christmas, and the two chatted amiably for a few minutes, seeming to have forgotten that Nina was there. This gave her the courage to lean forward slightly, when the car was stopped at a traffic light, and say, "May I know, please, where you are taking me?"

The officer on the passenger side twisted in his seat to look back at her. "To the bus station. You're on your way home."

Her relief, her joy, were too fragile to bear the press of another question—if she had misheard, she didn't want to be corrected; if the officer had meant *home* but not *home to stay*, she did not want to know. So she kept silent.

At the bus station, the officer who had spoken to her in the car placed his hand under her elbow, in the manner of a gentleman, to offer her guidance. Her ticket, it seemed, had already been ordered, as it was handed over the moment the officer asked at the reservation window. He showed her the ticket, pointing out that she would have to get off in Columbus, where there would be a two-hour delay before her bus to Newman, but he thought there was a diner there where she could get a sandwich and a cup of coffee. A few minutes later, he was steadying her as she climbed the steps into the bus. She took a seat near the back, next to a window, and sat stiffly, still afraid that if she made a sound or even relaxed her shoulders, someone—the officer who was still standing in the boarding area, the bus driver just getting on, another passenger—would realize a mistake had been made and she would be hauled off the bus and dragged away again to that terrible, barren room where Parks and his note-taking partner waited.

Or someplace worse.

She was aware that several more passengers got on the bus, but she had made herself a blank. To look at the other people, even in a neutral, curious way, might attract attention—and attention, questions. Any one of these people might have been put onto the bus for the purpose of watching her, or there might be someone waiting in Columbus to arrest her.

How changed she was.

Everything that had happened, including this unexplained release and the politeness of the officers, seemed designed to break her trust, to make her fear to take the smallest step, lest the ground give way at the touch of her heel. She would not allow her mind to turn to hope, she decided, until she was on the second bus, on her way home to Newman. From the Columbus depot, she would find a way to make a call or send a telegram to Otto, and then, though there might be someone, too, on that other bus, sent to watch her, at least she would know that Otto, Kurt, Gerhard, and two dear young friends would be waiting at the end of the journey. She would not be alone.

Just as the police officer had said, there was a small diner at the station. Outside the diner, there was one public telephone, but it was in use and four other people were already queued up and waiting, so Nina looked around for a Western Union sign. She found one in the main room of the depot, over a table well supplied with telegram blanks and pencils, so she could send her message without saying more than a few words to the clerk when she paid. She would keep the message short, for soon she would be in her own sitting room, beside the fire with her family, a cup of chocolate in her hands, able to say every word that came into her head. Someone had left a discarded form crumpled on the table, and she used this to sketch out her message, getting it down to the ten clearest words: "Darlings—Coming home tonight. Meet bus arriving Newman 9:20. Love."

When she opened her bag to get her coin purse, she glimpsed a green edge peeking out of her ticket folder. Three dollars—put there, she supposed, by the gentlemanly police officer. If she could find out his name, she would send him a Christmas card. And a box with a *Linzertorte* for his children. How sad it would be if a man like that— so thoughtful of a stranger—had no children of his own.

She walked to the diner, and by the time she had finished her meal, a roast beef special, she had only thirty minutes to wait before the bus came. Otto would have received her telegram by now, and if it was busy in the restaurant, he might get a little short with the customers, trying to hurry them along, until Kurt reminded him that even if the last group stayed right up to the nine o'clock closing, there would still be plenty of time to get to the station. Kurt would have to take over as host, for though Otto would see the truth in what his son said, reason could not calm his childlike impatience when happiness was nearly in reach.

There was enough room on the bus, and few enough passengers, that she was again able to have a seat to herself. For the first time since she had been taken away, she was neither hungry nor thirsty nor cold, and in this comfort, she dozed, dreaming in sweet brief moments of the cupboard Kurt had built for her—a masterwork of ingenuity, with a mingling of tiny doors and bins and drawers, each one perfectly suited to the herb or spice it was meant to contain. In the dream, she saw herself passing it on to Bess, bright-cheeked on her wedding day. She dreamed of Gerhard, at eight or nine, standing on the stage at his school, reciting the poem he had written about her hands and all the work they met with in a day. Last year, as a new gift to her, he had found the poem again and, with Hugh, had set it to music. And she dreamed of the great godly strength of Otto's shoulders and of the safe little valley of his breastbone, where her cheek just fit.

She woke as the bus slowed, making the turn onto Vine Street. At the end of the street, the corner of Vine and Baxter, was the new bus station, built only last year. She had thought it garish, then, all flat surfaces and sharp edges, but now, wrapped in light, the blue and white block gleamed like a river in spring.

The driver called out, "Newman, Indiana!" Nina stayed in her seat, waiting for a young couple with a child to make their way down the aisle.

In a moment. In only another moment.

She stepped off the bus and onto the curb.

"*Tante* Nina! *Tante* Nina!"

Bess and Hugh, their coats open despite the cold, were running toward her. Together, they fell against her so hard she staggered back.

"Dear ones, dear ones," she said, patting their backs, looking over their shoulders for Otto and her boys, but there was only a tall, slender man of sixty or so, slightly familiar.

Bess was sobbing. Nina hugged her more tightly. "It's all right, my girl," she said. "I'm home. I'm all right."

Hugh stepped back, clutched her hand between both of his, and kissed her knuckles. "*Tante* Nina." His voice was controlled, but tears flowed down his cheeks. "They're gone. They're gone."

The man behind Hugh stepped forward suddenly, catching her as her knees buckled. The three of them got her through the door of the depot and onto a bench, and she felt a paper cup being pressed into her hand. Bess was on her left, as close as a frightened child. Hugh knelt before her, his head in her lap. Mr. Beale—for she realized now the slender, white-haired man was Mr. Beale—sat on her right at a respectful distance.

"The FBI came," said Mr. Beale. "Your youngest—"

"Gerhard," she said. His name rang strangely in her head, hollow and mournful, like a distant church bell.

"Gerhard was just getting home from school. These two were with him, of course."

Of course. Of course. What a strange expression. As a matter of course.

Mr. Beale went on. "There were three men from the FBI. That's right, isn't it?" he said to Bess and Hugh. "Three?"

Nina felt the children's heads nod against her.

"Your elder son—Kurt—he'd been picked up at the repair shop, and he and your husband had been handcuffed and chained to a table in the dining room. One of the men was guarding them. The other two were upstairs, searching the apartment."

Nina lifted her head to look at him. "Searching for what?"

"They wouldn't say. Not to me. Or to Charlie Griffin—he's a friend of mine. An attorney." He took a long, slow breath. "They handcuffed Gerhard as soon as he came in, and then Hugh ran to the drugstore and called me, and I called Charlie. He tried to get a stay—some order that would stop them from taking your husband and the boys, at least until there could be a review or a hearing—but the judge wouldn't have anything to do with it, not when he heard it was the FBI."

Nina looked at her hand, surprised to see the paper cup still there, uncrushed. She took a sip from it. Water, tepid and stagnant. "Do you know where they have been taken?"

"Not yet," said Mr. Beale. "Charlie's trying to find out."

Perhaps, while she was dozing on the bus, dreaming of home, a police car carrying her good and lovely men, chained together, had passed her going the other direction.

"Did Otto receive my telegram? Did they know I was coming back to them?" She did not know which answer she wanted, which would be worse—a yes or a no.

Mr. Beale shook his head. "Those men—they made such a mess of everything. Hugh and Bess wanted to stay, to put things back in order as well as they could, so we were all at the restaurant when the telegram came."

Nina nodded. She drank the rest of the water, swallowing hard.

"I'm sure Charlie will find out where they are," said Mr. Beale. "By tomorrow, certainly."

"Will you take me home, please? I would be most grateful."

Hugh lifted his head from her lap. "Mama says you can stay with us."

"That's very good of her," Nina said. "But I would like to go home." She put her arm around Bess and reached for Hugh's hand. "Perhaps she would let you stay with me, yes? Both of you? Just for tonight?" She turned to Mr. Beale. "Could you persuade her?"

"Mrs. Aust, I—"

She looked from Mr. Beale to Hugh, lifting her hand to the boy's cheek, ignoring the new tears on her own. "Please say you'll stay with me."

"I would, gladly," Hugh said. "You know I would, *Tante* Nina. Bess, too." He looked away. "It's just—it's not safe. For you. While we were inside clearing up, a gang of boys—I didn't see who they were—"

She slid her fingertips over Hugh's lips. He need say no more. She could see it in her mind. Six or seven, maybe eight, enraged young men reenacting on a street in Newman what they had seen in a newsreel from Berlin. Bricks shattering the windows. A black swastika across the door. And in man-sized letters, painted across the fronting pavement in red—they would know to make it red—*Nazi, Nazi, Nazi.*

VII

M R. SNYDER, THE POULTRY MAN, refused to cancel the
Christmas order.

Nina saw him, leaning against his truck, even before she
saw what had become of her restaurant. When she unfolded herself
from Mr. Beale's car, the poultry man looked at her and then looked
at his watch, as if she'd been late coming downstairs to receive a delivery—something that had never happened, not once. Mr. Snyder
looked at her again and stepped over a berm of blackened snow onto
the sidewalk, pulling his order pad and pencil out of his pocket—just
as if this were any ordinary morning. As if the front door weren't
standing open. As if the flanking windows hadn't been smashed as
wide as gates.

Hugh and Bess slipped past her up the brick walk—someone
had cleared it. They stopped just inside the restaurant door so she
could see they were near. She murmured, "Thank you, no," to Mr.
Beale's whispered offer to deal with the poultry man in her place, and
then he, too, went inside.

Nina forced herself to count silently to ten. She put her useless
keys back in her purse. "Mr. Snyder." She nodded. "Good morning."

"Just stopped by to tell you," he said, "I'll have those geese to you
on Tuesday. Six of them—eight to ten pounds each. Like usual." He
turned to step off the curb again and walked around to his driver's

side door. "Mighty nice, this year," he said, waving his order pad at her. "The geese."

She counted again. "I'm afraid the restaurant will be closed for a short while, so I will not be able to accept delivery. I will contact you some days before we open again, so I can decide the week's menu."

He stood behind the open door of his truck, clinging to it like a shield. "No cancellations, Mrs. Aust. You know that. Take the geese or not, but you'll pay for them all the same."

"Since the time of your father," Nina said, "our agreement has always been three days' notice for cancellation. This is Friday. The order is for Tuesday. I count four days."

"No can do."

"Mr. Snyder. The geese are meant for the Christmas Eve dinner. It will not be possible, I think, to complete the necessary repairs before then. As you can see…"

He looked past her now, at the shattered windows, the name *Aust* on the sign smeared out with red paint, written over in black with *Kraut.* "Oh, I see," the poultry man said. "I see very well."

How like Parks he was. That same self-satisfied nastiness. *Smug*— that was the word in English. She'd heard Gerhard use it once to describe a classmate, a boy with a hundredweight of self-righteousness for every ounce of intelligence.

"Listen," Mr. Snyder said, "I'll cancel the standing order on eggs—and the chickens and ducks. But not the geese." He hugged the truck door more firmly against his chest. "I raise those special for you. Not another buyer in a hundred miles. Everybody around here wants turkeys for Christmas."

Nina had never liked him, the younger Mr. Snyder. His father had been a decent man who made no distinction between respectfulness and sound business. The elder Mr. Snyder—who, in private, they had addressed as their friend Heinrich—had been their first regular supplier, and in their third year in America, when Otto organized his singing society, Heinrich had joined, saying the singing reminded him of his father, also called Heinrich, who was not a singer but a storyteller. A story-song could bring Heinrich Snyder to tears, recalling a Germany he had not seen since boyhood. He had still been Schneider then, many years before the spring of 1915, when he would break his father's heart by changing the family name to Snyder. Heinrich had confessed this quietly to her and Otto one night over a final cup of coffee, long after the other men had gone home, having bid their weekly farewells by linking hands and singing "*Das Deutschlandlied*," pledging themselves once more to unity, justice, and brotherhood.

"*Schneider*—" Otto said, "to speak it is like a small symphony. But *Snyder*—what is that? A boy humming through his nose. Why should you change?"

"The war," said Heinrich.

How many men—how many women, too—over how many years had used those words? In America. In Germany. In England, France, Belgium, Russia. Two words too small to answer so much— and yet no other words would serve.

Heinrich tilted his cup to separate the last sip of coffee from the dregs. "In this country, to hold a German name in those days—it was like carrying the Kaiser's flag in parade. No matter that I could show my papers, prove I had been a citizen twenty years and more. But Americans—they care only for what shows on first look." He set the cup down, stood, put on his hat. "Always inside I am the same man—the same man my customers had been knowing a long, long time. But to keep them, I must change my wrapping."

This son was nothing like that good man, their loyal friend. The upstart who had inherited not only the business but the name Heinrich—a name their friend could count back, first son to first son, through nine generations—refused to be called anything but Hank. He'd named his only son Bobby. Except for being able to name favorite dishes passed down from the elderly Frau Schneider, these younger generations could speak no German at all. It was a point of pride for Nina and Otto that both Kurt and Gerhard spoke German as well as they spoke English.

"Very well," Nina said, fixing her gaze on Mr. Hank Snyder. "Have the geese here by seven o'clock on Tuesday morning. I expect them clean as eggs. No pin feathers. Fifteen minutes past and I do not pay. For every pin feather I find, I subtract ten cents from the bill."

"But—what will you do with them? You won't be able to serve them. Might just as well take the loss instead of wasting beautiful birds like mine."

So, just as she suspected, he had counted on doubling his money—making her pay while selling the geese elsewhere. She could almost see the names inside his order book.

"I will do with the geese as I choose," she said. "And from Tuesday, you may close the account for Aust. We will arrange for a new supplier."

She ignored the poultry man's curse and stepped into the dim light of the restaurant.

Bess crouched near one of the shattered windows. She had wrapped a dishcloth over her hand and was putting pieces of broken glass into a cardboard carton left over from a delivery of apples. Hugh and Mr. Beale were righting overturned tables and separating the sound chairs from those with snapped legs.

Nina wound through the rubble of the dining room, into the kitchen. There was too much loss to gather up in her mind—broken crockery, tablecloths soiled and trampled on the floor, the oven doors askew on their hinges, cupboards spilling out what was left of their wasted contents. The herb and spice cabinet Kurt had made for her, dashed to pieces.

She passed back into the dining room and walked toward the ruin of Otto's little office. The curtain had been torn down, rod and all; the drawers of his desk pulled out and thrown to the floor; all the account books gone; the cash box dented, open, empty—but she could fix her attention on nothing other than the empty space where the radio had sat.

"They took our radio," she said. "Why should they take our radio?"

Nina listened to the clink of glass as Bess dropped pieces into the carton. She thought of her St. Nikolas Sunday dinner guests, their celebratory clinking of cups—coffee, tea, chocolate—while they caroled.

"You'll need a list," said Mr. Beale.

"A list?"

"For the police. So you can report what's damaged, what's missing."

"A list." Nina shook her head. "How can I tell what has been done by the FBI and what has been done by others who came after? The police will not help me." She recalled the gentlemanly officer who had put her on the bus yesterday—could that have been only yesterday?—and she felt sorry for what she had said. "Please forgive me. It is difficult just now to remember there are many good people."

Hugh came to her and folded her in his arms. Squeezing him hard, Nina peered over Hugh's shoulder at Mr. Beale.

"Of what is missing," she said, "I care for only three—my Otto, my Kurt, my Gerhard."

Mr. Beale nodded. "I need to go put up a sign saying I'll open the store after lunch," he said. "I'm sorry. I wish I could give you the day. But, what with Christmas—" He brushed away the needles of wood clinging to his overcoat. "I asked Iris to let these two stay as long as need be. She'll call the school when she gets to work."

A little sob broke from Bess's throat.

Mr. Beale reached into his pocket and handed the girl a folded handkerchief. "As soon as I get that sign up, I'll go over to the lumber yard and get them to send somebody over here to board up those windows, check the door to see it locks all right. Charlie ought to be in his office by then, so I'll see what he found out. I shouldn't be more than an hour and a half—two at the most. If Charlie knows anything, I'll ask him to come over himself."

When he was gone, Nina stared without seeing. Her unwashed hair itched, and beneath her coat, she felt the oiliness of her clothes—

the same dress, the same slip, the same stockings she had been wearing when Parks and his men had come for her twelve days ago. Last night, when they'd gotten to the Sloans' tiny apartment, Iris had said, "I'm sorry, I wish I had a clean dress to fit you"—Iris Sloan was narrower even than Bess, slim and tough as a birch tree—but she offered to go around to the neighbors on their floor and ask them to leave the shared washroom to Nina for an hour. It was late by then, well past eleven, and, much as Nina wanted to feel clean, she wanted more not to draw attention to herself, to set those strangers asking questions. She had asked only for a cup of tea to warm her before lying down on the sofa. She hadn't slept.

Perhaps later, she would send Bess upstairs to look out some clean clothes for her, but she couldn't go herself. Not yet. The condition of the flat was probably worse even than the restaurant, and she wasn't ready to face what those officious, warrant-waving men had made of her family's private life.

From some deep place, her mind conjured the opening notes of a *Lied* the boys often performed. She wanted to push it back down, cover the dark hole with a stone.

But no—the sound was real.

She looked toward the piano. Hugh stopped mid-phrase, right where Gerhard's voice would have entered.

Strangely, the piano had been spared. The bench, too, where Hugh now sat. A cold gust, tunneling through the window, lifted and swirled fragments of torn sheet music around him like dead leaves. He reached up to settle the fall back over the keys.

"Let's have some music, eh?" Nina said.

"I can't," said Hugh. "Not without—"

"Maybe just for piano, then." Nina stooped to gather up some of the paper, hoping to piece together something—anything—but she found she couldn't bear to look at the black bars to match one leaf to another. "You know something from memory, darling?" she asked. "Play that for us. Please."

From the first measure, she knew it was Bach, the Prelude in B-flat Minor, ache of three voices on one note.

She closed her eyes, following those voices in their struggle to rise, to coil as one. But they failed, dropped like tears—until the first, breaking faith with the other two, slipped away to grieve alone. Then the second peeled from its fellow, seeking its own way. The three voices, drifting far from each other, as through a tangled wood, called out in fragmented echoes. Fainter and fainter, the echoes receded. Fading nearly to silence.

Her heart's memory knew what was coming—and there it was.

Soft pulses, growing stronger. The voices rose again. They called each other, in tones now edged like knives, drew in toward the center, and crossed—discordant.

Stunned, only one voice survived. It could be any of them.

Bereft in the silence, yearning after the others, who hummed now only as muted imagination, the single voice sang on, sang the primary phrase they had all shared at the beginning—*Where are you? Where are you? Where are you?* The voice sang until—the phrase too heavy to carry unaided—it sank toward its end.

A whisper clung, only the memory of longing.

But then—out of death: resurrection.

Breaking like paired shafts of sunlight through fog, the other voices rang out, pulling the lost one into their glow. They drew closer, closer, closer, straining to reach—and in a single note, interlaced their hands.

Nina felt Bess's hand slip into hers and together they moved to the piano and stood behind Hugh, each settling her free hand lightly on his shoulder.

He played on as, one step at a time—one weary step, one blessed rest—the three voices, united, climbed the mountain toward brightness. Reaching its peak, though spent, they hovered at the edge of hope—unable to see what might come next, knowing the journey might break them, but, nonetheless, resolving into harmony.

VIII

DURING THE GREAT WAR—THOUGH SHE was but a girl then and not yet Otto's wife, only his sweetheart—she had survived the days on days of not knowing by working. Working at perfecting all the skills she would need when Otto returned to their life—growing the food, preserving the food, cooking, baking, scrubbing, sweeping, tending neighbors' babies, teaching small children, managing accounts. She learned from her mother that to wait for a soldier a woman had to think of herself as a soldier, looking up often to mark in the distance, like a standard, the dream of one's life, but focusing on the battle of the moment.

It helped her now to think of Otto and her sons as soldiers, fighting somewhere in enemy country, trying to get back to her. She answered as their fellow, holding her ground. She took charge of the repairs, dispatching Hugh to the telephone office to bring someone to restore her service, for the telephone had been torn from the wall. She sent Bess with signed notes to the post and telegraph offices stating that, despite appearances, she was in residence and all deliveries should continue as normal. She used the telephone at the drugstore to call for the gas man to secure all the lines. She found a tinker to hammer out the dented pots and a handyman to tend to the plumbing, the small carpentry, and the sagging oven doors. Some of the workmen looked at her with sneering suspicion, like the poultry man had done, but when they came she showed them she had the money to pay, in cash, and they laid out their tools.

There was less damage upstairs in the flat—the locks on the two steamer trunks had been forced and a few dresser drawers knocked out of plumb when they had been flung to the floor—but the scene was more chilling. All the cabinets and closets, bureaus and bookcases had been turned out, every piece of their private lives examined, noted, cast aside or carried away. Their bank books had not been taken, but they had been rifled. Gone was the stack of newspapers, *The Freie Presse*, mailed to Otto from Cincinnati each week. The FBI was sure to make something of that, though the papers in the stack were plainly unread, still in their wrappers. Their books had been divided, only those written in English left on the floor, and she wondered if anyone in the government offices would know enough German to recognize that what had been seized were two Bibles, some children's tales, the works of Göethe, Hoffman, von Kleist, and a well-thumbed copy of *Das Nibelungenlied*, which Kurt and Gerhard, when they were small, would beg their father to read out to them in rousing performance. Kurt's high school diploma was missing, along with his letter of welcome from Purdue University. Gerhard's diary. Otto's Honor Cross. All their photographs.

Though she herself had no appetite, every day she cooked something—a pork roast, meat pies, potato soup, and bread, always plenty of bread—in case one or all should suddenly push through the door, free. She had tended to the matter of Mr. Snyder's fat geese by cooking a full Christmas Eve dinner for thirty, carried in a convoy organized by Mr. Beale to the convalescent home where Iris Sloan worked. Out of hope, Nina had kept back one roasted goose for Otto and her sons. The next day, she sent that home with Hugh and Bess and pounded steak for beef rolls. When she wasn't cooking, she sorted and tidied, laundered, pressed, and put away afresh all the clothes and linens. She polished every surface until it shone.

Afternoons, the lawyer, Mr. Griffin, would phone to tell her he had pulled another thread from the tangle and had made more calls, sent more telegrams, "But," he would say, "I'm sorry. I just don't know where they are."

When the repair and cleanup work was all done and nothing left but the ordinary housekeeping chores, Nina would find herself in the restaurant dining room, dazed and mute, looking out at the street as if she were sitting all alone in a strangely clean bus station that no one else used.

She was sitting there now, having just taken the morning's bread from the oven, when she caught sight of a man on the sidewalk opposite, whipping his head left and right, impatient to cross. It was Mr. Griffin. Nina sprang up to fling open the door for him.

"They're in Chicago!" he shouted as he jogged across the street. His face had gone a deep red, and he pressed a hand against his chest as if to quiet his heart. Nina stood aside to let him through and then scooted past to pull out the nearest chair for him.

"Telegram this morning," he panted. "They've been moved around a lot. One or two nights one place, then another—mostly small jails. It's why it's been so hard to trace them."

"I will go to them. It is allowed? May I go?"

The lawyer nodded. "I phoned the place before I came over. Wanted to verify they were there—that they were still there—before I told you. I talked to a guard and told him to expect you. It's your right—I checked that, too—and I'll send a notarized letter with you in case they give you any trouble."

"But how long must they stay? They can come home with me? Already it is nine days. I must pack a few things for them in any case. And I will take the fresh bread for them. I need a timetable. Will it be faster to go by the bus or the train? I will stay until they are released. It cannot be long now."

Mr. Griffin held up a hand to stop her rushing words. "You don't understand, Mrs. Aust. The telegram was about their hearings."

"Hearings? Why hearings? What reason?"

"Yesterday they all had hearings—if you can call them that. No representation. No chance to bring evidence or witnesses. No judge.

Just panels," he said, adding bitterly, "their minds already made up. And all three panels came back with recommendation for internment. Probably for as long as we're at war, unless…"

Nina's hands went suddenly cold and heavy, like blocks of ice. "You must tell me all, Mr. Griffin."

"There's always a chance they could be released later on—a few months, a year," he said. "That is if I can get them new hearings—real hearings. I'll try. But any one of them, or all of them, could be sent back to Germany."

"Without choice? While the fighting continues?"

"Without choice." Mr. Griffin looked out the window for a moment. "But so long as the war goes on, I doubt they would deport your sons. Wouldn't want to add any men to the German forces."

"And Otto?"

"He should be safe for now—from deportation, I mean. There's still too much confusion for the government to send back anybody who doesn't volunteer to go—and even that's difficult. You have their passports? The FBI didn't take them?"

"In a safe box at our bank. They are there."

"Good," said the lawyer. "Whatever you do, don't take them along when you go. But get them out of the bank. Today if you can. I can lock them in my office safe for you—better that than keeping them here. Now, about the bank— is your name on any account? As equal owner to your husband, I mean?"

Nina nodded. "We are joint in the account for the restaurant, and for a savings deposit. Our savings for our sons are in their own names."

"Here's the thing," said Mr. Griffin. "A lot of German-owned property was tied up during the last war. It could happen again. If the attorney general approves the recommendations for internment— that could be a few days, maybe a couple of weeks—you could lose access to the accounts." Mr. Griffin's face had gone red again, and he looked away. "The government wants to stop any money that might go to Germany," he said, "or that anybody could use for spying or spreading propaganda."

"I am not a Nazi," Nina said. "I am no spy for anyone. Nor are my husband and sons."

"I believe that, Mrs. Aust. I do. You asked me to tell you everything."

"What must I do?"

"You can't touch your sons' accounts, not without their signatures. You can set up a private account for yourself, but don't move any more money from the joint account than you can help. The more you can take out in cash, the better—but, again, not so much to raise questions. Keep good records of what you spend. Receipts for everything in case someone comes snooping around, demanding to know what you've done with the money."

She thought of the bankbooks, the pages roughly turned by strangers' hands. "The FBI," she said. Was there any sound uglier than that?

"Spend only what you have to. From the private account. I wish I could tell you something different, but the truth is, this whole situation is so unstable, changing by the minute, I can't promise you won't be picked up again yourself."

Nina trembled at the question forming in her mind, but she must ask it. "Is it revenge, Mr. Griffin?"

The lawyer raised his eyebrows. "Revenge? For what?"

Nina took a deep breath and looked down at her hands. "For us, this has begun as it began for the Jews in Germany. I mean not only for Germans here, but also the Italian and Japanese people. First we must register. Then we must carry special identification—and among ourselves, we ask how long before we are ordered to wear marks on our clothing. Then our houses are destroyed and we are arrested without cause. Our families broken apart. " She looked at Mr. Griffin. "Is it revenge?"

"Revenge for the sake of the European Jew?" Mr. Griffin shook his head. "No—Americans never do stir much when there's trouble for

Jews. You remember those riots in Germany, in '38? The night when the crowds smashed up so many Jewish businesses, burned synagogues?"

She did remember. Weeks afterward, Kurt had pointed out an article in the newspaper, only a single paragraph, reporting that many families had been forced to sell their property for a fraction of its value so they could pay the fines imposed on them for the cost of cleaning up the mess the Nazis had made. "And the Americans? Was there nothing done?"

Mr. Griffin sighed. "Roosevelt issued a statement with a few strong words, recalled the ambassador. Nothing else. Not even sanctuary for Jews trying to get out. Then six, seven months later, he turned back that ship of refugees at Havana." He looked past her, toward the open door of the kitchen. "It keeps me awake sometimes, thinking about what might have happened to those people—what might be happening to them."

He caught his breath for a moment; his lips trembled. "So—no, I don't think what's happening to your family has anything to do with a direct, eye-for-an-eye revenge." He closed his eyes and rubbed at his forehead. "Systematic repression is hardly exclusive to Hitler and his gang. Plenty of it right here—and always worse when there's a war. When people are afraid, they'll hand over their rights as willingly as they'd hand over pennies for bread. But not until they've handed over other people's rights first."

Mr. Griffin patted her hand and stood up. "I know you need to see your family. However you get to Chicago, you mustn't wait. The place where they are is just temporary. The permanent camps are scattered all over—Oklahoma, Texas, Nebraska, Maryland, a few others. Some Army camps, some run by the INS—but not much different, I imagine."

"They will go to a *Stalag*? You say to me, my husband and sons— they are prisoners of this war?"

"They're not soldiers, so you won't catch anybody in any federal office calling them that. But, yes, in a way, that's what they are. *Alien enemies*—that's the term they use. Potentially dangerous. It's what was in the telegram." He turned toward the door but looked back at her. "Like I said, don't wait. They could be moved any time—as early as tomorrow. Today, even. I'll go back to the office and call everyone I can think of who has any pull—try to get a delay on the transfers for at least a few more days. But they're all going, Mrs. Aust. That's certain. And soon. Come by when you're ready, and I'll give you the address and that letter to show the guards."

Standing in the open door, she watched him cross the street. On the corner, the children—Hugh and Bess—stopped him, and she could see him shaking his head, gesturing back to where she stood. Then they ran across to her, hugged her hard, and forced her back inside the restaurant, into a chair. Bess sat before her, trying to rub warmth into Nina's hands, but she could barely feel the girl's touch.

"Do you remember that last day? When we were celebrating St. Nikolas?" She could hear the singing, smell the winter spices, see the revelers helping themselves to sweets, lifting their cups as Otto, Kurt, and Gerhard wove among the tables. "It is not yet three weeks. Everyone so happy until we stopped for the radio. When I think of that day, it is like to me—" She clutched at a breath that was half a sob. "It is like one of those planes, the planes with the bombs, came here. To pour down fire before going back across the sea."

For the first time since Hugh and Bess had come in, Nina looked into their faces—stunned, as if she had slapped them. "You will help me?" she asked. They nodded, and she kissed them both. "Come upstairs with me, then."

She gathered all the cash she had and handed most of it to Bess. "Go and get me three plump chickens," she said. "And buy as many sausages as you can with the rest. All kinds. I have bread, cheese, mustard, jam, pickles, plenty of potatoes and onions for a salad. I will pack a feast for them."

She handed the remaining bills to Hugh. "Take this. They must all have plenty of fresh soap. For shaving and for washing. And when you come back, while the chickens are cooking, you can both help me with the packing. They will need all their clothes."

Bess shoved the money deep into her coat pocket and hurried down the steps, but Hugh stayed where he was, staring at the bills in his hand.

"Do you think it is not enough?" Nina asked. "I am going to the bank for more."

"It's enough."

"You know what kinds they like best?"

"Yes, I know." Still, Hugh didn't move. "But *Tante* Nina? Please. Bess and I—we want to come with you."

No. No. The word burned in her mind.

She could not share this journey. Time was too precious, their final hours together as a family. Their last, perhaps, for many years. Perhaps the last of all—

She took Hugh's hand. *I am sorry*, she meant to say. *You will understand, my young friend,* but the pleading in his eyes clutched her heart. This pain was not hers alone.

"Please, *Tante* Nina."

She nodded. "If your mother agrees—yes. Yes. We will go tonight. We three."

IX

WHEN THE TRAIN REACHED CHICAGO just before dawn, they pushed through the crowd to the taxi stand and squashed into the backseat of one of the cabs, so that the brimming hamper Nina had packed could ride up front. They traveled in silence along the shore of the lake, just beginning to burn blue and orange in the breaking morning light, and when the driver pulled up to the curb and repeated the address they'd given him, Hugh sprang out, hauled the hamper from the front seat, and met the driver at the back. While he and Bess lifted the suitcases from the trunk, Nina counted out the fare. None of them had really noticed where they were until the taxi had gone—a quiet street lined with houses, ornate and towering.

"This cannot be right," Nina said. She looked through an ornamented iron fence—taller even than Otto—at the grand house beyond. Surely the taxi driver had brought them to the wrong place. Her own strange prison, with the Good Shepherd sisters, had been a simple farmhouse, large but starkly utilitarian. This edifice of golden brick, like a fantasy castle carved from brown sugar, was deliberate art.

Hugh touched her arm and pointed to a plaque, affixed to the gate, where the complete address announced itself in brass. And then the newly assigned purpose of the house was clear—for just behind the plaque stood a hastily built shed, out of which stepped a uniformed guard, rifle held at the ready.

Nina lifted her chin and strode toward the guard. "I am come to see my husband, Mr. Otto Aust. And my sons, Kurt Aust and Gerhard Aust." She passed her identification card through the iron bars and with a slight tilt of her head indicated Bess and Hugh, who stood behind her. "And my sons' friends have come as well. My attorney, Mr. Griffin, telephoned here yesterday to make the arrangements."

The guard lowered his rifle and took Nina's identification card. When he handed it back, he asked her to spell out, slowly, the names of the others. "Do those two have some kind of ID with them?"

"They do."

"Okay," the guard said. "I need to let them know inside. All of you stay right here by the guardhouse so I can see you. Don't move."

Nina motioned Hugh and Bess forward and they all three stood together, their arms linked.

The guard walked toward the entrance of the house, where two other armed men sat in the shadow cast by the portico, flanking the door. The first guard spoke to the others and then, when those two went inside, he turned to watch the visitors, shielding the door with his body. Several minutes passed before the guards returned. One resumed his position at the door, while the other came toward the gate with the first guard.

"You," he said, pointing to Nina, motioning her toward an area near the guardhouse. He told Hugh and Bess to step back to the curb. One at a time, they were each brought forward by the guards, who examined their identifications and asked questions about where they were born, where they lived now, if they worked, where they worked, how they had traveled to Chicago, how long the trip had taken, what towns they had passed through, and why they'd come. When they had all been questioned by both guards, the two men collected their identification and stepped inside the guardhouse.

"I am sorry for this trouble," Nina whispered. All through the long train journey, she had felt confident in her vow to Iris Sloan that she would let no harm come to her children.

"I really don't like them being mixed up in all this," Iris had said, "but I guess it's too late for that." The words burned Nina, though she knew Iris had spoken out of fear, not cruelty. Had the circumstances been reversed, had Bess and Hugh been her own children, Nina was sure she would not have allowed them to go off on such an uncertain journey with only Iris to watch over them.

Hugh pressed Iris again, saying, "I wouldn't feel right letting *Tante* Nina go alone. Not after all that's happened."

"And what about what I'd be going through, sitting here worrying?" Iris asked. "It's like you're always forgetting I'm your mother. Me. I am." She sank onto a rusted metal stool in her tiny kitchen, deflated by a sigh. "It's not that I don't understand. The Austs have been good to you both." She looked at her children, standing shoulder to shoulder. "I could forbid you to go. It's what I want to do. But you'll be eighteen soon, so you'll tell me a few months won't make any difference. If I say no, you'll go anyway—that's plain."

"I will look after them," Nina said. "I give you my word."

She had braced against Iris Sloan's doubts, but now she trembled. Those rifles—anything might happen. Or what if, when they finally got inside, she was arrested again? She had given each of the children more than twice the money they would need to get back to Newman on the train, and they had Mr. Griffin's phone number and knew how to send telegrams—but would that be enough? "I'm sorry," she said again. "I should have come alone."

"We wouldn't have let you," Bess said. "Would we, Hugh?" Her voice wavered beneath a weak smile.

"Of course not," Hugh answered. In spite of the biting cold, his forehead and the bridge of his nose shone with sweat.

When at last the guards reemerged, the first one opened the gate and called for the hamper and the suitcases Nina had brought. When these had been thoroughly searched, the guard ordered them to come through the gate, pick up the cases, and line up behind him, single file. The second guard locked the gate behind them and attached himself to the end of the line, his rifle raised.

They passed by the third guard, through the door, and into a high-ceilinged entry hall that could have swallowed the dining room of the Aust Family Restaurant. The house's fine façade had been deceiving. Except for the magnificent staircase, which split at a broad landing to lead to opposite wings of the house, there was little left of the original grandeur. Deep cracks vined the plaster walls and from the ceiling a perpetual frost of dust drifted over them. The red oak woodwork was badly in need of oiling, and Nina and Bess had to step carefully across the ruined mosaic floor so as not to catch the heels of their pumps in the divots left by missing tiles.

"Stop right here," said the guard who had led them, and he signaled to a fourth guard who had just stepped out from another room. That guard quickly mounted the steps to the landing and shouted out, "Aust—Otto. Aust—Kurt. Aust—Gerhard. Report!"

And suddenly there they were, coming from the corridor on the left, walking hurriedly, looking bewildered and nervous—but then Otto caught sight of her, and they all called out, their three voices blending to one. The pounding of their feet on the staircase seemed to shake the house, and she heard the guards shouting, "No touching!" even as Kurt, who reached her first, caught her in his strong arms and swung her off her feet. Gerhard captured her as she landed and buried his face in her neck, and Otto had to pry the boy loose so he could draw Nina to him. She nestled her cheek against his breastbone.

One of the guards tapped her shoulder hard and said, "Move away. No touching," but Otto held her tighter and said quietly, "Please, sir. She is my wife. Please."

"Don't try anything," the guard said, stepping back. "I'm watching. Just keep your hands where I can see them."

Nina closed her eyes and pressed her cheek deeper into Otto's chest, mapping his warmth, breathing in his smell, humming to the beat of his blood.

Secure in his arms, she listened for the joy of those she loved. The hoots of welcome, the clap of arms around shoulders, the tinkle of Bess's laughter when Kurt sang out his play-name for her, "Bess the Blest!" and then crooned more softly, "My Bess. My Bess." She heard Gerhard and Hugh, murmuring in voices paired like violin strings— and then Kurt's voice again, slashing through theirs, "What, Hugh? No handshake for me?"

Nina opened her eyes and saw Gerhard and Hugh, knotted. Kurt pulling at his brother's shoulder. Bess trying to wrap all three boys into one great hug. One of the guards pounding Hugh's back, shouting, "Enough. That's enough!"

Otto released her and stepped toward Kurt and the others. "Come! Come!" he boomed. "You must show what you have brought us!"

The cluster broke apart, and everyone backed away, their faces red and damp, their eyes darting. Bess pushed her hair from her eyes and bent to flip open the hamper. "Food! We've brought you Sunday dinner. Four kinds of sausage. Chicken. Bread and cheese. Come see!"

"Kurt, call down the others," Otto said. Turning to Nina, he added, "There are seven more like us." He knelt on the floor beside Bess, who was unloading the hamper, laying everything out as if for a picnic. He lifted up a loaf of bread and a tray of sausages, showing the guards. "You will join us, please? Plenty enough for all."

And then that great grim shell of the entry hall filled with men whose names slipped past Nina like the Rhine, thanking her in loud, happy voices for bringing this feast.

Nina took Otto's arm and whispered, "Will they let us speak alone?"

Otto shook his head. "We are to be sent on a train today, Kurt and I—within the hour, they say. When the guard called us out, we thought it was for that. When he called Gerhard's name, too, we thought it must mean he would be going with us to the same place."

"But where are you going? I can follow you."

"To a camp somewhere. The guards say they do not know. Perhaps they tell the truth. They say I can write to you—so I will write the first day if they will let me."

"But Otto. What happened? Why are you to be sent away?"

He shrugged. "Three men behind a table asked me questions—a quarter of an hour, no more. They asked me if I should like to see Germany fall, and I said, 'No. Of course, no.' They asked me if I should like to see America fall, and I said, again, 'No, I would not.' And then they asked me whether, if the American government commanded I should do so, I would fire a bomb at my uncle's house in Koblenz. I told them I would follow no one's command to murder my uncle, my cousins—not anyone of my blood."

"Otto…"

"They asked many more questions. I could see they wanted only for me to say that I have no love for Germany or for the German people. That I had shaken its dust forever from my feet when I came to America. It was much the same for our sons. Only hatred for Germany would answer."

Only hatred would answer. How could such a thing be so? Had she been the one to face these questions, Nina knew that, just as Otto and her sons had done, she could never have said she wished to see Germany, her homeland, fall in this war—not even if she knew her freedom depended upon such a lie.

But after all that had happened, what would she do if one of those guards demanded to know, this moment, if she would like to see America fall?

She looked at Bess and Hugh—children she loved almost as her own. She thought of the kindness of Sister St. John; and of Iris Sloan, despite her fears; and of Mr. Beale, though they were nearly strangers to each other. And she thought of all Mr. Griffin had done, a man who owed them nothing, a good and decent man outraged by so much injustice.

"No," she would say to the guard. "Not Germany, no. Not America. Not the people of either. I want none to fall." And then she would say, "But these men of power who hate so narrowly, who so love to make war? Yes." She saw them as monstrous yews, sprung up to poison neglected fields of rye. "Yes—I should like to see them fall, taking with them only the saplings they have sheltered."

What would these guards do if she should answer this way? How many of them, how many of their families, would wish the same? For only the warmongers to fall, and for the ordinary people of both nations, of all nations, to grow strong and straight in the sun?

Everyone—her family, her friends, the other prisoners and the guards—now sat on the broken floor of the great hall, eating, talking, even laughing at times, in the way of tourists who meet by accident amid the crumbling walls of an ancient citadel. She moved nearer and stood watching them. Kurt ate one-handed so he could keep his other arm around Bess. Gerhard and Hugh sat side by side, their heads nearly touching, in the language of best friends. And Otto was holding court with a mixed group of Germans and guards, daring them to discover for him a better cook, a truer wife, than his beautiful Nina.

There was no hatred here. Only good people—many good people caught and twisted in the same black net of others' making. Good people sharing generously with other good people.

She tried to think of something to say; something everyone here could carry with them, wherever they must go, whatever they must do; something that would preserve this fragile peace in all their hearts. Speech seemed too weak.

Years ago on the ship, when they had made their long crossing from Hamburg; through a spring, a summer, an autumn at Franz's farm, when the boys, still too small to understand, were fretful for the sounds and smells of home; in those first years at the restaurant, when she and Otto, putting the boys to bed, were too tired to weave stories—and in all the years since, in trouble, sadness, and joy—it was music that had bound them to each other and to the beloved land they'd left behind.

It was with music they had comforted their friend Heinrich, grieving the loss of his ancestral name. It was with music they had opened the doors of the Aust Family Restaurant, and music—music and rich, warming food—that had led so many of the people of Newman across the threshold of bitterness left by the Great War and into fellowship.

Like food, music had the power to strengthen, to heal. She could bring music to this moment, to join her family to the other Germans here, and to lead the guards, in friendship, into the deep, fertile goodness of Germany. A *Lied* all this company would recognize, but hear anew. Yes. Haydn's melody would carry them through the fields and forests, into meadows and across mountains, down rivers and along the banks of lovely old towns. And even those listeners who could not understand the century-old words were sure to feel the poetry.

She stepped to the center of that faded entry hall, the staircase spreading behind her like wings, and sang:

Deutschland, Deutschland über alles,
Über alles in der Welt.

Everyone fell silent. Then Kurt leapt up and, grabbing her hand, sang out with her:

Wenn es stets zu Schutz und Trutze
Brüderlich zusammenhält.

One of the guards scrambled to his feet and shouted, "What do you think you're doing!"

Gerhard and Hugh understood, and they rose, threw their arms around each other's shoulders, adding their voices to finish the first verse.

Nina squared her shoulders and stood straighter. They were singing the *Lied* as it was meant to be sung, restoring it to its true purpose as a testament of pride and hope, scrubbing away with their voices the stain of Horst Wessel, wresting the words and music from the proclamation of arrogance and hatred Hitler and his Nazis had made of them.

"Stop!" The guard looked toward his comrades and cried, "Don't you recognize it?"

Nina sang more brightly. Her joy would teach the guards that this anthem exalted life and brotherhood. It was nothing like the American celebration of bursting bombs, nothing like the French's *Marseillaise*, glorying in fields watered by enemy blood.

Two of the other German men stood and sang with them. Three more sat with their heads down. Another turned his back and moved slowly toward the staircase. The group sang on, uniting their harmonies. Nina smiled at the guards, beckoning them to the Germany she loved.

In Bess's eyes, she could see the welling of tears, could see her shaking her head and mouthing, "Please, *Tante* Nina. No."

Nina answered by reaching open arms toward her. Bess shook her head, covering her tear-streaked face with her hands.

The guard who had shouted was talking now to the others, waving his arms and pointing angrily at the singers. And then it seemed the other guards heard him at last. They put down their food and stood. They straightened to attention.

Otto neither joined the chorus nor stood with the guards. He was the wide, calm river between, dividing them, connecting them.

The guards pulled at their rifle slings, bringing their weapons to the front.

Pivoting wildly between the guards and the singers, Bess screamed, "No! You don't understand! Stop, please! You don't understand!"

Then Otto became the ferry crossing the river, and the king who had launched it. He stepped in front of the singers, facing the guards—bold, welcoming.

And as they opened the second verse, Otto's big voice rained down over them all, nourishing their roots, resurrecting the soil Hitler had decimated. Their voices rose higher, stretching toward the light as they sang, proclaiming the glories of German women, German wine, German song, and of fidelity and noble deeds.

1942

I

DESPITE THE COLD, THE SAME three men walked the north fence, their heads bowed for the triple purpose of hearing the others' words, of shielding their faces from the insult of the dry wind, and of preventing their hats from being whipped up and away by a gust.

As Otto watched them through the high octagonal window in the dormer of Barracks 32, he found himself wishing to see the hats carried away. To become, for a moment, like brushed-felt birds. And then, as if in answer to his wish, one of the men took his protecting hand away and the hat was swept up, up—soaring as high as Otto, caged, soared in his imagination. Faster, higher, and farther flew the hat-bird, riding the air—until the cruel wind, a gasp short of carrying the fugitive free, reversed and rested, dropping its prey into the waiting maw, three rows of barbed wire teeth rimming the cyclone fence.

"He has lost his hat," Otto said to no one in particular. A dozen other men were in the room now, occupying themselves with writing letters, reading tattered adventure stories, playing cards, or lying curled or stretched on their cots, their faces to the wall, while they waited for the midday count. They'd learned it was easier to be at their bunks well before the guards appeared, ordering them to attention, rather than having to scramble back across the snow from the laundry or one of the workshops when the signaling siren blared. One man not in his appointed place meant, for the rest of them, hours locked inside the barracks while the miscreant was hunted down.

"Who has lost his hat?" asked Max Kuehn. He sat on the bunk nearest Otto's window, whittling a bar of soap with the nib of an empty fountain pen into a chess piece, a pawn.

"The short one."

"I believe you wish to join them, Otto," Max said.

Otto looked out again at the trio, who called themselves the *Wanderkameraden*, the hiking comrades. "They are educated men," he said. "I hear them talk of Schopenhauer and Stravinsky, of European history from before the Romans. What do I know? How much to charge for *Wurst* and *Spätzle*."

Still, Max was right—partly. Otto did want to walk—but not with those men. With Kurt. While they had sat shoulder to shoulder in the prisoners' mess, he had said to his son, "We could make a pattern for ourselves—just we two—and talk as we like."

Kurt grasped the stale hard roll from his plate and with a violent twist, tore it in half. Staring down at the pieces, he said, "Too much of the habit of home, *Vati*. Too much like Gerhard, walking with Hugh. We'd be left waiting for their singing, for the smell of *Mutti's* bread. For Bess. I couldn't stand it." Kurt looked toward the window facing into the center of the compound, one red brick corner of their barracks just visible. "Besides—you're forgetting about the microphones on the fence."

Otto now left the dormer, the one place in the room where he could stand at his full height, and bent to pick up one of the soap pawns Max had already finished—smooth and well balanced, remarkably fine carving considering the materials. Max was a tool and die maker from Seattle who had been arrested at work, trundled at gunpoint across the factory floor in front of all his coworkers.

This is how the men in the camp knew each other: profession, American home, and manner of arrest. A plumber from Detroit, a baker from Milwaukee, farmers from Iowa, Nebraska, a salesman from Pittsburgh. From different cities all over California—tailors and accountants, teachers and engineers, shop owners and architects, photographers and ministers. Each man's story an outrage—some snatched while walking to work or getting off a bus or coming out of the post office or sitting at a drugstore counter drinking coffee; while milking a cow or carrying a basket of potatoes from the root cellar; while patching a roof or unstopping a drain or repairing a furnace; others dragged from ransacked homes at 4 a.m., clung to by half-dressed wives and bawling children.

From the first day, Otto too had slipped toward this labeling—a restaurant owner from Indiana. When he spoke of his arrest, he said, "I was taken with my sons," but liked to add, "Some hours before, my wife was freed." There was hope in that—small, yet possible. Any of them might be released too, like Nina, without warning. Without apology or explanation, either—but Otto thought a man could wait for that, so long as he was free.

What he would not confess, even to Kurt, was that he feared Nina had been arrested again. And if that were so—what hope for them? What hope that their family, their home, could ever be restored?

In Chicago, the guards had broken up the singing, jabbing at them with the butts of their rifles. They ordered Nina to the end of the great hall and surrounded her while the prisoners were hurried back up the stairs. When they reached the landing, two guards held Gerhard between them, and Otto and Kurt were told to put on their overcoats. They were handcuffed, a chain leashing them together, and led back down the steps. Bess and Hugh sat on the floor, huddled against a wall, collapsed on each other like whipped young dogs. Otto could not see Nina at all—only the tight ring of the guards that held her within. Kurt had called out his farewells, but only Hugh responded with a despairing look and a wave of his hand.

Otto placed the pawn back on Max's cot. "How will you tell the white from the black?"

"I'll find some black paint," said Max. With a wry smile, he added, "Perhaps, along with the black, I should paint them with red and gold, so everyone knows these are the true Germans."

"Imperial colors," Otto mused. "And the other side?"

"I'll leave them as they are. What would you call this color? Not really a color at all, this gray-yellow—just as it comes from the mixing pot."

Otto returned to his window to watch the walkers, wondering if the three continued their talks when the cold drove them back to the barracks. He wondered if they welcomed other men into their circle, if they appreciated the good fortune of discovering friends in unfortunate circumstances. Perhaps Kurt felt something like that toward the German seamen, held on the west side of the compound—men he would never have met, had he never known this place.

Again, Otto wished he had urged his son to follow him to this room and take a bed beside his, so they could talk quietly after lights out. But when they had been herded with sixty or seventy others into Barracks 32, Kurt had stopped on the second floor, turning down a hall. When they reached the third floor and saw how the sharply slanted ceiling would force them to stoop, the taller men behind Otto went back down the stairs to seek out other beds, but, satisfied, Otto claimed a cot with his hat. Here on the third floor, because of the low ceiling, the cots were single, not in stacks of two as they were in the rooms below, so, while he might knock his head if he sat up in the night, he would not have to sleep either above or beneath any other man. And here, though the windows were small and few, the room got the best of the feeble winter light, too high for the North Dakota snow to reach, even when the drifts on the deep porch roof covered the second floor windows.

"Perhaps," Otto said to Max, "you will invite the *Wanderkameraden* in to play chess when you have finished. And all of us could talk."

"Perhaps," said Max. "Perhaps two."

"Not all?"

Max stopped carving. "Do you not know, Otto? One of them is a Jew."

"Why should this matter? You are no Nazi, I think."

"Of course not," said Max. "I do not wish the Jews any trouble, you understand. I am not a man for the *Pogrom*. But one need not call himself Nazi simply because he does not wish to mix with Jews." Max sighed and fixed Otto with the look of a weary schoolmaster correcting a dim child. "Really, my friend, I think you cannot have been very long in America if you imagine those people find more welcome here than in Europe, in Russia. Tell me, in that town where you have your restaurant, how many men do you know—how many who count themselves American men and Christians—who would invite a Jew to sit at table with his wife and children?"

"I would welcome a Jew to my table. To any of my tables."

"And soon you would have no customers at all. They would pass your door, and in this way, say to you, 'Let the Jew stay in his place.'"

"Would you have the whole of the world marked off in blocks, Max, like your chess board? Where is your place? Where is mine? And who shall decide?"

Max leaned out from his bunk and traced his gaze around the room. "It seems our place has been decided for us." He took up his carving again, shaping the head of a new pawn. "But it is no matter," he said. "Three cannot play chess. Nor four. And talking is no good when the mind is needed for strategy, so let those others keep to their walks. I need only one opponent. So—you, Otto? Do you play?"

"I learned a little during the war. But you must ask Kurt—my son. He plays very well." Otto smiled to show he would drop the quarrel. "At least he tells me this is so."

"And where is this boy of yours now?" Max's tone was not kind.

In the last ten days, Kurt had twice missed a count—one at midday and one at lights out. Both times, the guards had found him in one of the barracks assigned to the seamen arrested last spring.

Among them were several Nazis, a small but vocal leadership who called themselves *Die Schlageter*, after Hitler's martyred hero. Though it could be said that everyone in the camp had benefited from the *Schlageter*'s demands regarding their treatment, with militant attention paid to the bylaws of the Geneva Convention, it was plain to them all that the guards watched with greater suspicion anyone who mixed with the seamen.

Just yesterday, Otto had asked Kurt, "Why do you go so often to those men?"

"To learn what I can about Germany."

"I will tell you of Germany. I *have* told you."

"I mean Germany now," Kurt said. "The way it is now. You can't tell me that, *Vati*. You've been gone too long. Everything's different. All we get here is the American view of things—the Roosevelt view. And you see where that's brought us." He shook his head in disgust. "You know, those guys—they're not soldiers. Most of them are merchant marines. Some of them even worked on ships for Standard Oil. You see? An *American* company. And still they've been stuck here, first under surveillance and then in these camps. Two years it's been going on. And all that time, Roosevelt was telling everybody he was going to keep America out of the war—so why does he take prisoners?" Kurt looked him hard in the eye. "The whole time, *Vati*. Do you understand? He's a liar."

"My son, these men speak to you from their anger. I too believe this anger is deserved, but even so, it narrows what they see, and what they will tell you, of Germany." He placed his hand on the back of his boy's neck and pulled him closer. "Listen to me. To look through one's anger is to look through a hollow reed. You must throw it down."

"I just want to hear the other side, that's all," Kurt said. "Especially if they send us back. You've heard the talk. We're like dollars in the bank—waiting to be paid out in ransom for any Americans who didn't bother to get out of Europe and got stuck behind the lines."

"Rumors," Otto said. "Rumors only."

"Maybe. But it makes sense, doesn't it? They can't give us real trials, fair trials, because they'd never be able to convict us—we haven't done anything." Kurt pressed his fingertips along his forehead, rubbing hard, angrily. "I used to believe in the law," he said. "But I see now it's nothing but sand. Try to hold it and it drains through your fingers. Wet it and you can mold it into any shape you like."

Otto could not disagree, so he said nothing.

"I just want to know the other side," Kurt said. "That's all, really. I'm not saying I believe that, either—not altogether."

"You say 'the other side' as if you believe there are only two," Otto said. "So much trouble comes from men who see only two faces—the self and the enemy, right and wrong. It is the way of power. And, Kurt, you must not give yourself whole to power." He pressed his palm over his son's heart. "Do you hear my meaning? Not to any power."

After breakfast this morning, Kurt hadn't come back to the barracks—likely again with his seamen friends, so many of them young men like himself, their lives suspended—but Otto did not want to stir more trouble for his son by admitting his suspicion to Max. Instead he said, "Perhaps today the mail will come. Bundles of letters for us all."

"You say that every day, Otto."

Otto attempted an easy laugh, "Every day, it may be true. Why not today?"

Nearly six weeks had passed and, still, there had been no mail for any of the men who had been on the train with him and Kurt. The journey had been like a single, terrible, continuous moment, as in a nightmare. The windows had all been barred and sealed with dark blinds, denying them so much as a glimpse of the country they were no longer free to roam. For those two days and nights, they all sat rigid in their seats, facing the mounted machine guns pointed to the center of the car, fearing that in the dusky light even the simplest movement—smoothing back one's hair, scratching one's nose—could be mistaken for a threat.

Otto's only relief—and Kurt's too, he learned, when they were able to whisper a few words to each other—was that they were together, each able to confirm with his eyes that the other was safe—but the relief was frail, for Otto could not look at Kurt without his mind slipping to a vision of Gerhard, alone, locked into stillness by guns on another dark train.

To lift himself over these thoughts, Otto imagined writing to Nina, of first writing her name, one precious character at a time, and then thinking of what he would say—nothing of this wretched journey, but instead words that would carry her with him into a shared day of their past, just as if they were lying in their bed, heads touching, saying to each other, "Remember..." As the train clacked on and on, he finished, in his imagination, his first letter, written with the finest phrases he could turn, and saw himself nudging the thick pages into an envelope, sealing tight the flap, slipping it through a brass-plated slot, and then, as if suddenly blessed with a sorcerer's vision, he could see the letter traveling to her, into and out of the hands of postal clerks with their inked stamps, under the supercilious eyes of Postmaster Jackson in Newman, into the bag carried by the thin fellow with the mustache who brought the mail to the restaurant, and at last into Nina's small, plump hands. Her busy, lovely hands.

He saw her reading, smiling, perhaps blushing at his charming wit. He saw her writing her reply, heard her voice as she wrote it, and then his own second letter, her reply, and on and on through a correspondence that, letter by letter, recalled all of their days together, every one.

On the train, Otto asked Kurt, "Will you write first to your mother or to Bess?"

At the mention of the girl's name, a smile flicked at Kurt's lips, then quickly disappeared.

"Your mother—she will understand," Otto said. "She has been the sweetheart, coming before a mother when it was time for writing letters. So you may write first to our Bess. She is your sweetheart, I think?"

Kurt's smile returned, with a spark of mischief. "Remember that car I wanted you to buy? A little privacy on wheels."

On the third morning, Otto stepped down from the dismal carriage onto a glacial platform cordoned by armed guards standing four feet apart. He ignored the pain in his legs, stiff from days of sitting, and walked toward the end of the platform. Stopping directly before a guard, he said, "I would like to post a letter to my wife. How may I do this?"

The guard swung up his rifle, holding the end of the barrel half an inch from Otto's chest. "No talking!" He cocked his head to the left. "Over there."

Otto joined the mass of men who had gotten off the train ahead of him. They stood for a long time while the train guards flung their luggage into rough piles and consulted with the platform guards about whether to unload the remaining cars or wait until the first group was processed. The men huddled together, each one listening for his name to be called so he could move back toward the train, find his luggage, and carry it to an old stationmaster's hut that had been commandeered for the search. Inside, the men had to hand each item to a guard, who would hold it in the light, squeeze, prod, shake, or pull it. The guards even tore openings in the linings of jackets and hats, determined to discover anything that might have been concealed.

After many hours more on the platform, Otto saw a line of tarp-covered Army trucks approaching, followed by three or four smaller, open-bed trucks and a few cars—all of them weaving about, trying to pass the Army trucks. Standing in the open beds were many men, and, despite the cold, the great speed, and the drivers' wide steering, they remained steady on their feet, holding rifles high above their broad-brimmed hats. Other men stretched their bodies out the open windows nearly to their hips, shouting, beating against the cars' roofs and doors with clubs.

As the first of the Army trucks drew up beside the platform, the cars and open-bed trucks swung past, skidding to a stop around the stationmaster's hut. "Nazis! Traitors!" men shouted as they tumbled out of cars. "Blow 'em up! Ship their ashes back to Krautland!" From the open bed trucks, men leapt down into the snow, chanting, "Out! Out! Out! Out!"

On the platform, the Germans shoved forward, trying to get to the waiting Army truck, but they were forced back by a line of guards barking, "One at a time! Single file!"

"Out! Out! Out!" The chant grew louder. "Move the traitors out!"

A rifle shot. Another. But Otto could not tell from where—the guards or the jeering men.

He pushed Kurt deeper into the knot of bodies, and lifting his head high, tried to see beyond the platform. Most of the guards were on the ground, now, shoulder to shoulder, blocking the mob and pushing it back to the cars and open-beds, keeping their rifles aimed until the intruders, still cursing, had slammed their doors, sped back across the tracks, and turned onto the main road.

When all the Army trucks were loaded, they drove as a gray-green convoy into the gloom, and, after a long while, through an iron gate into this fenced wasteland, where the men were unloaded and lined up like spiritless horses before the camp commander, Mr. Hudson.

To the old soldiers among them, like Otto, Hudson struck a strange figure—a man of military mien wearing a civilian's brown tweed coat with the hat and boots of a matinee cowboy. He explained the roll call, taken three times daily, plus random bed checks at night. He pointed toward the guardhouses, the mess hall, the barracks, and recited the rules governing them. All detainees were expected to help with the daily operations of the camp, he said, with rotating duties assigned in the kitchen, the boiler room, the laundry, and so forth. Men with special skills as medical workers, plumbers, carpenters, blacksmiths, or mechanics could request their permanent assignments in those areas. They would each receive three dollars in camp scrip every month, he told them, to trade for things in the little canteen, like tooth powder and tobacco.

"There's plenty to do, for any man who likes to keep busy," Hudson went on, informing them that, if given clearance, they could work beyond their assigned duties in the canteen or any of the other areas for ten cents an hour.

At last, he spoke of the mail. Two letters out per week, per man—each no more than twenty-four lines on one side of a single page. Four postcards, no more than seven lines each. If they insisted on writing only in German, their allowance was reduced to one letter and one postcard weekly. The letters had to be brought to the office unsealed, to make matters easier for the censors. All the mail—outgoing and incoming—would of course be read by the censors, every package searched.

"You can write that it's been snowing," said the commander, "but never how much snow fell in one day or anything more specific about the temperature than something like, 'It's very cold today.' No particulars about the camp—no numbers, not the number of guards or staff or detainees. No estimate of size. No names beyond first names. No details about where anyone is from or where and why they were arrested." A few of the men snorted at this—who, among them, knew *why*? Hudson barked, "Quiet!" and went on, "Nothing of what you might see coming into the camp—deliveries and such—or going out of it. Nothing about transfers in or out—yours or anyone else's. Nothing of what you might hear about the surrounding area—like what's going on in Bismarck or on the farms or in the towns beyond."

From the experience of having many of their early letters returned by the censors, the men had learned that they must also not complain—not of anything. Not of the barracks made frigid by wind that screamed through great chinks between the bricks, nor of the insufficient fuel for inadequate stoves. Not the indigestible food, nor the yearning boredom, nor the humiliation of being marched here and marched there, counted like livestock, watched and listened to and judged without ceasing. They could say nothing of the light that flooded away the darkness with the glare of a hundred perpetual full moons. Nor could they despair of the flat landscape of white white white relieved only by the expanse of gray fence, ten feet high, and the black guard towers that, like seven hideous giants, dwarfed even the fence.

From the dormer window, Otto could no longer see the *Wanderkameraden*. They had moved on, abandoning the hat, trapped out of reach in the teeth of the fence.

"Over here!" someone shouted from a lower floor in the barracks, followed by other loud voices and pounding feet, enough to rouse two or three of the men from their cots. These and a few others hurried out of the room and down the long corridor to the back of the building, where men from other rooms were already clumped around the window. "Come look!" one of the men called. "More trucks. More prisoners."

Max took his overcoat from the peg board, then reached back for Otto's coat, tossing it to him. "Let's go down," he said. "We can show the new ones we are alive, eh? Still men, and strong."

They joined a crush of others on the stairs, spilling out onto the porch. There were so many men pushing through the deep snow that by the time Otto and Max got outside, there was a leg-plowed path around the barracks. They followed the path across the service road, past the canteen, and beyond the boiler house, where they joined a crowd of their fellows, many dozens of them, facing the fence that enclosed them to the south. A separate fence, ten or twelve feet beyond, mirrored theirs. Behind that fence stood two groups of seven long and narrow clapboard structures separated by a field, where the new men were being lined up as they stumbled down from the trucks.

For assemblies, Hudson insisted on rows of twenty-five, and Otto quickly counted six and a half rows already formed, enough additional men approaching to fill four more—and still trucks poured through the west gate, beneath the arch of iron that spelled out to the new prisoners where they had been brought: *Fort Lincoln*.

When Otto had first seen those low flimsy buildings on the other side of the fence, snow drifted nearly to the eaves, he had thought they must be storage sheds, but last week he'd been assigned to a work detail inside the buildings, helping to set up rows of stacked bunks along the walls. Though the single stove at the center burned dangerously hot, Otto, working in his overcoat, shivered, pitying any men who might have to sleep in that room. Now he shivered again, for he could see many of the new men had only thin overcoats—some of them only suit jackets—and many more had no hats, scarves, or gloves. Snow buried their trouser legs halfway to their knees.

Otto pushed through the crowd, trying to get closer to the fence so he could see if his boy, his Gerhard, might be among the new arrivals on the field, hunched against the bite of the wind.

"Japanese," someone near him muttered. "They're all Japs."

This awareness ended the interest for most of the group, and they turned to make their way back to the barracks. Even the hiking companions, who had stopped along the south fence to watch the unloading of the trucks, now cut diagonally across the compound toward their barracks. Otto stayed, moving closer to the fence.

More and more men staggered out of the trucks, some with small suitcases, many with nothing—all of them huddled and pinched, their faces cast down. In his hurry to get outside, Otto had left his own hat and scarf behind, and now he was reminded of a paradox: the deepest cold burns the flesh.

Still, he stayed. He wanted, somehow, to show these men they were not alone in their trouble, that it was possible to endure—just as Max Kuehn had suggested—but he did not know how to communicate this. He wanted them to know he considered them part of the same brotherhood with him, a brotherhood of men imprisoned without cause. He dared not call out or even wave his arm, lest the guards accuse him of sending some coded signal.

The others were all gone. He stood alone. He stood straighter. At least by this he could show the men on the field and the guards who aimed their rifles at them that he, Otto Aust, stood as witness.

The siren for the midday count sounded, but still Otto stood.

"Back to barracks! All you gawkers! Back to barracks now for the count!"

Otto turned and saw two of the mounted guards, cantering and wheeling before the complex of wooden bungalows and brick barracks where the seamen were housed. A great mass of them, well beyond a hundred, stood in formation, facing the field of Japanese men. The guards shouted again and again, "Back to barracks! Fall out!" but the seamen stood deaf.

Otto looked hard at the formation, trying to see some glimpse of Kurt—hoping suddenly that he would see his son there with those honorable young men, united in strength. A swell of pride made him stand taller still.

More guards entered the field on foot, their teargas-loaded billy clubs raised and ready. The seamen did not move.

"Stop! No running! No running! Stop now!"

Otto looked toward the shouting. Who was running?

He saw Kurt near the boiler house, standing still, his back to Otto, hands raised as two guards approached, fingering their holstered pistols, pointing their gas billies at his face. One of the guards spotted Otto and signaled for him not to move. They stopped before Kurt, and Otto watched the pantomime of their questioning him, demanding what was in his hand, examining, consulting, and finally nodding sharply. One of them pointed to Otto and shouted, "You! Back to barracks for the count!" They turned away from Kurt and headed toward the other guards, who were still uselessly ordering the seamen inside.

Kurt waited for Otto to make his way across the snow. "Look," he said, holding out his hand when Otto drew near. "Letters. Six for me. Three from *Mutti*. Two from Bess and one from Hugh."

"Letters? We have letters?" Tears pricked Otto's eyes. "Nothing from Gerhard?"

"Maybe there will be something in our letters about him," Kurt said. "They wouldn't let me take yours, but you have some in the office. I don't know how many. A package, too, they told me." He divided his letters and held out half to Otto. "Here—for now you'll share mine. But, wait—" He plucked away one of the three he'd given to Otto, addressed in Bess's hand, and replaced it with the letter from Hugh. "You start with these, *Vati*, and after the count, we'll go and get yours. Together. Okay?"

"Perhaps your mother has sent us a fruitcake, ripened in brandy."

A great gust of wind slammed them and they nearly lost their footing. Otto took his son's arm, and they braced against the next gust. "See?" Otto said. "If we walk as one, we are stronger than the wind."

II

THOSE FIRST FEW LETTERS HAD been like a breach in the dam, and after that, as the censors caught up, the mail flowed in steadily—cards, letters, packages—sometimes three and four a day per man. Each delivery brought a small stack for both Otto and Kurt—mostly from Nina, but with regular letters from Hugh and Bess, and one or two from the lawyer Charlie Griffin, seeking to assure them he was doing all he could on the family's behalf.

But nothing from Gerhard—not even news of him.

Though the letters that finally came into their hands were nearly empty of substance, so much of the content blackened out or scissored away, each was as a small voice singing *You are not forgotten.* That fear—the fear that they were forgotten men—had proven inescapable, settling into their bones, against all reason, after two months on this plain of ice. Held fast in the grip of dim days and floodlit nights, dawn and dusk became meaningless. The camp was shut off from everything that could help the men mark time—radio, newspapers, magazines, even ordinary conversation among the guards—anything to remind them a living Earth turned beyond this realm of white and wired gray.

But as the flow of mail swelled, the men in the barracks grew friendlier, brighter, talking of their families and their work, remembering their own value, sharing generously from parcels filled with extra shirts and trousers, sweaters, woolen underwear, new bootlaces.

And food—dried sausages, cracker bread, hard-baked pretzels, waxed cheeses, and dense, long-keeping cakes.

Otto and Kurt now stood before a long table in the camp office, the contents of a bushel carton Nina had sent spread across the table, dozens of pound-sized white boxes open for examination.

"You're telling me all this is candy," wheezed the young guard who had been put in charge of searching and cataloging the prisoners' packages.

"It is, yes," Otto said. "All kinds—honey, ginger, cinnamon, licorice, sage, mint, lemon, raspberry, sour apple." Nina identified her flavors by color, but every box was a delight of mixed shapes—jewels, buttons, bows, leaves and acorns, blossoms of daisies, violets, roses, snowflakes, seashells, tiny fish, sleeping lambs and little birds.

The guard couldn't be more than a few years older than Kurt, but his sunken chest and raspy breath explained why he was here rather than in a military unit. "I've never seen any candy that looks like this."

"Have a taste." Otto surveyed the boxes, choosing one. "This," he said, offering the box. "My wife worries for my chest in such weather, so she has sent three batches."

The guard leaned in. "Where'd it come from?"

"My mother makes it," Kurt said, a little too sharply. His fingers tapped a wild drumbeat against the sheaf of letters he held, nine between them. "She makes all of it. That one's good for congestion—head and chest. Puts to shame anything you'll ever get from Smith Brothers."

"So that's medicine," said the guard. "You can't have people sending you medicine."

"Made with two kinds of mint, ginger, and cinnamon," Otto said. "And sugar, of course." He reached for another box. "Or perhaps you care for licorice? Also good for the throat."

"You think I'm fool enough to put one of those in my mouth?" said the guard, just as Commander Hudson came in.

"What's the trouble here?" Hudson glanced over the table, read the label on the carton. "You are Otto and Kurt Aust? Which is which?"

Otto laid his hand on his chest. "I am Otto." He nodded to Kurt. "My son. My elder. This parcel comes to us from my wife. All homemade."

"He claims it's candy," the young guard said. "Tried to trick me into eating some. Confiscate it?"

Hudson looked at the table, shook his head slowly, and Otto thought he saw the hint of a suppressed smile. "From your wife, you say? Fine work. Does she run a confectionary?" Hudson pointed to the box in Otto's hand. "May I?" He plucked out a piece, held it to his lips, and sucked gently. "Reminds me of some my grandmother used to make as soon as the weather turned cold, only this tastes a lot better." He popped the candy into his mouth, held it there for a moment, and then patted the base of his throat. "Feel it working already." Hudson surveyed the table again. "Now—why so much? You know you can't set up a business in camp."

"No, no," Otto said. He showed Hudson the bundles of small wax paper sacks Nina had included and handed him the note she had taped to the top layer of boxes: *To Share.* "My wife is most generous." No doubt she had emptied the restaurant's entire sugar store to provide them with such a surprise. Otto pulled a few sacks from the bundle and held them out to Hudson. "Take what you like. Please."

Hudson shook his head, his eyes showing obvious regret. Probably a violation to take anything from a prisoner, even when freely offered.

He turned to the guard. "Make an inventory, have them both initial each item and sign. Then, for God's sake, let them go." He started back toward his office, then stopped, turned. "Aust..." He lingered over the sound, as if studying it. "I know that name. You two wait here for a minute."

The back of Otto's neck prickled. He glanced at Kurt. His son's face had paled slightly, and he had stopped drumming at the letters, but he still stood with his head high and his back straight, solid on his feet.

Hudson returned, reading something from an open file folder. "Yes," he said, without looking up. "Report from one of the guards. A walkthrough a couple of days ago, late afternoon. Kurt Aust, 4271869, talking in German, writing in German, with 2150921, Egon Merkel." He stared at Kurt. "What was that about?"

"It's about staying in touch with his family," Kurt said. "Just like I told the guard."

Sheathe your tongue, Otto urged silently. There was nothing he could do. Any small signal, like a tap on his son's elbow, could easily be misinterpreted.

"Never mind what you said to the guard. I want you to tell me. Now."

Kurt sighed. "Herr Merkel…"

Hudson raised an eyebrow, so Kurt began again.

"Mr. Merkel's over seventy. He can't read or write in English. His children and grandchildren can't read or write in German."

Hudson slipped a page from the back of the folder and laid it on top. "Hard to believe Merkel doesn't know English," he said. "He entered the States in 1897."

"And that whole time he's worked on his farm in Wyoming," said Kurt. "Never more than twenty or thirty miles away from it until you—until he was arrested. His wife learned English and she took care of all the translating. She died last year."

"You still haven't told me what you were saying and writing for Merkel."

"I translate his mail for him. I take his family's letters, write them out for him in German so he can read them as much as he likes. Then he writes in German what he wants to say back to them, and I rewrite the letters in English."

Hudson grunted. He took the pencil out of the guard's hand and made a notation in the folder. "Is this Merkel the only one?"

"There are four others in our barracks," Kurt said. "Barracks 32. I can't speak for the rest of the camp."

"You're translating for all of them?"

Kurt nodded. "Mostly. My father helps when there's a lot of mail at once, to cut down on the wait. Depending on the dialect—"

"Dialect? What do you mean?" Hudson asked. "Different dialects of German? How many? You know them?"

"I'm learning," Kurt said.

"And they're still used, these dialects?"

"By the old ones," Otto said. "The country people, yes."

Hudson made another note.

Kurt said, "If you're going to tell me there's a rule against this, too—against helping old men with English—then the blame's on me. Nobody else."

Hudson eyed Kurt but said nothing. He handed the pencil back to the guard, keeping quiet while the inventory of the candy was finished, initialed, signed, and the boxes repacked in the carton. Finally he said, "Tell Merkel and the others to keep all the letters they receive in English. You keep dated copies of whatever they write in German, and copies of everything you write for them—German and English. Any time, I might tell you to hand them over to our translators."

"And for the two who can't read or write? What do I save for them? Should I bring them to the fence and stand under a microphone so you can listen in? We could set up a time—call it *The Epistolary Hour*."

"Watch your step, boy." Hudson drew another page from the file. "Are you translating for those Nazi sailors, too? It's been noticed you spend a lot of time in their section."

"They're not all Nazis," Kurt said. "And it's not a lot of time."

Hudson snapped the file shut. "Answer my question. Are you translating for them?"

"I'm not. Most of them speak English, anyway. The seamen. They don't need me."

Hudson grunted again. "I'll tell you once more: remember where you are and why. Your freedom to move around this camp, your mail, these packages—they're privileges, not rights. So watch it." He turned and strode back to his office.

When Otto and Kurt stepped outside, they were blinded by the snowpack, bleached to searing white by the sun. Kurt, carrying the carton, stopped at the edge of the porch, blinking against the rays.

Otto had meant to speak to Kurt about governing his words and tone when answering Commander Hudson, but he was awestruck when the sunlight sharpened the manly beauty of his son's face and made his hair glow red as embers ready to break flame. He remembered the evening, perhaps two weeks ago, when he'd walked past the open door of the first floor sleeping quarters and had seen Kurt sitting on a bunk beside Egon Merkel.

His son's face then—this he would never forget: intent and gentle while Herr Merkel spoke. His strong, lean hand on the old man's shoulder.

The lesson in restraint could wait. "I see how like your mother you are," Otto said, a small sun swelling his chest, spreading its glow to the top of his head, like a crown. "Myself—and Gerhard, too—when a need rises before us, we try to help. I hope we do." The thought of Gerhard ached in his throat. "But you and your mother," he said with some difficulty, "you think of what is wanting before the need shows itself, and strive to meet it before the need becomes too great." Otto swallowed back the ache. "What a fine man you are, Kurt. I am proud to call you my son."

III

THE GROUND WAS STILL HALF frozen. Otto liked it this way. Each thrust of the spade shivered through his shoulders—a challenge to his strength that would reward him with greater strength tomorrow. He liked the silvery sound that rose when he turned over each clump of earth and broke it apart with the tip of the spade, iron shattering ice. And he liked looking back at the neat row he had already dug along the eastern wall of Barracks 32, without the help of a plough.

Nearest the wall, he would bury seed potatoes, and in front of them, onions, cabbages, peppers, and tomatoes. The seedlings were already growing in wooden flats inside the barracks. But first he would prime the rows by sowing beets, spinach, and peas, loosening the ground for his tender-rooted plants.

Because this ground had not been broken—not for decades, if ever—Otto dug deep, nearly two feet, and with each slice of the spade, he wondered what he would do if he poked through the ceiling of someone's tunnel.

Every man held inside Fort Lincoln—on the German side at least—had heard the story of the truck, loaded with scrap concrete, that had dropped through the rain-softened ground to its axles, revealing a tunnel so long it reached a dozen yards beyond the south fence. And they had heard of the young officer from a scuttled oil tanker who had escaped through another tunnel and was said to have made it all the way to the Missouri River before he was captured. None of the prisoners knew the story beyond that, for the officer had been immediately transferred to another camp—a punishment camp, some whispered darkly, a *Straflager* for troublemakers.

Now there were rumors of new tunnels, recently found, and everyone was under suspicion. Some said three tunnels, some said five, some as many as twenty, but no one would admit to knowing where they were, and no one would point the finger of blame. Conscious of the microphones, the prisoners snapped off their talk when walking near the fence, and in the barracks, whenever Otto heard the word *escape*, he looked away deliberately so as not to fix that idea on any one man.

It was because of the tunnel diggers that Hudson had brought in the dogs, a pair of splendid German shepherds with erect ears and intelligent eyes. Otto could see them now with their handlers on the parade grounds, leaping barrels, knocking down men made of straw and rags, finding handkerchiefs buried in ash cans and wood piles.

As Otto watched, a lone man walking the fence line came into sight—the last member of the *Wanderkameraden*. Otto called out, but the man paid him no heed. His two friends—the Jew and the physician who had given the trio its name—were among the few who had been paroled. Like scores of others, this man's appeals for a second hearing had been denied again and again.

At first, news of paroles had sparked hope in the camp, but most of the prisoners—undistinguished men like Otto, Kurt, Max Kuehn, Egon Merkel—quickly realized there was no such hope for them. Those freed few, those very few, had lucky connections—six or seven professionals with American-born wives, like the fence-walking doctor; a handful with high-ranking relations in banking or industry; and a loud, swaggering fellow from Venezuela who had told everyone he was a diplomat.

Others had disappeared from camp, but these were the transfers. For weeks, a man on the point of parole carried his notice everywhere he went, walking briskly and speaking buoyantly, spending his days writing letters to associates on the outside and taking long, unregretful leave of camp acquaintances. But a man being transferred might be pulled from a meal or his work detail and told he had three minutes to pack. More often, he was taken off sometime during the night, his bed stripped, his few belongings boxed up by a guard the next morning, leaving the rest of the men to speculate *Where? And why?*

Otto watched for a moment longer before finishing the row. When it was done, he leaned the spade against the brick wall, rolled his shoulders and his neck. He stretched his arms high and wide and flexed his hands.

"Aust! Otto!"

He turned toward the sound. Two men were coming from the direction of the woodshop. One was Kurt, carrying a bundle of stakes to mark the borders of the garden patch. The other, Otto could now see, the one who waved his arms and again called "Otto! Otto!" was Johan Cappelmann, a woodworker from Idaho. Johan had been arrested on New Year's Day, along with his wife Liese, who had been sent to a women's camp in Texas with their five-year-old daughter, Sofie.

It was Johan's way to start speaking as if he were already in the middle of a conversation, and he did just this when he was still twenty feet from Otto. "Liese writes again and again that I must keep up my work or my hands will become like blocks of wood. So, I have had a talk with Mr. Hudson, and I am to build an extension to the canteen, large enough for many tables and a counter for selling coffee and tea—perhaps bread and pastry. A café."

Otto held out his hand to greet Johan, nodded, and, unsure of what to say, said, "Indeed—a good project. A deal of work, I should think."

"So it is, my friend," Johan said, clapping Otto's back while Kurt laid the stakes on the ground. "But not so much if you Austs work with me! You have a restaurant, so you must help me with the design, show me what will be most convenient." He squatted beside the freshly dug row and sifted the soil through his hands. "We could serve your vegetables, Otto." Seeing that Kurt had already set the first stake into place, Johan took the spade, and with a perfect strike drove the stake deep. "Kurt," he said, "I have heard you tell of building things for your mother, and I know you can draw the plans—so you will be my first assistant."

"Can you teach me to make dovetail joints?" Kurt asked, steadying the second stake. "Mine never hold."

"Of course!" Another perfect strike. "Otto—can you manage a hammer and saw?"

"A hammer, yes—but not so well as you. A saw, only if you mark the wood. A garden I can measure—who cares if it is a finger's breadth too wide or too narrow?" Otto laughed. "Hand me a saw if you like. But truly—if you are wise, you will never trust me to cut the wood. It is because I talk too much."

Johan and Kurt quickly set the remaining stakes. "We'll begin with what is easy," said Johan, returning the spade to Otto. "The materials for the café must first be ordered, so we start with the stage."

"A stage?" Kurt said. "You didn't tell me anything about a stage. Where? What on earth for?"

Johan pointed to the boxy warehouse where, once or twice a month, the men lined up folding chairs to watch a film cast onto the windowless back wall. "Yes, yes, a stage," he said. "Think of it—soon we can have real performances. Theatre, music, and not just those terrible American movies." Johan slapped his hand against a stake to test its firmness. "With this, too, you can help me. Before we had to turn in our radio, my Liese and I used to listen to the opera from Berlin. I enjoy the music but cannot follow the story. Otto, you know of these things," he said. "Often I hear you singing softly. Kurt, too. I am no singer, but I want to know the words, and I want to know the stories. In this, I will be your apprentice." He tested another stake. "A good trade, I think."

Otto's grief burst upon him—memories of Gerhard singing, sometimes even in his sleep, as if the boy breathed music. Letting the spade fall, Otto turned toward the barracks wall and covered his face.

Behind him, he heard Kurt explaining quietly, his own voice unsteady, "My brother is the one you want—the classical singer. The expert. But my father and I can tell you the stories. And we can teach you the drinking songs—they help the work go faster, especially the hammering." Otto heard the chuck of the spade breaking new sod. "And the digging," Kurt said. "Don't you think so, *Vati*?" Kurt spoke again to Johan. "We still don't know where he is—my brother."

Johan said, "Every day in this place, there is something to remind us of our sorrow. I am sure to miss my little Sofie's birthday."

Turning back toward them, Otto asked, "She is your only child?"

Johan nodded. "A few days before we were arrested, my Liese told me she believed she carried another, but she was not yet sure. In her first letter to me, from the camp, she said she had not been well—a day in the hospital. But no more has she spoken of expecting a child." With his heel, he broke apart a large clump of freshly turned soil. "It is best to keep busy," he said, "so we do not think too much on things we cannot help."

While Otto rested with his back against the wall, Kurt worked the ground. Johan went to the storage shed where the hand tools were kept and returned with two more spades. For the rest of the afternoon, the three men dug. Johan told them he had already found the supplies for the stage, so they talked about design and seating and when they might begin building. They talked of the café and customers and cooking. They talked of woodworking and the opera and their families. And for those hours, so long as they did not look up to the towers or across the compound to see the horses trotting past with their mounted guards, they could feel like ordinary men, like good neighbors sharing labor.

They finished digging the garden patch a few minutes before the siren for the evening meal sounded, and while they changed their clothes and scrubbed their hands, they told their barracks' mates about the theatre. By the time they reached the mess hall, men were reciting their favorite poems to anyone who would listen, and by the next morning, they were scouring the camp library for books of plays, writing scenes and skits of their own, practicing songs and folk dances, bickering about who should take the women's parts.

Over the next few weeks, in the afternoons, after they had finished their required work, Otto, Kurt, and Johan laid the stage floor and built the frame for the proscenium arch. "Our stage shall be as grand as we can make," Johan said. "And for the arch, we must seek out the finest decorative painter in the camp."

In the evenings, in the hours before lights out, though their backs ached and their hands were needled with splinters, Otto and Johan worked on plans for the café while Kurt translated letters for Egon Merkel and the other four men with little English. It pleased Otto to hear the long-absent brightness return to his son's voice as he talked with the men, in German, about their children and their farms, and about Germany as it had been forty, fifty years before. In turn, the men asked Kurt about his schooling, nodding in approval when he told them he'd been accepted for study at university. One of them, a sugar beet farmer from Montana, said he didn't know where Indiana was, and this prompted another man to wonder how far his own mail had traveled from Oregon.

"We should draw a map," Kurt said, "so we'll know where our friends are, after we've all gone home."

In his son's eyes, Otto saw a flash of boyish delight. When Kurt was small, he'd made a game of mapmaking until he could draw a perfect Germany—Germany before the Great War—without checking a book or asking a single question.

"I have something you can use," Otto said, and he hurried upstairs to his bunk and came down again, a little breathless, and offered a sheet of brown paper Nina had wrapped around the wool socks she had sent him. Kurt smoothed it across a table in the first-floor common room and sat for a long time, his pen hovering.

"Maybe I should have paid more attention in geography, huh?"

Otto squeezed his son's shoulder. "Begin with what you know."

Kurt touched the tip of the pen to the paper and quickly drew what looked like the petals of a wilted lily. "The Great Lakes," he said. "Sort of." He used the finger dip of the center lake to mark the northwestern corner of Indiana, made a straight line down the right side and then angled to show the southern border, jagged along the river. "This is where we're from," he said, marking an X. From that jagged borderline, he shaped Kentucky, then sketched in Ohio to the east and Illinois to the west, topping Indiana with Michigan, tucking it into the embrace of the lakes. "Now," he said, "any of you from Illinois—come tell me what's around you."

After the stage was finished, while they waited for the supplies to work on the café, Kurt spent most of his free time in Barracks 32. Whenever he retrieved the map from under his cot and unrolled it across the table, the others would break from their rehearsals, their reading or writing, their cards or their chess boards, and join him. Working on the map became for them a game, a great puzzle they all had a hand in solving. Sometimes they chuffed each other in vibrant debate before agreeing on precisely where a state belonged or how large it should be. Then, when all the states were in place, the men helped fill in their own with what they knew of cities—of how long it took to drive from one to another, where they sat in relation to deserts, forests, mountains, rivers, and roads.

One evening, a stranger appeared in their barracks. Otto had noticed him before, a man who, despite all lack of privacy in this place, had managed to keep to himself, as if he moved about inside his own tiny room. He stood at a window to eat his meals, his plate and cup resting on the sill; he turned away from conversations during work assignments; and he walked alone, always with his chin level, his eyes focused rigidly ahead. Now this man draped his coat over the back of a chair where another man was sitting, pushed his way to the table, pressed his finger down on the shape representing Ohio and said, "Springfield. There I am Professor of German language and literature. Wittenberg University."

"Like in *Faust*?" Kurt asked.

"Just so."

"Then you are a teacher," Otto said.

The man smoothed his wispy red-gray hair and gave a quick tug at the hem of his waistcoat to make the buttons lie flat. "I am Professor Spannagel."

"My father means no offense," Kurt said. "There are men here who could use some help learning English. I've been translating for them—letters, mainly—but they'd have an easier time if there were a regular class."

Spannagel now looked even more offended, if that were possible. "My own work absorbs my time. There are insufficient English translations of Germany's greatest poetry. To translate Göethe alone is the effort of a lifetime. It is most taxing."

"You are permitted German books?" Otto asked.

"Of course," said Spannagel. "When I arrived, I composed a report to make my position known to Mr. Hudson. He understands who I am, and that it is a mistake that I should be here. My scholarship is too valuable to suffer interruption. While I wait for this error to be corrected, I must continue, just as I would in my rightful place at the university." Spannagel looked around at the men in the common room, refusing to conceal that he was judging their skills and intelligence—and the justness of their imprisonment—by their appearance. "Surely you can discover a man suited to your task, a schoolmaster by profession."

"Right," said Kurt, his voice twisting toward sarcasm. "I'll ask around for someone more qualified." He dismissed Spannagel with a nod and turned back to the map, muttering, "Pompous old coot."

Several of the men near Kurt pounded the table, laughing in approval. With a dramatic flourish, Spannagel swept his coat from the chair and strode out. The open door caught the wind and flung wide, the frozen hinges squealing under the strain.

Otto stepped onto the porch, drew the door closed, and rejoined the group.

"What a performance," said Kurt. "Can he repeat it, do you think? Johan—tell him he could do it on stage. To impress Hudson."

Otto laughed. "Yes, yes. Invite the professor to recite some of his translations as a centerpiece for our revue. Tell him his Göethe shall be the stone in the pot that begins our hearty soup."

Everyone laughed again, and after a few more jokes at Spannagel's expense, Max Kuehn said, "This is not a bad notion, Otto. Americans, I think, could do with a little Göethe."

Someone imitated Spannagel's strut, then was joined by another, and another, until half a dozen of them had formed a chorus line of strutting Spannagels. As a great round of applause faded, the group took up the chant again, urging Johan to invite the professor into their theatrical plans. When at last Johan had agreed, the men broke away into friendly trios and quartets to study the map, to dream of companionable evenings in the café, and to rehearse their scenes and songs.

IV

NINA WALKED THROUGH THE HOUSE to see what the FBI men had left to her. Most of her clothes, some soap and shampoo, and a single large suitcase lying open on the floor of the bedroom, as if to give notice that she was expected to depart within the hour.

The men had come well before dawn, five of them shouting and pounding at the door, flashing badges as they shoved her aside—still in her night dress—to root, rifle, break. To strip and strip and strip. They'd brought a moving van this time. They emptied bureaus, chests, a wardrobe and a china cabinet into crates, which they carried out to the van, and then they carried out the furniture. They took all the garden tools, along with the hammers and screwdrivers, jars of nails and fasteners, a box of hinges. Cans of paint.

If she hadn't shipped the carton yesterday, they would have gotten Kurt's books—physics, calculus, geometry—along with his drawing pencils, his protractor, triangle and slide rule. All the things he needed for his engineering studies. As it was, they took every other book left in the house. They took the boys' school papers and their desks. They took the preserve jars in the cellar. They took her kitchen knives, her saucepans and baking sheets.

She kept them from taking her mother's porcelain chocolate pot. When she had seen one of the men eyeing it in the kitchen, she had lifted it down from the shelf without a word and carried it to the back porch. She sat on the swing, though it glistened with frost, and held the pot on her lap. Every few minutes, one of the FBI men would open the door leading from the kitchen to the porch and stand and stare at her before going back inside. She did not look at them. She said nothing. She had decided that if any of them asked a question or gave an order, she would respond as they required, but, though at times two or three of them seemed to be discussing her behavior, none of them approached her. They had finished before the downtown shopkeepers and office workers began their day, and when the FBI men had taken everything, they left without a word, not bothering to close the front door.

She had telephoned Mr. Griffin, knowing he could do nothing. "I understand now the house must be sold," she told him. He'd broached the subject with her weeks ago, explaining that because her bank accounts had been blocked, she'd have to offer the house as a cash sale.

She'd said then she wanted to try once more before giving up, and she'd painted a sign announcing the restaurant would open again for lunch every day beginning March 18. Tomorrow. How she had wanted to write Otto and Kurt about it. How she had longed to assure Gerhard, when at last she learned where he was, that he, his father, and his brother had a home waiting for their return.

Well, the FBI had seen to that. It was probably why they had come. Someone had seen the sign, had not liked it, and had made up a story, perhaps, about codes or secret meetings. Or perhaps not. It was impossible to know.

"How much can I get for the house, Mr. Griffin?" she had asked.

"Probably no more than half its value," he said. "I'm sorry. The advantage is always with the buyer in a cash sale."

And when the seller is a spy, a fifth columnist, a dangerous alien enemy, Nina thought, but she did not say it.

What she did say was, "With half I can finish the mortgage and a few remaining bills. When the house has been sold, I will rent a room for myself. From today I must look for a job."

But how to find either? Nina sat down on the bed—they had left her that. She rested her feet on the rim of the open suitcase. How to inquire for a job or a room when, everywhere she went, she was met with an unbearable silence if she dared to ask a simple question—*What price to mail this package? Have you sewing thread in this color? What day was this cabbage delivered?* How, when people she'd known for years looked past her or through her, their faces smooth as stone? When regular customers, hailed with a wave, blanked their eyes and turned their backs? Stock boys and clerks at the greengrocer's, the hardware store, the druggist's. Teachers who, season after season, had praised Kurt and Gerhard at awards assemblies. Everywhere she went, she felt herself pushing against a current of unspoken suspicion and condemnation.

She recognized this feeling—a shadow of it—from years before, when the boys were small. On a late September evening, nearing dusk, she'd noticed a black family on the walk in front of the restaurant, the man leaning to one side, as if trying to peer through the window into the dining room. The restaurant was nearly full because of the early dinner crowd that always came on Wednesdays, before the evening services at the Baptist and Methodist churches. Gerhard had come home from school with a fever, she remembered, and Otto had just gone upstairs to take him some hot broth. Kurt was in the kitchen, dishing up the orders.

It was the sudden silence in the dining room that made Nina look out the window. Everyone, even the small children, had stopped talking. As she walked toward the door, she felt an electric pressure on her skin, as if a thunderstorm were about to break.

The pressure followed her outside, pushing at her back, draping around her shoulders, though the sky was clear and the setting sun had cast a golden glow across the garden. She smiled at the family—a man, a woman, three little boys—and said, "Welcome! We are open for dinner. Please, come inside."

One of the children took a few steps forward, but the man caught him and pulled him back. "I'm hungry, Daddy," the child said.

With a laugh, Nina said to the couple, "Always hungry, the little boys. They grow so very fast. I have two. Won't you come inside?"

The man looked at his wife, but Nina couldn't read what passed between them. He looked back at Nina, without quite settling his eyes on her. He nodded slightly. "We got to be moving along now."

"Please," Nina said, "my family and I wish you to be our guests."

A look of outrage flitted across the man's face. "I have the money to pay."

"Of course, of course," Nina said. "Even so, we should like to invite your family for this evening."

The woman whispered something to her husband. He shook his head and turned again to Nina. He met her eyes this time, but the look of anger had passed, replaced with an expression mingling strength, weariness, gratitude, and sorrow. A look that could burst a heart.

She watched them go before returning to the dining room. Everyone was chattering again. It was as if the storm had passed and the air was fresh and calm. And suddenly she understood that all those people believed she had sent the family away. This was what they had wanted, what they had expected. Believing she had done this, they approved of her, counted her as one of them.

She should have said something—should have faced the crowd and said, "I invited them in. They are welcome here always." But she had not done it. The shame she felt then burned deeper, now that she understood in her bones something of what the black couple must have felt, standing outside looking in.

Every day, more and more posters appeared—in shop windows, on buses, outside churches. There was the helmeted Hun with his menacing gaze and the warning *He's Watching You*. The declaration *It Can Happen Here* beneath the image of Nazi jackboots treading on factories. A fist punching through a swastika bordered by the demand to buy more war bonds. A German soldier thrusting a bloody dagger through a Bible.

Among these were variations of the leering, big-toothed Japanese soldier—inclining his elephantine ear to a keyhole because *Open Trap Make Happy Jap*; clasping his hands and begging Americans to *Take the Day Off*; emerging from fire, stooped as a gorilla, with a naked white woman flung over his shoulder.

And everywhere, the drowning American sailor pointing a finger directly at her: *Someone talked.*

Then there were the dignified little banners with the blue stars—for a husband, a son, a brother gone to war. Some stars had already been changed to gold. So many stars—in the windows of houses, apartment buildings, even offices—fixing her like dozens of accusing eyes. When the first banners had been hung, her heart had ached in fellow feeling. As a wife. As a mother. But now if she stopped to look at one, she felt stares boring into her—stares shielded by downturned hats, a twist of the head, a twitching curtain—turning the banners to placards all with the same message: *Enemy. Enemy.* She fought the urge to stop people on the street and demand to know, *Where am I to find such a banner, to show the cost I have paid in this war? My husband. My sons. Our home.*

Once, she would have thought the other German people they knew in Newman would help her, but it was not so. In the days before Christmas, even before she learned where her family had been taken, she had made a list of those who might write letters of support to the attorney general, to the president himself, in favor of Otto's and the boys' release. But whether she telephoned or went to their doors or met them on the street, they all interrupted her. They had heard about the arrests. No, they would not write, could not write. A letter, what good was that? They could do nothing. A few said outright that she and Otto—even their sons—must have committed some wrong, perhaps unknowingly, but wrong all the same. Others, in saying it was not for them to judge, implied she and her family had brought the trouble on themselves.

All of them were afraid.

Jan Mueller, one of the members of Otto's singing society, who at the last St. Nikolas feast had raised his glass to Otto, saluting him as the best of friends, said to her, "Always Otto has talked too much. You see what has come of it." Martin Sauber, the butcher who made their sausages, upon hearing her first words had snapped, "Don't call again" and hung up the phone. Father Emil Kraus, who for twelve years had unfailingly ended his Lenten fast with a platter of Nina's roasted pork and potatoes, promised to pray for the family, but added, "What more can I do? Do you want them to come for me next? I must think of the church."

She had even called Otto's cousin. As soon as she said, "Franz, this is Nina. Nina Aust," he handed the phone to his wife, who whispered, "He is still bitter about the farm. And it will be of no use to ask Peter or Albert," she added, referring to her sons. "Franz has told them Otto is a man not to be trusted."

Of all these—friends, neighbors, customers, passing acquaintances, strangers—how many had spoken against her family, had told lies, large or small? Lies that the president's secret police, led by that Mr. Hoover, could twist into damning evidence. In her mind, she asked the same question of every face that turned away. *Was it you? Was it you?*

So long as she had her home and a small hope of reopening the restaurant, Nina had believed she could endure, surviving in a small, honorable way until her men were returned to her. Now that hope was gone. Perhaps she should go to another town entirely. But where? Where would her name, her way of speaking, her identification card in its angry red folder not mark her as an enemy?

She latched the suitcase and grasped the handle so she could move it back to the closet. When she lifted the case, something dropped away from it. She reached for what had fallen—a packet of seeds. Her cornflower seeds.

Otto had planned to sow them in the front garden as cooling drops of blue amidst the orange fire lilies and the poppies of scarlet and sun. The first spring after they'd bought the house, while she and Otto scraped and sanded away the dull white from the siding, repainting with the blue-green tint of fir trees after rain, they had talked of flowers. In summer, Otto told her, when their guests stepped from the city pavement onto the brick walk leading to the restaurant door, they would, for the space of five meters, believe they were passing through a mountain meadow painted by a happy god.

She put away the suitcase and carried the packet outside with her. It was almost too late now to sow the seeds for summer blooming. Otto would have tended to his task on the first day of false spring, which always came in February. For fifteen summers, she had longed for the cornflowers, but the seeds couldn't be found in Newman. Then, last November, Otto surprised her with the packet on a snow-dusted morning. When she asked how and where he'd managed to find the seeds, he pinched her nose and said, "No matter, my sweetheart. This summer, you shall have your blue jewels."

She stood on the brick walk, looking at the house, trying to remember the feeling of the happy years, when, because of Otto, always Otto, the deep weariness of each midnight vanished with the next dawn. If Otto had been the one left behind in Newman, instead of her, he would have managed to save the restaurant somehow, would have planted the cornflowers as a pledge of faith in the future. She was sure of it. His spirit had always been brighter than hers, always more eager, more hopeful. More accepting. More patient. And few could resist his good cheer. Otto could make friends of enemies.

If she had it to do over, if she could go back to the Good Shepherd sisters or even back to that grim room with Parks and his partner, she would give them what they wanted. She would make a confession of guilt. Guilt for what did not matter. If she had it to do over, Nina would confess to anything at all if doing so could have spared Otto and their boys. *Cloister me forever*, she would have said, *or send me back to Germany, never to return. Only let my husband see our sons safely into manhood.*

She had tried to do this in Chicago, tried to take all the responsibility onto herself. And it *was* hers. She had started the singing. And she had kept on singing even when Bess begged her to stop. A terrible, terrible mistake. She had said this, said all this and more, *The fault is mine alone*, but they had chained up Otto and Kurt in spite of her, marched them away, and told her she was forbidden further contact with Gerhard until he was assigned to a permanent camp.

She was responsible, too, for the trauma she had caused Bess and Hugh—hours of interrogation punctuated by threats of blacklisting, threats of jail and prosecution, all at the point of a rifle. When they were back in Newman, Hugh came to her the next day, just as he always had, and every day after, morning and evening, but not Bess.

Watching out the window, Nina would see the two of them across the street, but when Hugh started toward the restaurant, Bess would stop, turn right or left, toward school or home. Sometimes Hugh would catch her sleeve and try to hold her back; sometimes they seemed to be arguing, but, in the end, Bess pulled away and Hugh crossed the street alone.

"What can I do?" Nina asked Hugh one morning. "What can I say to her?"

Hugh shrugged and, head down, made his way to the piano bench. "She's scared."

"Of me? Of my family?"

Hugh played a few mournful notes. "She says she doesn't know what to believe anymore. Who to trust."

"She doesn't trust me?"

Hugh shook his head. "But she misses you. I know she does." He played on, working out a sad tune he had invented. "She almost came with me yesterday."

Bess did return at last, just three weeks ago. She trotted across Elm ahead of Hugh, breezing into the restaurant, tossing off her blue coat—cornflower blue, Nina now realized. Last winter, she had helped the girl choose it. And then, as if there had been no lapse at all, Bess asked what

help was needed in the kitchen. Nina longed to explain herself, to again
ask Bess's forgiveness, and she longed to ask Hugh how he had persuaded
his sister to come. But in the way the girl would avert her eyes if Nina
looked too long; in the way Bess would abruptly ask about the amount
of flour if the talk turned to the arrests, or to the letters from Otto and
Kurt, or to the lack of news about Gerhard; and in the way Hugh went
quiet and watched his sister anxiously at such moments, Nina understood that silence on the matter had been part of the negotiation.

Gently, Nina pressed the packet between her fingers so she could
feel the hard little cylinders of the seeds, like tiny bullets. Perhaps
she ought to sow them, a ceremony of parting. By the time the little
meadow bloomed this summer, the house would belong to others.
The Aust Family Restaurant, their home, would be no more.

No—whoever came next would not have her cornflowers.

She would save the seeds for herself, for those she loved, for those
who loved her. And if she could see no hope of planting them, she
would pass them on to Bess to store away for some precious someday.
That was the wonder of seeds, holding their glory in trust for decades
so long as they were kept dark and dry. Only a few needed to survive
to assure the next generation.

She put the packet of seeds in her pocket and pulled up the stake
holding the sign announcing the restaurant's reopening. It seemed a
nasty joke that the FBI had left this, of all things, untouched.

"Mrs. Aust."

Iris Sloan had slipped up behind her on the brick walk. Nina
hadn't seen her since Hugh had pleaded to go to Chicago.

"I had to work the night shift at the nursing home," Iris said.
"I've only just heard. Everett called me—I guess Charlie called him."
The woman's unbuttoned coat revealed an aide's uniform, rumpled
and spotted. "I asked Everett to go pick up the kids before they set
out this morning and take them on to school. So I could talk to you."

"Come," Nina said, letting the sign fall to the ground. "I can give
you coffee. And some bread. Please."

They passed through the restaurant dining room, the remaining tables and chairs scattered like skeletons. In the kitchen, the cupboard doors stood open, only a few cups and plates left inside, but the smell of yesterday's bread, freshening in the warm oven, swirled around them and filled the hollows.

Iris's face, already drawn with exhaustion, now drained of color. "I had no idea. What happened?"

"That which the palmerworm hath left," Nina said, "hath the locust eaten. The Book of Joel, I think." She held the swinging door open with her shoulder and looked at the empty place in the dining room where the piano had sat. "I am worried for Hugh that he will not find another instrument for his practice. He must not lose his practice."

She let the door swing shut, pulled out a chair for Iris, filled the kettle with water, and set it on the stove. She put the chocolate pot on the table and spooned in ground coffee. She took the bread from the oven, cut two slices, smeared them with butter, and brought them on a small plate. When the water boiled, she poured it in a gentle stream over the grounds and put the lid on the pot.

"Bess told me about this once," Iris said, hovering a fingertip over the flowers encircling the lid, each a separate, tiny sculpture. "I never imagined it was so beautiful."

"A wedding gift to my mother—1882." Nina looked around her ravished kitchen before settling her eyes again on the pot. "Better it would have stayed in Germany."

Iris drew her hand back. She took a bite of the bread, chewing slowly. "I'm sorry I haven't come before," she said at last. "I couldn't. I mean—I couldn't because I was so angry with you. More than I've ever been with anyone in my whole life. If I'd been there—in Chicago—if I could have gotten my hands on you…" She shuddered, as if slashed by a frigid wind. "When I let myself think of what could have happened to my kids…" Iris closed her eyes and tilted her face to the ceiling, whispering a prayer for strength. "I'm not saying I've always done the best for them, in spite of trying. Far from it. But I do know what it's like to be treated like poison everywhere you go because of one or two choices other people have made up their minds were wrong. People who don't know a thing about you except for the gossip they've heard. So I try not to do that. I try."

Nina swirled the coffee in the pot, thinking of the times that she, from the sanctuary of her own family, had looked out on Iris with a condemning eye for choosing to leave her children in the care of another while she went out dancing with some lithe young man. She set down the pot so the grounds would settle and thought of the many times she had heard others—in the restaurant, in shops, at school functions—ridiculing Iris for not being able to hold her husband, mocking her for refusing security in the form of a marriage proposal from a stodgy widowed deacon of the Baptist church. Nina had not joined in, but neither had she spoken up in defense.

If she had it to do over again, Nina would say to Iris, *How strong you are. How splendid you are—to have been left alone with so many burdens to carry, and yet to rise up.* She could say it now. Nina lifted the pot carefully, so as not to disturb the grounds, and poured the coffee, silky black and fragrant, into the waiting cups. "I am sorry to have no sugar or cream," she said.

"You know, I was going to come anyway," said Iris. "Soon—even if it hadn't been for all this. I'd made up my mind to it because my children love you. And I love them. More than anything." She wiped tears from her cheek and tipped her head back again for a moment, then met Nina's eyes. "They want me to make my peace with you." She held out her hand. "So here I am."

V

ANOTHER CAVE-IN—THE THAWING GROUND HAD simply given way this time, taking part of a wooden delivery platform outside the camp bakery with it. Several men, a tailor and a watchmaker from Barracks 32 among them, had been hauling fifty-pound sacks of flour from a supply truck, hoisting them onto the platform when it collapsed. The diggers hadn't gone deep enough. Someone had taken a lot of trouble to gain access to the crawlspace, creating a false floor for a large cupboard in the pantry, but whoever was responsible for the digging had left a mere foot of earth, unsupported overhead, as he tunneled beneath the loading platform toward the southwestern corner of the fence. The tailor told how he and the others were still rescuing the flour from the hole when the siren blasted and guards fanned out across the compound, shouting and waving the prisoners back to barracks.

There were four counts that day. In between, the barracks doors were locked from the outside. A man couldn't look out any window without seeing armed patrols. After the third count, a pair of guards dropped down from the bed of a truck, pulled out pails of milk and coffee and a crate filled with bread, which they set on the floor, just inside the door. Otto calculated quickly, protesting the supply was less than half what was needed. "You must bring more," he said, and when a dozen others pressed forward in support of Otto's demand, the guards turned and forced the prisoners back with threats of tear gas. Just past dark, as the guards finished the fourth count, Commander Hudson himself came, ordering everyone in Barracks 32 into the common room for an announcement.

"All optional work is stopped until further notice," Hudson said. "All recreation outside the barracks is suspended. Assigned duties for camp maintenance will carry on as usual."

As Hudson turned to go, Johan pushed his way up the staircase so he could be seen and called out, "Sir! Mr. Hudson, sir. You do not include the building of the café, I believe. The materials are ordered. And you will not stop the theatre—we are nearly ready to fix a date for the opening."

"I've made myself clear," said Hudson. "I won't be hearing appeals on this."

The next morning, notices were posted all over the camp, in every barracks and work area, saying the parade ground would no longer be available for soccer matches or group calisthenics. The gates between the barracks and the workshops would now be locked during the day, with each man required to present his identification at the guard house before and after his assigned work. When the wood for the café arrived a few days later, it was pulled from the truck, stacked, and covered with a tarp, quickly coated by a sheen of spring ice.

Meal times were reduced to twenty minutes, leaving men at the end of the serving line as few as five minutes to eat. The number of guards for each work detail was doubled and all nonessential communication forbidden, preventing conversation among prisoners housed in different barracks. Otto tended his warm-weather seedlings inside, but he was refused permission to work in his garden patch. Whenever he could, shielded for a moment by a group of other men who were also passing the garden, he dipped his hand down to pluck away weeds threatening the young plants.

The stream of mail slowed again, and everyone's allowance of weekly postcards was cut from four to one. Though the men could see their packages being unloaded from trucks and carried into the camp office with the same frequency as before, they received almost none of them. The few they were allowed to collect were searched more rigorously, with more items confiscated without clear reason—anything with a German label, even if it was as harmless as a hairbrush; glass jars of preserves; sheaves of clean writing paper; postage stamps.

In one box, Nina had sent the books and drafting tools Kurt needed to keep up with his engineering studies. After more than half an hour, first reasoning, then pleading with the wheezing guard not to destroy them, Kurt insisted on speaking to Commander Hudson himself.

Hudson came, but he held up a hand against Kurt's arguments. One by one, he examined the items, dropped them back into the carton. Then he scrawled a note in red, *Contents banned,* and tossed it in. "Return to sender," he said to the guard.

When Kurt told Otto what had happened, the old fear crept in again. They were suspended, like birds in a bell jar. Each day with the incoming letters, however many or few there were, men all around him learned of babies born, wives or parents or children ailing, furnaces faltering, roofs sagging, businesses stalling—and they could do nothing, absolutely nothing, about any of it.

Still, Otto opened every envelope with a hunger for news of Gerhard. But week after week, he found nothing more than a sentence or two, increasingly more pained, to say that there was no news. Gerhard was not with Nina. She had not heard from him. She had no address to share.

Nor could Otto make out what was happening with the restaurant. Was Nina managing? Were there were enough customers? Had she reopened for business at all? In each letter he wrote, he prodded for information, but he could not tell if his wife was avoiding answering, or if her letters with the details he wanted were the ones that came with great sections cut out, the remaining pieces taped incongruously together.

He studied her words, studied the slope of her handwriting, searching for unarticulated messages, but all he could fully understand were her questions about his health, whether he was sleeping enough and eating enough, or what he would like her to send him. From time to time, she offered tidbits about the coming marriage of Iris Sloan and the jeweler Everett Beale. Always, she ended with warm assertions of her love and a promise that she would write again tomorrow.

Sometimes, he wanted to tell Nina to stop writing because the letters were becoming part of the monotony—mere tricks of light suggesting movement where there was none—but when he saw he'd written the words "no more letters," he crumpled the page and threw his pen to the floor. He would miss the day's outgoing post if he didn't write something, but he had nothing to say—nothing that would pass the censors intact. He picked up his pen and reached for a postcard. Seven lines he could manage: *How I wish I could be with you now, drinking coffee, eating your walnut cake, talking of spring. Tell me if the daffodils are blooming. Little grows here. Write of color. Please send news of our youngest. –Otto*

What was the date? Lately Nina's letters had been coming to him thirty-two or thirty-three days after she'd written them—the one he'd received yesterday had been dated the twenty-fifth of March—so he was always uncertain now of what day it was. He rose from his own bunk and, stooping to keep his head from hitting the ceiling, he crossed the room to Max Kuehn's cot. "Max, may I see your calendar, please?"

A day or two after they had arrived in camp, Max had sketched a tiny calendar, lightly in pencil, on the wall above his cot. The columns of numbers were so fine, so vaporous, they might have been spider webs or specks of dust, and even if someone knew the calendar was there, it was impossible to see from more than a few inches away.

Otto knew of no rule meant to prevent Max from keeping his calendar, but secrecy had become natural to them. Their brief fellowship of sharing had faded as the mail slowed and the guards' paranoia spread like cholera among them. When they wanted to open their suitcases, they created a screen with a coat or a blanket. They hid bits of bread in their pockets when they left the mess hall, tucked their already censored letters and the books they'd borrowed from the small camp library under their mattresses or inside their shirts. When Max could not hide his calendar by sitting on his bunk, he propped the chess board he'd made from the bottom of a cardboard box against the wall and lined up his soap chessmen as guards. Instead of marking out each day with a cross, he wetted his thumb and wiped it from the wall.

Max shifted aside and Otto leaned in. The twenty-seventh of April.

Otto nodded his thanks and wrote *27 April 1942* on the postcard. Four months since he had heard Nina's voice, Gerhard's voice. The hyacinth and daffodils in the back garden would already have bloomed and faded and nearly all the trees would be in full leaf again. The tulips would have begun to set their heads for blooming and the spears for irises and summer lilies would be piercing the ground. He would send the card anyway, he decided. Perhaps eight weeks would pass before he held Nina's reply to this card in his hand. By then, the poppies would have stretched thigh high, their bright blossoms perched on the stalks like greedy cups gulping the sun.

He stopped on the second floor to look for Kurt, and when he couldn't find him there, he looked in the common room. Four men were playing cards at a small table they had pushed up to a window to get the benefit of the weak light filtering through the overcast sky. "He's outside," one of them said, nodding to the window. "On the steps. He never came back in after he went to pick up his mail."

The steps had not yet been fully cleared of a wet morning snow, but Kurt sat there anyway. Otto bent to take hold of his son's arm. "Come inside. You must change to dry clothes."

Kurt shook Otto away. He held a letter—typed, on heavy paper, partly open, showing a large round seal enclosing a fierce winged creature that clutched a shield in one foreclaw and a lamp in the other.

Kurt did not resist when Otto tugged it from his hand. "What is this letter? From Purdue University?" Otto read the letter quickly, then once again, more slowly, and sat down on the step next to his son. "We must let your mother know," he said. "Perhaps she can telephone someone and explain."

"She knows." Kurt stared off across the compound. "She forwarded it." He handed Otto another letter, this one from Nina. She wrote that after the letter had come, first she and then Charlie Griffin had phoned the university, with Mr. Griffin finally speaking to a dean, who cited the uncertainty of Kurt's situation as reason not to hold his place in the School of Civil Engineering.

In Otto's hands, the pages had become as lead. "So they have canceled your enrollment." He put his arm around Kurt's shoulders. "Never mind. When all is sorted, when we are home again, you will apply once more. You can write today and tell them so. Come."

"It's time to stop dreaming, *Vati*." Kurt reached inside his coat, brought out two more envelopes, both marred with the familiar bruises of censors' stamps, notes, initials, and resealing tape. Kurt tapped the top envelope. "This one's from Mr. Griffin."

"And the other? That is not your mother's writing, I think," Otto said, leaning closer.

"No," Kurt held up the letter to Otto. "It's Gerhard's. He's in a camp in Tennessee. There's an address."

"Gerhard!" Otto pressed the letter to his chest and let his tears spill freely. "Come! Come!" he cried, tugging at Kurt's arm. "Our lost one is found!" He stood and turned back toward the barracks door. "We must write to our Gerhard today. Now. Come inside."

Kurt stayed on the step. "My little brother's a prisoner," he said. "I'm glad you think that's good news." He put his head in his hands and sighed deeply, as he always did when he had said something he was sorry for. "You keep that one, *Vati*, but please give me the others."

Otto handed the letters back.

Carefully, as if to preserve them, Kurt refolded the pages, re-placed them in their envelopes, and stacked them, lining up their edges. Then, quick as a stab, he ripped through them. He laid the halves of the envelopes on the step beside him, and, taking them up one at a time, he tore them into bits. When he'd shredded the last, he gathered all the fragments, holding them in his open palm until the next gust of wind carried them away.

"I do not understand," Otto said quietly.

"What's to understand, *Vati,* except that we're not wanted here?" Kurt stood up, beat the snow from his coat and the seat of his trou-sers, turned his collar up against the wind, and headed across the compound toward the seamen's barracks.

VI

NINA WAS LAUGHING—THEY WERE ALL laughing—as they left the judge's chambers, and they kept on laughing as they spilled into the hallway and down the stairs to the marble-floored rotunda. A bright amber and rose-tinted light poured down from the stained-glass dome, sparkling like heavenly champagne. When Nina offered her outstretched hands in congratulations to Iris—now Mrs. Beale—Iris pulled Nina into a great hug, breaking free with a kiss on her cheek.

Then everyone was hugging everyone else—two, three, even four at a time—and when Charlie Griffin tried to wave the party into place for photographs, they could not stop hugging. Mr. Griffin snapped away, catching Everett Beale striking a dance pose with his bride; he caught Iris between her children, their hands joined and arms swinging high as if in a playground game; Everett grasping Hugh's hand in a manly shake; and Everett beaming on Bess like a proud father while lifting her hand to his lips for a kiss. Mr. Griffin made them all pose together three times—Nina, too—shifting their positions for each photograph, and then he waved to a woman who had been standing beside a column and gave her the camera so he, too, could be included in the picture.

When the woman had taken several more photographs, she handed the camera back to Charlie Griffin and disappeared through a side door, returning with a brown paper sack filled with rice. Nina reached in, dipping up as much as her hand could hold, and followed the children to the outside landing—Hugh, so lean and crisp in his blue suit, and Bess, blooming in lilac chiffon. Charlie Griffin rushed out ahead of the bride and groom and down the steps, his camera poised for the next scene.

When the newlyweds pushed through the doors and Nina raised her arm to toss the rice, she saw Iris's face in a snapshot of joy. Her expression had nothing to do with her children, nothing to do with the security Everett would give her. Hers was the face of a woman who adored a man and who knew herself to be adored in return.

On the sidewalk, everyone laughed and hugged again before turning to walk in happy parade back to the restaurant. The new owner would take possession on Thursday, but today Nina would play hostess one last time. With Iris's help, she'd borrowed enough mixing bowls, cooking pots, and baking pans from the kitchen of the convalescent home to cook the ham, to make the meatballs for the wedding soup, and to bake the cake. Everett had borrowed table linens from the Elks' Lodge, and Mr. Griffin had brought his late mother's good china, silver, and crystal out of storage.

Nina linked arms with Hugh and Bess, one on each side of her. "We must go quickly," she said, "so we can arrange the food before the other guests arrive." Nina did not know these others—two or three of Iris's coworkers, a few of Everett's fellow Elks—but she would welcome them all as dearest friends of her dearest friends. *If you must bid farewell to a beloved place,* Otto would have said, *then only a jolly party will do.*

From a bench across the street, in front of the Army recruiting office, a girl about Bess's age waved at them. "There's Ruth," said Bess. "I want her to see my dress." She broke free and ran across the street, reaching the other girl just as three young men stepped out of the recruiting office.

Nina felt Hugh stiffen beside her, and then he was off across the street too. She called out, "What trouble?" and started to follow, but had to wait for a passing car.

When she reached the opposite curb, she could see one of the young men standing too close to Bess. His arm was around her waist, and she was trying to twist away. Hugh had his arm around his sister's shoulder and was pulling her, but the boy held her tightly. The girl, Ruth, red-faced, was trying to get a grip on the boy's arm. "Cut it out, Bobby!" she cried. "Let her go!"

Bobby Snyder—Nina recognized him now. The poultry man's son.

Still holding Bess, pulling her even closer, Bobby Snyder flung back his free arm, knocking Ruth to the ground. He ignored her cries and said to Bess, "So, what about that graduation dance?"

Nina ran to help Ruth to her feet while the other two boys laughed.

"You've already graduated," said Bess.

"Leave her alone, Bobby," said Hugh.

"Nobody's talking to you, faggot," hissed Bobby. He leaned his head against Bess's head and said, "You and me. The dance. And after. It's your patriotic duty."

The other two boys howled at that, clapped, and one shouted, "Aw, hell, Bobby, forget that one. That Nazi Aust has already occupied that trench!"

Nina turned to face him. "To say such ugly things! You should be ashamed."

"What's it to you, granny? Who the hell are you?"

The third boy said, "Don't you know Frau Hitler when you see her?"

Nina raised her hand to slap the boy's face, but Hugh was already on him.

The other two boys tackled Hugh, pinning him to the sidewalk, punching and slapping, the third one still on his feet, kicking at Hugh's ribs while the girls screamed and tried to help Nina grab at shirts, arms, belts—anything to pull the boys off Hugh.

"Stop it! Stop it!" cried a woman's voice—Iris, on the sidewalk now, trying to step in. Charlie Griffin and Everett pushed ahead of her and got the boys by the shoulders, yanking them up and back, shoving them away. Hugh sat up slowly, his head and face bloody, his breath coming in raspy patches.

"I know every one of you," Charlie Griffin said. "Don't you forget it. I have a good mind to walk right into that recruiting office to tell the staff sergeant just what kind of trouble he's signed up. Disgraceful."

"Go to hell, old man," said Bobby Snyder. He spat in Hugh's direction. "Better warn the sergeant off that one. Can't even fight his own fights without a couple of old geezers to back him up. Goddamn fairy."

"Watch your mouth, boy!" Everett grabbed the front of Bobby's shirt and shoved him so hard he stumbled backward into the other two. "Get out of here. All of you. Now."

For a moment, no one moved. Then one of the others said, "C'mon, Bobby. She ain't worth it."

Bobby clacked his heels together and snapped into a mock Nazi salute. He made an obscene gesture at Bess. "Whore," he said, and stalked off after his friends.

While Iris and Everett helped Hugh to his feet, Nina took Bess in her arms. The girl Ruth had slipped off after the boys.

"Better get on," said Mr. Griffin. The wedding party knotted together, Hugh and Bess in the center, and silently walked on toward the restaurant.

VII

THE ARGUMENT STARTED AT THE wedding reception. Not loudly or intrusively. Not in any way that would set the guests to asking questions. No harsh words were spoken— not in Nina's hearing. This was a quiet dispute. A softly uttered but firm disagreement where agreement had been expected.

Back at the restaurant, after the fight outside the Army recruiting office, everyone had thought Hugh should rest upstairs in the flat. His suit was ruined—the trousers filthy and torn, the jacket blood-spotted around the shoulders and on the sleeves—and so at the very least, he would have to stay back from the party until Charlie Griffin returned with some clean clothes.

Downstairs, Bess laid out the food while Iris and Nina took Hugh upstairs to assess and tend his wounds. After a few minutes, Everett knocked lightly on the door and said the first guests had arrived. Standing at the foot of the bed, he took a long look at Hugh and said, "Not too bad." The boy's right eye and cheek were already puffing up, red underlain with purple, and his lip was cut. His hair was matted here and there where the women had sponged the blood away.

"Very proud of you, son," Everett said, "the way you stood up for your sister." He sat down on the edge of the bed and offered his hand to Hugh. "Now don't you mind what those boys said about you. Foolish talk—I know that."

Hugh shifted in the bed and fingered the edge of the blanket Nina had draped across his legs. "Yes, sir," he said.

Everett went on. "I've got a friend working down in the Navy recruiting office—the son of an officer I served under in Cuba in ninety-eight. You and I can go into town tomorrow morning, and he'll see you're sorted out."

"Everett—" Iris took a quick step to the bed and grabbed his shoulder.

Everett reached up and patted her hand. "We can delay our trip for one day," he said, looking at Hugh. "If you sign up right away, you can be ready to go to training next month, as soon as you graduate. Be at sea by September."

"Everett—" Iris said again.

"Mrs. Beale, this is between me and the boy here."

"Everett, this isn't the time."

"It is," he said. "He's eighteen."

"Everett, listen to me."

He did not. "A good man answers his country's call. He doesn't wait until he's ordered. Hugh knows that."

"Everett—our *hostess*."

Nina caught Hugh's eye. He had the look of wild creature, cornered. "Mr. Beale, please," he said. "Not now."

Nina picked up the basin with the blood-smudged cloths and moved toward the door. "I must see to the food. Bess will need my help."

Iris and Hugh gave slight nods but Everett kept his eyes on Hugh. "Nina's our friend. She understands these things," he said. "We're talking about nations, not particular people." As Nina opened the door, Everett continued, "Now, Hugh, it's decided. We'll go down to the Navy office in the morning." As she pulled the door closed, she caught Hugh's reply: "No, sir. I won't."

It was a long time before the Beales came downstairs. So long that the guests began to joke that the newlyweds, eager to start the honeymoon, had sneaked away before cutting the cake. When at last the couple did appear, they moved stiffly, forking apart at the bottom of the stairs to greet their guests separately.

There was so much food, so much punch, so much laughter and handshaking and hugging and backslapping that no one besides Nina and Bess—who had slipped upstairs to deliver Hugh's clean shirt and trousers—noticed anything was wrong.

The next morning, the Beales left for Fort Wayne, as planned, to spend two weeks visiting his people there, none of whom had met Iris. After school, Hugh and Bess came to the restaurant to help Nina move her things into the room Charlie Griffin kept in his office building as a housekeeper's lodging. The former tenant, a girl half her age, had gone off to Indianapolis with hopes of a high-paying job in a war supply plant. Now Nina would live in this little room, more cramped still when the bed was pulled down from the wall, and, in the evenings, after the close of business, she would clean Mr. Griffin's office and the offices of another attorney and an accountant who rented from him.

"You can't live here," said Bess, when she saw the room. "It's terrible. We'll help you look for a better place."

Nina squeezed Bess's hand. "It is a change." The room was rather terrible, but there was no better to be had, not for her. She had walked the streets of Newman for weeks in search of a job and a new lodging, but she knew on the first day she would find neither. As soon as she presented her identification card, so clearly marked *Alien Enemy*, every door closed to her. Mr. Griffin had offered Nina the room and the job, obviously embarrassed at having nothing better to give. "You must not be sad for me," she said to Bess. "I am grateful to Mr. Griffin, so you must be grateful as well."

"Then you have to stay with us while Mama and Mr. Beale are gone," said Bess. "Doesn't she, Hugh?"

Hugh murmured his agreement, but Nina could see his thoughts were elsewhere.

"Not to sleep," Nina said. "That would not be correct. Your mother has not invited me. But there is food left from the reception, and it must not go to waste. I would enjoy having a kitchen for a few days more." Her room had a two-burner oil cooktop, a sink, and a small icebox.

Bess and Hugh helped her clean the offices, so the work would go faster, and then they collected the rest of the food from the restaurant and took it to the house, still an unfamiliar place to the children, who had spent only one night there.

Nina made a pudding to finish the stale bread, and while it baked, filling the kitchen with the sweetness of cinnamon, vanilla, and warm raisins, the three of them nibbled at cold beef and spooned up wedding soup, gently rewarmed so as not to spoil the noodles.

"I'm glad they're gone," said Bess. "But I don't know what it's going to be like when they get back. They argued all night. They closed their door and tried to whisper, but we could hear it all the same. He kept on at Mama, saying she was going to have to convince Hugh to enlist, but she said she wanted him to wait for the draft, and that since he didn't even have to register until he was twenty-one, the war would probably be over before they got to him."

Nina glanced at Hugh, but he was staring into his plate.

"Mr. Beale said Mama couldn't possibly be paying attention to the news if she thought the war would end before 1947 or '48," said Bess, "and then he said the draft age was sure to drop to eighteen before the year was out, just like last time. 'So he can wait until then,' Mama said. She tried to settle him by saying that when Hugh did register, he could select for the Navy, but that just started Mr. Beale off again about duty and how embarrassing it would be for him to have a son who was a shirker."

Hugh's ears and cheeks burned red.

"And Mama said, 'He's my son, not yours.'"

Bess tapped the edge of Hugh's plate so he would look at her. "Did they say anything else when you drove them to the bus station?"

"Nothing else," Hugh said. He lifted his bowl to his lips and drank the last of the soup broth. "Just more of the same until Mama called for a truce." He got up from the table and carried his dishes to the sink. "I hope it holds. Mama deserves to have a nice trip."

Nina started to do the dishes, but Bess bumped her aside, took the apron from her, and led her out to the back porch. "You've earned a good rest," she said, firm and clipped, like a young nurse. "And you, too," she called to her brother. "When he came outside, she touched her fingertips to his bruised cheek. "Keep *Tante* Nina company while I do the dishes. I'll bring the pudding out when it's ready."

A short brick wall with a concrete ledge framed the porch, setting off the neat yard beyond, which lay in the day's last glow of the sun. The scent of lilacs floated on the breeze, though none grew in the Beales' yard. Everett was an orderly gardener. All the shrubs had been trimmed to the same size, so the slender, eager limbs of the forsythia would never be permitted to outreach the roses, the burning bush, or the azalea. All the flower beds had been kept under command as well. Gladiolas, hollyhocks, sweet William, pink yarrow, columbine, tulips, and violas were all ranked in order of height, with the tallest at the back, forming a protective wall. In its own way, the garden was appealing, brimming with color—but bereft of wildness, under Mr. Beale's charge.

Hugh sat on the swing and reached out his hand to draw Nina down beside him. He started them on a gentle sway.

"What will you do?" Nina asked.

The rhythmic creak of the chain sang out like a distressed lark.

"There's something of a choice if I enlist," Hugh said. "At least if I was on a ship, I wouldn't be seeing Germany for the first time through the crosshairs of a rifle." He closed his hand around the chain and looked out into the garden. The fireflies were just beginning to spark. "But then, on a ship I might be the one who has to launch the torpedoes." He stopped swinging. "Do you think it's better or worse not to see the faces of the people you kill?"

The words trembled through her. All over the world, there must be young men tortured by this question.

Hugh sighed deeply. "If only I could talk to Gerhard." He pulled his hand free and rubbed at his eyes. "I've never had to decide anything without him. All along I've been getting through by telling myself they'll let him go soon—let them all go. But now, even if they do, it looks like I won't be here. I can't see a way around it." He rested his head against Nina's shoulder. "All I can think about is that I'll never see him again. And how can I stand that? It's like looking in a mirror and not seeing my own face."

It was dark now, except for the tiny blinking lamps of the fireflies and a soft pool of light that slipped out the screen door from the kitchen. Nina could hear Bess inside, moving about quietly, humming low. Crickets chirped in the grass, the call of a persistent bobwhite piercing their song. Without lifting his head from her shoulder, Hugh whistled back to the bird in perfect mimicry.

Nina stroked his hair. What could she say to comfort him, to make an impossible choice possible? Better if Otto were here, for he, too, as a young man had suffered over knowing he would have to kill, that his Kaiser commanded him to kill.

After the war, many years after, one night when they were putting away the restaurant dishes, their boys safely asleep upstairs, Otto recalled for her an August day in Koblenz. Everyone had gathered along the *Löhrstrasse* for the parade of volunteers. As the crowd sang and stomped and cheered the men on their way to the train station, Otto had looked long into the faces of those he loved. His mother; his small sister Elke, who rode high on their father's shoulders. His aunts. His aged uncles, who searched the passing crowd for their younger brothers and their own sons. And Nina. She'd been standing beside him.

As Otto spoke, Nina remembered how, that day on the *Löhrstrasse* as the parade passed, he had suddenly turned to her, put his hands on her cheeks, tilted her face up to his. The look in his eyes had warmed and chilled her, filled and emptied her, drowned her. She was but a girl and couldn't understand, and Otto, hardly more than a boy himself, could not form the words to explain. They could not know that years would pass before they could begin to speak truthfully of that time—not until they had grown into a woman and a man who could see how very little war left behind. Only heaps of fragments. Nothing whole.

Working side by side in their kitchen, surrounded by the lingering smells of spices, fresh herbs, roasted meat, and plentiful bread, Otto told her something he had never told her before. At that long ago moment in Koblenz, when he looked at her, when he looked at his family, he saw at once there was no one save himself to stand between them and harm—whether from the French, from the English, from their war-fevered neighbors, or from Germany's own offended dictator.

Nina let her head rest gently against Hugh's. She could tell him of that day in Koblenz—but perhaps her remembrance would not ease his struggle. Perhaps hearing it would make his struggle worse.

Otto had recognized what he must do—but, troubled as this knowing had been, it had been absolute. At eighteen, Otto had only to look in one direction to see all that mattered. He, unlike Hugh, had not yet been torn between two countries, two families, two selves.

VIII

COMMANDER HUDSON WAS GONE, REPLACED overnight by a lean man named McCoy who, unlike the showy Hudson, would have been indistinguishable from the other guards except for the rusty trail of tobacco spittle he left in the dirt as he walked about the camp.

The day after McCoy took over, Johan Cappelmann had gone to headquarters to ask permission to open the theatre and begin work on the café. When McCoy said he would need time to review the matter, Johan convinced him to make the carpentry workshop available to men who wanted to build useful items for the barracks—extra chairs, reading tables, storage chests—and perhaps even small gifts for their families. Then he persuaded Kurt to give up hours every day to learning dovetail joining, decorative carving, and inlay, urging him to make a writing box for Bess.

"I am grateful to you, Johan," Otto said. The two men stood together in the workshop, admiring Kurt's finished piece, the wood shining like wildflower honey. Kurt had gone in search of unwanted cloth to wrap it in.

Johan ran his fingertips along the wooden inlay, stained two shades deeper—just her name, *Bess*. "Slight, but I can feel the edge," he said. "One more sanding was needed. It is good. The next will be better."

Otto placed his hand where Johan's had been. If his eyes had been closed, he would have thought he was stroking silk laid across a slab of polished marble. He could feel no seam.

"His sweetheart will certainly write more often when she has such a box," said Johan. "And when we build the café, Kurt can help me with all the fine work. A handsome place it will be. What pleases the eye also pleases the soul."

The little writing chest was a marvel. A carved vine of ivy bordered Bess's name, and when the front latch was released and the box laid open to reveal its writing slope, the ivy pattern repeated itself, framing a blotter of burgundy felt. In each corner of the slope, Kurt had carved little wells, sanded smooth as water, so one could lift it up from either side on its internal hinge to reach the storage space—one side to hold writing paper, the other with its own separate, lidded compartments for ink bottles and pens.

The boy had built it for an heirloom, a piece both useful and beautiful, that would bind him to Bess for generations. Otto had let himself hope that he would one day see Kurt's child, his own grandchild, learning to write on clean paper laid atop the wool felt. The wood was straight and sound, durable enough to survive the war as a bridge between the young lovers, the joints tight enough to span centuries.

"It is nearly time for the count," Otto said. "Perhaps Kurt has returned to the barracks." He secured the latch and picked up the chest by its recessed iron handles, perfectly balanced. "I'll take it to him there."

Johan said he wanted to finish sanding a tiny rocking horse he'd carved to fit inside the dollhouse he'd made for his little girl. Every day he made a new piece—a person, a cat, a bed, a pie safe for the kitchen—so when at last he was able to give her the house, it would be a miniature home spilling over with happiness, and from this, Sofie would know her father had remembered her each day they were apart.

When Otto reached the guard station, he handed over the writing box for examination and asked permission to linger outside the barracks for a few moments to inspect his garden. At Johan's urging, Otto had gone to speak to McCoy about it, and the commander had said, "Go on with it, of course. I won't see hard work or useful skill wasted here." On McCoy's desk, next to a pencil cup, sat an empty can labeled *Kuner's Tender Garden Sweet Peas.* While Otto thanked him, McCoy picked up the can, spat into it, and said, "Be sure to check in at the station every time. Log in. Log out."

After he had passed through the gate, Otto could feel the guard watching him, so when he reached the edge of the garden, still in plain sight of the guard house, he took off his jacket, laid it on the ground, and set the writing box on top before stepping across the spinach and cabbages to get to his tomato seedlings. Just three days ago, he'd planted them up to their necks so they could develop fresh roots, and already they had thanked him by sprouting fresh pairs of leaves on their sturdy fat stems.

McCoy's determination not to waste skill extended to the dogs. At dawn and dusk, they tracked across the compound, searching for slight disruptions of the landscape, hints of tunnels or breaches in the fence line. At night they ran the alley between the fences dividing the Germans from the Japanese. In this way, and others, McCoy had rapidly and firmly asserted his control.

In recent days, notices had appeared throughout the camp proclaiming all escape attempts had been foiled. At the bottom of the notices were two drawings implying internee informers had helped stop the tunnelers. The scenes were so crudely drawn they were almost comical. The first showed half a dozen prisoners in a barracks— five of them, all with expressions suggesting wickedness, leaning in toward each other across a small round table. The sixth man, likely meant to look pure, but who instead had the foolish expression of a cartoon half-wit, pretended to read a book while inclining sideways toward the men at the table. To mimic sound waves, the artist had sketched three short curved lines in the air beside the half-wit's ear. The second drawing showed the half-wit, mouth open, babbling, shaking the hand of a smiling, heavily armed guard.

Some of the notices had been modified by another hand, placing a blindfold around the half-wit's eyes and a noose around his neck.

Schlageter appeared as a signature on a few of these, but the word could have been scribbled by someone else, anyone else—even Mc-Coy—who wanted to suggest that refusing to be an informer branded a man a Nazi puppet.

The violent image disturbed Otto, but he saw the same irony the second artist had surely noticed. They were in this place because the American government had presumed them to be spies, and now that same government wished them to spy.

Despite the notices and the presence of the dogs, the guards had lately become edgier, their tempers more capricious. Three or four times a week, someone was arrested and confined to the stockade for several days—often more—for refusing to peel potatoes or wash windows, for brawling or pocketing a packet of cigarettes in the canteen without paying. One man on Otto's floor was confined for twenty days for having cut up his camp-issued blanket in an attempt to make shades for the windows. He was accused of trying to signal planes at night and of attempting to conceal secret midnight meetings from the guards, who watched with binoculars from the towers, suspicious of any movement. When two others spoke up for him, saying he was only trying to block out the glare so they could sleep, they were confined for five days.

Was it the same, Otto wondered, for the Japanese on their side of the camp? Surely there must be men among them who longed for their wives as he longed for his Nina. Men sometimes overcome with fear for absent sons. And yet, despite all this loss and uncertainty, had some of them found new friendships in the camp, as he had—men with whom they could play cards and sing songs? Did they have a Johan Cappelmann, who dreamed up theatres and cafés and bravely asked to build them? Did they have a young man like Kurt on their side, volunteering to write the letters they could not write themselves? Did any of them dream of taking the risk to tunnel to freedom? He would like to speak with them of these things, but he only ever saw the Japanese from a distance, filing glumly toward their separate wing of the mess hall or standing at the fence in a long, listless line, their fingers laced through the chain link, never lifting their eyes to the Germans who stopped to stare at them.

Otto finished in the garden, again signed the guardhouse log, and returned to the barracks. He found Kurt sitting on his bunk, the map half unrolled beside him, open letters in his lap. He took no notice when Otto sat down at the end of the cot. Only an hour before, in the carpentry shop, Kurt had been laughing, performing a loving pantomime of Bess's delight when she unwrapped the writing box, so pleased with himself he made no bother with false humility when Johan praised his work. But now in his face, his eyes—turmoil.

"Could you find nothing for wrapping the package?" Otto asked.

"What?" Kurt looked up at him, struggling after the question. "What? No. No."

"Likely someone right here will have what we need," Otto said.

"No," Kurt said. "I mean—" He looked away again, seeming to deliberately swallow the sentence. He put the letters down on the cot and drew the map closer to him, pulling part of it across his lap. He ran his fingertips over the surface—Indiana, Kentucky, Tennessee. "*Vati*, do you remember who helped fill in the places in Tennessee?"

Otto shook his head. "We have not many cities marked there, do we? The information came from travels, I think. Not from anyone who lives there."

"What do you think it's like? For Gerhard? It must be warmer. Maybe it isn't so bleak." Kurt touched the eastern edge of the wide, slim state. "If he's in this part, then he'd be in the mountains." He moved his fingers to the opposite border. "But over here, I think it's all flat. I don't know about the middle. Valley, I suppose, but what kind? Would it be farmland or paved cities?"

"New men have joined us since you drew this," Otto said. "We will ask if they know anything of Tennessee."

Kurt showed no sign of hearing these words. "Wherever he is, I hope he can see trees—lots of huge old trees."

Otto picked up the letters. On top was the one that had arrived from Gerhard, just days ago. "You will not find your answer in this," he said. "You know he cannot tell us about the camp."

Otto scanned his son's words. Gerhard described the food he missed most—the first dipping of the sauerkraut from a freshly opened crock, spread over bratwurst fried with apples, and then he wrote, "You know how, when we were kids and didn't feel like talking, we'd sing a line or two to say how we felt? Today, I'm like this—" Gerhard had, Otto supposed, written a phrase or a title from a *Lied* Kurt would have recognized, but a censor had blackened out the words.

The other letters Kurt had taken out were from Nina and just as unsatisfying as Gerhard's.

"Always you are welcome to read the letters I receive," Otto said. "But I am afraid you will not find more of worth in them than you find in your own. We must instead think of when our family is together once more. We will not stop talking, even to sleep—not for many weeks."

Kurt drew a sharp breath, as though he had been suddenly struck in the chest, but the distant look in his eyes had not changed.

"I have brought back the writing box," Otto said.

Kurt looked at him as if through fog. "I don't know if they'll let me send it. After the business with my books, I thought I'd better ask first. You know McCoy still hasn't let Johan send Sofie's dollhouse."

Otto waited, but Kurt seemed to have lost his thread. He nudged his son's elbow. "What was the answer? May you send the box to Bess?"

Again, that strange, fogged look. "I didn't even get to the postal counter," Kurt said. "When I was on my way over there, one of the guards stopped me and said he'd been sent to get me. Said McCoy wanted to see me."

"But why?"

Kurt's eyes suddenly cleared. "Oh—nothing worth bothering about."

"Is it about the seamen? Did you tell him you have been going among them much less since you have been working with Johan?"

"You think McCoy doesn't get a daily report on what I'm doing? How many men out of the hundreds here do the guards know by sight?"

"Tell me," Otto said. "What did the commander say to you? What does he want?"

Kurt looked away, toward the window that faced onto the parade grounds where the dogs were still training. He tapped his fist lightly against his closed lips. "Nothing," Kurt said. "I have nothing to tell you."

Otto thought again of the notices—the official and the defaced. "He wants you to tell him what your seamen friends say. Is that it? Is this what he wants of you?"

"That's what he wants from all of us," Kurt said. "To spy on each other. No news there."

"What news, then? What does he want?"

Kurt rolled the map, gathered the letters, and got up from the cot. He slid his suitcase from under the bed, put the letters inside, returned the suitcase to its place, and laid the rolled map neatly alongside it. "I can't tell you that, *Vati*," he said. "I just can't."

IX

B Y THE START OF McCoy's fifth week in command, most of
the *Schlageter's* leaders had been plucked out and transferred to
other camps. Their spokesman, Stengler, a ship's captain and
an avowed Nazi, had been the first to go. The *Schlageter's* unification
through rigid drills and resistance to negotiation had kept all but a
few of the German civilians from openly joining their cause, but most
quietly admitted that Stengler's unrelenting protests against injustice
had benefitted all of them.

Now McCoy had firmly shut his door against all complaints,
saying he would hear no more until the detainees—all of them, not
just the seamen—had elected a more objective liaison.

For days, the men in Barracks 32 debated McCoy's decision. Otto
stayed out of it, and for the most part, Kurt did, too, but Otto could
see his son still churned from whatever the commander had said to
him in private. Since finishing the writing box for Bess, still unsent,
Kurt had returned to spending his idle hours with the seamen.

He came in one evening, an hour before lights out, just when
the debate had bubbled up again, with the majority loudly defending
McCoy's order for an election.

"It's a put-up job," Kurt said. "Can't you see that? If McCoy
doesn't approve the choice, his door will stay closed. He's like Roosevelt—comes in all hail-fellow-well-met, making a show of walking
among the serfs—but he's just a tyrant in democratic clothing."

"Bravo!" cried Professor Spannagel. "I have seen my Mephistopheles!"

The theatrical performance was on again. Amidst all the bitterness and uncertainty, McCoy had made that concession to morale. Without invitation, Spannagel had come into their barracks to join the election debate, and until this moment, he had remained quiet, nearly forgotten. Now everyone stared at him.

Spannagel looked only at Kurt. "You are a young scholar, are you not? Destined for the university?"

Kurt reddened. "I wouldn't be too sure about that," he said, moving off.

"Wait, please," said Spannagel. "I want to talk with you about the theatre."

"I don't have anything to do with that, apart from helping build the stage." He looked around, saw Johan and pointed to him. "There's your man. He's organizing everything."

Spannagel ignored Johan. "It is my idea to present two early scenes from Göethe's *Faust*. I have translated them to English, to appease our commander. I myself will take the role of Faust," he said. "Mephistopheles first manifests himself to the doctor in the form of a traveling scholar. The role must be played by a young man, for Faust mistakes him for a pupil. You see Göethe's cleverness, do you not? That the great and learned Faust, longing to know the secrets of the universe, bends his knee to a seeming boy? You must stand as Mephistopheles."

"You want me to play the devil?"

"I want you to play the Light," said the professor. "Mephistopheles is the Light without which Faust cannot see the Truth. Without which Faust cannot be redeemed. Light is not Truth, you understand—too many make this error. Light only reveals. The great risk of seeking Truth is that, before the lowly man can see it, the Light of Revelation may strike him blind."

"Like our floodlights? I think we'd all agree we've had light enough to blind us." Kurt laughed drily. "Whatever else you call Mephistopheles, Professor, his job is to collect Faust's soul. What would I do with another soul to look after? I have enough trouble with my own." He patted Spannagel's shoulder briskly. "Find another devil, Doctor Faust. As for me, I'd settle for one good long night of real darkness."

Hours later, lying on his cot—unable to stop thinking of the debate, of McCoy and the election, of Kurt's words about Roosevelt, of Göethe and Faust and the demon Spannagel called the Light—Otto was the first to hear the dogs.

Sharp barks pierced the walls like javelins, chased by wind-chill howls and then a mix, one barking, the other howling, building to such violent alarm there might have been ten dogs instead of two. Otto got up and went down the hall to the back window. A few others, wakened by the noise, came out of their rooms. Without clocks, it was always difficult to tell the time, but the sky was at its blackest beyond the blaze of the floodlights, so Otto thought it must be around three o'clock.

"What is it?" someone called. "Otto, what do you see?"

"The men—the Japanese—they are coming outside. All in their sleeping clothes. Some have blankets around their shoulders. Many guards are running." Someone pulled the cord for the overhead bulb. Otto cupped his hands at his temples to block out the extra light and pressed closer to the window. "Trucks are there—two, three. And there is another coming, just now, from the hospital."

The hall light was turned off again. Several men crowded up to the window, taking turns, reporting to those who had no view. It was as if they were sharing a telescope trained not on the stars but onto a great amphitheater. The focus of the spectacle was the entry to one of the clapboard buildings. Its inmates, now gathered outside, and those who streamed from other structures, lined the edges of the main stage as extras.

After a long while, one of the men at the window said, "They are carrying a stretcher inside," and a few minutes later, "The stretcher—they are bringing it out again. Fully covered."

"Another heart attack, perhaps," said Otto, recalling the whispered news leaked two weeks ago from the Japanese compound and spread to their side by a German hospital orderly. Word of that death had sobered them all. Among the civilians, most of the men were, like Otto, more than forty years old. Several were over sixty, and a few, like Egon Merkel, past seventy. The ordinary threats of old age—heart disease, strokes, cancers—became extraordinary here. The cold and the terrible wind, along with their depression, made them more vulnerable to illnesses of the lungs, like pneumonia, which could carry a man off in a few days. Even a young man. Any one of them could be boxed and buried under this desolate land for a month before their families learned they were ill.

At breakfast, the men spoke with each other in low voices, saying as little as possible, waiting for the truth of what had happened in the night to travel through the dining room. When the details reached Otto, he drew back, as if he'd been slapped. According to the German orderly who worked the night shift, the man had hanged himself in the washroom.

"Suicide?" Otto turned to the man on his left, a grocer from Oklahoma. "It must have been the fence sickness. Too much to bear."

Gitterkrankheit. It was one of the *Wanderkameraden*, the physician, who had diagnosed the illness as he walked the fence with his companions. Otto had known the symptoms before he'd known the word: displacement, confusion, festering worthlessness.

Then—eruption. When a man would madly run, scream, strike out, destroy. No cure, no escape, no hope of reprieve, only the damned fence. Lining the east, west, north, south—so straight and so far that its outlines, punching through the gray horizon, might have stretched across the whole of America. And no matter what a man might do to distract himself—build, make plays, grow vegetables, write letters—the fence was there, ringing the camp like an endless adder, many-headed, piercing with another drop of slow venom each time he stepped out a door or looked through a window. *Gitterkrankheit.*

"I spoke to the orderly myself," said a man from another barracks. "He tells me the other prisoners made a celebration for him, for the suicide. Before. A farewell festival."

"How can this be true? I cannot believe it," Otto said. "That a man's friends should know of such a plan and not fight to stop him. Impossible."

"Why should they stop him?" said Max Kuehn. "Always you believe in brotherhoods, Otto. There are times when I think you must be younger than this boy of yours. Are these yellow men even men at all? Men fit to stand with Germany?" He turned his head toward Kurt. "What do you say, young *Schlageter*?"

Otto flinched at the label, but he saw no sign that it had disturbed Kurt. He glanced up to see if any of the guards had noticed.

Max needled him again. "What do you think, boy? Are they proper men or savages?"

"We don't know what happened," Kurt said. He scraped the tines of his fork across his empty plate. "We don't know how differently they might think about things. Different thinking doesn't make a man a savage. Maybe he was doing something for them. Maybe it was a kind of sacrifice."

Max laughed. "Like a primitive blood offering to a pagan god? Is this what you believe?"

Kurt turned sharply on Max, ready to fight. "I don't know what I believe." He pushed up from the table and headed toward the door. Otto followed.

A month ago, when the last of the snow had finally melted, the rain started, leaving the camp a sodden brown, a great mudflat wrapped in wire. The ground sucked at their shoes. Otto and Kurt passed a fallen beam someone had tried to erect as a maypole. When it had been pulled down, McCoy ordered the guards to let it lie, a Nazi symbol rotting in filth. A few strips of cloth—black, red, white—still clung to the beam, and Otto wondered how the man had come by the cloth, the red especially. He wondered whether the man had been caught, and if he had, what punishment he'd faced.

"Kurt, you should not let Max upset you," Otto said. "He wants us to believe he still serves the Kaiser, but anyone with eyes can see Max Kuehn serves himself alone." He put his hand on his son's shoulder. "And you are right. We cannot judge what happened. I was wrong to speak as I did."

Kurt stopped. "*Vati*, how can a man know if what he chooses is right? How—when the choice is irreversible?"

The words struck like arrows. "What is troubling you? Tell me. Please."

Kurt shrugged away. "It's nothing. I was just thinking about the suicide." With his right foot, he dragged a line through the mud, then dragged his foot through again, and again, until the line became a trench. "Suicide's an irreversible choice."

Otto could barely get his breath. "You would not do such a thing?"

"No, *Vati*! No, of course not!" Kurt put his arm around his father's shoulders, and they walked up the barracks steps together. "I would never slit my own throat or hang myself in a washroom. No, *Vati*."

There was no mat, so they scraped their shoes on the sharp edge of the porch, as others had done, leaving clots of mud that would remain until the next rain.

Kurt opened the door. "Who would ever think it could still be so cold in June?" he said.

X

WHILE EVERETT PARKED THE CAR, Nina and Iris walked into the high school and turned toward the auditorium. Before they reached the doors, Nina heard the band strike up a chirpy tune that had been inescapable for months, even for someone who no longer owned a radio. As the band finished the first turn through the melody, four girls wearing crisp, homemade uniforms and perky caps marched out of the wings to center stage to stand behind a boy fitted out in olive drab, and when they started singing—the boy first, and then the girls in answer, all of them keeping up the march and snapping salutes—Nina recognized "We Did It Before and We Can Do It Again," a song suggesting war was just as thrilling and easily managed as a football championship. Most of the audience had gotten to their feet and were bouncing or clapping along.

Iris linked her arm through Nina's, and, drawing her close, set the pace for their walk up the aisle to their seats—slow and deliberate, in defiance of misplaced joy.

There were many speeches—by the mayor, the principal, the class valedictorian, and three or four others whose importance Nina could not discern—one speech running into the next as the orators declared that all Americans shared the responsibility of winning the war. They urged the graduates to take their part as full adults in this responsibility, to enter the armed forces, the auxiliary services, to put on coveralls and take jobs in factories or on farms, and to never complain about long hours or shortages, always knowing that everything they produced and everything they sacrificed would play a part in helping brave American boys axe the Axis.

Had Iris not been sitting beside her, Nina could not have borne it. She lost count of the times her friend's hand wound around her own. Everett sat to Iris's left, a portrait of noble contradiction. From the time he had knocked on the door of her little room, he had been unfailingly warm to her, considerate of her pain, quietly acknowledging that this graduation day was to have been Gerhard's as well. He'd even brought her a little corsage in the school colors, white carnations with purple ribbons, to wear in her son's honor. Then, when all the veterans in the audience were asked to rise, Everett had stood erect, tipping his head at the reading of his own name. When the principal asked the graduates who had already enlisted to step forward and be recognized, Everett lowered his eyes to avoid looking at the stage, where Hugh and one other boy remained so conspicuously seated with the girls.

While the new enlistees held their places near the edge of the stage, the principal directed the audience to the backs of their programs, where they would find the words to "Once to Every Man and Nation." A fanfare of trumpets, quickly joined by an organ pitched to Resurrection morning brightness, set the tone and tempo. Then came the celebratory flutes, with voices like angels rejoicing. Some in the audience were so eager to begin, they anticipated the entry by several beats. Their faces glowed with passion as they sang, glorying in the idea of having but a single moment in a lifetime to decide, once and forever, between good and evil.

Surrounded by people who were cheering more than singing, Nina felt her smallness. And she felt terribly afraid. They beat the air with their fists, drumming for a regiment guided by the torchlight of burning martyrs. Four verses they sang, their eyes blazing with certainty that they were marching in the footsteps of God.

When the organist reached the coda, the singers wiped their eyes or mopped their faces with handkerchiefs. Some turned the program about in their hands as if looking for another verse. As the last notes sounded, the audience cracked into applause so thunderous the principal had to call several times for quiet.

Though everyone finally sat down again, they shifted restlessly in their seats, impatient for the ceremony to end. Seeming to sense this, the principal read the names on the graduates' roll too quickly, so they all had to quick-step across the stage to receive a diploma before the next name covered theirs. Nina's heart clutched when the principal moved seamlessly from the name of Mary Abel to the name of William Berry, without so much as a fluttering pause to note where Gerhard's name should have been. Tears burned in her eyes when Bess's name was called and the girl turned to Hugh, offering her hand so they could walk the stage together.

After another round of applause, the graduates were released from the stage and sent down the center aisle in processional, accompanied by the full band tooting "You're a Grand Old Flag." Most of the graduates fell into step, though a few chose their own pace, including Hugh and Bess, who let all the others pass them. The audience stood to attention once more for "The Star-Spangled Banner" before the principal reminded everyone about the reception on the school lawn.

Outside, tables were laid with silver trays stacked high with finger sandwiches, already beginning to droop in the afternoon sun. Between the trays, instead of flowers, were bouquets of little American flags, like the one Otto had wanted to put on display the day after the attack in Hawaii. The day she lost everything.

Everett went to get the ladies some lemonade, and on his way, he stopped Bess, now free of her graduation robe, and bent to kiss her cheek. She joined Iris and Nina in a small patch of shade cast by a young pear tree.

"Where's Hugh?" asked Iris.

"He came out with me," Bess said, "but as soon as he saw *that*, he disappeared." She pointed to a trio of buses parked at the curb— recruiting buses, one each for the Army, the Marines, and the Navy.

Iris glanced at the table where Everett was waiting for a woman in a wide-brimmed hat to pour out the lemonade. "I imagine he's set off toward home," she said. "You know how he loves to walk. We can pick him up on the way back, if we see him."

"Perhaps he has gone back in," Nina said, nodding toward the building. "I'll look." When she turned back to Bess, she noticed something pinned to her collar—a deep blue V flanked by red and white eagle's wings, spread in flight.

Bess slapped her hand over the brooch. "They were attached to the ribbons on our diplomas," she said. "When we got outside, all the girls were putting them on."

Nina took Bess's free hand into her own and gently drew the other away from the brooch. She kissed the small soft hands and, looking into Bess's eyes said, "Darling girl. Congratulations."

Stepping back inside the school shocked Nina—the darkness, the silence, the unstirred air, heavy and damp, as if she had stumbled into a tomb. The lights had all been shut off, and the fans, too, to conserve electricity.

When her eyes adjusted to the low light, she turned left down the corridor, the first of three that led to the auditorium. Her footfalls echoed, multiplied, and she kept turning to see if anyone was behind her.

She passed recruitment banners, signs celebrating the graduates, oil portraits of the school's principals—four in its seventy-five-year history. She passed a wall of glassed trophy cases, but did not look in a second time. Already she had seen that the framed photograph of Kurt, accepting the state's highest honor for achievement in mathematics, 1938, had been removed.

At the end of the final corridor lay the auditorium. Half the double door stood partly open, wide enough to admit a slender boy—and, unspooling through the gap, the soft cry of a solo piano.

Nina opened the door a little wider and stepped over the threshold. Rivulets of light leaked through the high, narrow windows where the walls met the ceiling.

Hugh was on the stage, playing inside the darkness, fused with the piano into a gray silhouette, the boy inseparable from either the music or the means. He was the notes, the phrases, the hammers and strings. He was the reverberating case.

Nina listened. She closed her eyes, reaching for the memory of Gerhard's voice answering Hugh's notes. But what poured from Hugh now did not bring her son's voice to mind. This music was Hugh's alone—solemn as the *Dies Irae.*

Nina opened her eyes and watched Hugh. What was this piece? Familiar, centuries deep—but not the medieval chant of judgment. Mournful chords shrouded slow, heavy footfalls of melody. *What was it?*

She reached again, stretching far—and caught it.

The same melody that, not an hour ago, the crowd around her had sung with martial joy.

A discarded program lay just beyond the door. She picked it up and, tilting it into the weak light, she looked at the words, following them when Hugh reached the top of the melody. The same words that had terrified her before—the meaning now utterly changed.

Once to every man and nation
Comes the moment to decide,
In the strife of truth with falsehood,
For the good or evil side.
Some great cause, God's new Messiah,
Offering each the bloom or blight,
And the choice goes by forever
'Twixt that darkness and that light.

This was no march. It was a grave hymn. A hymn of human agony, sung alone at the moment of reckoning. The wretched soul cried out, knowing he must choose good over evil, light over darkness, truth over falsehood—or be forever lost.

But what was good? What was light? What was truth? The answer had been written on air, whispered in water.

This was the music of pained prayer, the music of Christ's pleading in Gethsemane while his disciples slept. A prayer full of longing for the burden of terrible choice to be lifted. A prayer to a God who answered pleas with silence.

Hugh played on, leaning into the music, as if emptying the vessel of his whole life into the river that flowed at God's feet. God stood, unmoving, already decided. The decision was stone. The stone was fate.

And in Hugh's playing, smooth as air, soft as water: recognition, resignation. Each note sounding another small cry of agonized acceptance.

There was no choice. This cup would not pass from him.

XI

THREE WEEKS AFTER THE SUICIDE, following an unexpected count conducted in eerie silence, the news spread through Barracks 32: another tunnel had been discovered, with mud-caked shirts and trousers found inside. McCoy's dogs had tracked the clothes to the seamen's barracks, to two young officers from different ships.

Otto had just had the story from Max Kuehn when he heard Kurt's voice coming from the stairwell, emboldened with special knowledge. He leaned over the railing and saw Kurt on the landing below. He was telling how the two ships' officers had laughed when the dogs, pulling hard at their leashes, herded them into a corner and growled.

Kurt threw his head back, clearly enjoying the tale. "One of them saluted the guards and said he was pleased to see even Americans could recognize the superiority of the pure German strain."

Otto shoved past Max to get to his son. "You were there? When the guards came with the dogs?"

Kurt hesitated. "No—not then. I heard after. I ran into a guy I know when we changed shifts in the laundry. He told me."

Otto grabbed Kurt at the back of the neck, hard, and forced him down the steps to the second floor. There were men in all the rooms, several of them lingering in the doorways, making little effort to pretend they wouldn't listen, so Otto pushed Kurt down the corridor to the south window, the favored nook of late-night smokers. It was the most private place he knew, provided nothing worth watching was happening on that side of the camp. Now, he could see only a few men trudging to or from the canteen, the post office, or their work stations. One man was entering the shoe workshop with a pair of boots tied together at the laces. From this window, made hazy by smoke, the men below looked like characters in an old bioscope, their forms frayed at the edges by sunlight.

Still holding the back of Kurt's neck, Otto pulled his son's head close to his own. "You must sever yourself from these men." He did not want to name the *Schlageter*, lest the others hear.

"Why?" Kurt did not bother to keep his voice down. "Really, *Vati*, you're as bad as the rest. They're not all Nazis. Some of them even want to stay here." He muttered, "In the US—though I can't think why." He shouldered Otto's hand away. "They're just men who love their country. Men who want to go home to fight for Germany. *For Germany*. Do you understand? Not for politics. For home. They're worried about their families. Especially now with all the bombing."

"Bombing? What do you know of bombings?"

The word brought the men in the doorways out into the hall. Others followed.

"Nothing," Kurt said loudly. "I don't know anything." He turned slightly to move closer to Otto and whispered, "A few of the guys built a radio. Only a receiver—" and held up a hand to still Otto's questions. "I don't know how. They keep it stashed under the floorboards, move it every few days—different rooms, different barracks."

"You know of this," Otto said quietly, "and still, every day you go there. Why will you not see the trouble you bring on yourself?"

"I didn't build the radio."

If Kurt the boy had spoken to him so rudely, Otto would have struck him across the mouth. But Kurt was not a boy, he was a man—a young man and sometimes a foolish one, beyond a father's reprimands.

Fiercely, Kurt whispered, "I'm no informer."

"And I would not have you be," Otto returned sharply. "There is no honor in that. But neither is there honor in a man who chooses to misshape another's meaning as you misshape mine."

"Don't you even care that the RAF is blowing up Germany? It's been going on for months."

"Yes, I care. Of course, I do," Otto said. "But—can you be such a boy in this? Did you think no one would fight back?"

Kurt ignored the question. "Lübeck—a lot of people killed there. Münster. Köln. And most of Essen's gone."

"Yes, son, yes—it is all very troubling."

"Hamburg," Kurt said. "At least twice so far." His hands were in fists. "You can bet the Americans will be in on it soon. All those new planes. Think of it—people we know setting fire to the people we came from."

Otto thought of his father, his mother. Were they still there, in Hamburg? His sister, Elke. She was still a girl when he'd left Koblenz. Just sixteen, skinny and dour, barely nodding goodbye when he kissed her cheeks and said he would miss her, but in the years since, when he'd thought of her, he'd remembered the plump four-year-old who shrieked with terrified delight when he leapt out at her from under the kitchen table, playing the ogre with a passion for cherry preserves—before he'd gone to war. Elke had children of her own now, perhaps a brave little girl who also loved cherry preserves enough to face down an ogre.

It had been such a long time—two years, nearly three—since he'd had a letter from any of them. Elke's husband, his brother-in-law, was probably in the *Wehrmacht*, and so it would be just Elke, left alone to look after their elderly parents and her little children. Though Otto had never seen the small flat they all shared in the city, he could see them there now, clutching hands in the dark, alarmed by each other's faces when for an instant the room was lit by a shock of fire.

"Aren't you angry, *Vati*?"

Oh, yes, he was angry. But how to explain to his son that his anger was as vast and varied, as dense and tangled, as the forest of Thüringen? How to tell Kurt—how to tell any young man this? The young, who believed the source of their anger could be fetched down like a ripe plum and obliterated with a hammer-aimed fist.

With a deep sigh, Otto said, "We must not argue, you and I. We can do nothing about these bombs." A strange feeling settled at the back of his throat, as if something he'd swallowed had stopped long enough to make a tiny fissure. If his heart beat too fast, he thought, he would split inside, like a weak seam, straight down through his center. He grasped Kurt's hand. "And, just now, we can do nothing to help those we love—nothing except bind ourselves to each other. We must look to our own family, first and always, the four of us. And Bess, too, when you marry her."

Kurt turned to the window, pressing his fingertip hard against the glass, dragging it through the smoke grime, writing his name, then making small shapes Otto could not quite see. "Gerhard wouldn't like you leaving Hugh out of the family portrait," he said, and then added suddenly, "I've been thinking I should probably end things with Bess." His voice wavered, but he caught it, steadied it. "Everything's changed. It wouldn't be fair to keep her hanging on, waiting." Kurt swiped his hand across the window to erase all he'd drawn there. He pulled his handkerchief from his pocket and rubbed at his dirtied palm.

"Bess loves you," Otto said. "She loves us all. One day, you'll see. You will be with her again. I am sure of it."

"And what makes you so sure? Tell me even one thing that's happened since we were brought here that makes you sure. Six months, and all we really know about Gerhard is that his mail comes from somewhere in Tennessee. The restaurant's gone. The house is gone. *Mutti* is mopping floors for strangers. Are you going to say you're sure it will all work out? Everything will be just fine?"

"We must talk no more of this." Otto said. "Come, let's find Johan. Today he is meeting with Mr. McCoy about starting the café—already he has approved the program for the revue. Very soon, we may have work again to keep us busy."

"I'm not doing any war work."

"What war work? These things we make—my garden, the stage, the café—they are for us, for all our friends. To make this time easier to bear. For yourself, you should consider taking up Professor Spannagel's offer. He is a bit ridiculous, perhaps, but learning the role would occupy your mind."

Kurt turned away. "Don't you see that's just what they want us to do? To not think? Every time we take up a task, every time we drive a nail, or borrow a book from that dime-store library, or make some absurd toy—Max's chessmen, Johan's dollhouse, a fancy writing box—our keepers win. Cooperation, quiet acquiescence—it's all capitulation. I won't do it." Kurt strode down the hall, down the steps, and out the front door.

Otto wanted to follow, but he did not know how he would answer Kurt. Everything his boy had ever stood upon, leaned against, reached for, had been torn away as by a great wave, tossed and broken on the sea. Staggering and confused, threatened by the next wave he saw gathering on the horizon, Kurt stumbled toward what he believed to be a seaside fortress, seeing only the great stone walls, blind to the beasts lurking behind the battlements. How was a father to persuade this emerging man to join hands and, with the trust of a child, walk with him into the darkness—a father who, himself, could not struggle free from the tempest surf and sliding sand?

A shaft of glaring sunlight struck the window, revealing clear outlines of what Kurt had written. His name—supported by a platform of tiny swastikas.

Quickly, before anyone could see, Otto blocked the window with his body, spat on the glass, and rubbed at it fiercely with his sleeve, scrubbing and scrubbing until he had removed every trace.

XII

HUGH HAD GONE WITHOUT A word to anyone. A few minutes after the clock in the dining room chimed five, Iris, awake but still in bed, had heard the front door close. This wasn't strange, she told Nina, so she went back to sleep, believing Hugh had only wanted one of his early morning walks before catching the bus to the shipyard in Jeffersonville. He'd taken his small grip with him—it was gone from his room—but there was nothing unusual in this, either. On work days, he packed a change of clothes in the case, along with his lunch. But at half-shift, his foreman phoned to say Hugh had never clocked in. For the past two months, Hugh had worked at the shipyard—sometimes twelve days at a stretch—and though he'd never missed and never been late, the foreman was angry.

"It's the pressure of war production," Everett said. "We need those ships, and the man has quotas to meet."

The Beales told Nina all this when they came to her room to ask if she'd seen Hugh or if he'd said anything to her—anything that might provide a clue about where he'd gone or why.

Nina knew nothing, except that the boy had looked progressively more grieved since graduation. But this was not what the Beales wanted to hear. She hadn't seen him since Tuesday, nearly a week ago, when he and Bess arrived at her door before breakfast, as in the old days. Bess worked in a factory assembling flight packs for airmen, and, for the first time since they had both taken jobs, they'd managed to coordinate their time off. "We're taking you to the fair," they told her. "No arguments."

It was a glorious day—the only unmarred joy the three of them had had all year. The children treated her as if it were her birthday, insisting on taking her on all the rides, into every show, stopping her hand when she reached for her purse to pay. As they'd walked around the fair, pinching off strands of cotton candy, they'd laughed at silly things, teased each other playfully, told old stories and sung favorite songs, often through tears—but, looking to each other for strength, they managed to leap over the tears back into laughter, as if they'd made a silent pact that this day would admit no sorrow.

Nina wished she could say something now to help Iris. She'd never seen her friend in such a state—white-faced and shaking, frantic as a moth trapped behind a window. Though Nina was sure it was not Everett's intent, she could see he was making Iris feel worse when he said, "He's probably gone to enlist. Just didn't want to do it here, since he's made such a point of refusing. He'll let us know when it's settled and, when he does, we won't make a fuss. He'll have done the right thing, so that will be an end to it."

Nina refilled the teacups while Everett spoke, and when he'd said his piece, she laid her hand over Iris's and said, "Hugh will be back. Whatever he's done, whatever he has decided, he will come home to tell us."

Four days later, in the still-dark hours of Friday morning, Hugh did return—not to Mr. Beale's house, but to Nina. Travel-stained and weary, he looked more like a roughed-up man of thirty than the eighteen-year-old boy who had proudly draped her with three long strands of imitation pearls, his prize from the ring toss game.

"I've seen Gerhard," he said.

Nina hugged him with all her strength. She kissed his cheeks, kissed his hands, hugged him again and wept against his shoulder. Trembling, she pulled away and, pointing to her short, narrow bed, told him to lie down and rest while she made him some breakfast. "Sleep first. Then eat. Then—tell me."

Out of all the dishes she cooked, Hugh best loved her potato pancakes with applesauce. While he slept, she cut up apples and set them to simmering. She grated potatoes and onions. And she readied herself to hear whatever he would tell her about Gerhard. There could be no happy news, so, while she cooked, she measured degrees of bad news, trying on each one, adding a few layers, testing what she could bear.

After she had fried a *bratwurst* and brewed coffee, she called for Hugh. He ate slowly. When he'd swallowed the last of the coffee, he said, "His voice."

His voice. "Tell me," said Nina.

"He coughs, and he's always fighting to clear his throat, and then when his voice comes—it's like rust. He's had pneumonia twice. The whole place is wet—heavy rain from March through June, Gerhard said. And since then, mosquitoes." He pushed up his sleeves, revealing dozens of bites. "They live in these little clapboard huts shaped like tents—dozens of them, lined up like crops. No proper roof, just a tarp and a dirt floor, he told me. Dirt that's mud most of the time because the rain floods in. He said they're always having to re-dig the drainage ditches around their huts because there's so much water. Everything smells like mold. It didn't rain while I was there, but the air is so heavy it's hard even for a healthy person to breathe."

Nina listened, feeling that foul, steamy air enclose her.

Hugh described the vicious fences of barbed wire, in double rows so that anyone who might get through one would be stopped by another, trapped between them, his skin gouged with every movement. Three more rows of barbed wire, angled in toward the enclosure, threatened anyone who might risk climbing the ten or twelve feet with the hope of jumping over. But no one could get that high, Hugh said, because of the snipers in the towers, three times higher than the fence. "The second day I was there," Hugh said, "I heard someone on the loudspeaker shout, 'Away from the fence! Get away from the fence!' I wasn't even near where they keep the prisoners. I was inside the station at the entry gate, but still, I could hear it. There was one more warning—'Away from the fence!'—and then three or four shots. "

Hugh fell silent, leaving Nina to imagine Gerhard, so depressed and lonely and angry that he had lost his reason and tried to climb. She saw her son reaching high, tearing his hand, reaching again. She squeezed her eyes shut, pulling the curtain on the scene, and tried to remember him singing, but the curtain rose again, and there was Gerhard, trapped like a song thrush between the barbs.

She blurted out, "His clothes—are they torn? How are his clothes? He will not answer this when I ask in my letters. Should I send him some? What does he need?" She reached for Hugh's hand. "How can I help him? Please."

Hugh shook his head. "He says he doesn't know what happened to his suitcase. There was some promise about storage, but he doesn't know. This place—it's an Army training camp. Gerhard has to wear fatigues like the soldiers—they all do—but with *Prisoner of War* in big letters on the back."

"Are there many men held in this camp?"

"Hundreds, I'd say—and, from the look of it, they're making room for thousands more."

"The guards, are they always with guns?"

"Every one I saw had a rifle."

She imagined Gerhard in filthy olive drab and thought of the other men branded across the back as criminals. So the guards could see clearly whom to shoot.

Nina leaned across the small table. "Please, darling Hugh—tell me all you know. You were so long away. You saw him every day?"

Hugh looked down at the table. "They wouldn't let me past the gate for the first three days. Said my name was on a list—because of what happened last time. Chicago."

Another stab of remorse. "I'm sorry," she whispered. "I'm sorry, I'm sorry."

"When they finally did let me in," Hugh went on, "they gave us only half an hour. Said that was all that was allowed. They put us in this grungy little room, put two guards in with us, and made us stand six feet apart, behind lines that had been marked on the floor. We couldn't get any closer—not even to shake hands. The guards told us if we said a single word that wasn't English, that would be it—I'd be kicked out."

He pressed the heels of his palms against his eyes. "There isn't much else I can tell you, *Tante* Nina. We couldn't say anything we really wanted to—not with the guards listening. I'm grateful that I saw him, but trying to talk—it was even worse than the letters."

Hugh got up from the table and walked over to the room's single window, which looked out on a narrow alley.

"He's lost a lot of weight. There's plenty of food, he says, but he hasn't eaten much because he's been so sick. He told me there's a good doctor who's looked after him—a German, interned like the rest of them. But it's hard to get the right medicine." Hugh turned back toward her. He smiled feebly. "Gerhard said this German doctor taught him how to dig black widow spiders out of their nests and trap them."

"These are poison! Why does he do this?"

"He says they're all over the place. Their hut was full of them. He shares with four other men, all Germans. He's heard there are Italians in the camp, too, in another section. Anyway, this doctor has developed an antidote for the spider venom, but he needs the spiders to make it, lots of spiders. When Gerhard was in the hospital, the doctor told him he'd have to be especially careful not to be bitten, since his lungs are already so weak from the pneumonia. That's how the doctor got him digging out the spiders. He uses some kind of knife to get below the nest to force the spider out. Then he has to act quick to trap it in a jar. He nearly got bit the first couple of times, he says, but now that he's got the hang of it, he doesn't mind it. He's not strong enough to do any of the heavier work, and this makes him feel useful—helping the doctor make medicine that might save somebody else."

Nina made more coffee and poured Hugh another cup. She poured a cup for herself and sipped at it, picturing her boy in that place, thinking she might now be better able to read between the lines of Gerhard's letters and understand the thoughts and feelings he was not permitted to write.

But what good was understanding, when one could do nothing? Her hand trembled so strongly she had to put down her cup. She looked at Hugh. He had left his job without a word. He had set out on this uncertain journey because he wanted to see for himself what Gerhard could not say. For Hugh's sake, for all his sacrifice, she had to believe that what he had learned made a difference.

After a long while, Hugh said, "Some of the prisoners started a newspaper. They call it *The Latrine*—a good name, from what I saw." He smiled bitterly. "Gerhard's had to spend so much time in bed that he's started translating *Lieder* into English for the paper, so he won't forget them. He can't sing, so he writes. Everything in the paper has to be in English, so he writes them out in German first, for himself. He said doing the translations forces him to work out the relation between the words and the music, and that's started him writing poems."

"Poems?"

"About everything that's happened." Hugh slid his empty cup away, then drew it back again and turned it between his hands. "He says when all this is over, when we're together again, we'll put the poems to music, maybe enough for a whole cycle—a *Liederkreis*, like Schumann's. To tell all the layers of the story." He sighed, and in the sigh, Nina heard the rattle of a deep sob. "I think that might need an opera."

Slowly, Nina slid her hand across the table and laid it gently on Hugh's wrist. "You have not yet told all your story, darling. You say for three days they turned you away. What happened? What changed?"

He slumped back in his chair. "They told me if I wanted to see Gerhard, I first had to prove that I was loyal to America."

"How?"

"I enlisted," he said. "I took the bus back to Nashville, found a recruiting office, brought my papers back to the camp, and they let me in. For thirty minutes."

Tears burned in Nina's eyes, spilling over.

"I wanted to tell you first—so you'd know I only did it so I could see him. Gerhard doesn't know. When I write, I'll have to find a way to tell him—but I won't tell him why. It wouldn't be fair. You're the only one who knows the real reason." He pushed away from the table and stood up. "But I'm not sorry. Don't think I'm sorry. I'd do it again if that was the only way to get to him."

He took a few steps toward the door and stopped, his face washed in dread. "I had to see him. I don't know how I'm going to explain to Mama. I as much as promised her I'd stay on at the shipyard and wait for the draft. She's going to be so angry. And Bess. And Mr. Beale. But all for different reasons." He closed his eyes for a moment, and then held out his hand. "Will you come with me? Some of the fire's likely to fly at you, too. But will you come anyway?"

The sun had been up for about an hour. Had there not been a war on, with ever-rolling shifts at factories and longer hours for all the supporting businesses, the streets would still have been quiet—a few people stepping out for newspapers or the early post, trimming hedges or tending their kitchen gardens before the day's heat settled in. As it was, there were so many cars going by, so many people clipping down the sidewalk, bursting into sprints when they saw their buses half a block ahead, that it might have been noon on the day after a bank holiday. Several times, Nina and Hugh were jostled by people pushing past them in a rush, but no one paid them any attention. The war had brought thousands of strangers to Newman, eager for the high-paying jobs needed to feed the insatiable battle machine. If the previous tenant of Nina's room had waited only a few more weeks, she would have had no reason at all to run away to Indianapolis.

Despite the boom, Everett had not altered his hours at the jewelry store, so his car was still in front of the house. At his insistence, Iris had quit her job and had since made it her habit to delay her errands until her husband left for work. Neither Nina nor Hugh could guess whether Bess was home at this hour—her shift at the factory was always changing.

"Hugh!" Iris was running down the walk toward them in her bare feet, an airy bed jacket thrown around her shoulders in a failed attempt to cover her silky nightdress.

Everett stood on the porch, shirt collar open, a green tie waiting to be knotted. With one hand, he reached out as if to catch his wife; in the other, he clutched a pair of ivory satin slippers. "Iris! The neighbors! Let the boy get inside." But Iris ignored him and flung herself against Hugh.

"Your feet, Mama," Hugh said, his cheek against her hair. "You'll cut your feet." He dropped his small case onto the grass, lifted Iris in his arms, and carried her like a hurt child to the porch, where Everett—rather roughly, Nina thought—collected his wife, carried her inside, and plopped her onto the sofa. She righted herself and patted the cushion beside her.

"Where have you been?"

Hugh put his arm lightly around Nina's shoulders and guided her to the sofa. He stood behind the wing chair but made no move to sit down. Everett paced the room.

"Is Bess here?" Hugh asked.

"She worked the overnight shift," said Iris. "It'll be at least another hour before she gets home—maybe more, depending on how the buses are running."

"Don't keep your mother waiting," Everett said. "She's been through enough, can't you see that?"

"I'm sorry, Mama," Hugh said. "This was something I had to do."

He began his story again, looking down the whole time, delivering a shorter version that emphasized the guns and barbed wire but that left out the guards' demand for proof of loyalty. Before his mother or Everett could ask any questions, he said, "I've enlisted."

"You promised to wait," Iris cried weakly, while Everett clapped Hugh on the back and offered his hand to shake.

"So you're in the Navy!"

"No, sir. Not the Navy. The Merchant Marine."

"The Merchants!" Everett shouted. "What were you thinking, boy?"

Hugh ignored him, keeping his eyes fixed on Iris. "I leave for New York in a few days—Hoffman Island, for training. I came back to say goodbye."

Everett was pacing again, in long, circling strides. "We can fix this. We'll get you into the Navy yet."

"There's no fixing it," Hugh said.

"Of course there's a way. Always strings to pull if you know the right people—and I know a few. The Merchants, they're not real military. And you're not the first boy they've tricked into signing on. They can't hold you. Not against an order from the Navy."

From her place on the couch beside Iris, Nina watched Hugh holding himself steady and calm, waiting for Everett's storm to blow over him.

"We'll fix it, we'll fix it," Everett said, picking up the telephone.

"No one tricked me," Hugh said. "Sir, please put the phone down."

"You don't know what you're doing," Everett said. "That's a bad lot you've signed on with." He shook the receiver at Hugh. "Slackers. Draft dodgers. Communists. Criminals. *Mercenaries*, for God's sake—only in it for the money!" He dialed the phone, and while he listened, waiting for someone to answer, he said, "You've been slow about it, but I know you're a decent young fellow."

Everyone was quiet. They could all hear the faint rings in the distance. Everett slapped the receiver back into its cradle.

"Ridiculous," he muttered. "Office isn't open yet. But it's better we go down in person. You get yourself cleaned up and we'll head out."

Hugh didn't move.

"Come on, Hugh. Get moving. Bring whatever papers they gave you."

"Everett, look at him," Iris said. "He needs to sleep. He must be starving."

"I'm all right, Mama."

Everett walked back over to Hugh, speaking more slowly. "You didn't like me pushing you the way I did, I understand that. So now you've taken a stand and gotten back at me. I'm glad you did—shows what you're made of. We can respect each other as men, now. But there's no need to ruin yourself with a rash decision."

"It wasn't rash," Hugh said. "The Army made it clear they didn't want me. Said they had no place for my sort. Same with the Marines and the Navy."

"What do you mean—" Everett began.

"I mean I went where I was wanted. Where the only questions they ask are about whether you're fit enough for the work."

Nina watched Everett. His face had changed from the redness of ordinary anger to a terrifying vein of fury, pulsing just below the skin. Iris had stopped breathing.

"I know what this is about," Everett said. "It's that business from Chicago. I blame myself. I should have stepped in and stopped you from going, but—" He looked at Nina. "None of us could have predicted how things would get out of hand." He turned to Hugh again. "They've put you on a blacklist of some kind, but all it'll take is a bit of explaining. So you have a connection with some interned Germans. A lot of people do. We can still fix it."

"There's nothing to fix, sir," Hugh said, but Everett wasn't listening.

"We'll get it sorted out. Now, I know that boy is your friend. But I expect the Navy will demand a promise from you to break off contact with him. Probably the whole family. No more letters—and for damn sure no more visits. Be ready to swear to it."

"No, sir. I'll not break my friendships for anyone." He faced Everett with a resolved gaze, confident and unwavering.

Everett was the first to look away. He looped his tie into a loose knot, buttoned his collar, and slid the knot into place at his throat. "I think your mother's right. You're too worn out to talk about it now. We'll discuss this again when I get home."

A few minutes later, Everett was gone. Hugh dropped heavily into the wing chair.

"We were going to get jobs," he said softly, as if to himself, in a private dream. "Both of us. After graduation—for a year, maybe two. We were going to go on living at home, save everything we didn't need for our expenses. Every penny straight into the bank, so that I could go to the conservatory, too." He closed his eyes and let his head fall against one of the chair's wings. His breathing grew deep, and for a moment, Nina thought he had fallen asleep. But after a few more breaths, Hugh opened his eyes and looked at his mother. "I think I'll check into a hotel until it's time for me to leave for New York. As soon as I find a room, I'll let you know, and you and Bess can visit me there. You too, *Tante* Nina."

Iris moved from the couch to the arm of Hugh's chair. "I think that's best, dear," she said, stroking his hair. "But there's no hurry. Everett will be out all day, so you go on upstairs, have a hot bath and then a good long nap. If he calls, I'll tell him you're sleeping. And when he gets home, I'll tell him the hotel was my idea."

"He won't let it alone, Mama."

"Leave it to me," she said. "So long as you're doing war work, he might be angry, but he'll know he isn't quite in the right. After all, the Army, the Navy, the Marines—they can't do their jobs unless somebody carries the supplies, can they?" She clutched her throat, stifling a sob. "It's just like what we talked about when you took the job at the shipyard, remember? The country's gone so crazy it's impossible for anybody to stay out of the war altogether. Every day, we all have fewer choices. While we can, we have to look at the choices we still have, find what we can live with, and do that until the war's over."

"I'm not a coward."

"I know that," she said. "I know it. You know it. Nina knows it. Bess will know it. And I don't have any doubt Gerhard knows it. Because we all know you. What does it matter what anybody else thinks? Now go upstairs and rest."

"I didn't tell you before," Hugh said, looking at neither of them. "Gerhard says every day a bunch of the other prisoners shout at him, corner him sometimes, trying to get him to say he'll leave off translating the *Lieder* and do marching songs instead. He tells them no. He tells them the art songs will live as long as there's a human soul to understand them. But the marches—they'll die the moment their loudmouthed leaders fall."

Nina gasped. Hugh looked at her.

"I thought that was brave—to tell me about it in front of the guards, but even more to say it to those men. He's braver than I knew." He covered his eyes with his hand. "But it terrifies me. Who are they, those men that want marches? What sort of people is he locked up with?"

Iris leaned down, pressing her cheek against her son's forehead. "I think it means," she said quietly, "that cruelty and injustice grow soldiers—and maybe even Nazis—where there were none before. Remember your graduation." She kissed his hair. "Gerhard is very brave, to stand his ground as he does. And so are you."

He clutched her hand and held it against his cheek. "I think I will have a bath, Mama." He groaned as he pushed himself up from the chair. "But I want to see Bess when she gets home. I can sleep while she sleeps."

When he reached the third step, he turned around and said, "Did I tell you, *Tante* Nina? Gerhard says he's going to write a poem about our half hour. He recited a few lines of one he was working on about the spiders—but I've forgotten them. All the way back on the bus, for as long as I could stay awake, I said them back to myself, but when I woke up, I'd forgotten." He shook his head bitterly. "How could I forget?" Nina saw his knuckles go white as he gripped the railing. He turned again to face the stairs and seemed to pull himself forward, bending lower with each step, as if struggling up a mountain.

When at last Hugh reached the top and disappeared down a hallway, Iris returned to the kitchen and busied herself with collecting Everett's breakfast dishes and wiping the counter. She worked silently, as if she had forgotten Nina's presence.

"I should go," Nina said.

"No, don't," said Iris. "Wait for Bess." She stopped her work and cocked her head toward the stairs. Nina heard a distant door click shut, then the glug of water from the tap. This seemed to be what Iris had been waiting for.

"You know about Hugh, don't you?"

Nina did not know how to reply. Hugh had asked her not to tell his true reason for enlisting.

"Everett doesn't," said Iris. "If he did, he'd never have allowed Hugh in the house."

"Never allowed? I don't understand."

"Don't you?"

Images of Gerhard and Hugh together rushed at Nina—their morning walks, the tenor of their laughter, a brush of the hand, a private look, the way they clung to each other in Chicago even as guards beat their backs. She saw Hugh alone—the attack in the street, Bobby Snyder's foul words. And then—the two of them, facing each other in a tiny grim room, forced apart by guns and hostile eyes, longing to touch. She saw what she had not seen before.

"He's such a kind and tolerant man in so many ways, Everett is," Iris said. "But not this. He's bound up inside that foolish notion—that men like Hugh aren't really men but some sort of monster to be stamped out." She pulled the top off the percolator, knocked the muddy grounds into a small crock on the counter, and rinsed the basket. "He'd never have married me if he knew. But then, if I'd known how he really was about it, I don't think I'd have married him. Strange—I've been on my own for so long, I'd forgotten how little you really know about a person until you marry him." She rinsed out the percolator pot and scooped fresh grounds into the basket. "I know most people think the same way Everett does about this—I just never thought I'd love someone like that. And I do love him, Nina."

"Yes," Nina said, finding her voice at last. "And I will not forget how good Everett has been to us. Without him, I would not have the great help Mr. Griffin has given me. I would not even know him."

Suddenly, Iris embraced her. "Oh, Nina—Everett's been pushing Hugh so hard about enlisting these last few months, I've only been able to think about him, afraid Everett would figure out how the boys feel about each other. Do you think Hugh's visit will have made things worse for Gerhard? It already sounds so terrible. If those guards realized—" She buried her face in Nina's shoulder and cried, "Please, God, may it not be so."

Nina went cold and weak. Dizzy. She reached behind her to grasp the back of a chair. Iris held onto her tightly, steadying her as she lowered herself into the chair. When Nina was seated, Iris turned to set the percolator on the stove. She brought cups, a sugar bowl, and a small pitcher of cream to the table and sat down across from Nina. Without a word, the women joined hands. Listening to the watery jangle of the perking coffee and the small sounds of Hugh's movements upstairs, they waited for Bess.

XIII

HALF AN HOUR BEFORE THE performance was to begin, Otto, Johan, and six others hurried back to the barracks to collect extra chairs. Even so, several dozen men had to be turned away with the promise that they would be the first to receive tickets for the next show.

For Johan's handsome proscenium arch, the painter had created lush, receding landscapes filled with robust young men and women, the passion of intelligence firing their eyes as they piped flutes, strummed lyres, laughed, sang, and danced beneath whispery clouds of a gold-bordered heaven. He'd finished it only yesterday, and as he climbed down from his ladder, the others, who had been rehearsing or arranging the set, stopped to gaze on his work.

"Beautiful," Johan said. "Magnificent! A noble hall, indeed!"

Hearing those words, Otto burst into a chorus from *Tannhäuser*, singing the celebratory dedication for the restored palace of music: "Joyfully we greet the hall, where art and peace alone may dwell!" He and Kurt taught the others, and they all sang the chorus six times through, with increasingly hearty joy.

Now, as they moved into their places, two or three of the men hummed or sang the chorus in low voices, and soon most of the rest joined in, as in a private overture. The stage was so small that the wings could accommodate only three or four waiting players, so the rest of the performers bunched into the triangles of floor space on either side, between the audience and the stage.

Otto stood next to a tall, round haberdasher from Poughkeepsie, who had taken the stage name Hartke for his role in a comic routine inspired by Laurel & Hardy. Less than a month ago, his partner Laurenz had been suddenly transferred to another camp, but one evening last week, when Hartke sat in the common room lamenting that he'd have to cancel his part, a slight, narrow-shouldered fellow—one of the camp's new arrivals—asked if he might try. Because of their dark suits, Hartke and his new Laurenz stood nearest the stage, ordered by Johan to wait there with the other soberly dressed actors and musicians, as a shield against the jugglers and dancers, whose brighter costumes might distract the audience from the action.

Since it required the most elaborate set, the evening's entertainment was to begin with Professor Spannagel's scene from *Faust*, in which Kurt would play Mephistopheles. When Otto asked his son how Spannagel had managed to persuade him to take the role after all, Kurt had shrugged, given a smile with a shadow of private knowing, and said, "You'll see."

There was no curtain to conceal Faust's study, dusty and dark. Aside from a narrow cot—borrowed from one of the barracks—the only furniture was a low stool and a small table dressed with an oil lamp and stacked high with the most imposing volumes the camp library had to offer. More books were scattered on the floor, many of them fanned open. A few lay caught in odd angles at the far reaches of the stage, suggesting that the great doctor had flung them away in frustration. To make the study appear even grimmer, like a dank cell, Kurt had used olive drab tarps to cover the bare bulbs overhead, rigging the tarps with pulleys so they could be drawn down when the lighter-hearted acts took the stage.

Someone in the wings blew a whistle and called for quiet. Johan stepped out to make his introduction, which was Otto's cue to maneuver his fellow singers to the steps at stage left, where they would await their entrance. They were to travel as a group downstage to the apron and, ignoring the study behind them, make gestures of happy companionship while they sang a rollicking song celebrating the delights of spring. They were a band of peasants on their way to an Easter festival.

"Welcome! Welcome!" Johan boomed. He turned toward Mr. McCoy, who sat in the front row on the right side, and thanked him for allowing the theatre to open at long last. McCoy responded with a nod. Then Johan addressed the whole audience, saying, "We also owe our thanks to the commander for permitting the building of the café. Finishing is now a matter of a few weeks—by the first of October!" With another slight twist toward McCoy, Johan started a round of applause, which most of the audience joined—but not without, Otto noticed, a number of wry smiles, especially from the three dozen seamen who sat in rank immediately behind McCoy.

When the applause subsided, Johan unfolded a page he had taken from his pocket. "Our story begins in Heaven," he read, "where Mephistopheles, the wisest of the defiant angels, tells God he should have denied mankind the Heavenly light of Reason. 'For it is by Reason,' says Mephistopheles, 'that man becomes more bestial than any beast.'"

Murmurs of assent rippled through the audience.

"In counterargument," Johan continued, "the Lord points to Doctor Faust, his devoted servant, ever searching for truth. At this, Mephistopheles scoffs, inviting the Lord to make a wager."

Here, from far back on the dark stage, Kurt's voice sounded: "You'll lose him yet, I offer bet and tally. Grant me leave, your Honor, to lure your Faust up *my* alley!"

The answer came from a voice Otto recognized as Max Kuehn's, and he chuckled softly, imagining the gleam in Max's eyes when Professor Spannagel asked him to speak the words of God.

"As long as Faust on Earth lives," said Max, as the Lord, "you shall not be forbidden. Try him. Strive to estrange his spirit from its primal source. And stand ashamed when you must confess the worthy soul *knows* its appointed course."

While the Lord spoke from the outer darkness, Spannagel had appeared on stage and now sat bent over the desk, opening first one book and then another, gazing into each for only a moment before snapping it shut and shoving it aside. With a great sweep of his arms, he sent all the books tumbling to the floor, crying, "O, boundless Nature—how to seize you in my clasp?"

Kicking at books, beating at the table, the lauded scholar raged over the failure of philosophy, law, medicine, and theology to satisfy his greatest hunger: to know the secrets of the universe. Turning, he grasped an invisible vial from an invisible shelf and, with the vial cradled in his hand, walked downstage so the audience, too, might see the small vessel of poison. Holding it high, he proclaimed, "To other shores I am beckoned. Uncharted orbits! New dominions!"

He cradled the vessel in his palm, caressed it with his fingertips, then hoisted it once more in a final toast. He pulled the stopper, but just as his lips kissed the vial's rim, an angelic chorus rang out: "Christ the Lord is risen! Christ has broken every chain!"

Otto and his troupe took the stage. Faust threw down the vial, watching the peasants in wonderment, entranced by their simple joy. But when the band moved on, the cloud resettled across Faust's brow.

Suddenly, the audience erupted in laughter.

An absurd dog, made shaggy with a fringe of black rags, had lumbered onto the stage. The dog sniffed. The dog howled. The dog tilted its head when it looked at Faust, approached the doctor with its head low, and then lay at his feet. Faust patted the dog, asked if it had lost its master, then called the dog to follow him back to his study. At the promise of shelter, the dog pranced, and the audience roared again.

Otto could see McCoy was laughing, too, clapping his hands in delight, the smile fading from his face for only a moment when a guard leaned down to speak in his ear. Without looking at the guard, McCoy nodded, and then he laughed again at the happy pooch, now in Faust's study, rolling on its back and paddling its big feet in the air.

Faust, a new hope lighting his face, picked up one of the books and opened it.

The dog whined and pawed at the floor.

"Cease your riot!" cried Faust. "Go lie behind the stove in quiet." He laid the open book on the desk, took the only pillow from the cot, and beckoned the dog. "My finest cushion shall be yours." He dropped the pillow on the floor, and with a complaining cry, the dog sprawled across it, covering it completely.

The audience laughed.

Faust patted the dog once more. "End your gambol, take your rest, and be welcome as my *silent* guest."

Faust drew up the stool to the small table and, stroking the pages of the book he'd left there, said, "Again I yearn to trace life's course— life's very springs to know."

The dog, from its inadequate bed, protested.

"Stop growling, poodle!" Faust bent over the open book. "'In the beginning was the *Word*,'" he read. "I must translate it differently."

The dog's growl became a steady grumble.

"In the beginning was the *Sense*," said Faust. "Is sense in fact all action's spur and source?"

The dog barked sharply three times, but Faust ignored it.

"In the beginning was the *Force*." Faust took up an imaginary pen and seemed to write the words before him on the air. He shook his head, swiped his hand across what he had written, and said, "Lo, the way is freed. In the beginning was the *Deed*."

The dog rose to its feet and howled. It turned about in wild circles.

"Poodle, cease your barking!" cried Faust.

The dog stopped its wheeling.

Faust backed away in horror. "How it does swell and rise—the beast is neither canine form nor size!"

The dog was shaking, growing wider and taller by the second. Unfolding itself.

The dim lights of the theatre snuffed as candles, and every man in the audience held his breath. Just as suddenly, the lights flashed on again, far brighter, blinding everyone.

Kurt now stood at center stage, dramatically tossing away the shroud of the black dog. The whole audience was still. Spannagel's face was blank with shock—for what had happened had turned him back to himself. He was Faust no longer.

Otto's face poured with sweat. He longed to run onto the stage and cover Kurt again with the cloak of rags, but he could not move his feet.

His son wore white trousers—from one of the seamen, no doubt—with red crepe-paper streamers hung from the waist to mimic stripes. Above, a cutaway coat crudely fashioned from threadbare blue serge. And on his head, a frowzy wig of white rags, resembling the fringe of the dog's costume. Fixed to his chin was a long, narrow beard of cotton wool, and in his hand, a top hat made of cardboard, painted blue and scattered all over with white stars.

As if on cue, three dozen seamen stomped and clapped as one. "There is your Yankee Doodle Devil!" someone shouted. "Your Uncle Sam in tatters!"

Kurt took an exaggerated bow, and the seamen rose to their feet, cheering. Johan tried to pull Kurt into the wings as McCoy leapt from his seat and onto the stage.

"Out! Out! Everyone out now!" McCoy shouted. "Back to barracks!"

His shouting had conjured guards, who surrounded Kurt and Johan. Another pair shoved Spannagel back toward center stage.

Otto struggled to make his way to Kurt, but the tide of bodies was too swift and powerful, and he was swept along with it, up the aisle and out the door into the floodlit compound, turned to greasy gray mud by a sudden downpour.

There was no porch where he could wait, so he took shelter beneath the narrow overhang of the roof, pressing himself as flat as he could against the side wall. He unpinned the blanket he had worn as his costume, a peasant's cloak, and held it over his head, but the rain spurled off the edge of the blanket, splashing his face and soaking him. A few guards came out of the theatre, but they did not see him, intent on herding the angry audience back toward the barracks.

From the center of the compound, the siren blasted twice, signaling a count, but Otto did not move. He would not fan the flame of McCoy's anger by going back inside the theatre now, but neither would he run away, leaving Kurt and Johan behind. This was his theatre as much as theirs. He had helped to build it, had encouraged his friends to perform. But worse, he had shuttered his mind against the depth of Kurt's disillusionment. He must remain and accept his portion of blame.

Johan and Spannagel emerged together, arguing. But no Kurt.

"Johan!" Otto called. "Where is Kurt? What is to happen?"

Spannagel shoved Johan aside and blocked Otto's path. "What is this you teach your son!" he shouted. "I tell them I have nothing to do with this, that it is a nasty joke by you meddling Austs, but still they suspect me. Me!"

Johan took a step nearer. "Otto did not know." His voice was confident, but even through the rain, Otto could see his friend's questioning eyes seeking confirmation.

"That is so. I did not know this plan," Otto said. "But the fault is mine. Something has troubled Kurt these last months, since the end of spring—something more than losing his place at the university. I am his father. I should have forced him to tell me."

"You have ruined me, you Austs! Ruined me!" Spannagel threw his arms out in enraged despair, as if he were playing Faust again, and splashed off toward the barracks.

Johan plucked at the locks of hair that had slipped down his forehead and tried in vain to wipe the water from his face. "The professor thought the play would win his freedom. Only now he declared to Mr. McCoy that his translation of Göethe was proof of his superiority and that he should not be held prisoner among the common worms. Foolish man."

The door of the theatre opened again, and out came a guard carrying a large, soft bundle. Amidst the raggedy black mound, Otto caught a glimpse of white, a flutter of red falling away into the mud.

"We must go back," Johan said, taking Otto's arm and pulling him in the direction of the barracks.

"No! I will wait for Kurt."

"Please, Otto," Johan said. "McCoy will not like for you to interfere."

"I should go inside."

Johan's strong grip stayed him once more. "You will make matters worse for Kurt if you do," he said. "You must allow your son to speak for himself in this. And if it comes, to take the penalty." He took a few steps toward the barracks. "Please."

Otto settled the blanket, heavy with rain, over his head like a shroud, its coldness easing the violent pain that throbbed in his head. Then he followed his friend, making the way back in silence, stepping lightly, picking his way around the channels and small lakes the rain had cut.

XIV

THE COMMON ROOM WAS DESERTED except for Egon Merkel, who sat in the chair nearest the door, obviously waiting for them. He rose and helped Johan peel off his drenched jacket. Otto draped his sodden blanket over his arm and worked at the buttons of his wet shirt with trembling fingers.

"The others wait at their beds," Herr Merkel said in German. "You heard the siren? The guards have not yet come." The old man took the blanket from Otto. "Whatever the trouble, I will stand for Kurt. Rolf and Kaspar also," he said, referring to two of the other farmers whose letters Kurt translated. "They have sworn." He held the jacket and blanket at arm's length. "Now we all need dry clothes."

Johan's bed, like Herr Merkel's, was on the first floor, so Otto climbed the stairs alone. When he reached the landing on the second floor, he saw two men positioned like sentries at the doorway of the room where Kurt slept. They did not turn their heads toward him, but he could feel their sidelong glares. The third floor hall was empty, and all the doors were closed. Coming to the room he shared, Otto knocked lightly and announced himself before turning the knob. The others were sitting on their bunks, some of them facing each other and talking in low voices. Max Kuehn was playing chess against himself, strategizing an advance for the black side, his Imperial army, before rotating the board for a counterattack by the yellowish opponent.

Otto sensed a deliberateness in the way the men did not look at him, the way they appeared not to hear him and not to notice the damp trail he left, or the wet, rusty odor of the mud splashed heavily on his trousers. He moved quickly toward his cot. He cringed at every sound he made—the small sucking of wet boots pulled from his feet, the creaking of the bunk's foot rail when he laid his wet shirt across it, the scraping of leather on tile when he slid his suitcase from under the bed.

He tried to muffle the clink of buckles and hasps as he opened the case, but suddenly he was furious. To silence himself was to accept the unjust punishment the others had imposed upon him. He would not.

He took out his dry shoes, held them waist high, and dropped them. Knowing his silver-backed clothes brush was rolled inside his clean trousers, he yanked them from the case, letting the brush clatter to the floor. He flipped closed the lid of the suitcase when he was done, securing the clasps with a rap of his fist. He dropped heavily onto his bunk and loudly sang *"Der Rattenfänger"*—flinging himself into the role of the traveling singer determined to clear the town of weasels and rats.

He stopped singing when he heard a guard shout from downstairs, signaling the start of the count. Normally, at night, the guards quickly ticked off each occupied bunk by number, not bothering to verify who sat or lay there, but these two worked slowly, having every prisoner state his name and identification number.

The following morning, the guards returned, ordering them to the common room with three short, shrill blasts of a whistle. The men jammed into the halls and onto the staircase in various stages of dress, some still struggling to fasten their trousers. A guard on the second-floor landing alternately blew his whistle and smacked the stair rail with the butt of his billy club, shouting, "On the double! On the double!" Another stood at the bottom, crying, "That side!" waving everyone to the right with his club.

A third guard held a clipboard. "When I call your name, line up over there." He pointed to the empty west side of the room. "And wait."

He called for Abel, Ackermann, and Artz, making marks with a pencil as they crossed the room. He called *Aust*—caught himself starting to say Kurt's name, and then shouted, "Aust, Otto!"

Name by name, the men lined up, the first group pressing against the wall and into corners to make room for the others. Voss, Weiman, and Zellweger were crossing when the door opened and five more guards entered, followed by the two shepherd dogs with their handlers. The dogs stopped in the center of the room and sat, erect and waiting. Slowly, Otto wedged himself through the crowd to get a clearer view. Both dogs noted his movement with low growls.

"Which bunk?" asked one handler, and the guard with the clipboard leaned in and silently pointed to his list.

The handler held out for his dog a bit of white cloth, greyed from too much washing. Kurt's undershirt—Otto recognized it. The kind his son preferred, with the collar he could unbutton when he felt too warm.

"Find!" the handlers ordered. Fresh from the scent, the dogs pulled toward the stairs, their necks stretched, ears flattened, tails parallel to the floor. The guard with the clipboard and three others spread out to watch the assembled men, while the rest followed the dogs and their handlers up the steps.

Overhead, there was bumping, scraping, thudding, slamming— so like the sounds Otto had heard back in December, when he'd sat chained with Kurt and Gerhard to a table in the restaurant while FBI men searched their flat. One of the dogs barked twice. Otto heard feet shuffling, then the strike of heavy footfalls approaching the landing.

The handlers and the dogs came down first and went outside. Three other guards followed, one clutching a roll of brown paper. Kurt's map. Another carried Kurt's suitcase. A third, the writing box meant for Bess. The last one came several steps behind them, and, reaching the final landing, drew his gun.

The procession stopped in front of the men, still crushed to one side of the room. The guard holding the map unrolled it and held it high.

The guard with the pistol swung the gun toward the map. "Who was in on this?" he demanded. "It's not the work of one man. Speak up." He trained the gun on the men for a moment before easing the barrel to the floor.

Some of them stared at the guards. Others glanced to one side or the ceiling. No one looked at the map. No one spoke.

"Come on. Who else? Kurt Aust has admitted it's his work, but we know he had help."

Otto stepped forward. "I urged him to draw it. It was I who provided the paper and I who identified some cities in Indiana."

"You?" With the pistol, he waved Otto to the empty side of the room. "Who else?"

A knotty, liver-spotted hand on a thin arm rose from the mass's center. "Wyoming," said Egon Merkel. "My farm, outside Wheatland town."

"Step out," said the guard.

Kaspar Pfenning followed Herr Merkel out of the crowd. "I am Nebraska. Near to Garland."

Johan emerged to claim southern Idaho. Everyone else kept his silence.

The guard with the pistol ordered Otto and his friends to stand against the wall farthest from the door, dismissed the others, and sent the rest of the guards away. Otto rolled his shoulders back and breathed deeply, expecting an interrogation, perhaps a forced march to headquarters to face McCoy, but after the guard had written their names and identification numbers in a small notebook, he left. For a moment, the four men looked anxiously at each other.

Johan broke the silence. "Perhaps this means nothing."

"Perhaps everything," said Kaspar Pfenning. "But it is done."

Otto sighed. "How can I thank you? Good friends. Brave friends. To speak up, not knowing how our words might be corrupted against us."

Herr Merkel patted his shoulder. "Come, come, Otto," he said quietly in German. "A man deserves censure for falsehood, not praise for truth."

How eloquent the old man could be when free to speak his own language. And how lucky his family must have felt when they received his letters, written in Kurt's hand—for Kurt would have taken care to capture Herr Merkel's thoughtful, measured voice. The letters Otto had translated for Merkel, when the load was too great for Kurt to manage, must have seemed like the work of a clumsy imposter.

Otto pulled out a chair from the table and sank wearily into it, but—as if burned—he leapt up again. "All Kurt's things—they mean to transfer him. To the *Straflager*, do you think? Because of a farce? For a schoolboy's map? I must speak to Mr. McCoy."

"Don't, Otto. Not in haste," said Johan. "You must not give the commander any reason for a mark against you. This will not help Kurt. Go with us to breakfast, to show the others you are not afraid, then go to your work assignment—and after, you can see the commander."

"Listen to Johan," said Herr Merkel. "If McCoy means to send Kurt from here, already it is done. You cannot stop it. But if it is still possible to move him, time to think and time to cool your anger will leave you better able to speak well on Kurt's behalf. And if McCoy is decided—time will strengthen you to meet whatever comes."

During the breakfast mess, word spread that Spannagel had disappeared from the camp. Still wearing the robes of Doctor Faust, he'd been stopped by a pair of guards as he was entering his barracks, bundled into a waiting truck, and seen no more. An hour later, a single, rain-soaked guard came in, walked straight to Spannagel's bunk, stuffed Spannagel's well-brushed Trilby and his neatly folded clothes into his suitcase, and walked out again. All without a word. The professor's books were left behind.

Similar stories circulated about a group of seamen—twenty at least, who were said to have been among those who cheered Kurt's Mephistopheles—and it was rumored that still more of the seamen would be transferred within the week.

Despite his fear, Otto followed the advice of his friends and went on to his assigned work in the laundry, glad for the steam that would obscure the faces of his fellow workers and even gladder for the noisy machines that would make it hard to hear what they spoke of. On his way there, he saw a guard throwing books into a fire that shot up so boldly from a metal barrel that the flames could not be troubled by the steady rain. Later—at dinner, perhaps, or at breakfast tomorrow—he expected to hear Spannagel's barracks mates report that the professor's private library had vanished.

When his shift was done, Otto trudged through the downpour to headquarters and asked to see Commander McCoy.

"Denied," the clerk said, and when Otto asked again, the clerk showed him a list with names of men McCoy wanted turned away. His own name was at the top.

"Then I should like to see my son, Kurt Aust. What paper must I sign to make a formal request?"

"No way that's going to happen," said the clerk. "Prisoners in solitary aren't allowed visitors."

"Solitary confinement? For how long?"

The clerk looked around as if afraid he was being watched. He opened a ledger, quickly flipped several pages, and closed the book again. Quietly, his voice barely above a whisper, the clerk said, "Forty-five days. No mail, either. Anything that comes will be returned to the sender unopened, marked with a special stamp."

Otto felt as if the air in his lungs had turned to cement.

Solitary confinement. Forty-five days. He thought of his boy, without company day in and day out, without air and sunlight, without letters, without room to walk more than three paces in one direction, and with nothing to eat but American bread, pale and tasteless.

By the time Kurt was released, Fort Lincoln might again be covered in snow. Forty-five days in a cage within a cage—but not transferred. Not yet beyond reach.

"That's forty-five days, pending investigation," the clerk said.

"He could be released sooner?"

The clerk shook his head. "More likely transferred. Or deported. But you didn't hear that from me."

The next day, rain gave way to sun—unclouded, hot sun, baking every drop of moisture from the ground and trees. Each morning, Otto stayed behind from breakfast to tend his garden before the plants, rejuvenated in the cool of the night, weakened again in the heat. At the beginning of summer, the guard named Lewis, a native of Bismarck, had warned Otto of harsh weather, often violently shifting, and advised him to collect as much packing straw as he could to layer over the soil and protect his plants against late frosts, buffeting wind, too much rain or too little, and the naked sun. Mr. Lewis—whom the staff called Lew—was the only guard universally respected by the men in Barracks 32 because he had troubled to learn their names, and because he called them Mr. Kuehn, Mr. Cappelmann, Mr. Merkel, Mr. Aust. Kurt he called "Mr. Aust the Younger," and Kurt answered in friendliness by calling him "Mr. Lew."

Now it was the second week of October—Kurt had been confined for thirty-two days—and Mr. Lewis, whose gardening advice had proven excellent, cautioned Otto not to trust the more temperate days. A killing frost could strike on any clear night.

In the evenings, no matter whether Otto sat at his bunk or in the common room, he could not escape overhearing the talk from clusters of men, renewing their complaints to one another that the actions of a few were sure to bring grave consequences to the many. "Already we have seen this," said the Poughkeepsie haberdasher, whose hopes of minor fame through his Laurenz & Hartke routine had disintegrated with the abrupt closing of the theatre. "A handful of spies, a few agitators—and the rest of us are suspected."

Sometimes the talkers posited complex conspiracy theories to explain the disappearance of the seamen—two more groups, smaller than the first. More often the subject was Professor Spannagel. The men who spoke of him never seemed to tire of saying, *A spy if there ever was one, probably a double agent,* though Otto could think of Spannagel as little more than an arrogant fool.

But in thinking this, he would again chastise his own foolishness—for prodding Spannagel on that first night when he came strutting into their barracks; for making sport of him behind his back; and, more than anything, for urging Kurt to accept the demon's role.

When the talk turned to Kurt, Otto was certain the men deliberately raised their voices. Why was Kurt still in the camp, they wondered. And why so mildly punished? *A solitary cell, that's barely a slap on the wrist for such a dangerous malcontent.* When they said, *All the Nazis must be flung out like bad fruit!* Otto wondered if McCoy appreciated the extent of his victory—so many decent men transformed into mindless machines, spouting the popular lie that any German who dared to protest his imprisonment must certainly be a Nazi.

Every night, hearing such things, Otto spent all his strength struggling not to rise. He wanted to pound the wall and cry out, *Show me these consequences you speak of!* just so he could point out that not a single one of them had suffered any punishment or loss of privilege. Johan had even been permitted to finish the café, which was now open nightly for the men's enjoyment, featuring some of the musical performances and recitations from the ill-fated revue.

In the mornings, when he was alone in his garden, Otto calmed again, and, reflecting on how shared food could heal, he filled anything available—pails, empty flour sacks, discarded boxes, sometimes even sheets fresh from the laundry—with glossy peppers, fat red tomatoes, and new potatoes, crisp and sweet, but except for Johan, Herr Merkel, and two or three others, the men in Barracks 32 refused his food, so he took to leaving his harvest silently outside the doors of other barracks. Once, with the help of Mr. Lewis, he sent two brimming half-bushel boxes over to the Japanese side. When he reached his garden the next day, he noticed about thirty Japanese lined up at the fence, apparently waiting for him. He waved his arm in greeting, and the men bowed to him deeply. He bowed in response and they all bowed again, quite low, before silently returning to their barracks.

On the thirty-eighth day of Kurt's confinement, a guard appeared at the garden and said, "Come with me. Commander McCoy wants to see you."

Silently, the two men crossed the compound. As soon as they entered headquarters, Otto could see McCoy's office door was open and that the commander was standing behind his desk. The guard called out, "I've got him!"

"In here," said McCoy, and the guard gave Otto a little shove.

A large sheet of brown paper lay across the desk. Holding down one corner was the same can Otto had seen before, *Kuner's Tender Garden Sweet Peas,* the label now so worn that the image of the peas had rubbed away. McCoy sat down and, looking at Otto, tapped the paper and said, "Tell me what you know about this."

"It is our map," said Otto. "Among Kurt's things, which the guards took away. We made it, Kurt and I, and some others in our barracks."

"When?"

"We began in the spring—before you came here."

"Why? Why did you make it?"

"We had been talking of our families and our homes. The map was to help everyone see the places described."

"Any more of them? Maps?"

"No," said Otto. "It is the only one. For all to share—like a mural."

McCoy opened a drawer and tossed something into the center of the map. "And what about this?" Another paper, of lighter color and heavier stock, folded to the size of a passport, but thicker. "Go ahead. Have a look at it."

Otto picked it up. There was fraying along the creases. Beneath his fingers, the structure of the paper felt weakened, as if it had been kept in the damp. Carefully, he worked open the folds.

"What do you see, Aust?"

Another map. A quarter the size of the one Kurt had drawn, but otherwise the same. A replica, to scale.

"What do you know about it?" McCoy spat into the can, and Otto caught the sharp, dank smell of rotted tobacco.

"Nothing," Otto said. He looked at McCoy, whose face was a blank. A tarry drop of tobacco juice clung to his lower lip.

"Your son's work."

Question or statement—Otto couldn't tell. He looked at the map again. "I don't know that it is."

The features of the map, though smaller, were familiar—but somehow not. The lines were bolder, more urgent. Otto bent closer to study the writing, the names of towns and rivers, mountain ranges, deserts, and lakes. "This is not my son's hand," he said. He pointed to the larger map, where Kurt had marked an X and written *Newman*. "See here? My son wrote this first. See how he shapes the letter *N*? Kurt writes in the American style—far simpler than this one." He held out the small map, indicating the spot. "This is a letter *N* made by someone schooled in Germany—long before the Nazis."

"Like you."

Otto turned the small map face down and slid it back toward McCoy. "Ask me to write the name of any marked place. You choose. You will see it is not my hand on this paper. When they were boys, my sons taught me the American way of writing because my suppliers could not read my orders. Call in your censors and ask for the letters I posted yesterday. Look in your files for all the forms I have filled since being brought here."

"No need," said McCoy. "You didn't know about it, that's clear."

"Have I been accused?"

McCoy shook his head. "Just a little test. To be sure." He picked up the small map, refolded it. "I know whose work this is. I have the confessions. Part of a plan to escape. Thought they could get themselves to the Gulf of Mexico—the fools." He held the map up for a moment before dropping it back into the drawer. "Discovered the night of your little revue."

Otto remembered—McCoy clapping and laughing while Kurt, dressed in the rags of the black dog, pranced absurdly across the stage. A guard bending to speak in McCoy's ear, the message wiping his face of its smile. McCoy laughing anew, louder than before, as Kurt rolled on his back and paddled his big black feet in the air. Then—Kurt's unveiling. McCoy's swift rage.

"This will be destroyed," McCoy said, rolling up Kurt's map. Again, he spat into the can. "The staff all know not to bring any maps in—but I guess when the rules were being drawn up in Washington, it didn't occur to anybody that the internees might make maps of their own."

The fools, Otto wanted to say, but he held his tongue. He pressed his palms into his thighs and stretched his fingers, fighting against the instinctive curl of fists. "Mr. McCoy," he said, mindful to blunt his tone, "my garden has grown very well. This morning I have many tomatoes ready to pick—a fine, sharp flavor. Perhaps you would like some for yourself? Perhaps you will allow me to send one or two to my son?"

"He isn't here anymore."

Otto's legs went weak. He wanted to drop into the chair behind him, but he would not bow to asking McCoy for permission to sit. He pressed his palms harder into his thighs. "Where? May I know where?"

"No reason not to tell you, since you'll know as soon as his first postcards go out. With the transfer, so long as he controls himself, he'll get his mailing privileges back. I don't agree with it, but that's the rule." McCoy turned his attention to papers on his desk. He picked up a pen, made a few marks, giving the impression he had forgotten Otto was still in the room.

"Where has my son gone?" Otto stared at the top of McCoy's bowed head. "You said I might know. Please? Sir."

With that word, McCoy looked up, leaned back in his chair with a small, self-satisfied smile. "He's on his way to Texas." McCoy flicked his finger against the rolled up map. "You know where Texas is, of course. Another camp there—Kenedy, it's called."

Otto nodded.

"You can go now. You'll be late for your work assignment, but you can make up the time this afternoon. Tell the guard I said so."

"A moment more, sir, please?"

McCoy glared with annoyance, but he didn't order Otto out.

"Among my son's belongings was a writing box he built for his sweetheart. If it has not gone with him to Texas, I would like to have it, so I can send it to her. She will be worried, not having heard from him for so long."

McCoy waved dismissively. "That was smashed up weeks ago. Had to make sure it wasn't concealing any messages." He looked past Otto, toward the lobby. "Paxton!"

A guard appeared instantly.

"Get him out of here," McCoy said. "Make sure he goes on to his work assignment—but before that, take him by his garden. Aust here has promised me the best of his tomatoes."

When the guard called Paxton shut the office door behind them both, Otto thought the punctuating thud had been directed not at him but at McCoy, though he would never be sure.

"Not so fast, Aust," Paxton said. "Your mail. Do you want it?" Without waiting for Otto's answer, the guard tossed a single envelope onto the postal counter.

Gerhard's clear American script dominated the center. Three censors, instead of the usual two—one for each camp—had framed the address with their initials. He slid a finger under the censors' tape, breaking the seal, but, feeling Paxton watching him, he took the letter outside—that was still his right.

Leaning against the building, Otto unfolded the page. "I'm still waiting to hear from Kurt about the theatricals," Gerhard wrote. "He said you were both performing in—" The last word was blacked out. Ridiculous. Of course he had written *Faust*. Hardly an inflammatory secret in this camp. Otto read on. "He promised to write, but the letter must have been lost." That was prisoners' code for *disallowed*. "Tell him to write me again, but you tell me, too."

What could he tell his young son? The price his brother had paid for a bitter error in judgment? Would that be allowed? No.

"Did I tell you I've been writing songs? Well, not songs so much as poems with some elementary music. Enough for Hugh to work with, I hope. I've written three more in the last couple of weeks. Nothing else to do when I'm confined to bed. But don't worry—I feel stronger today. I know the tunes aren't right. I'm trying to hear the music in my head, but I might be able to work out what's going wrong if I could sing them. The best I can do is croak a little. Nothing you could even call a note—not one anyone would want to hear, anyway. I wish you and Kurt could sing them for me. And *Mutti*, too."

What reply could he possibly give? Gerhard was ill—perhaps gravely ill—and in need of *what* from his father? Encouragement? Reassurance? Faith? Hope?

For all Otto knew, Kurt might be ill as well, gray and wasted from his confinement, made weaker by a long train journey in chains—and he, as father, as head of their family, had nothing to give. He might as well be dead for all he could reach either of his sons.

He crushed the letter in his fist. That, at least, he could feel.

He would write his boy another page filled with empty words—a bit of blather about his garden. By the time it reached him, they both might have had a note from Kurt, with no news except that he was alive and in another camp.

Yes—he would write as if he had never seen this letter, had never known that Kurt had written his brother about *Faust*. Let Gerhard think that this one, too, had been lost.

XV

NOVEMBER GRAY HAD SETTLED IN—ABRASIVE, naked limbs of trees flayed against the ashy sky, its low, heavy clouds melding with the asphalt and concrete. Nina thought the wind, too, was more bitter and persistent than usual, but she might be misremembering because November had always been an especially happy time in the Aust Family Restaurant, filled from opening to closing with customers driven in by wind and drizzle to the comfort of succulent beef rolls with gravy and potato dumplings, spicy sausages and red cabbage stewed with cloves, mounds of bread, and *Apfelstrudel*, warm and flaky-crisp.

Nina caught herself just before she turned down Elm Street in the direction of the restaurant, now called the Victory Café, which daily emitted odors of overcooked onions and scorched frying oil. She pulled her scarf up higher around her face and crossed the street with a crowd, taking the long route that would keep the café out of her sight as she headed to her private door at the back of Charlie Griffin's office building.

Now that she considered it, she realized she had few memories of being outside in Newman in the winter months—only short walks with Otto or the boys or Bess or Hugh, brisk, bracing walks that refreshed her between long hours in the hot and fragrant kitchen. These days, she walked for want of occupation—and because if she stayed too long in her cramped room, she found herself sobbing.

Until these last few months, in the whole of her life, she had never spent a full day without the company of at least one other person. Being so much alone was unnatural. How did people bear it, year in and year out?

Last winter and spring, those first, grim months, she had been buoyed by hope that her men would soon come home, by the companionship of Hugh and Bess, and by the flowering of her friendship with Iris. Back then, she had still felt close enough to Otto and her sons' lives to find substance in their hollow letters and to infuse her own with scents of home. But since Hugh had told her of the terrible fences and the rifle-armed guards that threatened Gerhard in that bleak and moldy camp, she had ached even more for him, for Otto and Kurt, too, unable to prevent herself from conceiving troubles they could not tell her. And then when her letters from Kurt began to come back, unopened, and his letters to her stopped entirely, she had thought the weight of her imaginings would drag her straight down to the center of the earth.

Hugh had left for his training by then. Bess—whose own letters to Kurt had been returned as well—had taken on extra shifts at the factory to save herself from being destroyed by the circular, unanswerable question: *Why? Why? Why?* Once or twice a week, Iris dropped in for an hour, but Nina knew Everett had begun discouraging their visits—and, in any case, Iris had her own fears to carry. Hugh would be at sea early in the new year.

Relief had sparked two days ago—a postcard, instructing her to send Kurt's mail to a different camp. Proof he was alive! Proof he was well enough to write his name clearly in his familiar hand! But quick-storm questions extinguished the infant flame, and those new, churning *whys* had driven her out of her room this morning. Kurt had filled in his own name and identification number in a blank marked *Interned Alien Enemy*, but the address in Kenedy, Texas, had been written by a stranger. What did that mean? Why had Kurt been sent to another camp? And what did this mean for Otto? Would their family be forever split—drawn and quartered, each member dragged alone to some desolate tract of the country? All in the name of protecting Americans?

She unlocked her door. Four envelopes had been dropped through the slot, and without bending, Nina could see they included two letters from Gerhard, a letter from Otto, and one from Hugh. Two carelessly folded notes—one on heavy white paper, the other on airy blue—had been dropped through the slot as well. The blue note was from Bess: *I'm on half-shift today. Mama thought you might want to go with us to the pictures tonight. Mr. Beale has a meeting, so it would just be us girls. We'll come get you at 7:00.*

The white note was from Charlie Griffin: *Come around as soon as you get this. Read your letter from Otto first. I have new information.*

Otto's letter was shorter than usual, as if he had imagined it would fly to her more quickly if it were lighter.

My Sweet Wife—There is to be a family camp organized. I am told we are not counted a family without a mother's presence. Mr. Griffin can make a petition. I am sending him a letter today. If you agree to come, I can join with others who will go from here soon to help build at the new camp, and we can all four be together, after the New Year.

Nina cried out. Her heart pounded. She read the letter through again, terrified she had misunderstood. Could it be true?

She hurried to Mr. Griffin's office. His private door was closed. Her hand was already on the knob, ready to turn it and push straight in, when the secretary called sharply, "He's with another client, Mrs. Aust. You'll have to wait."

Nina paced in front of the secretary's desk until the young woman, obviously annoyed, insisted she sit down.

She took the chair across from Mr. Griffin's door, sitting on the seat's edge, her weight already on her feet so she could leap up the moment the door opened. She watched the clock on the wall. Five minutes. Ten minutes. Fifteen.

At last the door opened and she stood up. Only a glance from Mr. Griffin and a softly spoken "A moment" prevented her from running at him. She waited while he accompanied his other client into the hallway, spoke a few more words to him, shook his hand, and wished him good day. He returned to Nina, nodded toward his office. "Please, come in."

"I want to be with my husband and sons," Nina said before the door was fully closed behind her. She pushed Otto's letter into Mr. Griffin's hands. "He says there is to be a camp for families. He says I can go there, too. That they three cannot be together unless I go there, too."

Mr. Griffin nodded, offered her a chair, and walked around his desk to sit down. "Your husband has written to me," he said, a note of anxiety lacing his voice. "It's a new scheme, still being worked out. I've made a few other calls to get more information." He sighed, stretched his arms out before him. "I'll write the petition—but only when I'm sure you understand what you'd be agreeing to.

"You'd be designated a voluntary internee—which means you'd be agreeing to imprison yourself, in exchange for being brought back together with your family. Your sons are of independent age, interned under individual orders, and so your husband is right about the possibility of reunion resting on your shoulders. Without you, they're considered three single men, and, as such, can be moved around at the government's pleasure. With you—if you're accepted—you're a family, and the intent of this plan is to keep families together.

"If you volunteer, you'll be tied to Otto's internment order, so, even if one or both of your sons were to be paroled, or to enlist in the service, or if either was repatriated or deported, you and Otto could likely stay together." He picked up Otto's letter to her, refolded it, and set it down again.

"Do you understand, Mrs. Aust? The length of your internment depends upon Otto's, so you will remain in US custody as long as he does." He looked at her. "None of us knows how long this war will go on or what the aftermath will be—on either side. I have to know you understand what you'd be committing yourself to. You're free to go in—but not to come out again. Not until the government decides when and under what conditions. You could be a prisoner behind barbed wire for years. Years."

It was as if he'd thrown her into a freezing river. She had come into his office thrilled and certain, thinking only of having the family together again, but Mr. Griffin's words had flung her back to memories of the FBI, the basement interrogation, and the Home of the Good Shepherd. After Parks, and then that horrible, cold woman, the nuns' house had been a haven—but what remained with her most keenly was fear. Fear that pumped through her body still, like blood. Never would she be fully free of it, this fear, which had been created by an imprisonment of only twelve days—not months, not years.

Could she bear a confinement so undefined, so unbounded, that it could endure the rest of her life? Who could say it might not? Now, this very moment, she could go outside and walk if she liked. She was free to go to the bank or the public library, the greengrocer or the butcher shop; free to sit in the park; free to go to a movie house with friends. But she was not free to do any of these things or a thousand others without fear—fear of being jeered at, shoved aside, pushed down, beaten, or arrested again.

Alone and afraid, as she was now. Or together, but at the will of a soulless bureaucracy. From these, she must choose. She thought of the double barbed-wire fence Hugh had described—wrapping around the prison camp, ready to trap a man, or a woman, in the narrow space between, tearing flesh at every breath.

"There's something else," Mr. Griffin said. "Your husband also asked me to file an appeal to reverse a deportation order for Kurt."

"Kurt? To be deported? When? Why?"

"That's what I'm trying to find out. All I've been told so far is that he said or did something they claim caused a disturbance in the camp—he's being blamed, anyway. In times like these, small things like holding up a sign, muttering a bitter word or two—singing a song—can set people to shouting *Traitor*. But you know that."

Mr. Griffin refolded Otto's letter and gave it to her. "Before I can appeal, I have to know more. That will take weeks, at least. Probably much longer. And I might not get what I need at all. Once the family camp is fully operational—February or March, I'm told—the director will give priority to parents of young children, and to those who agree up front that the whole family will be returned to Germany. So the best chance—maybe the only chance—for your family to be accepted is for Otto to join that building crew. This has to be settled right away—ideally today. I'll send a telegram saying a petition is being filed immediately for your voluntary internment, if that's what you decide."

He slid a gummed notepad to the center of his desk and took a pen from its holder.

"These are all things you need to think about, Mrs. Aust, I know that. Only there isn't time to think. I've explained what you'd be agreeing to: an undetermined amount of time in US custody, no boundaries to the government's authority over you. I have to tell you, too, if the appeal fails and it's decided Kurt is to be deported for cause, he won't ever be able to return to this country. If you don't go into this camp, you may never see him again."

She was numb—but, with the numbness, the pain of entrapment had faded.

"Send the telegram now," Nina said. "This moment. I will go."

Mr. Griffin nodded. He wrote the message, showed it to her, then opened the door and gave it to his secretary, telling her to deliver it immediately, by hand, to Western Union. He returned to where Nina was sitting. "I'll start on the petition right away, and it will be typed up and ready for you to sign first thing in the morning."

"Where is this camp, Mr. Griffin?"

"Someplace isolated, where there's a lot of undeveloped land. It's not decided yet. A couple of locations are still being scouted." He put his hand on the phone. "If it makes a difference in your decision, I can catch my girl at the Western Union office and stop the telegram."

"No," Nina said. "It does not matter." She would go to that camp if it were built on a volcano. She would go if it were in a cave under the sea. She would go if it turned out to be nothing more than a concrete room where, forced to stand, she could, if only for a few moments, look into Otto's and her sons' faces, feed on the sound of their voices. This must be what Hugh, desperate to see Gerhard, had felt.

She returned to her room, read her other letters, and wrote replies. To Hugh, a full explanation of all that Mr. Griffin had told her.

To Otto: *Yes, yes. I will come.*

To Gerhard and Kurt: *Your father will write soon with hope for us to be together.*

Iris and Bess were prompt. Nina opened the door and Bess came through first, chattering. "You will come to the movies, won't you, *Tante* Nina? It's Bette Davis. Mama's crazy about Bette Davis—aren't you, Mama?—but Mr. Beale doesn't like her, so we have to take the chance to go tonight. It's not a war picture—nothing about the war. I checked the paper this morning. If you don't want to listen to the newsreels, you can slip out until they're over, and Mama and I will save your seat—won't we, Mama?" She caught her breath and looked at Nina. "They'll be selling war bonds in lobby, of course, like they always do—but that doesn't bother you, right? You're so used to it."

Iris moved quietly past her daughter and put her hand on Nina's arm. "What's wrong?"

"Not wrong, exactly." Nina showed her the card from Kurt. "He has been moved to another camp," she said. "The address means we can write again. Otherwise, why send it? This is good." She held the card out to Bess, whose cheeks had gone red. "Take the card, darling. Probably you will get one too—but take it in case yours is lost. Already I have saved the address in my little book."

Bess studied the card. "There's nothing here but an address." She turned the card over. "Look at the postmark. Not even two weeks ago."

Iris returned to Bess's side. "That sort of thing wouldn't have to be censored, honey."

"But what about the rest of the time? Where has he been since August?"

"You know how inefficient offices can be," Iris said. "Maybe there was a backlog and this didn't get sent when it should have. Think of poor Kurt, waiting to hear from you."

"But *we* haven't moved," Bess said. "Why hasn't there been any mail for us?" She raised her eyes to Nina. "Why hasn't he written? What's going on?"

Nina smiled to blunt the sharp edge of the girl's questions. "Don't wait," she said. "If you write tonight, Kurt will get a few letters before he is moved again.

"Again?" asked Iris. "What do you mean? How do you know?"

"Because we are all to be moved." She smiled weakly. "We will be together."

"Oh, Nina—is it true?" said Iris. "What's happened?"

Nina asked them to sit with her on the bed. She explained about the family camp.

"You're not making sense," Bess said. "If you know all about this family camp, then you must know more about Kurt. More than you're saying."

"I don't," Nina said. She had promised herself she would not bring up Kurt's deportation order.

"You *must* know!" Bess waved the card at Nina. "Why would they move him now if they're only going to move him again? It's not logical."

"I learned just this morning of the family camp," Nina said. "From Otto. And from Mr. Griffin. I could not agree to what I did not know." She nodded toward the card in Bess's hand. "Kurt, you see, was transferred before any of this was decided."

Bess's eyes brimmed with tears. "You're not going to do it? Go to that camp?"

"I must," Nina said. "I must be with my family if I can—whatever the terms."

"You'd leave me? Alone? First Kurt. Gerhard. Then my brother. How can you think of going, too?"

"Always there has been the possibility the FBI would arrest me again. You have seen it. You know how they come for no reason and give no warning."

"But this is a choice." With the heel of her hand, the girl wiped furiously at her eyes, as if to blot out vision itself. "You're making a choice!"

"Bess, please understand. I don't want to leave you, darling. But you will not be alone—your mother is here. And Mr. Beale."

"Huh!" Bess tossed her head angrily and started to get up, but Iris stopped her, leaning across her daughter to clasp Nina's hands.

"We'll miss you," said Iris. She looked at Bess. "But of course we understand."

"Don't answer for me!" Bess leapt up, knocking the women's hands free. She raked her fingers through her hair and paced as if Nina's room were a cage.

"Let's go on to the show," Iris said, standing. "We can talk about this later, when it isn't so new."

Nina nodded and stood up, too. Bess stopped and turned. A strange, troubling look had settled in the girl's face.

"You said wives can go?"

"Mothers," Nina said carefully.

"Then I'll marry Kurt. I'll go with you to wherever it is. Kurt and I will get married, and I'll live in the camp, too."

"Honey," said Iris, "think what you're saying."

"No, Bess," Nina said firmly.

"I will."

"Bess—no. You cannot. Listen to your mother. What you are dreaming of is not how it will be."

"Hugh told me all about the camp. I understand the way it is. How would my being there with Kurt be any different from your being with *Onkel* Otto?"

Nina shook her head. "Don't be foolish. You know it is different."

"Because we're young?"

"Because it is impossible!" She had not meant to shout. She pressed her hand to her chest and drew a slow breath. "Because what is to come for him—for all of us—is too uncertain," she said quietly. "Because already too much has changed. Because you cannot know how Kurt has changed."

"Changed toward me?" Her face had gone white. "Changed toward America?"

"Changed in himself," Nina said. "That is my meaning. Only that."

"But won't *Onkel* Otto have changed? Would you let that stop you from going to him?"

"He will be changed, yes," Nina said. "As I am changed. Though we have been apart, we have suffered this trouble together. It is not so for you and Kurt. You have not lived what he has lived."

"What has Kurt done? Tell me. What's he done?"

"Nothing," said Nina. "You know this."

"I *don't*."

She wanted to take Bess's hand, to touch her cheek, but the girl had gone stiff, her body like armor, so Nina kept her distance. "I hope you never have to know what it is to be suspected," she said, "to be hated for what you did not choose and cannot change."

"There it is again!" Bess cried. "I'm so sick of that argument. Yes—you're German. Yes—America's at war with Germany. But that can't be all there is to it!" She paced again. "You want me to believe every person in the camps is as innocent as a dove. But I don't! All the things I hear. All the things I read. Are you going to tell me everybody on the radio, everybody in the magazines, everybody at my job is lying about the danger? And the president—is he lying, too?" She shook her head hard. "I can't believe you anymore. Innocent people aren't kept in prison. Not in America. Maybe sometimes there's a mistake—but it's been almost a year and no sign of it ending. If there had been a mistake, it would have been discovered by now. So you tell me—what has Kurt done? Why has he been transferred?" She stopped directly in front of Nina, glaring into her eyes. "What have *you* done? Why are you really going into the camp? It's not a choice, is it? It's another arrest. Is somebody going to follow us to the movies?"

How had things gone so wrong, so quickly? Nina saw now that Hugh had been the shield, protecting her from Bess's doubts. "Possibly," Nina said. "All this year, I have never stepped outside without wondering if I am followed."

"What are you hiding? Are you a Nazi?"

"Bess!" cried Iris. "You go too far!"

Nina stood her ground, glaring back—into the eyes of a hostile stranger. "I see you take the American view," she said coldly. "You believe that to be German is to be Nazi. To be Nazi is to be enemy." The words were bitter in her mouth. "We are German."

"There are plenty of other German families in town. They haven't been arrested. Why yours?"

Nina turned away, walked slowly to the table, and sat down. She gathered her letters into a neat stack. "Why this family? I cannot tell you. You must ask the FBI. When they have told you what we have done that makes us too dangerous to live among respectable people, you can feel proud of yourself for escaping marriage with a criminal. And on the Fourth of July, you can hang your head in shame for ever having believed you loved a traitor."

"Nina," Iris said through tears, "that's not fair." She grasped Bess by the shoulders. "Didn't I tell you now wasn't the time to talk?" She pulled her daughter in and hugged her tightly. "It's so easy to say things you can never take back."

Bess struggled free. She walked to the table and held her hand out to Nina. Clamped between her fingers was the card with Kurt's address. "I won't need this." She whipped around and yanked open the door.

Through shards of sleet carried in on the wind, Nina saw Bess's cornflower blue coat suddenly bloom in the light of the streetlamp, then wither into the darkness.

Trembling, Iris said, "Give her a few days, Nina. I'll talk to her. Please don't be too angry with her." She pushed the door closed but kept her hand on the knob. "Try to remember what it's like to be young, ready to start your grown-up life just when a war comes."

Nina nodded. "I remember. I'm sorry. Tell her I am sorry."

"I'll see you soon," said Iris.

"Soon," Nina nodded again, and Iris was gone.

She waited, just as Iris had asked. She waited for three days before going to the house, but Bess wouldn't see her. She tried calling, but Bess wouldn't come to the telephone. She posted a letter, but the next evening, when she was busy cleaning the offices, the envelope was dropped back through her mail slot, unopened. Twice Nina went to the factory and waited outside for Bess's shift to end, but both times, the girl saw her, turned her head, and walked in the other direction.

Ten days after the argument, Iris came to Nina's room and told her Bess had left with her friend Ruth for Cleveland, where they'd heard a factory that produced parts for military aircraft was hiring at top dollar.

1943

I

IN THE END, NINA DECIDED to leave her mother's porcelain chocolate pot behind—so she wouldn't have to see it stolen or smashed
to chalk. During her last hour in Newman, she bought a yard and
a half of new linen and cut it into three pieces—a small square for the
lid, a wide strip to wrap the fragile handle, and the largest for swad-
dling the pot with its secret cargo, her packet of cornflower seeds. Mr.
Griffin was able to spare a sturdy black hatbox, which he kindly filled
with a deep nest of excelsior.

While he held the lid of the box, Mr. Griffin asked, "Are you
sure?"—just as he had asked her four weeks ago, when her petition
was approved, and just as he had asked her each week since, when he
brought her the telegrams stating that Otto, then Gerhard, then Kurt
had arrived at the family camp in Texas. In this last week, he'd asked
her every time he'd seen her. "Are you sure?"

"I am," she said.

At the bottom of the hatbox, beneath the excelsior, she buried
the letters of the past year. The chocolate pot was next. Finally, on top
of the linen bundle, she laid a plain envelope filled with cash—three
hundred and twelve dollars. Her family's entire fortune in a hatbox.
She packed another layer of excelsior on top and let Mr. Griffin secure the lid with three passes of heavy twine. She watched as he set
the box on the lowest shelf of his safe and slid it all the way to the
back, where it disappeared in the darkness, as he had intended. He

had given her the name of his own attorney, the only other person who had the combination to his safe, and he had taken the extra precaution of writing the name in separate letters to Otto, Kurt, and Gerhard, as well.

"If I do not come back," Nina said. "If none of my family return, the money must be yours. Too small a payment for all you have done for us."

"I'll get everything back to you somehow," Mr. Griffin said. "Whatever happens."

She placed her hand on his arm to still him. "The chocolate pot goes into Iris's keeping, for Bess—should a time come when she can again think on the Austs with happiness."

She and Iris had said their farewells early that morning. When her friend stepped inside the little room, now scrubbed and swept, the only remaining signs of Nina's occupancy were her two suitcases, set neatly beside the door beneath the wall peg that held her coat and hat.

Nina asked about Bess, and Iris shook her head. "I can't stay long," she said. "I've brought you something." She set her handbag on the table, opened it, and drew out a packet wrapped in tissue paper. "I made one for each of us." She pulled back the tissue and revealed a small rectangular banner of red silk, fixed at the top with a slender, polished dowel and a length of gold braid, for hanging. A smaller rectangle of white silk was finely stitched into the center of the red, and in the center of the white, a deep blue star.

"Everett was furious when I put mine in the front window. He said it would be an insult for me to display it, since Hugh's not in the proper military. I told him I didn't care if President Roosevelt himself was insulted—my son's in service, too, and in just as much danger as anyone else's." She sighed. "It was a terrible fight." Tracing the blue star with her fingertip, she said, "Mine's still in the window—but I thought it best not to tell him I'd made one for you, too."

"Iris." Nina swept a tear from her cheek. "Is it all right, for me to have this? So beautiful—thank you. But is it all right?"

"Of course. Of *course* it is." Iris threw her arms around Nina. "I want you to have it. I know you probably won't be able to put it up," she said, her voice wavering, "and you mustn't feel bad if you don't. But Hugh is almost as much your son as he is mine—much more than he'll ever be Everett's."

For a long while the women clung to each other, sobbing, not trying to find the words to say goodbye.

"I have to go," Iris said at last. "Write to Bess again, once you're settled. It's always worth trying." She kissed Nina's cheek and, with a final squeeze of her hand, said, "Be well, my dear friend." Nina stood in the door, watching her friend go. Iris was nearly to the walk that fronted the building when she stopped, turned, and called out, "She came back to you once before. Don't forget that."

Mr. Griffin spun the dial on the safe and tugged at the handle. He looked out the window. "Taxi's here." Helping her on with her coat, he added, "If you're sure."

Not wanting to deliver her into the custody of a government escort, Mr. Griffin had requested permission from the attorney general to accompany Nina on the train to Cincinnati.

At the Cincinnati station, while she checked in with an armed man who identified himself as an agent of the Special War Problems Division, Mr. Griffin saw to it that her two small bags were properly loaded. Returning to her, he cried out upon seeing the large tag she'd been ordered to fix onto her coat, labeling her as a parcel belonging to the family Aust, bound for Crystal City, Texas.

When he helped her up the steps into the designated car, clasping her hands as tightly as she clasped his, he repeated his question—"Are you sure? Are you sure?"—even though they both knew it was too late for her to turn back. He, stretching up, she, reaching down—they tightened their grasps as the train began to move, and, when they had no choice but to let go, Nina wept, as if parting from her dearest brother.

II

THE OTHERS, INCLUDING KURT AND Gerhard, had chosen to wait inside the nearly finished community building, which had been designated as the check-in point for the wives and children, but Otto stayed in the carpentry shop, where he had a better view of the main road. The setting February sun was hot on his face, as hot as it ever got in July in Indiana, but without the shade. In Newman, the trees were so lush that each one entangled its limbs with its neighbors, creating a canopy. Here, hours from now, the heat would rise and disperse into the cloudless sky, and it would feel almost like winter again—a mild one, but cool enough in the black-walled shack to hold his Nina against his heart, through the night, and to the dawn.

A light wind stirred the dust, and Otto closed his eyes to protect them from the stinging, fine-grained sand. When the wind settled, he looked again to the incoming road, squinting into the sun. The air was so hot he could smell the oily dust of the road and the scorched grass that had struggled up the other side. He could smell the powder of ancient clays, upturned by his and other men's shovels, and the brittle skins of snakes disturbed from their dens.

He stared into the flaming sun, and, through the lens of the wavery heat, the scrub brush on the plain twitched, like kindling stripped to ash in the furnace blaze. *But what was that in the center?* He blinked five times, bathing his eyes with tears.

As if spit from the flames, a dull yellow spark—*Was it really there?* He closed his eyes once more, opened them.

Yes! A yellow bus, long past the hour for schoolchildren. A yellow bus, borrowed to bring their families to them—how he hoped.

Much as he wanted to break and run to the others, he did not want to raise a false alarm, so he stayed where he was, waiting in happy agony for the bus to slow.

Waiting for the bus to turn onto the camp road.

Waiting for the bus to roll through the gate.

And it did!

With a great whoop of joy, Otto ran out, leaping and waving his arms as the bus passed, then running behind it, still whooping and waving, urging it on toward the community building. As it slowed to a stop, he called out to the others inside, "They're here! They're here!" then stopped, his sweat pouring, his lungs burning, his eyes fixed on the bus's door.

It opened.

A teenage boy was the first to step off, turning back and reaching up to steady a woman carrying an infant. Two smaller children, one holding tight to the other's belt, followed her. Another woman, younger, clutching the hand of a little girl. More women, more children, some of them breaking free and crying out, *Papi! Papa!*

He stepped closer. Two more teenagers, a girl with golden hair and a boy almost as tall as Kurt.

And there—at last. On the top step.

On the second step.

Framed in the door.

To her chest, she clutched a burden—a winter coat, a thick cardigan, a hat.

"Nina!" Otto cried. "*Liebling! Mein Liebling!*"

She dropped her bundle in the dirt, hurtled toward him, was caught up in his arms.

Heaving with laughter and tears, he squeezed her tighter, tighter, tighter, until she was pouring into him. Melting into him. Until she was putting down roots in the safe little valley of his breastbone, where her cheek just fit.

The pressure of his arms around her, the small circles of his fingertips in her hair, the coarse weave of his shirt, the sharp smell of his sweat—a mingling of earth and minerals and wood dust—and beneath this, his own private scent of juniper bark, fallen oak leaves, and spring wheat: Nina took it all in, like droughted land taking in rain.

Somewhere, beyond this stronghold, other voices called for her, but they were too far away, as faint as birdsong beyond a mountain. She pressed harder into Otto, and in answer, he wrapped her tighter still.

Then, Otto's voice, stirring her like gently urgent music: "Your sons are here, my love. Your sons. Your sons."

My sons, my sons, my sons—the phrase tinkled above the anchoring beat of Otto's heart. *My sons!*

She opened her eyes, turned her head—and there they were, slightly blurred through the glass of her tears, reaching for her, both of them at once, enfolding her like boards of a book, and as they did, she felt Otto there, too, making the spine.

"My darlings. My family," she breathed. "My loves, my loves."

III

FTER THE INITIAL CLOUDBURST OF reunion had passed—
the shouts, the tears, the helpless laughter—and after Otto
had finally released her to Kurt's and Gerhard's arms; after
Nina and the rest of the newcomers had surrendered their luggage
for inspection; after the four Austs had moved as one into the community building; after they had mingled among the other families
without anyone absorbing anyone else's name; after they had settled
at a table to eat sandwiches and hear a terse address from the camp
commander; Nina, her husband, and their sons—none of them willing to let go, kicking up dust with every step—crossed in a clumsy
clump to the lodging assigned to their family. Squashed together and
singing, they might have been mistaken for a band of jolly drunkards.

When they reached a cluster of what looked to Nina like garden
sheds, Otto broke free, turned, and, with a great flourish and a deep
bow, waggishly declared, "Behold, dear wife, your noble cottage!"

Beneath the fierce glare of the searchlights, Nina took it in—the
wide, rough planks, the tiny windows, the tarpaper roof, the whole
structure balanced a foot or two above the dirt on flimsy-looking
stilts. Some small creature of the night, probably confused by so much
light, had darted beneath a neighboring shack at their approach. She
turned back toward the buildings she had taken for sheds, and, beyond them, Nina could see the signs of similar dwellings rising from
the dust—dozens of them.

Grasping the doorknob, Otto said, "We on the building crews are fortunate. In exchange for our work, we have been given the private houses."

Nina looked down at their long shadows and up at the fence, lined with floodlights. "Private?"

"I mean with one family only," Otto said. Still he had not opened the door. "Already we have plans for improvement." He smiled, but, as he said this, the smile vanished with a wave of shame. "Forgive me."

Once inside, Nina could see the reason for his shame—though of course he was blameless, as were her sons, who now hung their heads as well.

She stood on a bare concrete floor in a room perhaps seven paces deep and four paces wide. The walls were black, made of the same tarpaper that covered the roof, held in place by unfinished beams. As she looked, her eye caught something scuttling up a beam, and when she peered harder, she saw several of the strange and horrid little beasts near the ceiling.

"Scorpions," Kurt said.

Yes—she had once seen a drawing of a scorpion, like a fat amber worm that had slipped into a translucent suit of armor and sprouted legs.

"We've been killing them, Gerhard and I," Kurt said, "when they come out at night. We knock them down with a broom and slice them with the strike of a hoe. But—just to be sure—before you get in bed, let us shake out the sheets for you, and in the morning, we'll check your shoes."

"Look," Otto said. "I am collecting scrap planking to cover the walls." He pointed to one corner, where planks of varying lengths and widths had been nailed, seeming to rise up the beams in a precarious stack. "It's like a puzzle. But when I have finished, you will not see the seams. And we can paint. Perhaps white. Or a happy yellow?"

"Something light," Gerhard said, "to set off the scorpions."

"First spiders and now scorpions," Nina said, smiling painfully at her boy. "Hugh told me."

"There are black widows here, too." His voice was raspy. "I've already talked to the staff at the hospital, told them I'm an expert. They'll pay a quarter for every spider—to get the venom." He stifled a cough and tried to smile. "So I can make my fortune."

She realized with a start that Gerhard had not joined in the singing. She had seen the brightness in his face. She had seen him moving his lips, swinging his head to time. But she had not heard his sound. Quickly, so her son would not see her look of alarm, Nina turned toward the end of the room. Beyond a badly scratched wooden table and four metal chairs stood an icebox, a three-burner kerosene stove, and a sink.

"I'm better, *Mutti*, really," Gerhard said, stepping around her into the tiny kitchen area to stand beside Otto. "The dry air here has helped." He coughed hard and couldn't stop for several seconds, though Otto pounded his back. Gerhard's eyes watered and his cheeks and forehead had gone a purplish-red. "Except for the dust," he rasped.

Instinctively, Nina reached for her handkerchief before remembering that her overcoat and her pocketbook were both with the guards. She let her useless hands drop to her sides. "You do not work with the builders? Surely you are not yet strong enough for that?"

Gerhard wiped his eyes with the back of his hand and shook his head. "I'm learning to repair shoes. Heels, soles, half-soles." His smile was a bitter one. "Another useful skill, like spider trapping."

"And the poems? For the *Liederkreis*? You write them still?"

He nodded. "But I'm not sure how useful that is."

"Nina, come look," Otto said, opening a cabinet over the sink. Gerhard pivoted to change places with her.

"To start," Otto said, "there are three pots, a teakettle, some plates." He touched each of the items in the cabinet for emphasis. "The building for a general store and a market has begun. Our monthly allowance will not be enough for all the necessary supplies, but we can work beyond our assigned time to earn more. Kurt and I have been working as much as allowed and have saved six dollars and forty cents so far. A little extra—so you can buy what you need when the store opens."

Nina looked inside the kettle, ran her hand over the pots. Everything was heavily used, but in acceptable condition. She wondered if some of her own kitchen things, stolen by the FBI, would turn up for her to buy again. She forced a smile. "So I can cook for you?" Tears clogged her voice. "And we can eat here together, as a family?"

"Yes," Otto said. "Yes, together. We'll write a list of what you need."

"I could use a Dutch oven," she said. "Iron, if it can be got—which I think it cannot be." She nestled one of the smaller pots inside the largest one. "But until then, I can bake bread this way, if you find me some flat stones to put between. Perhaps a brick to hold the cover down?"

"Anything you want," Otto said. Then, with a note of defeat, he added, "Anything possible."

"What I want is for the extra work to stop," she said. "From tomorrow. I can find my way around the cooking—but you three I cannot spare. We have lost too much time."

Otto took her hand and showed her the two bedrooms—each so small there was space for little else besides the beds, but, Otto pointed out, they both had doors that closed. "The new lodgings will have only curtains to divide the sleeping spaces." On their bed, hers and Otto's, lay two small, thin towels, a cotton nightdress, and a brown and green print housedress. Otto saw her looking. "To guess the size," he said, "I pretended we were dancing." He slipped his hands through the sleeves of the nightdress, held it out from him, and did a little two-step.

Nina laughed, and Otto tossed away the nightdress, grabbed her by the waist, and waltzed her one turn away from the bed, one turn back—there was not space for more. He lifted the edge of the housedress, showing her that he had also thought to get her fresh underclothing.

"This is not all," he said. "There is a toilet and a sink." He opened another door, one step from their bedroom. "And a laundry tub on a little porch outside the back door. Most families still to come will not have these—not even the bedrooms."

"How many people?"

Otto shook his head. "Now we have orders to build for five hundred families—two thousand people at least. Later, perhaps a thousand families. Possibly many more before the war is finished. But when the first group is returned to Germany—" A stunned look shot through his eyes. He glanced anxiously over Nina's head toward the boys. She turned to look at Kurt, but his back was to her, his face tilted up at the beams, as if keeping watch on the scorpions.

"For showers," Otto went on, his voice strained, "we must use the shared bathhouse." He closed the toilet room door. A small sob broke from his chest. "I am so sorry, my darling. So sorry to bring you to such a place."

"Otto!" she cried, reaching up to stroke his cheek, his hair. "You must not say so. You must not think so." She put her arm through his. "Show me the rest."

He led her out the back door to the tiny covered porch, where the laundry tub sat. He looked to the sky, as if to gaze at the stars, but there were only pocks of darkness amidst the blaze of yellow-white. "In another hour," he said, "the heat will go and the night air will be pleasant. We could go for a walk. Or take the chairs outside?"

She thought of how the lights would expose them, even more than the noon sun would.

Otto was watching her, waiting for her answer. She put her hand on his chest and looked into his distressed eyes. "Whatever suits you best."

He looked out across the camp, then back at her. "It is perhaps too late for a walk," he said. "Tomorrow we can go—just we two. Tonight, we will open the doors and the windows to get the breeze, and we'll sit as a family at our table and talk."

"Then I would like a wash first," Nina said. "The sink will do for me."

Otto nodded. "The boys and I will go to the bathhouse. If you don't mind."

She did mind—she did not want to be alone here—but she did not say so.

"A quarter of an hour," Otto said. "No more."

When they had gone, she filled the sink, stripped off her clothes, washed quickly, and slipped the clean nightdress over her head. She stood for a moment, eyes closed, enjoying the feeling of the crisp cotton against her skin. This must be her practice, she decided, to be grateful for the small things of worth and comfort—for they would be few in this wasteland of red and yellow dust. She imagined the wicked prankster—what else could he be?—who had christened the place with such a ridiculous, storybook name: *Crystal City.*

For modesty, she draped the housedress across her shoulders like a shawl, gathered her soiled things, and carried them out to the laundry tub to soak them. She'd add the men's clothes when they returned.

Standing on the porch in that intense light, waiting for the tub to fill, she looked at the fence—really looked at it.

It was just as the one Hugh had described, with rows upon rows of flesh-hungry wire. She felt an impulse to go closer, to study the fence and learn its secrets, but when she turned to step off the porch, she felt a tower looming over her, much closer than she had realized—fifty, perhaps sixty feet from where she stood, rising from the ground like an immense devil's tree. Squinting into the light, she thought she could see a guard moving about inside, stopping, inclining toward her. Suddenly her white gown seemed like a flag of surrender.

She darted back through the door, closed it, and leaned her whole feeble body against it. The curtainless windows stared at her. *Prison*: now she understood the word.

She thought about the dinner in the community building: the unsmiling man in the off-the-rack summer flannel suit who had mounted a small platform at the head of the room and given his name, Collaer—Camp Commander Collaer. While they all sat at the bare tables, chewing on spongy sandwiches and pouring water from sweating pitchers, Collaer instructed the mothers to keep close watch on their children, the husbands on their wives. "It'll take time to learn the rules of the camp," he said. "But know they've been in force—and the penalties for violating them—from the moment you passed through the gate."

While he spoke, Nina let her eyes travel over the page of camp regulations that had been left on every table. She hadn't fully taken them in, but one phrase stopped her again and again—*under orders to shoot.*

After the meal, as she walked in the embrace of her family, she spotted a mounted guard, dressed like a movie cowboy, stopping his horse along the fence. The horse's hooves were slightly sunk into the rake-scored border, eight feet wide, they must never step across. On the other side—the free side—stood Collaer, holding a child's rubber kickball, his head tilted up to speak to the guard. Beyond Collaer, in a flood of yellow light, a little girl in a blue and white checked dress ran toward the men. "Daddy," she cried, tugging at Collaer's arm. "Throw it again!" Whatever else Collaer might be, he was also the commander of the guards who, every day, would line up other people's children for counting—the man who had placed his guards under orders to shoot anyone who crossed the raked boundary between camp and fence.

Her nightdress clung to her with new sweat. She pulled the brown and green dress from her shoulders, returned it to the bedroom, and patted herself as dry as she could with the damp towel. In the kitchen, she found four glasses. The water that poured from the cold tap was warm enough to proof yeast, but in the ice box there was a small but sufficient block remaining—enough to chip apart for cool water. Standing at the sink, she drank two glassfuls, then filled the others, filled her own again, put them all on the table.

The moment she sat down, weariness, deep and wide, overcame her. Through those three days on the train, ever conscious of the guards with their rifles and pistols on display, she had slept only in fitful patches, sitting upright on the hard bench seat, wrapped inside the sour odors of unbathed bodies, nauseated and feverish children, and fouled diapers.

She should sleep—and so should Otto and her sons, for they had worked in the heat all day. But what if she closed her eyes, only to wake and discover she had dreamed her family, as she had done so many times before?

No—she would not be able to sleep until they had talked enough to become real to one another again. But where to begin? There was at once too much and too little to say.

She took stock—replacing the memory of the men she had lost with the tangible flesh of the men she had found. All three were sunburnt. All three were thinner. A sallowness underlay Gerhard's burn, and his cheeks looked as if they had long been sunken and had only just begun to plump again. Beneath Kurt's bright red was a pallor of gray, and around his eyes, his jaw, through his arms and chest, a tightness another turn of the rack could snap. Otto shone like red gold, and he was as lean as he'd been on their wedding day—but where Kurt was coiled, Otto sagged, as though his own body were too much to carry.

And Gerhard's voice—his perfect voice—catching like a badly scratched phonograph record. What could she do to help? Tomorrow she could look about for herbs to make a soothing tea for his throat and chest. Or if she could get garlic, some mustard, she could make a poultice. She could see to it that he didn't overwork himself. With good food, rest, and her watchful eye, she could drive the yellow cast from his skin—but his voice. What if the damage was too deep for any remedy? She couldn't see far enough ahead to snatch at hope.

But tonight, for Kurt, she could act. He might be deported—who could know when? She must make him tell her what had happened, make him tell her anything that could help Mr. Griffin fight the decree.

She heard them coming, singing three-part harmony, low but brisk, the chorus of "Stout-Hearted Men"—a tune they had picked up from a silly film pretending at opera. The song dropped away when they opened the door.

"Don't stop," Nina said, looking hopefully at Gerhard.

He shrugged, coughed, and said, "I sound worse than Nelson Eddy. That's a little scary."

Kurt, still humming the chorus, took the wet towel and dirty clothes from his brother's arms and carried them out to the washtub. Otto followed with his own bundle. When they returned, Kurt, said, "It's nearly time for the siren, *Mutti*, so brace yourself. Shriller than Jeanette MacDonald. For the first few days, it'll freeze your heart."

A few moments later, in spite of Kurt's warning, she gasped when the piercing howl struck down through her chest.

"You'll get used to it," Gerhard said. "I have."

"I haven't," said Kurt.

Even when the siren stopped, it hummed in Nina's skull and coursed through her veins.

They all sat down at the table, and for a long while, but for the sounds they made as they sipped their water, they were awkwardly silent, as if they were strangers.

"In the morning," Otto said suddenly, "you will meet the Cappelmanns. Our friend Johan—Kurt's and mine—with his wife and child. Liese and the girl came only a week behind us, from another camp." He spoke rapidly, almost desperately. "They have invited us to breakfast in their cottage, but we must carry our own chairs. Kurt and I will take them."

He paused, wincing, seeming again to force back tears of shame.

"After breakfast," Otto went on, speaking more slowly now, "when we go to work, Liese will show you around the camp if you like. Little Sofie has made a great favorite of Kurt—never does she willingly let him out of her sight."

A smile twitched at Kurt's lips, and Nina smiled back to encourage him. He shrugged. "She just likes it when I carry her on my shoulders."

"She calls you her sweetheart," Otto said, "but I think you are more her slave." He laughed and looked at Nina. "Never does he refuse her."

"You knew this Johan before?" she asked. "In the other camp?"

"It is because of him I was able to join the builders. He taught me—when were together at Fort Lincoln. A true friend he has been to me. And to Kurt." He stood up suddenly, picked up his glass, and went to the sink. Only then did he seem to realize his glass was still nearly full. He clutched the edge of the sink, drank the water, and refilled the glass.

Slowly, Otto returned to the table. "Someday, I should like for you and Gerhard to know our other friend, Herr Merkel. He is a farmer." He sat down and stared into the newly filled glass. "I would not have thought it possible," he said quietly, as if to himself, "but he has become to me more than my own father. To part from him—" Otto shook his head, unable to say more.

After another long silence, Kurt asked Nina if anyone had come to see her off at the train.

"Mr. Griffin closed his office and came with me as far as Cincinnati," she said, fearing her own voice would break. "It was a great favor."

"No one else?"

"I could not expect it. Everyone now must work such long days." This was the truth, but it felt like a lie, so she added quickly, "On the last day, Iris called on me before breakfast, to say goodbye. And of course Hugh is at sea." She looked down at the table. "Has he written?"

"Yes," Otto said, "a good letter for my birthday."

"The mail has only just caught up with us," Gerhard added. "The last I got was sent right before Thanksgiving. Have you heard from him since?" His voice rose with hope. "Did you bring his letters?"

"I was not allowed," she said, "but the letters are safe, stored with the last of our things, in Mr. Griffin's keeping." She thought of Hugh's letters, tucked with the others into the hatbox beneath her chocolate pot, and she tried to put his news in order. "He also is writing music. Did you know?"

"No."

"He is," Nina said. "Music perhaps to mix with yours, or to make another song cycle. He tried to send me one, as a test, but everything in the letter was cut away. I received only the first and last paragraphs, taped together."

"Somebody must have thought it was a secret code," Kurt said.

"It's why I've never copied any of my poems into letters," Gerhard said. "They make it pretty clear they don't want anyone outside to know what it's like in the camp—or even for anyone inside to have a way to remember it later on. I had to smuggle the songs out of Camp Forrest."

"How?" Nina asked.

"I wrote them all out in German and mixed them in with the *Lieder* I'd been translating for the newsletter. When the guard searched my things, I opened my notebook to show him a few—the German and English versions side by side—and I compared those to copies printed in *The Latrine*. Then I flipped through the notebook and told him the rest were the German songs I'd written from memory but hadn't gotten around to putting into English. I knew he wouldn't be able to tell Göethe from Aust."

"Was this not dangerous? What if you had been caught?"

Gerhard shrugged. "I didn't want to lose them. I knew if the guard figured it out—or even if he suspected—he'd take the notebook, but I had to take the risk. I was already a prisoner. I decided any punishment beyond that couldn't be as bad as losing the poems, however poor they are."

"These songs," Nina said. "You mean for them to be in English? Why not German?"

Gerhard sighed. "Because everything that's happened to us has happened in English." He slumped back in his chair. "I understand why you didn't—but I wish you'd tried to bring the letters."

"I have something else," Nina said, "if the guards do not take it." She told them about Iris's blue-star banner.

"We can't hang it in the window," said Kurt. "Not unless we want a brick through it."

Otto agreed. "Some of the guards and some of the prisoners, too, would be glad to see this appreciation of Hugh's work. But many— Americans and Germans both—would take great offense."

"What about inside?" Gerhard asked. "Can't we put it up in here, so we can see it?"

"Better to keep it folded up under your mattress, brother," Kurt said. His breath caught and his face went pale. "No—we can tack it inside the kitchen cupboard, so that, if it's found in a search, we can show it belongs to all of us." He hung his head. "I'd like to have it in plain sight, too. But you know how things are."

Nina watched Kurt. A dark veil seemed to have fallen over him. He was brooding, no doubt about a great many things, but one of them was surely Bess. She didn't know how to begin to tell of what had happened between them, so she spoke on about Hugh. "He also writes that he has done well with his training—not at the top, he says, but well enough to 'pull the weight'—that is his phrase, I think."

"Pull his weight," Gerhard said.

"That's the one, yes. He was a few days from his first voyage, when last he wrote—that was in January, the middle. He was meeting his new shipmates. Such a mixed people he would meet nowhere else—two or three as young as himself, some much older than your father. And all kinds—black men, Mexicans, Chinese, Italians, even some Germans."

"The discards and the misfits," Kurt said bitterly. "Our boy fits right in."

She shot her eyes at Gerhard and then back at Kurt. "Through the summer it was very hard for Hugh—every day people stopping him, demanding that he tell them why he did not wear a uniform. He worried for the draft, worried that it would come soon and he would be forced to fight against Germany, which he could not bear. This is why he joined the merchant seamen." She reached for Gerhard's hand. "He must have written you about this last autumn, in some way that would not trouble the censors."

"He did," Gerhard said.

"And Bess?" Kurt burst like a hastily stitched wound. "Why don't you say anything about Bess?"

Since the day Nina had learned she could rejoin her family—the last time she'd seen Bess—she had prayed that all would be repaired before this moment could come. But here it was.

"You have not heard from her? Any of you?" Nina herself had written them that Bess had taken a job in Cleveland.

"Christmas cards," Kurt said. "The same to all of us."

Nina knew the card—clearly one of thousands supplied by the factory owners to their employees. On the back, the name of the manufacturer was printed beside a small image of a fighter plane being waved off by children wielding American flags. On the front, a four-color sketch of boys and girls in blue and red frock coats, trimmed in white fur, skating toward a snow-covered church, behind which rose, instead of the sun, a great V, striped and starred. Inside, a fill-in-the-blank message: *Miss Elizabeth Sloan wishes you a happy Christmas*. No personal note, not even a simply signed *Bess*.

"And before that?" Nina asked. "When was the last?"

Immediately she was sorry for the question. All Kurt's frustration collapsed inward, and he seemed to shrink before her eyes. Gerhard stared at the table, running his thumb back and forth along the edge. Otto reached toward Kurt and, like a gentle bear, clasped the back of his boy's neck.

Looking at Nina, Otto said, "Your letters to Kurt—some of them came back?"

"Yes, many. I never knew why."

"Since that time, from August, Kurt has had nothing from Bess except for the card. She continued writing to Gerhard—but then the letters stopped, until the Christmas card. Nothing after."

Gerhard nodded to affirm his father's words.

"The last I had from her," Otto went on, "was marked the fourth of November. At first, she wrote to me every week, asking why she did not hear from Kurt, why her letters were returned, but I could not tell her he was in the stockade. Any such letter would have been stopped."

"Stockade? Kurt—what happened to you?"

Without lifting his head, Kurt said, his voice defeated, "Why doesn't she write, *Mutti*? Why didn't she start again when you did, when you knew I'd been transferred?"

Nina took his hand and squeezed it with all her might. "Bess loves you greatly, darling. This I believe. The day I received your father's message about this camp, Bess said she wanted to come here, too—to marry you and live here with all of us. This is the truth."

"But—" Kurt rubbed hard at his forehead. "No. No."

"I told her it was not possible, but she would not understand." There was no other choice: she must tell the rest now. "Kurt," she said softly, "I had only just learned from Mr. Griffin you were to be deported. How could I explain this to Bess when I did not know the reason? Still I do not know it." She tried to take Kurt's hands, but he pulled them out of reach. "Bess was upset, confused and angry. From this, she said a great many hurtful things—words I believe she did not mean in her heart."

Was that the truth?

Kurt seemed to stare through her, as if he had drawn the memory from her and was now watching the scene play out. "What did she say?"

"I will not repeat. I, too, was angry—and I am ashamed to say I answered her with that anger. I tried to mend it. But she would not speak to me, and a few days later, she went away. Her mother gave me the address, and I wrote to her many times, but she did not reply. Like you, I've had only the Christmas card."

Kurt drew a sharp breath, turned his eyes back to the floor, shook his head. "It's just as well," he said at last, his voice so sad that Nina longed to pull him onto her lap and rock him as she had when he was small. "She doesn't need to be mixed up in my trouble."

"But what is this trouble?" Nina asked. "Tell me of the stockade. And why you are to be deported. Mr. Griffin could learn only that you are blamed for a disturbance, but he could get no one to explain what kind of disturbance. What happened?"

Kurt stared on at the floor, saying nothing. Quickly, Otto told her about Kurt's translations for some of the old men—Herr Merkel among them—and of his friendship with the disenchanted seamen. He told her of the map and of the play, describing Kurt's satirical portrayal of Mephistopheles. "The play was stopped. He was arrested. Even I was not permitted to see him—not until I saw him stepping down from the truck in this place."

"Still I do not understand. Such small things—and all were known by others, including the officials? You are to be deported for these?"

"It's more tangled up than that," Kurt said. "Tangled up in things I can't tell you."

"But you must tell me. Perhaps Mr. Griffin can help—but he cannot if he does not know all. Can you not write to him at least?"

"No, *Mutti*, I can't. And I can't tell you why."

She turned to Otto. He answered in a whisper, "He has not told me."

Kurt stood up and walked to the end of the room, his eyes on the ceiling. "C'mon, brother," he said. "Time to get at those scorpions, or none of us will get any sleep."

Gerhard took the broom, Kurt, the hoe. With an eerie rhythm, they swept and sliced, swept and sliced, going wordlessly about their deadly business.

IV

THE NEXT MORNING, WHILE NINA was pulling the brown and green dress over her head, the ice-pick siren rent the silence. Startled, she twisted violently, breaking some stitching around the dress's left sleeve. With her luggage under guard and her travel clothes soaking in the washtub, she had nothing else to wear.

She waited for the siren to die. "Otto, have you a needle and thread?" She showed him the torn seam.

"No time," he said. "We must go outside, before the guard comes." He put his arm around her shoulder and guided her the five steps from the foot of their bed to the front door. The boys were already standing outside, facing the narrow dirt road. Otto steered her into place next to Gerhard, and she grasped her son's hand.

The sun was just coming up—or, Nina thought it was, but she realized she couldn't parse the dawn from the floodlights. The air was full of the sharp, sticky odor of tar, and it felt like an oven an hour after baking—dry, with pockets of heat that hadn't dissipated. Everything was quiet now that the siren had stopped, so quiet she heard the soft thump of horse hooves in the dirt and the slap of a horse's tail beating flies from its flank. She turned her head to watch the horse bob toward them.

The rider perched painfully straight in the saddle—perhaps because of the rifle slung on his back, pointing up as if to fire upon God. Like an enormous tumor, the great lump of a holstered pistol grew from his hip. Propped against the saddle horn was a clipboard, which the guard consulted as he rode. As the horse approached them, barely lifting its feet, the guard peered at them from under his hat and shouted, "C-15. Four!"

Were they meant to answer? Otto and her sons remained silent, so Nina did too.

The guard yanked the reins hard to the left, turning the horse back down the road, and shouted again—this time at a knot of people who stood before another shack across the lane of packed dirt. "In line!" He waved his hand sharply. "In a line! C-14!" He stopped the horse. "Six! C-14! Where's the other two?" He shifted in the saddle, preparing to dismount.

"Coming!" cried the panicked voice of a woman. She stumbled out the door, carrying an infant, naked from the waist. A clean, unfolded diaper was slung over the woman's shoulder.

Nina pressed forward, wanting to help the woman, but both Otto and Gerhard held her back. The woman joined her family in line. No one spoke. Even from this distance, Nina could see the woman was shaking as she clutched the baby tighter to her chest.

The guard resettled in his saddle and shouted in a different tone—an audible check mark—"C-14. Six!"

Watching the swishing tail of the horse recede, Nina asked quietly, "Is this every day?"

"Three times," Kurt said. "Except when there's more."

"Now I can find you some thread," Otto said, explaining that they must wait for a short blast from the whistle, signaling the count was finished, before they could go to the Cappelmanns'.

Nina returned to the bedroom to take off her dress. In a moment, Otto brought her a Lucky Strike package, empty of cigarettes but holding a needle secured in a scrap of blue cloth, along with two small cardboard winders wrapped sparsely with thread—one white, one black.

"You are not smoking?"

"Oh, no," Otto said. "This I carried from Fort Lincoln. I asked for it the moment I saw the man draw out the last cigarette. He would have crushed it in his hand." He sat on the bed beside her. "I have drained the washtub," he said, "and put the things aside. We have some washing powder. Should I put your clothes back in now? They will not be so dirty as ours."

"Later," she said, snapping a length of black thread with her teeth and guiding it through the eye of the needle. "I'll wash everything after breakfast. Where can I hang them?"

"Only across the chairs for now—so it will have to be after breakfast." A wry, half-laugh popped in his throat. "Today I will look for a clothesline, and tonight Kurt and I will consider how to put it up without making trouble."

She stopped sewing and looked at Otto. "What do you mean?"

"In the camp before this, Johan's wife met a woman who had been accused of signaling airplanes with codes, made according to how she put her laundry on the line."

What could a person say to that? Nina stared at him for a moment and then, looking back to the dress, she took three more stitches. "At least the woman knows what she is accused of, however ridiculous." When she was finished with the seam, she whipped the needle through again, catching the edges where the cheap fabric had frayed as it tore. It wouldn't hold long, but it would have to do.

The whistle sounded. She put the dress back on and met her men outside.

Otto and Kurt each carried two chairs. Gerhard brought a box that held their four plates, glasses, and cutlery, topped with a shallow bowl in which he had settled seven hardboiled eggs, cushioned with small blocks of yellow cheese. "We've saved all our eggs for the last two weeks," he told Nina. "Just for today."

"You have not been going hungry?"

When Gerhard shook his head, she saw the scrawniness of his neck. Noticing her stare, he reddened, grinned, and knocked her playfully with his hip. "We were glad to save the best bits for you. After all, you're our best bit." He stopped for a moment and leaned his head against hers. "Thank you for coming to us, *Mutti*."

How could I not? The words were there, in her mouth, ready to be spoken, suddenly dammed by fear that she had made the wrong choice. To have come: would this be twisted against her, against all of them—taken as an admission of guilt, as acceptance that this imprisonment was right?

"I love you, my darling," she said. It was her only answer.

She heard some hoots and vulgar whistles and looked about to find the source. Four men, young but old enough to know better, waved and swished as they passed, kissing their hands—to Gerhard, she realized—calling, "Good morning, *meine Freundin*! Come see me later, *Schatzi*!"

Nina took a tight hold on her son's arm. "Who are they?"

"I knew them in Camp Forrest," he said. "Well, they knew me— or thought they did. When I first got sick, one of the guys from the hospital would bring soup to me in the tent. That's when they started up." He turned his head slightly to glance over his shoulder. "Don't let them worry you. They're Nazi idiots."

Up ahead, Otto and Kurt had stopped in the road. "Wife and son!" Otto called cheerfully, "Catch us up! We are here." Kurt stared, his face rigid, and Nina followed the direction of his gaze. He was watching the hecklers disappearing between the rows of huts. When Nina and Gerhard got closer, Kurt nodded at his brother and Gerhard nodded back.

The Cappelmanns' lodging sat by itself across from the community building, in sight of the gate she'd passed through on the bus yesterday. The small house was watched over by an American flag ten yards from the front door, the pole rising higher than the fence, higher than the floodlights, higher even than the guard towers. Because of Johan's position as head of the building crew, Nina had expected the Cappelmanns' quarters to be far better than their own, but it was just another rough-hewn hut, its tarpaper roof still wet-looking from yesterday's melting sun.

All the differences were inside. Like Otto, Johan was piecing together a wall from scrap lumber, but the odd pattern as it rose from the floor seemed planned rather than haphazard, while the one finished wall, though unpainted, was so tight and smooth Nina would not have been able to tell one plank from another had it not been for the nail heads. The windows had curtains, which matched the cushions on a small settee and armchair arranged in the corner nearest the front door. On the floor between the settee and the armchair sat a blue and white dollhouse—two stories with a gabled roof and a pair of grand pillared porches. On one porch, three tabby cats kept watch on the steps, while a black and white dog lay stretched beneath a swing, cushioned identically to the real furniture.

From that lovely fantasy, Nina looked to the kitchen. Next to the stove, there was a perfectly fitted work counter with shelves beneath. And the stove itself had a small oven, which Liese Cappelman was now opening, drawing out a pan of bread rolls.

While the men arranged the chairs and set the table, Nina squeezed past to the kitchen. "Mrs. Cappelmann," she said, "I am Mrs. Aust, Otto's wife."

"Nina!" The young woman startled her with a hug that brought Bess to mind—the action instant, open and hearty. But as Liese clung to her, Nina thought instead of Iris, whose way of embracing balanced their strength, as if together they made the fulcrum on which the whole world rocked.

"And here is our Sofie," Johan said.

For all the adult bodies crowded into the tiny space, Nina could not see the child until Kurt lifted her onto his back, his arms hooked around her skinny legs. Sofie flung herself forward so she could press her golden cheek against Kurt's. Her arms hung down over his shoulders, her hands clasped over his heart.

"This is my mother," Kurt said to Sofie. "Say hello."

Sofie pressed harder into Kurt, claiming him. "Hello."

Liese directed them all into chairs, and, standing behind Johan, she handed the dishes over his head, waiting while they were passed around. When each plate had a portion of everything—bread, cheese, an egg, half an orange—she set down a pitcher of water in the center of the table and took her own chair. Pressed shoulder to shoulder, everyone talked about the day's tasks—all but Nina, and Sofie, who kept watch on her.

When most had finished eating, Johan turned to Nina and said, "Now that you're here, I want you to join me in my plan of persuasion."

"Not now," Liese said, giving her husband a sharp look.

"Now is the best time," Johan said irritably. "From the time she goes to collect her luggage, the staff will urge a return to Germany."

Sofie, leaning into Kurt's lap, stuck her tongue through tight lips and made a disgusting, sputtering sound. "Germany!"

"Hey, Noodle," Kurt said, lightly rapping his knuckles on her forehead, "that's where I was born, you know."

"No."

"There, we were all born," Liese said, "except for you."

"I don't believe you," Sofie said to Kurt.

"It's true. I've got a label and everything: *Hergestellt in Deutschland*. Made in Germany."

"Where? Let me see." She pulled at his shirt, trying to look down his collar.

"Nowhere you can see," he said. "There's a shipping label, too: *Return to Sender*."

"Mr. Cappelmann," Nina said. "Johan. What do you mean? Persuasion to what?"

"Urge your sons to enlist. For America. Otto, he is too old. I think they will not take him. But your sons, of course, because they are young. Me, I am but thirty-two, strong—so they will want me, also."

"Stop it, Johan," said Kurt.

Johan turned to him. "It's the way to our freedom, don't you see? How could they hold your parents if you were a soldier?'

"Go talk to the Hauptmanns," Kurt said. "C-27. They have a son in the Army."

Johan shook his head, "No, no. You overlook that Hauptmann purchased the *Rückwanderer Marks*."

"That was an investment," Kurt said. "So they'd have some money in the bank when they went back to visit."

"Hauptmann can name his act as he chooses," said Johan, "but to purchase the marks, he had to swear his intent to return permanently to Germany."

Kurt leaned over the table, his eyes fixed on Johan. "Don't you ever talk to people? Hauptmann bought US war bonds, too—every paycheck." He pushed back his chair and stood. "How do you get your information, anyway? Same way as the FBI—exaggeration, invention? Making up what you want to be true? Tell me—why are you here? Why is Liese here?"

"It is for this kind of talk you are assigned for deportation," Johan said. "What difference now if you say you will fight against Germany? It is a chance—a chance to free your family."

"Leave it alone," Kurt said sharply. "You don't know what you're talking about." With three strides, he was at the front door.

"Enough, Kurt!" cried Otto. "You will not fight with our friends in their own house. And you will not leave here until you make it up."

Nina watched Kurt as he pressed his back against the door, squeezing his eyes tightly shut. He released a long, slow breath. "Johan, you mustn't think I'm not grateful for all you've done for us. For me. For how much you've taught me. But this decision is mine." He came back to the table. "Don't let him get to you, Gerhard." He bent down to kiss Nina. "I'm going to work now."

Sofie broke from the table and ran to the door ahead of him. "Take me!" she demanded.

"Not to work," Kurt said gently, stroking her hair. "You have school."

"*Kindergarten*," she said. "For babies."

Kurt patted her cheek. "Then go and teach them how not to be babies. I'll see you later."

When Kurt had gone, Johan turned to Nina. "For them to enlist," he said, "it the best way, believe me. No guarantee, of course, but the timing is right. Already since we have been here, the young men have been given two or three opportunities to reverse and answer that they are now willing to fight against Germany. Who knows which chance will be the last—but why keep asking if they do not mean to offer us a way out?"

"Pressure," Nina said. "Manipulation. A trick?"

"Nina," Otto said.

"I'm sorry, Otto. I have no wish to be rude to your friends—but all of us, we have been questioned and questioned and questioned. Never given clear reasons. Never ourselves allowed to question. Why should we trust that these questions have any purpose but to trap us? Why give up our hope for imagining there is a secret code that will open the gates, if only we can discover it?"

"Gerhard," Johan said, "What is your thinking on this matter? Will you say you are willing to fight against Germany?"

Gerhard gathered the empty plates and stacked them on his own. "At the hospital, they tell me I'm still 4-F for the draft, because of scarring from the pneumonia. So I don't have to answer. Not yet." He carried the plates to the sink. "But I do have to go fix some shoes." Pulling out his chair and the one Kurt had used, he said, "*Vati*, I'll help you take these." He looked at Liese. "I'll come back for the plates."

"No, leave all the things here," she said. "I mean to prepare lunch for everyone—Kurt, too, if he will come. And I'll send you home with something for dinner. You must let your mother settle in." She turned to Nina. "Stay a while."

Johan said goodbye with a solemn shake of Nina's hand; Gerhard, with a kiss on her cheek. Otto—after looking at her for a long moment, eyes glistening—wrapped her up as if he were a mountain cleaving to its own center. Murmuring in her ear, he said, "Only a few hours, wife. We rest when the sun is high and return to work after the second count."

As the men were leaving, another woman appeared in the doorway and called for Sofie, who skipped away toward the road before Liese could make introductions.

Closing the door, Liese said, "Mr. Collaer says there is to be a school, but probably not until September—seven months more to wait—so that lady you saw, she organized the *Kindergarten*. Several mothers of the small children take turns as teacher. Sofie would have begun in elementary school last year, so she is furious when someone reminds her she goes to the *Kindergarten*, but I will not lose the chance. I tell her she must go. When she is with the other children, she forgets her anger and enjoys herself."

Nudging Liese away from the sink, Nina said, "Last night, Otto told me of Sofie's fondness for Kurt. I see he did not exaggerate." She rubbed a wet cloth hard along the rim of a glass.

"He will make a wonderful father, your Kurt."

Nina dredged a plate in the shallow, soapy water and scrubbed it. "One day, I hope. But very long away, I think."

"Nina," Liese said. "Please do not think badly of Johan." She took the rinsed plate from Nina's hand, but, instead of drying it, held it dripping over the floor. "He fixes on a notion, then must make everyone else believe it, so he can believe it himself. When Kurt said, 'Why are you in this camp? Why Liese?'—he struck the bruise."

Nina knew this bruise well, struck anew every time she remembered Bess's accusing questions—*What are you hiding? Are you a Nazi?*

"We don't know why we have been punished," Liese went on, "or for what. Probably we will never know." She wiped the plate dry and set it on the work counter. "Before permission was given for our family to come here, Johan had to agree that we would all go back to Germany, but when he arrived, he would not sign the paper. It was the same for Otto—he would not sign."

"He did not tell me," Nina said. "Not any part of this."

"Neither did Johan, not until after Sofie and I had come," Liese said. "But now Johan is terrified we will be forced, so he looks for any reason to explain why others have been put in the camps, why others are to be deported, so he can compare and say, 'But this is not true of us.' For a long time, he believed Sofie's birth would be our protection from being deported, but here we have come to know one couple, with two children born in America, who are on the list. There are surely more."

"Your family is on this list? Like Kurt?"

"No—but it's a list that grows. While we wait, there is pressure, every day, to volunteer to return to Germany—pressure from two sides. The Americans want us to sign. But some of the Germans, after they have signed for themselves, try to make others do the same. People who say no, they sometimes find their names have been added to the list for deporting. They go to Mr. Collaer's office or they write to the attorney general or to Immigration asking if they are to be deported because they did not volunteer for repatriation, and every time they are told no—the reason is something else, the reason is classified and cannot be disclosed."

When the dishes were all washed and dried, the women reset the table and began cleaning the vegetables for lunch and dinner—a pound of parsnips, two fat bundles of glossy dark spinach. While they worked, Nina asked, "Will you tell me how it is to be here? What I mean is—inside with you now, and earlier, too, at breakfast, even when Kurt and Johan argued, nothing seemed so very strange. I knew how I should be, what I could say or do. But outside—with the fence, so many guards—"

Liese sighed. "You know I was in another camp before this, with Sofie?"

Nina nodded.

Liese picked up a parsnip and began scraping away the peel with a knife. "After a time, I don't know how long," she said, "you stop being afraid that you will be taken off in the night and shot. You don't stop believing it is possible. Yet you stop being afraid, because you cannot live at all if you are afraid. You go about your day, because you must." She nodded toward the window. "Everyone here—all but the small children—understands there is a war, and that we are America's prisoners. But we prisoners know nothing of how the war goes—only the fragments we get from someone new to the camp, someone who has been free in the world for a while longer." She looked at Nina. "You will tell me what you know? To add to the puzzle?"

"I will."

"When you are here, because you do not know what goes on outside this place, you lie awake in the night and think about how evil men can be—and women, too—when they fear to lose what they love best—people, land, power. And, lying there, you think how it would be nothing at all for a guard to shoot you: He has been given the right to shoot. As you walk through the camp, with each guard you pass by, your only protection is that man's conscience—the hope that, despite the rules, he does not believe he has the right to shoot."

Nina thought about Hugh, how he had trembled when he told her of the cry he'd heard, "Away from the fence!" and the shots that followed.

She would not tell Liese this. She would tell her of the food rationing, of the patriotic fervor, of the suspicion that had surrounded her every day in Newman for the last year; she would tell her as much as she had read about the course of the war—the rush to manufacture weapons, the battlefronts and estimates of losses.

But she would not tell Liese of the reports claiming that, in Poland, Hitler's Nazis were dragging Jews from their houses to shoot them against their own city walls. Nor would she tell her that, in America, mere weeks after being arrested, six German men—one an American citizen—had been executed as spies.

No, Nina decided. Let them be kind to one another. Let them tell of the worst they knew only when their sharing could help each other endure another day—ever watchful, but unafraid.

V

S*IXTEEN BOLTS, THIRTY-TWO SCREWS*—THE REFRAIN looped through Otto's mind like some torturous child's rhyme. The monotonous count of hardware for a single, so-called Victory Hut—a box of baked-white tin, sixteen feet square. Just as he had begun to feel proud to be called a builder, he had found himself at the head of an assembly crew. Johan had been reassigned to develop plans for the German school while overseeing the furniture workshop, and he had taken most of the other skilled carpenters with him. He'd wanted Kurt, but the boy had refused.

Commander Collaer, or someone above him, had determined that Victory Huts were the most practical solution to the rapidly swelling population of the Crystal City camp, which had quadrupled in the two months since Nina's arrival. Two or three men could piece one together in an hour—every hour another holding pen for yet another stunned family with an indefinite future. But no matter how fast the assembly crews worked, they couldn't keep up; the head count was expected to triple again by the end of May.

The sun, now directly overhead, flashed its burning heat off the white tin. Squinting against the light, Otto mounted the ladder and, by feeling for the connections, he secured the final bolts for the roof. Below, his two-man crew walked around the hut, twisting fittings another notch tighter. The men, both from Costa Rica, spoke little English, and whenever Otto addressed them in German, they looked anxiously toward the guard riding nearby, suggesting in whispers that they speak neither German nor Spanish, but instead make do with hand signals when English failed them.

He could not blame them for their fear. In the past few weeks, families like theirs had been trucked into Crystal City by the dozens: Germans, Japanese, Italians—not only from Costa Rica, but from Panama, Bolivia, Ecuador, Guatemala, Honduras, and Peru—turning the camp into a Plain of Babel.

Fragmented, in five languages, the newcomers' stories had spilled out and spread through the camp, patchwork narratives all eerily similar: men anonymously informed on, blacklisted, publicly accused as Axis spies or fifth columnists intent on disrupting or destroying Allied military and commercial interests. Some had been arrested immediately, while others had gone into hiding, driven to turn themselves in when their wives and children were taken up. While the men were dragged off to city jails without trial, their families were crowded into makeshift prisons at recreation centers, schools, and embassies, where food and clean water ran short and toilet facilities were quickly overwhelmed. Weeks later—or sometimes months—men, women, and children were forced at gunpoint onto ships bound for America, where they were again separated, stripped of their passports, charged with illegal entry into the United States, and sentenced to deportation.

With the collusion of countries they had believed to be their own, these people had been kidnapped by a foreign power, and, from the moment they had been dumped onto American shores, these mothers and fathers had to face a horrific truth. They and their children were hostages—hostages who would never be ransomed, only exchanged.

Six months ago, when he'd learned of this camp, Otto had clutched at the hope of restoring what had been lost, begging Nina to pass through the gates voluntarily, but he had succeeded only in leading his family into an elaborate trap. No longer could he pretend that Camp Crystal City had been conceived out of empathy, as a place to reunite and preserve families. Its sole purpose was to collect a great store of human currency—families threatened with dissolution, should they not willingly leave the country together. If somehow the Austs and other German-Americans managed to slip the snare and not be returned to Germany against their will, the price of their freedom would be paid by their Latin neighbors.

He and Johan had argued about it a few days ago, while they were sanding smooth the one fully planked wall in the Austs' cottage.

"Do you not see, Otto, their coming is better for us. These people have no claim on America. Never, like us, have they chosen it, or given their lives and work to it."

Otto shook his head. "What kind of country snatches up people from its allies and makes them prisoners? The way you speak, Johan—I think it is how our German neighbors spoke when we were arrested. *Better him than me. Better his family than ours.*"

"Don't be so grand, Otto. You would have said the same."

"No!" He slammed his fist against the wall. A short plank popped free on one end. Otto knocked it back into place with another strike of his fist. "I beg to God that this would not be so—or that I should be punished if it were!" He stepped back, trembling with anger.

A glimpse out a window—*the fence, the fence, the fence*—recalled him to where he was. Shouting could bring the guards. He lowered his voice. "Never will anyone hear me say there is justice in our being imprisoned. But Johan—you cannot believe it is not a much greater failure of justice to steal people from other countries, to carry them thousands of miles across an ocean, only to hold them until they can be shipped many more thousands of miles to countries they left years ago, that their children have never known, countries that are likely in these times to see them as enemies or traitors."

Johan brushed the wood dust from the section he had been sanding. "Rage at America will bring you nothing. You alone cannot repair these wrongs. Do you want to go back to Germany? To the Nazis?"

"To Nazis—of course not. They live only to destroy."

Johan smiled, as a winner who has won no prize. "What other choice have you, then, but to do what is necessary to remain in America? When we are released, we will start again. We can change our names, let our children teach us to quiet our accents. Or we can claim to be Poles. We can live in America as we would live under the roof of a hateful landlord: pay the rent, walk softly across the floors, complain of nothing, tend to the peeling walls and the sagging floors at our own expense."

Otto picked up his sanding block and rubbed it rhythmically along a seam. "You're wrong," he said. "I admit to you I have no other answer. But you are wrong. We should not look away when America turns its principles to lies."

"You ask too much, Otto. What country at war cares for principles?"

"But believing this—still you would offer yourself for enlistment?"

"Why will you not see that our best hope against forced repatriation is to show proof of loyalty to America? Any proof. Urge your sons to join me. And yourself, too—it could not hurt."

"You have said I am too old."

"Ach! They will not take you. And probably neither of your sons—Kurt has made a bad bed for himself—but the Americans, they will note the gesture. This could save your family."

"Salvation? To offer our blood to the disloyal? This is a dangerous game you play."

"When next the man from the Army comes," Johan said, "I will find him."

He meant the enlistment officer, who came weekly to pressure Japanese Nisei sons of Issei fathers to sign on as American soldiers. Johan had repeatedly insisted the man would soon call a meeting of the young German men, as he had done weeks ago for the Japanese, but he hadn't—not even for the German boys born in America.

They finished their work in silence, the quarrel hanging like a curtain between them. When they said goodnight, Otto could feel in Johan's loose grip that he was drawing away from their friendship.

With his sleeve, Otto wiped the sweat from his face. He stowed his wrench in his belt, came down from his ladder, and, nodding in approval at the work of his fellows, moved the ladder to the opposite side of the tin box. The sun was slightly behind him now, scorching the back of his neck as he climbed again. From this height, Otto could see people gathering on the North Road, near the cottages. Perhaps another band of volunteers preparing to march to the main guard station to request an audience with Commander Collaer on the subject of new elections. Collaer would refuse: he would hear no one but Karl Kolb, the elected leader of the German Internee Council, despite his unconcealed loathing of and impatience with the man.

Like Stengler at Fort Lincoln, Kolb counted himself a Nazi and made no secret of it. Kolb and the other members of the Council, whether Nazis or sympathizers, had been elected when fewer than forty men occupied the camp, nearly all of them zealous for repatriation. Kolb was fond of organizing showy rallies, where he would hold forth from a dais, flanked by his cronies, who hoisted hand-painted banners scarred with swastikas. Only yesterday, in the recreation hall, Kolb had hosted a birthday celebration for Adolf Hitler. Most of the Germans had stayed in their lodgings, avoiding even the latrines and showers, lest they be suspected by the guards of supporting the rally, or rounded up by Kolb's men and herded into the hall, forced to raise their arms in a Nazi salute.

While the Austs sat around their table playing cards, waiting for some sign that the rally had ended, Gerhard said, "They wouldn't even have been allowed to assemble at Camp Forrest, so I can't believe the guards will let it go on for long."

"I wouldn't be too sure of that, brother." Kurt laid his cards on the table, taking the trick. "Collaer has a different strategy. Maybe this commotion is just what he wants—proof that Germans are mostly Nazis." He rearranged the cards in his hand. "He writes up his report, complaining about the drum-beating, goose-stepping German machines, making twenty-six middle-aged men and a few boys sound like a battalion, so the bureaucrats in Washington can pretend they're throwing us out for real cause instead of because of their own paranoia."

Now, from atop another ladder sixty feet away, Kurt called, "*Vati*! Come down! It's time for lunch."

As he gave each of the roof bolts another hard turn, Otto called down to his men that they should return when they heard the afternoon whistle. When he dropped from the final rung, he grasped the ladder, opened the door to the finished Victory Hut, and slid the ladder inside, followed by all the tools. Lately, there had been several instances of vandalism—supplies stolen; bags of concrete punctured to be ruined by rain; screwdrivers and wrenches pocked by chisels, pounded awry by hammers, or smashed between stones. The round-the-clock guard claimed to have seen nothing, but they were happy to make raids on families, assuming guilt and assigning punishment if a handful of nails, a piece of planking, or a cutting of tarpaper were found stashed in the shack.

A new ruling, issued from Collaer's office last week, made the head of each work crew personally responsible for all the tools and supplies. Even the building scraps had to be taken back to the warehouse and catalogued, so they could be sold to prisoners who found them useful. Nina had told Otto she would rather live on with unfinished black walls than let the American government drive them further into poverty over wood scraps.

"Did you store the ladder?" Otto asked, when Kurt joined him. "And the supplies?"

"I did," Kurt said. He stared down the row of identical huts. "So many people, canned and caged. What a proud American victory."

Otto knocked his fist lightly against a corner, causing the tin to squeak. "A wind will bring it down, and nothing, I think, will keep out the dust—but the white will reflect the sun. That is some help."

To reach the road that lay between the four-family Quonset huts and the recreation hall, they had to pass the swamp. All morning the stench had been rising from the muck, foul and rotted. Otto listened for the sound of rattlesnakes and cottonmouths sluicing through the reeds. In the mornings before beginning work, he and the other men had to take extra care—the snakes, cooled in the night, came out of the swamp to stretch in dust the same color as themselves and lie pressed against the white tin, which warmed quickly in the sun.

"I've been offered a different job," Kurt said. He stopped walking, and nodded or spoke briefly to sweaty men from other work crews who plodded past them. When the others were well down the road, Kurt turned to face the swamp. "Apparently there's an engineer from Honduras—Italian, I think—who says it's possible to drain and clear all this to build a swimming pool." He smacked mosquitoes from his arms and neck. "We'll have to catch the snakes, pull out the brush, and then do all the digging by hand. God knows how long it will take."

"An engineer," Otto said. "To work with him will be fine training for you. Probably you would have many teachers. When they learn of the project, other engineers will surely join him. Better than university."

Kurt shook his head. "I'll be just a common laborer. I doubt the Italian will even ask my name. Accept it, *Vati.* There's nothing else for me—not for as far ahead as any of us dare to imagine." He looked again at the swamp, as if trying to see his way beyond the muck, the reeds, the snakes.

"Do you mind it?" Otto asked. "Do you no longer think, as you did before, that to help build this swimming pool—or a school, a library, a café—is to give in? What was your word—capitulation?"

Kurt sighed wearily. "It'll be nice for the little kids. If it can be this hot in April, what will it be like in August? And a pool might help keep the teenagers out of trouble." He looked at Otto. "I don't want to give in. But why should I make others pay for my taking a stand, especially the kids?"

Otto patted his son's back. "Perhaps there is room for me also on this crew."

"It'll be harder work," Kurt said. "At least at first."

"Gladly would I work harder, for the possibility of bringing pleasure," Otto said, looking back toward the Victory Huts, "rather than greater humiliation."

"C'mon," Kurt said. "Let's stop for the mail on the way back. Maybe there'll be something nice for *Mutti*. Or Gerhard."

"Or for you," said Otto. He knew that Kurt used at least half his weekly mail allowance writing to Bess—letters that had never been replied. Kurt rejected his thoughtless chirp of hope by saying nothing, and in that silence, Otto heard the strangled pain of defeat.

As they crossed to the path that would lead them past the recreation hall, Kurt stopped and pointed. "Look up there—just making the turn where the bakery's going in." He shielded his eyes from the sun. "They've got a few flags—not swastikas, and I don't see uniforms, so it's not Kolb's outfit. A lot of women, too. And some children. Wait—" He pointed again, and Otto saw two work-rumpled men moving up the road toward the marchers. "Are they the guys from your crew?" Kurt asked. "Those must be their national flags. What do you suppose it's all about?"

Whatever it was about, they did not want to get caught up with the marchers. They hurried across the road and slipped behind the Liaison Office, taking the long way around to reach the side entrance for the post office. They stopped just inside the door, glad to be out of the sun and enjoying the breeze from the ceiling fan.

Though the sign was out, indicating the post office was open, there was no one in attendance. Otto heard women speaking, and he leaned across the counter as far as he could, trying to locate them. He saw the older of the two, with short dark hair, standing alongside a window. "See the banners? Looks like they're setting up for some kind of festival."

Otto could not see the redhead who usually handed out the mail, but he could hear her answer. "Every day's a holiday for them. I'd like to show them what it's like to work for a living."

"Some of them work," said the other, turning her face toward the voice.

"But that's for extra. The ones that sit around on their hind ends all day get everything they need, just the same. You'd never believe the hunks of beef those German women carry off from that store that's been set up for them. I saw one of them with a roast that must have been two pounds."

"Think we can get ourselves locked up?" The dark-haired woman laughed dryly. "I'm getting pretty tired of rabbit." She sighed, drawing back from the window. "I don't think it is a festival."

"No—it's another protest," said the other. "They're all wearing labels around their necks—*Guatemala, Ecuador*. All those little Spanish countries. And look at the signs: *Innocent Mother. Innocent Father. Innocent Child*." Her red hair flashed into Otto's view as she moved closer to the older woman. "Did you see that one in the back? *Crystal City Kidnap Camp*. The nerve of those people."

Otto felt Kurt's hand gripping his shoulder, pulling him back. "Stand down, *Vati*," Kurt said. Only then did Otto realize his body was like an arrow notched in a drawn bowstring, ready to snap and shoot him over the counter at the two women.

Kurt rapped lightly on the counter, and in a smooth, bright voice, he called out, "Hello? Excuse me, please. We've come for our mail." He had pasted on his disarming smile. Anyone reading his eyes would see the smile was forced, but there was no danger there—the civilian staffers never looked a prisoner in the eye.

The women stopped talking, and then Otto heard them whispering to each other. A full minute passed before the redhead came out. The older woman appeared behind her, pacing like a watchdog.

"Mail for the family Aust," Otto said, straining to keep his tone gently neutral. "A-U-S-T—the names Otto, Nina, Kurt, Gerhard."

"Sign and date," the woman said, shoving the log at him. "I guess you know the date." A snide reference to Hitler's birthday, but Otto let it pass.

She snatched up the signed log and carried it beyond a partition. He imagined a small office beyond that, where censors with black markers and knife blades worked at long tables, joking with each other about the writers' private sorrows.

The woman returned with a thick stack of envelopes, sloppily banded. She laid them on the counter and looked at Kurt. "You're JURR-Hard?"

"Gerhard. My brother."

"Your *brother*?" she sneered, flicking the bundle across the counter, as if the letters were contaminated.

Otto said, "Thank you." The woman crossed her arms and turned her back.

Kurt grabbed the stack and pulled off the band. "From Fort Lincoln," he said, handing the top envelope to Otto. "For you—from Herr Merkel." Quickly, he flipped through the rest of the stack, plucking out one envelope Otto recognized as Charlie Griffin's office stationery, folding it into his back pocket. More slowly this time, he turned through the stack again. "From Iris Beale, for *Mutti*." After a third time through, he handed another letter to Otto. "It's from Hugh. There's one from him for *Mutti,* and one for me, too. The rest are for Gerhard."

He replaced the band around the sheaf belonging to his brother. "Hugh must be in port again—or he was, five or six weeks ago." He pinched the edge of the envelope in Otto's hand. "So what news? What does Herr Merkel say?"

Otto tore open the envelope and quickly scanned the letter. "He is to be paroled!"

"Hmph!" Otto heard from beyond the counter, but he refused to acknowledge the women again. He tilted the letter so Kurt could see and held his finger under the date the old man had written. "Is that February? This was more than eight weeks coming, so probably he is already there, on his farm. Perhaps at this moment, he is on his tractor, preparing the ground for spring wheat."

"It's a sweet thing to think about, isn't it," said Kurt.

Outside again, they looked around for the marchers. Otto spotted a bobbing block of color that looked like an apparition through the wavering haze. Sometimes guards rode out to surround protesters before they got to the gate, triggering the siren, an extra count, and confinement to lodgings, but it looked like these people were going to be allowed to stand and chant at the locked gate until they fell ill from the heat and had to disperse. "Come," Otto said, "we have good news to share with your mother. And the sooner Gerhard reads his letters, the sooner he will tell us what goes on with Hugh." He gave Kurt a light nudge. "And perhaps Bess."

Despite his dust-parched throat, his burning skin, his sweaty clothes, and his pulsing regret for persuading Nina to come, whenever he stepped across the hut's threshold to his wife, Otto felt happy, himself again. Each entry struck a pinhole through his memory of returning from the drugstore to discover that Nina had vanished. How many pinholes would it take to tear the image asunder?

Otto said to Kurt, "You first for the washroom," and Kurt handed him the letters. He watched his wife working in their little kitchen, the cabinet door open to reveal the pretty silk banner. From where Otto stood, Hugh's blue star seemed to kiss Nina's shoulder as she reached for the plates.

"So many letters for Gerhard," Otto said, setting the stack on the edge of the small work counter. "You have one from Hugh, also. And another."

Nina looked up sharply.

"From Iris," Otto said. Like Kurt, she devoted much of her mail allowance to writing letters and cards Bess never answered.

Her hands were full of plates. "In my pocket, please," she said. As he tucked the letters into her apron, he kissed her forehead, and she whispered roughly, "I hope she is well."

While Nina set the table, Otto scrubbed his hands at the kitchen sink, leaned over to smell the round of bread cooling on the slatted shelf he had added for that purpose. He lifted the lid on a pot to sneak a taste of leek soup with peas and peppers.

Nina came up beside him, took the spoon away, and pointed with it toward the bread. "I want you to make me a box, with two shelves." She spread her hands apart to show him. "Each shelf must be wide enough for two loaves side by side, and a handle on top for me to carry. When will the bakery be finished?"

"Another month," he said. "More if the ovens are delayed, which is expected." When the bakery opened, it would sell bread and pastry for camp tokens, but women who wanted to bake their own bread would be allowed to use the pans and big ovens three afternoons a week. Nina was already planning, no doubt weary from the scorching hours it took every day to bake a single loaf—not enough for them—on top of the stove in her makeshift Dutch oven.

"Make the sides with slats, too," Nina said, still thinking, "so the air can go through. I'll make a cover to keep out the dust when I carry the bread back."

"The box when filled will be heavy and awkward to carry. Kurt could make a wagon—useful for many things, not only the bread."

"The wood will not cost too much?"

"No—but why ask? This is needed."

Nina nodded crisply at a well-struck deal and kissed Otto's cheek.

Kurt came out of the washroom wearing a clean, dry shirt, his hair rinsed and slicked back, and as Otto slid past him in the tiny hall, he heard Nina calling, "Here is paper, son. Come and draw. You are to build me a wagon."

When Otto returned, fully clean and in his own dry shirt, he saw Kurt studying the cooling shelf for the bread, scratching away at paper he had spread on top of the ice box. Gerhard was back and was standing over the table. He had already slit the censors' seals on the envelopes and was sorting Hugh's letters by date written, claiming the spaces between the plates, bowls, and a centerpiece board holding sliced bread and a small block of cheese.

"How many?" Otto asked.

"Sixteen," said Gerhard. "I wonder where he was when he sent them—and where he was headed. In this one—" He held up one of the letters briefly. "He says it will probably be at least the middle of May before he can get mail out again. And that's if orders don't change." Gerhard gathered the open letters carefully, pushed his plate aside, laid the stacked pages on the table and pressed them smooth. "Figure May fifteenth. Add six or seven weeks for transport and censors." He sighed. "I guess I have to make these last until the end of June, or even into July."

"Put them on the armchair," Nina said, "or you will soak them with soup."

While Nina filled the bowls, Otto held up his letter from Egon. "Good news and hope for us all," he said. "Herr Merkel has been paroled and can return to his farm." He looked around at his family. "But here…" He tapped the final lines of the letter. "Kurt, I did not tell you this. He invites us to come live with him when we are released. 'Whether you come all together or one by one,' he writes, 'I will welcome you.'"

Everyone was quiet. Gerhard stared at Otto, his eyes wide. Kurt was drawing a spoon through his soup in small, slow circles. Nina looked back and forth between their sons and then at Otto. "Farming is a life's work," she said. "Already once we have turned away from it, because it was not right for us."

"He suggests only that he can give us a home," Otto said.

"But surely, Otto, he thinks of our young men and the help they could be to him—and you and me as well."

"He says nothing of work."

"But of course it is implied, between friends. You have told me he is an old man and a widower. A year in that terrible camp— more—and he will be much weaker than before the war. Of course he needs help. We could not live in his house without paying with our labor—and we would wish to pay. But after many months, perhaps a year or two, we could not leave him alone for a different life. To go would be promising to stay."

"He asks no promise," Otto said, though he knew well that Nina was right. He refolded the letter and put it in his shirt pocket. "I would have thought that after this, we would all want to look out across wheat fields—fields, Egon says, that go on for miles, with no fences except low ones to mark one farm from another and to keep out the grazing cattle. You cannot even see the fences when the wheat is high. Would that not be splendid?"

Nina looked at Gerhard, who, like his brother, was studying his soup.

"What troubles you all? Kurt?" Otto lightly slapped his son's leg. "What is left for us in Indiana?"

"For now, please," Nina said, "write to him our thanks, and tell him we will think about it. But, Otto, remember that even if we wished to go, we cannot know how long we will be here. And still we do not know if something can be done about Kurt—"

"We do know," Kurt said. He pulled the envelope from his back pocket, opened it, and dropped the letter into Nina's lap. "I didn't want to tell you until I was sure. He says we're out of appeals. I'm definitely going to be deported, eventually."

"Kurt—" Gerhard began, his voice catching. "Kurt, I'm sorry. So sorry."

"I expected it. For a long time, I've expected it."

"It's my fault. All of it. Our being here."

"You're mixing things up, little brother. You weren't even in Fort Lincoln. You're not to blame for me being deported."

"I think I am," Gerhard said. His breathing rattled like chains. "We'd all still be at home—if it wasn't for me."

Otto said, "What do you mean, son?"

"I should have told you in Chicago." He coughed badly and gasped several times. Nina rubbed his back and Kurt urged him to take a glass of water, but Gerhard shook them off. "It was that hearing. The first thing they asked me was, 'How old were you when you joined the Bund?' I told them I didn't know what they were talking about—that I'd never joined anything. To prove it, I said, 'How could I join the Bund? Only American citizens could join the Bund.' And they said, 'So you looked into it. You must have considered it.' After that they went on and on about Herr Vogel. I kept saying, 'He was my music teacher. That's all.'"

"The FBI," Nina said. "They asked me also about Herr Vogel, and would not accept my answers."

"They just wouldn't let it go—this idea that our restaurant was the local Bund headquarters. 'It is unreasonable,' they said, 'for us to believe that your family would so often entertain Nazis without being Nazis yourselves.'" Gerhard stopped for a moment to breathe. "I shouldn't have said it. I shouldn't have been sarcastic—but I was so mad. I said, 'Herr Vogel can't have been a Nazi. His favorite composer was Mahler—and Hitler hates Mahler. He banned his music.'"

Gerhard hunched with another fit of coughing. "Quick as anything, one of them said, 'How do you know that?' I'd have lied if I could have been sure the news had been in the paper or on the radio, but I was afraid, so I said, 'Herr Vogel told me.'" He gasped again for air, this time allowing Otto to stand behind him and gently pull his shoulders back. "That settled them. One of them said, 'That's just the sort of thing a spy would say.' I didn't know whether he meant me or Herr Vogel, but it didn't matter. The next thing I knew, the guy in the middle was banging a paperweight on the table and saying, 'Recommendation for internment. Unanimous.'"

Kurt had refilled Gerhard's water glass and brought it back to the table. "It's not your fault," he said. "They made a big deal about my engineering books, my tools, harping on why I was working on cars. They didn't really ask questions. They just said things like, 'Your drawings tell you where a structure is most vulnerable.' Or, 'Now that you understand engines so well, you'll know how to sabotage a car or a truck.'"

Still holding Gerhard's shoulders, Otto said, "They asked me, 'Why did you not become an American citizen?' But before I could answer a word, they said, 'You take a German newspaper. You have German books in your house. You lead a group of German singers. You brought up your children to speak German. You send money to contacts in Germany.'"

Gerhard's breathing had finally steadied. Otto stroked his son's hair, as he used to do years ago, and then returned to his chair. "We should eat," he said, and they did, slowly, because they needed their strength to face the afternoon's work.

When he had sopped up the last of his soup with a bit of bread, Otto began to gather the dishes. The boys moved to help, while Nina filled the sink with water. In a few minutes, working together, everything was washed, dried, and put away.

"I have thought on this for a long time," Nina said, closing the cabinet on the clean plates. "Now that we have been able to talk, I see I was right. They wanted each of us to believe we had brought the trouble on our family. They used our love, our desire to protect, to misshape our words into daggers. They wanted to make us doubt ourselves and each other. To crush our spirits."

She looked suddenly exhausted, as if all her blood had drained away. Otto led her back to the cleared table and sat down beside her. The boys took their own chairs again.

"The last time I saw Bess," Nina said, "she asked me, 'Why only your family? Why have other German families here not been arrested?' I see the answer now. It was to frighten other Germans into silence." She looked at Otto. "No one would stand with us. No one would even write a letter. They arrest only a few people, one family, in a town or a neighborhood, and this makes foolish Americans believe they have been rescued from silent danger." She reached for Kurt's hand. "Bess looked into my face and called us traitors."

Kurt stared at his hands for a long moment. When he looked up, he turned to Gerhard and said, "I do wish you'd told us in Chicago. Because then all of us—you, me, *Vati*—we would have talked about it, compared what happened. We might even have gotten some of the other men to talk. But that's not your fault either. *Vati* and I didn't talk about the hearings until we'd been at Fort Lincoln for months. Like *Mutti* says, they wanted to make us all afraid to say a word—afraid of what might happen to people we loved."

"You're not afraid now," Gerhard said. "To talk about it, I mean. So why can't you tell us why you think you're being deported? Maybe we can help somehow."

"This is different," Kurt said. "This really is my fault. Partly because of things I did, but mostly because—" He shook his head fiercely and wiped his eyes. "No. I'm not dragging you into it. Mr. Griffin has done all he can."

"You told Mr. Griffin everything?" Otto asked. "Even those things you will not tell us?"

Kurt sighed. "I couldn't, *Vati*. I can't. Everything I write to him I write to the censors. I'd only be making trouble."

"More trouble than this?" Gerhard asked.

"More," Kurt said. "So much more." He stroked Nina's hand. "You have to trust me on this, *Mutti*—and accept that I'm headed back to Germany." He shook his head and gave a soft chuckle. "Funny—I think I might like settling down on Egon's farm. But that's never going to happen. Not for me. So you three decide what's best for you, together or apart. I won't ever be able to come back."

Later, after Otto and his sons had finished their day's work, after Gerhard had settled on his bed to read his letters and Kurt at the table to write one, and after the sun had been down long enough for some of the heat to seep away, Otto asked Nina to take a walk with him along the fence.

"What news from Iris Beale?" Otto asked.

"You mean news of Bess." She quickened her pace. "Everett is thinking of selling his store, and the house as well. He wants to go north to Fort Wayne. He has family there."

"So when we are free, we will have no one left in Newman."

"There is Mr. Griffin."

Otto nodded. "No matter where we go when we leave this place," he said, "we will be starting again. Why not with Egon in Wyoming?"

"Why do you want so much to go there?"

"He is my friend."

"Mr. Griffin is my friend. So is Iris." She stopped and looked down at the ground, scraping the toe of her shoe through the dust as if she were looking for something she had dropped. "It is hard to remember that you don't really know them, not as I do. Never have I had such friends—so good, so true. Not even when I was a girl." Otto watched her, trying to read her face, but she took his arm and started walking again without looking up at him. "Of course I would choose again to come to you. You must not doubt this. But I would not have thought being apart from them would be so painful."

He drew her arm in more tightly and laid his hand over her hand.

"Still," Nina said, "I would not ask you three to follow me only for those friendships."

They walked from one light pole to the next, and then to another before Otto spoke. "I believe I know something of what Egon's farm means to him. His children saved it for him, changing the papers to protect ownership, paying the taxes, but not one of them wants to farm. More than forty years he has given to make a legacy his children do not value."

Nina slid her arm from his. "There is more. Those are Herr Merkel's reasons. What are yours?"

Otto pulled his handkerchief from his pocket and wiped his face. "Still it is so hot."

"Otto?"

He folded the handkerchief and turned it over in his hands, again and again, before returning it to his pocket. "When Kurt was taken from the performance, Egon was the first to stand with me. He was the only one never to back away. When Kurt was in the stockade, and after, when he was sent away, Egon was always with me. And always for Kurt. Never did he waver. Never did he doubt our son." He pinched the bridge of his nose and then coughed so Nina might think the tears in his eyes were from the dust. "I did doubt. There were times when I wondered if what the others said of Kurt might be true—that he was a Nazi, a spy, or simply one who was happy only when making trouble."

He saw himself again in Barracks 32, confined in those long hours between the evening meal and lights out, when the sounds of friendly argument rising from games of cards or chess did not include him, when the men who had once been his friends passed without looking at him. Even Johan had done this, turning away from Otto when he knew others were watching. At those times, Egon would lay a hand on his shoulder and quietly draw up a chair beside him.

"I should like to be such a good man—such a stalwart man," said Otto.

Nina stopped again. The bright light made her tear-filled eyes look as if they were encased in glass. She touched her fingertips to his lips. "You are the finest man I know."

Otto smiled. "You do not know Egon."

"I see, Otto. I do. I understand. But will you agree that first we must try again to keep Kurt with us? I will write to Mr. Griffin myself. Your Herr Merkel is so fond of Kurt, he will understand that—and now that he is free again, he could surely speak for Kurt. Be a witness. Then, if we are successful—if to go to Wyoming is what you truly want, I will go with you." She pressed her cheek into his chest. "But the boys must be free to choose their own lives."

Otto put his arms around Nina and squeezed, lifting her off her feet. "Kurt said he would like the farm."

"Gerhard, then."

"He will want to be with us."

"No. Gerhard will go wherever Hugh goes."

"But they cannot go on with their plans. Gerhard will not be able to perform again. Or not for many years, at least. And after the war, Hugh will surely want a long rest. Egon would welcome him as well, if he wants to come. We can get a piano. They could work on composing their songs, and the fresh air and hard work will make them both strong."

"Perhaps," Nina said, with a tone that meant *No.*

"Why not? It is possible."

She shrugged. "You cannot answer for them. It is for them to choose for themselves. Together. As you and I choose together."

"What do you mean?"

Nina took his hand again and started walking. "I mean that in this life, true friends are the rarest of treasures. It is why I respect your wish to take up your friend's offer—but it is also why you must respect that Gerhard will not bear to be separated from Hugh. They have planned their lives together since they were children. All you need to see is how many letters Hugh writes to know that this, if nothing else, will not change."

They had walked so far they were nearly in the Japanese section. They turned as one. Whenever they heard other couples or groups of friends coming up behind them, they stopped to let them pass.

After a long while, Otto said, "If we cannot stop Kurt from being deported, what shall we do?"

"I think we must go with him. Perhaps one day we would come back to America, but the first years for him, even if the war is over, will be terrible—more difficult than anything he has yet suffered. We cannot leave him to find his way alone."

"And Gerhard?"

"He will be with Hugh." Her voice broke when she said it. "In time, they might come to us, if all the conservatories have not been destroyed."

"Do you want to go back to Germany, Nina?"

"To a Germany that no longer exists. To the Germany that died in the last war. " She stopped and looked up at the sky, as if searching for stars, but probably she was trying to see the guard in the nearest tower. "Maybe it never existed, the way America has never existed—only an idea of freedom." Nina looked to the ground, and Otto's eyes followed hers to the barren dust. "Wherever we go," she said, "we will be beggars. You remember how it was before, Otto. People so poor, so hungry, they beat strangers from their gates. Sometimes even family. Here, in America—if the bombs and the soldiers do not come—we know we still have a few friends who will not turn against us." She laid her palm over his heart. "I want what you want, husband—for our family to stay together. But this, I fear, has been made impossible."

"Not yet," Otto said. "I will not yet accept it is impossible. We thought we had already lost each other, but here we are." He slipped his arm around her waist. "We must not give up."

VI

OTTO TOOK BREAD ROLLS AND dishes of pickles from Liese, rearranging the covered pots and bowls of potato salad and sauerkraut in Nina's wagon to make everything fit.

"It's too hot for a picnic," Liese said, handing Otto a clean sheet to cover the wagon.

"Here, it is too hot for anything," said Johan, "so it makes no difference."

Otto glanced at Johan. "Are you unwell?" he asked. It was strange for his friend to sound so bitter.

"Otto, where is your hat?" asked Nina. "You cannot sit in the sun without your hat."

He twisted to show her that his hat, secured by a string, had fallen down his back. Her pressed lips told him she would not be satisfied until he put it on his head.

"Where's Sofie?" Kurt asked.

As if she had been waiting for his call, Sofie bounced out of the house singing, "I'm a Yankee Doodle Dandy."

"Sofie!" snapped Johan. "Stop that singing!"

Sofie stopped. Locking eyes with her father, she began to hum the same tune.

Johan took a step toward her, but Liese got in his way. "Sweetheart," she said gently. "Do you know what this song means?"

"Yes!" chirped Sofie, like a prized pupil. "It means it's the Fourth of July!" She bounced again. Liese stilled her with a firm hand on top of her head.

"It is," Liese said. "But what does that mean?"

"Fireworks!"

"Not today, Sofie," said Johan. "No fireworks." To Otto, he said quietly, "You go on. We will stay here."

Otto kept his own voice low. "It is not wise," he said. "Perhaps there will be no roll call, but can you be sure? There will be many at the picnic who know you, Johan. If anyone should notice you are not there, and speak of it, the Americans will assume you are with the Nazis."

When the all-camp picnic had been announced, the Nazis immediately called for an Anti-American Independence Day rally in the recreation hall. They, too, would be paying attention to who was in attendance, but there was little they could do to punish the hundreds of Germans who, however unwillingly, had chosen the new commander's event. In May, Collaer had left Crystal City to take a job in Washington, replaced by Joseph O'Rourke. The Independence Day rally was his pet project, touted as "an old-fashioned picnic and ice cream social," promising games and prizes for the children.

"As you say," Johan said with a nod that showed, not agreement, but something else Otto could not name.

Gerhard picked up the basket of plates and cutlery. "It'll be nice to have a natural way to meet some Japanese." He colored when the others looked at him. "I mean, as natural as anything can be here."

"You want their stories," Nina said. "For the *Liederkreis?*"

"How many songs is this cycle to be?" Otto laughed. "I think singing it will take more hours than Wagner's *Ring*."

"Maybe," Gerhard grinned. "Or maybe in the end it will be very short—four songs. One for each of us. I need to work it out with Hugh." His smile faded. For days he had been expecting another bundle of mail.

"Well, you just make sure Hugh doesn't cut my part," Kurt said, and Gerhard smiled again.

Sofie jumped across Kurt's back, sending them both to the ground. "Hey!" Kurt rolled free of Sofie's wild limbs. He stood up and brushed himself off, while Liese knocked the dust out of Sofie's dress. "Okay, Noodle," Kurt said, kneeling so Sofie could climb onto his shoulders. "Let's go."

"To the fireworks!" crowed Sofie.

"I wouldn't count on that." Carefully, Kurt stood, and Sofie giggled as she rose higher and higher. "There'll be games, hot dogs, lemonade, and lots of ice cream. And I hear some Japanese are going to play baseball. You might make some new friends."

"I want sparklers," Sofie said. "I could see them from our house last time."

The adults looked nervously at each other. What Sofie believed were sparklers had in fact been torches at the summer solstice gathering, held in the open field behind the recreation hall. The so-called festival had begun with a few activities for the younger children—relay races for the boys and lessons in making wildflower crowns for the girls—but at dusk, Kolb lit a fire. When Liese saw his men gathering around a barrel filled with stobs, she lifted Sofie into her arms, said, "Here it is nearly your bedtime and you haven't had your supper," and, with Nina walking briskly alongside them, she carried her whimpering, flower-crowned daughter down the road. Other women, seeing Liese's hurry, took their own children in hand and slipped away before the torches could be lit.

The men had stayed—some out of curiosity, but most out of fear of reprisal. Though the entire German Internee Council, including Kolb, had finally been unseated in new elections, Commander Collaer allowed Heinrich Hasenburger to claim the spokesman's position, despite his having received less than one-quarter of the vote. Hasenburger was every bit the Nazi Kolb was, and, though the two were known to hate each other, they joined forces for public rallies to create the impression that the Nazis were in the majority and the leaders united in their cause.

Collaer's refusal to interfere had allowed the two factions to take control of all duty assignments, warehouses, workshops, and services, and to punish prisoners who resisted their will. Until Hasenburger decided otherwise, a violator was considered to be outside the community—which meant he or she could be denied work, clothing, bedding, household goods, milk, ice, food, or even access to showers and latrines for as many as ten days.

It was only for this that the greater part of the German community had come out for the solstice festival, and only for this that the men stayed. Forty torch-carriers marched shoulder to shoulder in a long line to the twilight of the lawn, then stopped and, as one, began to rotate the line—rigidly, as if they were a hand on a clock. After three revolutions, the ends of the line joined and became a circle. Three more revolutions, counter-clockwise, and the forty split into lines of ten, stomping one behind another toward the center, making a cross. Again, three revolutions, and they broke the arms of the cross at right angles, forming a burning swastika that turned and turned and turned.

After that, there were speeches that went on and on, until Otto was startled by a cheer. There at the center, hooped by torchlight, was Fritz Kuhn, the disgraced former leader of the German-American Bund, looking not at all disgraced. He looked just as he had in the dozens of newspaper photos Otto had seen—hawk-nosed, pot-bellied, arrogantly sneering. As he preached, Kuhn alternately beat his fist in the air and jabbed at the sky, vowing to lead the faithful into their triumphant return to the Fatherland.

In that moment, Otto knew Kurt had been right about Collaer's decision not to quash the birthday march for Hitler: such theatrics suited Collaer's purposes, and, now, it seemed, his successor's. Collaer's replacement, Joseph O'Rourke had proved, by his conspicuous absence on the night of the summer solstice, that he meant to deal with the Nazi element as Collaer had done, by keeping distant watch, stopping nothing, and so there were three factions now. Kolb, Hasenburger, and Kuhn spent their days separately strutting about the camp, each trailed by his minions.

O'Rourke was fond of walking through the camp, too, displaying an apparent fondness for children. Little ones began tagging after him, having discovered he could be counted on for a butterscotch or a stick of chewing gum. Older children might look up any time from their games and see Mr. O'Rourke on the sidelines, loudly cheering a well-cleared hurdle, a fastball, or a string of cartwheels. It was through the children that he had initially spread word of his American Independence Day celebration—turning up wherever the children played, giving them cellophane-wrapped lollipops glued to handbills announcing the event.

"There have to be sparklers," Sofie said now, her eyes gleaming. "And the paper says fireworks."

"It does not," said Johan, who, as he walked beside Kurt, appeared comically small.

"It does!" Sofie patted the top of Kurt's head and pointed at a poster-sized version of the handbill fixed to the flagpole.

"It doesn't *say* fireworks," said Kurt. "That's just decoration." The sign was spangled all over with stars and stripes, but the child had mistaken the Old Glory image—a flag waving on through the red glare of rockets—as a promise of fireworks.

Sofie wasn't listening. She turned her glee into a chant: "Sparklers! Firecrackers! Cherry bombs! Rockets!" Soon other excited children heard Sofie and took up the chorus. Calls from parents to quiet down made the children sing louder.

The picnic was being held on the west side of the camp—the Japanese side—near the young citrus grove where the American elementary school was to be built. As they passed the swamp, which he and Kurt were helping to clear of snakes and brush, Otto saw two groups of American women, all in crisp white or pastel dresses, forming a kind of gateway into the picnic area. At the back of each group, men held up hand-lettered signs that said *Meet Your Teachers*. All the women—presumably the teachers—carried clipboards.

Smiling vacantly, one stepped in front of Otto and quickly turned to Gerhard. "You'll have finished school," she said.

"I—" He hesitated. "Yes."

The woman nodded, looking past him toward Kurt. "And that one, surely. Graduated?" She didn't wait for an answer. "But that's not his little girl. Who does she belong to?"

"She's mine," said Johan, stopping before the woman. "What is it?"

Otto helped Sofie down from Kurt's shoulders and set her on her feet beside Liese, who draped a protective arm around her.

"We're enrolling the children in school," said the woman. "How old is your daughter?"

"What school is this?" Liese asked. She nudged Sofie toward Kurt and stepped forward to stand beside Johan.

"Federal Elementary," the woman said. "Operated by the state of Texas to ensure detainee children get a proper education."

"Cappelmann," Johan said. "C-A-P-P—"

"Stop, husband." Liese looked at the woman. "We have not yet decided which school our daughter will attend—German or American."

"Unlike the unofficial German school," the woman said, "all our credits are transferrable to any American school, and recognized in many other parts of the world." She looked past Liese and brayed, "What's your name, little girl? Wouldn't you like to come to our lovely school in September?"

"Madam," Liese said, slipping her arm through Johan's. "My husband and I must discuss privately. Have you a paper we can take away to look over?"

The woman glared for a moment before depressing the clip on the board and pinching up one of the pages. She held it out to Liese. "It's a simple enrollment form. No later than August fifteenth, or she might lose eligibility."

Liese thanked her, but the American said nothing. Instead, like a machine, she pulled her face into that empty smile and walked into the path of another family.

From Nina, Otto knew the Cappelmanns had not been able to agree on this matter. Like Johan, Liese wanted to go back to Idaho and one day build a real version of the dollhouse that sat in their hut. But she was worried; no family could be sure they wouldn't be added to the deportation list, and Sofie knew so little German. She feared, too, that the Council would punish them if they chose for their daughter an American education. Johan scoffed, saying they would have no trouble from the Council, as he had earned their favor by taking charge of building the German school. Now, he insisted, they had to demonstrate to the camp commander that they were loyal to America. "We must place Sofie in the American school," he said, "to prove we mean to stay."

When they got through the swarm of teachers, they entered heavy smoke billowing from four large grills. A little further on, dozens of tables had been set up, some of them marked for the buffet by galvanized tubs heaped with chunked ice. Several Japanese women were gathered at one end of the buffet, nestling their dishes in the ice, so Nina and Liese took charge of the wagon and headed toward the other end. Kurt swung a giggling Sofie up onto his shoulders again and, at her command, trotted toward the section where the games were being organized. Otto, Johan, and Gerhard debated the merits of various empty picnic tables before claiming one near the citrus grove.

After a few minutes, Nina and Liese returned, producing another clean sheet from the wagon. With one on each end, they snapped open the sheet and floated it over the table. Gerhard unloaded the basket and arranged the plates.

Sofie, squealing and chased by Kurt, came running to deliver a balloon and a sack into her father's keeping. "I'm in the spoon race!" Sofie ran a few steps toward the game area, but in mid-stride, she twirled on one toe and came back to the table. "I forgot," she said, plunging her hand into the sack. She pulled out a small flag and waved it wildly.

"Put that down," Johan said.

"We're all doing it!" Sofie protested.

"Put it down!"

Kurt dropped into a crouch beside Sofie and gently pinched the flag's stick above her clenched fist. "Just look at that pointy top," he said, pressing his finger to it and showing her the dent it made in his skin. "What did we decide about running with things like pencils, twigs, and forks?"

Otto had not heard such an exasperated sigh from such a small person since Kurt was a boy, stubbornly determined to take a heavy, sizzling pot from a stovetop higher than his head.

Sofie let the flag drop to the ground and grabbed Kurt's hand. "You come watch me." Ignoring her father, she turned her face to Gerhard. "You come, too."

"Sure, Sofie," said Gerhard, taking her other hand. "We used to do spoon races with eggs. What are you going to carry?"

"Cotton balls!" she proclaimed, breaking free from both of them and skipping off as lightly as if she were a bit of fluff carried on the wind.

Johan picked up the sack, glitteringly labeled *Compliments of Federal Elementary*, and spilled its contents across the table: a noisemaker, a plastic whistle, two jawbreakers, a paper crown, and a yellow box with eight crayons. The lid was torn, exposing the crayons, which had already begun to soften in the heat. "How cheaply they buy our children." He flicked the box down the table. Two crayons, violet and orange, fell into Nina's lap.

Liese picked up the flag, brushed it free of sand, and laid it on the table. Piece by piece, Otto quietly collected Sofie's party favors in the sack. He watched some children who had found their way through the fence surrounding the grove to play hide and seek among the trees. Their laughter was like cool water.

"She doesn't realize, Johan," Otto said. "You and Liese have protected her from our troubles. Can you not be satisfied—just for today—that these small things have made her happy?"

Johan did not reply. He was looking toward the game area, where the women with clipboards were cheering on the children, some leaning down to talk with them or shake their small hands.

Nina returned the escaped crayons to the box and set it before Johan. "The decision for her schooling still belongs to you and Liese," she said. "No one can force you."

Otto added, "If you wish her to go to the American school, we will help her to better her German. All of us." Uncomfortable with Johan's silence, he added, "Kurt and Gerhard studied all their years in American schools, so, if you choose for Sofie the German school, they will see she does not fall behind."

"Until you're all deported," Johan said.

The words knocked Otto back like a strike to the face.

"Johan," said Liese, "that was cruel."

Otto looked at Nina. She closed her eyes, holding them shut for a moment. Otto rubbed his jaw, as if he really had been struck. "Our sons will help," he said. "Nina and I will help. For as long as any of us are here."

"Help," Johan said drily. Without a glance, he set off into the crowd, breaking through the line of people waiting for lemonade.

Otto started to follow.

"Don't," Liese said. "He is having moods. I find I must leave him alone in these times." She lifted the small flag and rotated it slowly before her eyes. "Who among us can say we truly know our family—or even ourselves—after these two years we have lived? I cannot say from one day to the next what I believe."

For the next hour, Otto, Nina, and Liese walked about together, stopping to watch Sofie while she balanced a spoon mounded with cotton balls, and then with her leg tied to the leg of a skinny Japanese girl called Michi, whom Sofie announced was her new best friend.

They walked to the cleared ground that had been claimed as a baseball diamond and watched the game. Otto noticed O'Rourke on the other side of the diamond, miming a swing of the bat for five or six Japanese boys. Gerhard was there, too, on the near side, not watching the game but standing behind the crowd with a group of Japanese men, one of whom, they learned, was Michi's father.

When the game ended, the players and the spectators meandered back toward the picnic area. Meeting amiably at the grills, some of the Germans invited their new Japanese acquaintances to sit with them, a gesture reciprocated by many Japanese families. Sofie and Michi ate their first hotdogs with Michi's family and their second with the Austs and Liese. No one could say for certain how many glasses of lemonade or scoops of ice cream the girls had.

When the food was gone, two of the women who operated the *Kindergarten* went around gathering their charges, explaining to the children's mothers that they had arranged a drawing lesson and a music period so the little ones could relax from the excitement. Sofie, who seemed to have forgotten about the sparklers—and about Michi—took her place in front, padding away from the picnic with her head high like a goose marking the way for her goslings.

It was mid-afternoon now, too hot for anyone to say much. They all worked together to clean up, dumping the ice, clearing and folding the tables, gathering up the game equipment, and packing their own things. When there was nothing more to do except load the tables, grills, and other camp property onto waiting trucks, Otto told Nina and Liese to go on ahead with the wagon.

"We'll pick up Sofie," Kurt said. "She told Gerhard she wants us to hear her sing."

Johan had never returned.

"Where did he go, do you think?" Otto asked Kurt.

Kurt leaned in so no one but Otto would hear. "I asked around. Someone saw him walking off between two Council members—the ones that are always with Hasenburger."

Half an hour later, Otto, Kurt, and Gerhard made their way down the broad dirt road rutted from truck tires and horse's hooves. Before he'd left, Collaer had made a ceremony of naming all the streets. The path they were on now had been designated Lincoln Avenue.

"Is that Johan?" Kurt asked, pointing to a man who was pacing the ground beyond the flagpole, just north of the community building.

"I believe so," Otto said. He stopped and squinted. "Is that not where he has marked the ground for the school?"

"What's he doing?" Kurt asked. "He's pulling something up."

"It looks like a stake," said Gerhard. "Look—he's winding the string."

A few hundred yards from where Johan paced, a line of children, their hands linked, emerged from the community building, the *Kindergarten*. Instead of dispersing for home, the children formed a circle and sang "*Alle Vögel sind schon da*," turning and hopping about like the happy, nimble birds they sang of.

Though the children sang loudly, Sofie among them, Johan did not look up. He continued his slow walk, winding the marking string as he went, stopping and stooping to pull up another stake.

"What is he doing?" Kurt asked again.

A rumble like thunder. Otto turned sharply and shoved his sons off the road. Two horses, whipped to full gallop by their riders, pounded past them.

Otto was on the point of calling out to Johan when a great shouting—fierce, outraged, many-voiced—rose behind them. They all turned to look. Hasenburger's, Kolb's, and Kuhn's men were pouring out of the recreation hall as a mob. Within a few paces, they had formed into a brigade, marching in step, stomping their way straight down Lincoln Avenue.

Kurt pulled on Otto's arm. "What's that they're chanting?"

Otto listened. "English," he said. It sounded like *Down, down, down*—one word for every step—*bring the flag down*. "They are marching to the flagpole."

"C'mon!" Kurt broke into a run, and Otto and Gerhard followed. Kurt shouted, "Johan! Sofie! All you kids!"

A phalanx of mounted guards blocked Central Avenue. At a gunshot, lines of riders spurred their horses toward the community building, splitting around it.

The children scattered, leaving Sofie alone, screaming as she ran a few steps toward the flagpole, then a few steps toward the community building. She turned her back to Otto and Kurt, as if to run across Eighth Avenue to her family's cottage.

"Sofie! Sofie!" Kurt cried again. The child pivoted to his voice. Otto saw Johan's head snap up, and he, too, ran toward his daughter.

"Kurt!" Sofie screamed, her arms out, and in another instant he had snatched her up without breaking stride.

Otto flung his arm across Gerhard's back. He ran ahead, half carrying his son, whipping his head toward the guards and back at the chanting mob. "To the Cappelmanns'!" he shouted to Kurt, who darted across the road with Sofie as Liese stepped out the cottage door.

"Johan! This way!" Otto waved with his free arm. Together, he and Gerhard stumbled across the road. Liese and Nina met them at the door, helping Gerhard, coughing badly, into the armchair. Nina leaned over him, rubbing hard between his shoulders.

Otto turned back to scan for other children, grateful to see one of the teachers running with the last two into the community building and slamming the door behind her. With everyone inside, Otto stood guard across the open door of the cottage until Johan could reach it.

Johan came at him with such speed, such fury, he barely had time to move aside. "Out of my house!" he shouted. "All you Austs—go!"

"Johan!" Liese's face had gone white. Nina, equally white, sat rigid on the arm of Gerhard's chair. "Johan, what are you saying?" Liese cried. "Of course our friends must stay until this disturbance is over." She looked toward the small settee, where Kurt sang softly to the sobbing child, rocking her gently. "Sofie might have been trampled."

With two long strides, Johan reached the settee. "Give me my daughter," he demanded. "Sofie! Come to me!"

Sofie wailed, tightening her grip on Kurt.

"Sofie!" Johan grabbed the girl's arm, pressing his fingers deep into her soft flesh.

"Stop it!" Liese pushed her husband out of the way. She bent over Sofie, still in Kurt's arms, and stroked her daughter's hair. "Come to me, sweetheart," she said. "We must wash your face."

"Go on, Noodle," Kurt said. She slowly released her hold on him and leaned into her mother's arms. Liese carried Sofie past Johan, shooting him a fierce look before slipping into the tiny washroom and firmly shutting the door behind her.

"Get out," Johan said, glaring at Otto. From the corner of his eye, Otto saw Kurt rise and move to the front window.

"Can you make out what's happening?" Gerhard asked.

"Someone's gone up the flagpole," Kurt said. "He's just a kid! Maybe fifteen. There must be a dozen guards aiming at him. Come and look, *Vati*."

Otto turned to the window.

"Wait," Kurt said, "they're backing up the horses. He's coming down." Kurt looked at his brother. "I'm going over. I'll try to find out what's going on."

"No!" Nina cried. "You must not!"

Before Otto could stop him, Kurt was out the door.

"I have ordered you all from my house," Johan said. "Go."

Otto faced him again. "What makes you angry, Johan? Why do you strike at us? We are your friends."

"No friends of mine. You are no longer welcome in my house." Johan's eyes blazed with contempt. "Keep away from my family. All of you."

Otto searched Johan's face for any small sign of explanation. Finding none, he said, "When you tell me why you rise against me, against my family, I will leave your house. Not before."

Johan's red face poured with sweat. "You told the Council. If not you, then Kurt—or another from your house."

"Told them what? And when? Their meetings are closed, and you know I never speak to any member unless I am forced to ask his pardon for walking in his path. Why should I?"

There was a single rap on the front door as Kurt pushed in. He left the door open and came to stand beside Otto. Gerhard, still breathing hard, had risen from the chair.

"They pumped themselves up at that rally." Kurt said.

"About the flag?" Otto asked.

Kurt shook his head. "They're saying—the Nazis are saying—that a couple of guards came in during the speeches, ripped down the swastikas and shredded them. That's what set them off." His eyes darted from face to face. In a voice tight and cautious, he continued, "O'Rourke's out there now. The guards that did it have owned up—gloated about it. Now Hasenburger's demanding the American flag be taken down, saying something about how prisoners can't be forced to work under the colors of the captive power. He's the one who sent the kid up the pole to cut it down. I heard someone say it was his own son. But now it looks like it was all a show to get negotiations started. When the kid came down, he didn't even have a knife."

Kurt laid one hand on Otto's shoulder, the other on Gerhard's. Nina stepped up and took Otto's arm. Kurt said, "We'd better go home, *Vati*."

"Not until Johan tells us why he has ordered us from his house."

"Perhaps it was Kurt after all," Johan said bitterly. "Always he has a way of finding out what the Nazis are doing. Feeding information is a means for getting information."

"What are you talking about?" Kurt said. "What's wrong with you, Johan? Why were you pulling up the stakes for the school?"

"Go ask your Nazi friends."

"Not my friends," Kurt said. "More like yours. You're the one who works with them."

Johan drew a sharp breath, as if he had been stabbed. "In these last hours, I have been removed from my position as head builder. Eighteen years at my trade—all my skill cast aside. From tomorrow, like a boy, I am assigned to deliver the ice." His throat looked painfully knotted. "For days I have felt suspicion tightening around me, like rope. They called me traitor, because someone told them I planned to offer myself to the Army. Who else but you, or your father?"

Kurt shook his head. "I didn't tell anybody anything. And I know my family didn't."

Johan's voice was cold. "I told no one else."

"You've done nothing but tell!" Kurt cried. "For months you've been hounding every family with sons, spouting your scheme, urging the younger fathers to sign up. Anybody who thought about it could figure out what you planned to do yourself."

"It had to be you," Johan said. "For privileges, special consideration. Your new assignment."

"The swimming pool?" Kurt raked his fingers through his sweaty hair. "You accuse me of trading information with the Nazis—for *that*? You're crazy. I am slave labor clearing the muck. *Vati*, too. God!" Kurt took a step toward Johan, his arm raised high as if to strike. He stopped, breathing hard, and released his fist.

"You will not deny," Johan said, "that this work brings you into connection with those who can benefit you—several well-regarded engineers, whose lessons will assist you when you are returned to Germany."

"Johan, the only connections I'm making are with mosquitoes. I'll be lucky not to wind up with malaria." Kurt's laugh was sour. "Tell you what, old friend—I'll deliver the ice. Why should I work twenty times harder to get my ten cents an hour? You can trade places with me, since you think you're so good at spotting snakes in the grass."

"Enough," Otto said. "Kurt, come here." He grasped his son's arm and drew him toward the door. Gerhard and Nina followed.

Otto turned to face Johan once more. "When you come to see that neither I, nor any of my family, have done you a wrong, we will greet you again as our friend. Until then," he put his arm around Nina, "we go."

Outside, they blinked against the sun. As Otto pulled the door closed, the wail of the siren rose. The Nazis had been fully surrounded by mounted guards. Accompanied by neither jeers nor pistol shots, all chins lifted proudly—Americans, Germans, even the horses—the two groups moved as one, slowly and calmly, toward Central Avenue. The Austs waited for the strange parade to pass, and then, not trying to talk over the siren, pulling the wagon with its soiled dishes rattling with every rut, they made their way silently back home.

VII

WHEN THE SCORPION, LURKING AMIDST the plates, plunged its stinger into her palm, Nina screamed. She screamed from her fingertips, from the soles of her feet, from the dark moist skin beneath her breasts, from the blood in her belly, from the bones of her neck and the spaces between her ribs. Even as she screamed, she understood her clamor to be many times greater than the pain shooting through her hand and down her arm, but she could do nothing to quell it. Her scream could have drowned out the siren—she remembered thinking that.

She remembered Gerhard sweeping the scorpion to the floor with a spoon taken straight from a boiling pot, crushing the demon under his heel.

And she remembered Otto and Kurt, their faces masks of shock, locking hands beneath her, making a chair of their arms. Crouching low, in an almost-run, they carried her to the hospital, while she screamed that terrible scream all the way. Mounted guards had to pull up their startled horses. People inside buildings opened windows to look. Children playing in the dusty yard near the new German School ran for shelter.

She thought she remembered—but perhaps she had only imagined it—that, as they passed the flagless flagpole, Liese Cappelmann opened her front door and hurried a few steps after them, calling their names.

When at last they reached the hospital, Otto and Kurt set her on a bench in the corridor. While Kurt went to find a doctor, Nina leaned all her weight into her husband, her scream withering to exhausted tears. And she was ashamed.

In time, a Japanese doctor came, examined her, and called for an orderly to bring a towel filled with ice and a nurse to prepare a bed. Nina understood she was to be kept in the ward for a day or two so she could be watched for signs of allergic shock or infection, but as her clothes were taken away and replaced with an over-bleached gown, she felt sure the real reason for her hospitalization was the screaming.

She had heard of such things happening in Crystal City—to women, to men, to German and Japanese. In an argument over the last dress in the store, two women had scratched each other's arms and faces raw. A man had punched a woman in the face when she complained that his children had trampled her sunflowers. There were tales of teenagers hurling hammers at doors and smashing windows with stolen chairs; of a woman wildly razoring her head bloody because she believed fire ants had nested in her hair; of a man running naked toward the fence and being shot in the back, dying at the feet of neighbors, who had shouted their pleas to the tower guard not to shoot.

When Nina had been but a few weeks in camp, Otto told her about the fence-sickness—*Gitterkrankheit*, they had called it at Fort Lincoln—a reaction swelling and bursting out of proportion to the pain that sparked it. He had nearly succumbed to it, he told her, two or three times, but he had not.

She had. Hers was the wall that had cracked. And after only seven months a prisoner, not the twenty-one Otto and their sons had endured. How could she ever expunge the humiliation of her screaming, which had stained her family, too?

She remembered Mr. Griffin leaning over his desk, looking at her with his earnest eyes, and she again heard his voice, urgent and anxious. "Do you understand, Mrs. Aust? You could be a prisoner behind barbed wire for years. Years." Had she nodded or said she understood? But she had not understood, not really—not truly and deeply.

The hospital workers moved like ghosts through the ward, making only muffled sounds. From time to time, one would hold a finger to his or her lips and breathe, "Sshh," but there was nothing to quiet. No visitors were admitted, and no patient made any effort to talk to another. Instead, whether still or restless, those in the beds—male, female, German, Japanese—lay next to but apart from each other, coiled in their antiseptic cocoons.

It had become like this on the outside, too. Every family had narrowed, existing as a small country unto itself. Month by month, new families arrived, others were sent away, and anyone—whether from political embitterment or weary, disillusioned outrage—might fall into the Council's fascist trap. And so they all held doors for each other and exchanged polite banalities, but no citizen of any small nation fully trusted the citizen of another. To make new friendships in this place required too much strength, too much trust—and she had too little of both to spare.

For a long while, lying useless in her white bed, Nina thought of everything that had happened in two crowded, empty, hopeless, loving, bitter years. Years she could make no sense of. Her true friends— Iris, Mr. Griffin, and Hugh, beloved Hugh—every day seemed further out of reach. Mr. Griffin's last letter had carried a tiny needle of hope: he had found an attorney in Wheatland, near Egon Merkel's farm, who would arrange to take down a formal statement from the old man regarding Kurt's character.

"With new evidence," Mr. Griffin had written, "I have grounds to ask for a new hearing. It might take a long time to get a court date, but when I do, the decision will likely be quick. I'll be in touch the moment I know more." It had been six weeks since she'd received that letter, and the prick of hope was scarring over.

It had been even longer since Iris had written the words, "Bess won't tell me so, but I do think she reads your letters. Please don't stop trying." There had been other letters from Iris after that, many, but never another mention of Bess. Still, Nina had kept writing—writing and writing—trying to touch Bess's feeling.

After Johan's outburst, Nina had tried with Liese, too—in the beginning. A few weeks after the picnic, she'd heard some women in the shop whispering that Hasenburger had called for the Cappelmanns to be shut out, barred from purchasing anything for five days. Though no one could risk buying supplies on another's behalf, Nina had filled her own basket with enough vegetables to double her stew, and she dug into her small savings to buy an extra loaf of bread and three small pastries at the bakery. At home, she saved back only one cup of milk for cooking.

She watched until she saw Johan's ice truck reach the end of North Road and turn right onto Twelfth Avenue; then she put everything in her wagon and covered it with a pile of clothes so that, if stopped, she could claim she was on her way to the sewing room to do her family's mending. Walking purposefully, with her eyes straight ahead, she took a wide, indirect route to the Cappelmanns' back door. She ought to have left everything beside the washtub, knocked, and gone away, but she wanted to see Liese, so she waited.

Liese opened the door an inch and peered through. "Go away, Nina. You have to go away."

"I am here only to bring the food," Nina lied. "Please, take it." She held out the bread.

Liese shook her head. "How could I explain to Johan?"

"Say only that it was left," Nina said desperately. "Say you do not know who brought it."

"He is my husband. I cannot put a lie between us, even if I disagree with him."

With that, Liese closed the door, but as Nina returned the food to her wagon, she thought she heard a sob. She wanted to hurl herself at the door, to pound with all her might, crying out for her friend. Instead she had only leaned against it, quietly pleading until a mounted guard stopped his horse and stared at her.

After that, Nina had seen Sofie once, playing hopscotch with the little Japanese girl, Michi, from the picnic. Michi, waiting for her turn to hop, had waved and called, "Come watch me, Mrs. Aust!" Sofie froze in the middle of her course. In Nina's memory, Sofie's eyes had filled with tears, even though she knew she had been too far away to see properly. Perhaps the tears had been her own.

On the day the German school opened for classes, Nina had seen Liese walking with Sofie into the schoolyard. But their backs were to her, and Nina did not call out to them—despite having stopped near the school on purpose, in hope.

She was worn out with trying, worn out with hoping. That was why her wall had cracked, releasing her immense, leagues-long scream.

When she woke the next morning, she felt an untouchable, bone-deep pain in her arm. After the breakfast trays had been cleared, the Japanese doctor said she could go home if she was able to walk on her own to the end of the ward and back. A young German girl who had mopped the floor earlier in the morning offered to brush out and re-pin Nina's hair, and then led her to a screened area where her laundered clothes had been folded on a chair. "Do you need any help?"

Nina opened and closed her hand several times. Most of the numbness had left her fingers. "Not to dress," she said. "But to get to the cottage? It is a long way in the heat."

"Where would we find your family?" the girl asked. She wrote down the cottage number as well as where Otto, Kurt, and Gerhard were working. "When you've finished dressing, I'll take you to the sitting room off the center corridor. You can wait there until someone comes."

Two Japanese women were already in the sitting room. One had heavy strands of gray through her black hair. Both were bent over a table dabbing at something with tiny brushes.

The younger woman looked up, and Nina saw she was barely more than a girl—perhaps twenty. "Hi," the girl said, laying aside her work and rising. The older woman remained seated, but gave a slight bow. Uncertain of what to do, Nina nodded to both and said to the elder, "I am sorry to disturb you. My husband or one of my sons will come for me soon."

"My mother doesn't speak much English," the girl said. She came around the table and offered her hand to Nina. "I'm Masami. My mother is Mrs. Kimura."

Nina stepped closer to the table where the older woman continued her work. "Mrs. Kimura. I am Mrs. Aust." Mrs. Kimura bowed again and sat back in her chair, as if inviting Nina to see what lay on the table—a flock of small wooden birds, each shaped, posed, and painted differently. Nina recognized sparrows and finches, thrushes and larks, hummingbirds and swifts. Some had not yet been fully painted, and Nina could see that Mrs. Kimura had been at work defining the sapphire feathers of a barn swallow with narrow brush-strokes of black.

"Lovely," Nina said. "Most beautiful."

"My father carved them. Some here, some in the camp before—as a way to bear up." Masami picked up a plump thrush with a slim russet tail and a creamy, brown-spotted breast. "He did most of the painting. He's very ill now, my father. The staff tried to make us leave, but my mother's terrified someone will take him away from us again, so every day, all day, we stay as close as we can, carrying on his work. It helps."

"I'm sorry," Nina said. "I hope he will recover his health." She found it soothing to look on the precise and elegant birds. "My son—my younger son—writes poems that will someday become songs, with the help of his dearest friend. Every word is a labor. I had thought he wrote to remember—but I think, like your father, it must be for enduring."

Masami closed her eyes and turned her head away. Then she bent to the floor and brought up a sewing basket Nina had not noticed before. "Would you help us with something?" She opened the basket and took out a thickly folded white cloth, from which a bold orange tiger growled, exposing its sharp teeth and its blood-red tongue.

The young woman spoke to her mother in Japanese, and the older woman nodded. Turning back to Nina, Masami said, "My mother's making this for my brother. He left a few weeks ago, for training, and she wants to get this to him before he's shipped out." She unfolded the cloth, revealing a long, narrow sash on which lines of bright red knots seemed to shoot out from the central tiger like rays of sun. There were fewer lines on the left side than the right, but a threaded needle waited, securely tucked in the fabric at the point where the next knot should be set. "It's a tradition—to wish the soldier the courage and strength of a tiger, and to guide him safely home, like the tiger who has roamed far." Masami ran her fingertip over a line of knots. "There have to be a thousand knots, each tied by a different woman—a thousand women, tying in blessings for good luck and long life."

"You will allow me?" Nina asked. She wished she had something like this, an amulet with the loving power of a thousand women, to protect Hugh and bring him home. "I fear I will be clumsy." She flexed her right hand and showed Masami where the scorpion had stung her.

"I can twist the thread on the needle for you," the young woman said, "and you can pull it through with your good hand."

In a moment, the knot was done. Nina looked at it, praying for the safety of a boy whose name she did not know. "I would that I were in myself a hundred different women," she said, "to place a hundred knots."

"Thank you," said Masami. Lowering her voice nearly to a whisper, she said, "My father was furious when my brother enlisted. They didn't make up before he left, and my mother thinks that's why he's so sick now." She shook her head. "It's cancer, most likely. She doesn't want him to know about the sash. But I want him to see it—so maybe he'll realize my brother and I can be American and Japanese at the same time." She held out the cloth to her mother, pointing to the newest knot.

Mrs. Kimura smiled at Nina and gave another bow, deeper than before. "Please," she said. She floated her hand over the flock of painted birds. "Choose. Please."

Nina felt a warm blush rise in her cheeks as she looked on the birds. All but one was positioned to perch—a goldfinch, with its magnificent black-bordered wings spread in glorious flight. She did not have to ask, for Mrs. Kimura saw where her gaze had settled. With both hands, Mrs. Kimura cupped the little bird and offered it to Nina.

"*Mutti?*"

She turned to Kurt's voice.

"I am making new friends," she said. She turned back to Masami and her mother and said, "My son, Kurt. My elder." She explained to Masami that Kurt sometimes made lovely things from wood, and she showed him the goldfinch.

Kurt, too, leaned over the table, and for a long time he studied the birds. When he looked to Mrs. Kimura and said, "They're wonderful. Fine work," she patted his hand, then grasped it tightly and said with effort, "Good son."

They said their goodbyes. Kurt took Nina's arm. As he led her through the corridor and toward the door, she felt renewed in strength, but the instant they were outside, she gasped and staggered backward.

"What is it? Are you dizzy? Is it the heat?" Kurt pulled her into a patch of shade and held her up. "Maybe you need to go back in."

"I'm sorry," she said. "I cannot explain." Tears spilled so fast she couldn't catch them all. "I'm sorry. I'm sorry. I cannot explain." How could she tell her son of all that had suddenly overwhelmed her—anxiety for Hugh, the sad worry that Mr. Kimura and his son might not come to forgiveness before one of them was lost, the pain of having failed her family, the fear that the guards looking down on her from their horses and towers were laughing at the madwoman who had screamed all the way to the hospital. "I cannot explain," she said again.

"You don't have to, *Mutti.*" Kurt took her hand in his and looked, it seemed, straight into the loneliest part of her heart.

Arm in arm, they walked slowly, Kurt asking her now and then if she needed to stop and rest. Each time she shook her head, even though she could feel her small strength pouring out of her with her sweat. The air was well over one hundred degrees, and the sun was not yet at its peak.

As they made their way down Eighth Avenue, she looked toward the Cappelmanns' cottage, which appeared oddly lonely now that the flagpole had been removed. She longed for a glimpse of Liese. Kurt slowed their pace, but kindly gave no other sign that he had noticed her looking. When she faced forward again, she saw a group of men coming toward them—Fritz Kuhn, strutting, with six of his followers keeping step behind him. Among them, she thought she recognized two of the men who had insulted Gerhard as she'd walked with him on her first morning in camp. As the group came closer, she heard a voice say, "*Bundesfüher—*" and one of the familiar men trotted up beside Kuhn and said something else she could not hear. All seven stopped to watch them, and suddenly seven arms shot out in salute: "*Heil Hitler!*"

Kurt tightened his hold on her arm but continued his smooth steps, saying quietly and casually, as in ordinary conversation, "Don't look. Keep walking."

She could feel the men's rage billowing out, pursuing them.

"Aust! Kurt Aust!" one voice shouted as they passed. "Aust!"

Kurt kept walking a few steps more, until the shout came again. Quietly he said to Nina, "Forgive me," and he released her, turned about, and delivered a rapid but wordless salute. He took her arm again and quickened their pace.

Her head and chest pounded, and she could barely feel her feet connecting with the ground. *Why?* she wanted to ask him. But how could she? In an instant, he had inhabited another country.

When they reached the house, Kurt suggested she lie down until the afternoon count. "I came straight from work, as you can see," he said, plucking his sweat-saturated shirt away from his chest. "I'm going to change and put these things in the washtub."

"I'll start the water running," Nina said, taking a step toward the back door.

Kurt stopped her. "I can do my laundry for today. For as long as necessary. We've already put everything together for a cold lunch. There's plenty enough for dinner, too." He smiled. "All you've done since you got here is take care of us. Let us look after you a little." He was her son again, a citizen of the nation of Aust.

"Thank you, darling," she said, still hoping he would explain why he had saluted the Nazis. "Perhaps I will try to rest for a time." She stood for a moment, watching him. "In the hospital, I remembered something. Iris wrote that she believed Bess reads our letters. I think I did not tell you at the time, because I was afraid it would hurt you."

He did look hurt, but his pained expression quickly dissolved into another she could not interpret.

"I hope you can sleep a little," Kurt said. He kissed the top of her head and went to his room, closing the door after him.

She wanted to take off her dress, but her tingling fingers resisted grasping the tiny zipper. She slipped off her shoes and lay down as she was. The pain in her arm intensified every other discomfort, made the heat unendurable, and she felt nauseated and confused by the pungent odor of tar that seemed to be above her, ready to spill hotly down. The bald sun was leeching the sticky blackness out of the roof and walls.

She kept thinking she should get up, that she needed to get up, that she would be more comfortable if she would only get up and sit in the kitchen with a glass of water, but she could not make her body obey.

She must have slept, because suddenly, out of darkness, Otto was standing over her, telling her she must get up because a guard had come for her. He was waiting outside with a jeep.

"No," she said, reaching for him. "No. I will not go. I will not leave you."

He caught her hands and pressed them gently between his. "It is a telephone call," Otto said. "Only that. The guard says there is a call for you. Or that it is coming—by appointment. But there are only a few minutes."

He bathed her face with a cloth he must have cooled with ice, and when he helped her sit up, he held it to the back of her neck.

"I don't understand," she said. "A telephone call?" And then she did understand and scrambled to her feet. "Otto! It must be Mr. Griffin, calling about Kurt. The order will have been reversed. Bad news he would have saved for a letter."

Otto's eyes sparked with joy. "The guard did not say who was calling. I think he does not know." He found her shoes, turned them upside down, and knocked them against the bed frame. "But you must go. He is waiting now to drive you to the gate."

Both her sons appeared in the doorway. "It will be Mr. Griffin," she said, trying in vain to smooth the wrinkles from her dress. "I am sure of it. With good news for Kurt."

The boys laughed. "Maybe we're going to make it to Herr Merkel's farm after all," Kurt said. Nina's heart leapt at the hope in his voice. Kurt flung his arm around his brother's shoulder and said, "You'll come, too. At least once in a while?"

"Of course," said Gerhard, catching Kurt's spirit, "whenever Hugh and I can be spared from our world tour."

"Nina, please," said Otto. "The guard is waiting. You must not miss the call."

In another moment, she was outside, the sun straight overhead like an umbrella of fire. The guard looked at her warily. "Number and name."

Confused by the demand, she said, "Mr. Charles Griffin," and struggled to recall his telephone number.

"*Your* number and name," the guard pressed.

"Yes, yes." She shook her head to clear it and heard herself reciting her identification number. "Aust, Nina."

"Into the jeep." The guard swung into the driver's seat.

Otto had followed and stood near the back of the jeep, ready to climb in. "Sir, my wife has not been well. May I come?"

"Are you Nina Aust?" Without waiting for Otto to move away, the guard slapped the jeep in gear and spun up a great cloud of dust.

Nina was still coughing and wiping her tearing eyes when the jeep rolled through the open gate and jerked to a stop before the administration building. The American flag that had loomed over the Cappelmanns' cottage dangled limply from its new pole. Another guard was waiting, and when she confirmed her identity, he led her into the building and down the hall to a small office with only one desk.

The woman sitting at the desk stood up and said, not unkindly, "I thought you weren't going to make it in time." She pulled out the chair and waved Nina over. "You can sit here." She snatched up the phone before the first ring was finished and said, "Confirm the name? She's here." She handed Nina the receiver and slipped into the hall, closing the office door halfway.

"Hello? Hello?" Nina pressed the receiver hard to her ear, fearing the call had been lost. "Hello? Is that Mr. Griffin?"

"Nina. Nina," said a voice that seemed to be drowning. "Nina." It was Iris.

"Hello?" Nina gripped the edge of the desk. "Hello? Iris?"

"Oh, Nina," the voice choked again—and then a terrible wail filled her ear. Just as suddenly, the wail, shrill and wretched, fell away from the receiver.

"Hello?" Nina said, longing for Mr. Griffin's voice.

"Nina—" said another voice, a man's, trembling. "This is Everett. Iris can't—" His ragged breath was backed by that terrible, distant wailing. "It's Hugh." The tremble swelled into something like a cry. "His ship. Disappeared."

Through the phone, where Everett's voice should be, Nina heard a rattle like paper. "I don't understand," she said, wishing she did not. "Disappeared."

"Due in port the middle of July," said Everett, his voice strangled. "It never showed."

On the desk, a calendar was turned open to the new month. October.

"The telegram came only this morning," he gasped. "They would have been waiting for some sign of survivors. Or word of prisoners."

Would have been.

"Two days ago, some wreckage washed up." She heard the rattle again. "The telegram—the telegram says, 'Your son, Hugh Sloan, missing and presumed dead.'" Everett let his own sob go then, the great hollow sob of a father who has lost a son.

Iris, Nina tried to say. "Hugh," she did say.

With a sparking click, the sob and wail vanished, and there was only a strange, crisp female voice saying, "Your time is up."

Another click, and Nina heard only waves of her own blood crashing in her ears.

The woman stepped into the office again, but she stood patiently, with her head down. Somehow Nina got out of the chair, around the desk, and through the door, murmuring a thank you to the woman as she passed.

A guard was waiting in the hall. He said nothing, only pointed to show she was to walk slightly in front of him. Outside, she stopped and looked about for a jeep. The guard said irritably, "To the gate."

When they reached the gate, she gave her name again, and two guards pulled it open. It clattered shut behind her the instant she was on the other side.

She walked without seeing, walked without feeling the sun baking the sweat from her skin and the tears from her eyes. She walked thinking that at any moment she was going to tear off her clothes and run toward the fence, like the Japanese man who had gone mad.

If they shot her, she would not have to walk back to hut C-15. She would not have to open the door and see her family gathering around her, feel their desperation to know what she knew and did not want to know.

If they shot her, she would not have to remember that Hugh had enlisted for thirty guarded, touchless last minutes with her son.

If they shot her, she would not have to find the courage to take Gerhard's hand and say to him, *The boy you love is gone. Our Hugh— your Hugh—is gone.*

VIII

WHEN NINA TOLD GERHARD, WHEN she said the words, though her whole body burned, outside and in, she looked into his eyes. She would have wanted the same from anyone bringing her such news of Otto.

From her son's eyes, she saw his soul drain like water. She could feel it falling through his chest, pausing briefly in hands that tightened in hers before dropping down, down, down to his feet and through the floor, boring into the earth and driving toward the sea to swirl in deep currents, searching its mate.

He sank away from her, but Otto caught him, and in hoisting their son's body, he dragged the miserable soul back.

What happened next, she remembered as a long braid of motion and sound: a slap from Otto to wake him; Gerhard lunging for the front door; Kurt catching him around the waist; Gerhard twisting free, bolting for the bedroom; Kurt hurtling against the door's closing, then deranged wolf-cries, scuffling, knocking, and Kurt shouting, "Don't! Give it to me!"; Kurt staggering out, a mangled notebook in his hand, panting, "The poems. Get the letters away from him!"; the floor littered with paper leaves; Gerhard on the bed, trembling and silent; Otto leaning over him, saying, "Son, son," trying to release fists from a sheaf of letters, still whole.

Since then, for eleven days, Gerhard had lain on his cot, curled open-eyed toward the black wall. He answered nothing but the siren, three times daily rising like an automaton, standing for counting weak as a dead tree. He drifted by the rest of them as if their bodies were shadows and their words wind, then passed again over the threshold and returned to his bed. Perhaps once a day, he stopped to turn on the tap, drinking only as much water as his cupped hands could hold. If he slept, none of them knew it. They sat up in shifts through the night, the same terror crawling like spiders over their skin: if they failed in vigilance, they could lose Gerhard, too.

In the mornings and evenings, so as not to disturb him, Kurt and Otto quieted their steps and Nina took down and put away pots and dishes as carefully as if a breath could shatter them. Gathered at meals, or afterward in the sitting room, the three of them found they couldn't speak.

To talk of Hugh was impossible. To talk of anything other than Hugh was unthinkable. His death hung between them like something invisible yet massive—the dense, raw agony of meeting every new day with the realization that Hugh was not in it, and would never be.

There was no going on as before—not for any of them. In every calculation of their variable futures, Hugh had been a constant factor. They had to learn a new algebra now.

Today, Nina was determined. Gerhard would take some broth, if only two or three ounces, and that would be a start.

"Gerhard," she said quietly but firmly as she entered the room. His eyes, as ever, were rigidly open. She knelt beside the bed and set the cup on the floor. "I know you can hear me, darling." She rubbed his back between his jutting shoulder blades. "I cooked this broth all night. To get enough bones, I had to pay the rest of our meat allowance for this week, so you will drink it."

Gerhard did not respond.

"Come, sit up." She stood and bent to embrace him, with one arm under his shoulders. He was surprisingly heavy, and she strained to lift him. "Help me," she ordered. Gerhard groaned but obeyed. When he was fully upright on the bed, his feet on the floor, she sat beside him, ready to catch him if he swayed. She handed him the cup. "Drink it all."

It took a long while. Every swallow was followed by a gasp of effort, and after he had drunk half, he pressed his hand to his mouth and leaned forward, as if expecting the broth to come up again.

"It's all right," Nina said. "It is to be expected. You have eaten nothing for so long."

In a few moments, his breath had steadied. He lifted the cup and drank the second half as he had drunk the first—swallow, gasp, swallow, gasp.

Nina took the cup. "Good. In a few hours, you will have a little more, and then a little more. We'll get you strong again."

Almost imperceptibly, he shook his head. "What for?" he rasped. "I can't see my own life anymore."

She put her arms around him and held him with all her might. "Look harder. *Harder.* I am there. Your father and brother are there. Look deeper—you will see Iris, too, like a second mother." Her tears slipped between her cheek and his bare shoulder. "You must not go away from us. Each of us needs the others to endure this terrible pain—like none we have ever faced before."

"And Bess?"

She caught her breath and held it against a sob. "There is too much fog to see her now, but she is there." *Let it be true.* Nina struggled to see through that fog. *Let it be true.*

For several days she had sat with a pen in her hand, two blank letter forms before her, trying to think what words Iris would be able to bear when they reached her six weeks from now, and what words Bess would not despise her for sending. In the end, she had written the same message to them both: *I love you. Nina.*

"I still can't see it." Gerhard's head dropped forward, too great a burden for his neck. "Any future. I don't want to."

"Sleep," Nina said, slowly easing her son down. "No decisions of any kind without sleep. You are far behind with yours." She knelt again beside the bed. "Sleep now." He closed his eyes. She stroked his hair, and though outside the sun was high, she sang softly of a peaceful moon rising to light the dreaming woods. "*Der Mond ist aufgegangen, die goldnen Sternlein prangen....*"

"Don't!" Gerhard grasped her hand and clutched it to his chest. "Don't."

"Forgive me. Sleep now, my darling boy. Sleep, sleep, sleep."

Over and over she murmured her refrain, stroking his hair, gently rocking him forward and back, forward and back, and after a long while, his breathing slowed and his grip on her hand relaxed.

The next day, he allowed her to bring a cloth and a basin of water to wipe his skin, and, after that, he let her tear a bit of bread into each cup of broth before he drank it. In a few days more, he let Kurt help him to the washroom while Nina changed the sheets, and the next morning, with just the two of them in the house, he sat at the table to eat a coddled egg.

Twenty-six days after Nina had made those terrible words real by saying them, Gerhard, sitting at the dining table, greeted Otto and Kurt when they returned in the evening. He said to his brother, "If you'll help me, I think I'd like a shower."

"Let's go now," Kurt said. He rolled their clean clothes inside towels, tied the bundle with a length of rope, and slung it over his shoulder.

Gerhard's knees buckled as Kurt helped him toward the door, and Otto jumped up, saying, "I should come as well."

"We'll be okay," Kurt said. "He's just not used to his feet yet."

Otto wedged by them and stood at the door, his hand on the knob. "I also need a shower before dinner."

Steady now with the help of Kurt's powerful arm, Gerhard shook his head. "Please, *Vati*, I don't need a king's worth of servants."

"Of course you don't, darling," said Nina. With her eyes, she urged Otto away.

For a few moments, Nina and Otto stood together in the doorway, watching their sons move slowly down the road, their arms around each other. From a distance, it was impossible to tell that Kurt bore nearly all his brother's weight.

"You have a quick wash here," Nina said. "I want to talk to you while they're gone."

While Otto went to the washroom, Nina opened windows, more to release the heat than to let in any cool air. There was nothing but the calendar to tell them it was the first week of November. *A year*, she thought when she remembered. A year since she'd gotten Otto's letter saying, *We can be together*; a year since she had run to Mr. Griffin's office and told him she would go, that she would leave that very day if she could. A year since she had quarreled with Bess; a year since she had seen Bess's blue eyes full of love instead of suspicion; a year since she had come into her little room and found Bess's note, the last time she had heard the girl's voice lifting up out of words on paper. Almost two years since she had sent her whole family—Otto, Kurt and Bess, Gerhard and Hugh—into the morning with a breakfast she would have called ordinary then, but wondrous now. The memory set her reeling. Never again, never again. Never all of them again.

Otto came out of the washroom, buttoning his clean shirt. Nina pointed him to his place at the table, where she had left the letter. "I've had it for nearly a week." She sat down across from him while he read Mr. Griffin's explanation of the court's decision to deny Kurt a new hearing. The judge had deemed the testimony of Egon Merkel unreliable and irrelevant because, despite having been paroled, he had not been cleared of suspicion.

"According to the court," Mr. Griffin had written, "Mr. Merkel is still an alien enemy, potentially dangerous, and subject to rearrest."

She reached for Otto's hand. "There is talk of another ship going out in the New Year—with Germans this time." Two months ago, with little notice, more than half the Japanese in Crystal City had been deported or repatriated. Since then, hundreds more had taken their places, arriving from camps in the west. "If Kurt is on that ship," she went on, "we must be as well—otherwise we lose him." She took the letter from Otto and laid it on the table between them. "You know I am right. There is nothing left for us here. Kurt cannot stay." She breathed deeply and swallowed hard against a sob. "Gerhard has no reason to stay."

"Very well." Otto nodded. "I will write to Egon and post the letter in the morning. But for now, this stays between us. In a day or two, I will explain to Kurt, but I think Gerhard is not yet ready to hear it."

She agreed and asked him to put the letter in their room, in a place where their sons would not accidentally come upon it while clearing the house of scorpions. She set the table, trying to think of how Germany would look after years of this new war. Would they find still standing any place they had once known, anyone they had ever cared for?

A figure streaked past the front window and Nina heard shouting. "Otto! Otto Aust!" Fists beat at the door. "Otto! Come quickly!"

"Who is there!" Nina cried.

The door opened before she reached it, and Johan Cappelmann stumbled in, shirtless, breathing hard, his eyes wild. "Your sons! The Nazis—they are beating your sons!"

IX

A S THEY RAN, CUTTING BETWEEN huts, Otto tried to ask questions, but Johan, already out of breath, could manage only to point and pant out, "This way." Otto looked back for Nina, lagging many strides behind, but when she saw him slow for her, she waved him on.

Johan stumbled, fell. Otto reached for him and lifted, but his legs gave way and he slipped to the ground.

"Here, I'll get you up," Otto said.

Johan shook his head. "Showers," he gasped. "Middle building."

Nina reached them. "What does he say?" She ran a few steps on.

"With Nazis about, we cannot leave him, Nina!" Otto cried. "Stay. Let him get his breath." He saw terror in his wife's eyes—terror he wanted to drive out, but already he had lost too many steps.

Otto ran on, looking about for a guard. Why were there no guards? Why no sound of alarm? He ran across Ninth Avenue, too far from the fence to shout up to the men in the towers, though he knew they could see him—and whatever he was running toward.

"Kurt!" he shouted. "Gerhard! Kurt!"

A naked figure, hunched and hobbling, appeared between the first and second shower houses. It was Kurt, blood from his head running in rivers down his shoulders.

From the line of Quonset huts facing the shower buildings, a man dashed out with a sheet. "I heard the cries," he said, draping the sheet around Kurt.

Otto leaned over his son. "Kurt, where is Gerhard?"

Kurt tried to lift his arm, but gasped with pain. "My fault, my fault."

The other man pointed deeper into the center of the camp, toward the recreation hall. "That way. I saw several carry off another man."

With enormous effort, Kurt nodded.

"Go on," the man said. "My wife and I will look after him. Already some neighbors have gone for the ambulance."

Many others had gathered in front of the huts. Otto shouted, "Who will help me?"

Three men called, "Yes! Yes! I will!" and caught up to him, confirming the direction the other man had given. Together, they ran straight down Lincoln Avenue. Still there were no guards.

The recreation hall was in Otto's sight—all the lights out, the smell of burning somewhere near. "Gerhard!" he shouted. "Gerhard Aust!" The others took up the cry. One broke away to circle behind the recreation hall.

Ahead in the road, at the point where every morning Otto and Kurt crossed to help dig out the swamp, another man—slim, but not tall enough to be Gerhard—waved his arms. "Stop! Stop!"

"Gerhard!" Otto shouted again, determined to run on until he heard his boy answer.

The man shot his arms out to his side. "Stop! Stop!"

Otto's companions darted past the outstretched arms, but Otto pulled up short, his feet sliding in the dust, nearly knocking down the man, a Japanese. Otto doubled over, struggling for breath. "My son. Gerhard. My son!"

"Help is here," said the man. "Get your breath, sir."

Otto pushed himself up again. Beyond the stranger, many others—including two guards on horseback—moved around the perimeter of the muddy pit that was to become the swimming pool.

Suddenly, the Japanese man slammed against him, crying, "Out of the way!" An ambulance sped past them and squealed to a stop near the horses.

"What is happening?" With every hard breath, Otto drew in more dust. "My son." He coughed and coughed as the man grasped his arm to steady him. "Where is he?"

"Sir—it is very bad. But you see the ambulance has come." He called to someone else Otto could not quite see, and another Japanese man appeared by his side.

"Can you take his other arm," the first man asked, "and help me get him to the hospital? He believes the boy in the pit may be his son."

The pit. Gerhard, in the pit.

Otto felt the second man take half his weight. The three of them began to walk on the side of the road, away from where Gerhard must be. "What is happening?" Otto asked again.

"I was walking with some friends," the first man said. "We thought we saw a fire some distance ahead, so we walked on to see where it was coming from."

A barrel of fire for the Nazis' torches.

The man went on. "We heard a scream—most terrible. A moment later, the fire went out. We hid ourselves behind the pump house, but we could see. Four or five together, walking short steps, carrying something, we thought. They crossed the road to the swimming pool. We heard them count together—it sounded a count, in German—and they swung something large into the pit. We shouted at them, 'What are you doing? What have you thrown?' and they ran away, scattering all directions."

In his mind Otto could see his boy, naked as a flayed deer, flung high to drop fast and hard into snake-infested mud—and the brutal cowards, scuttling like rats.

"We ran to our houses for more help—more men, more lights," the man continued. "We took our lights, walked around the edge, calling and listening. Only a small sound, but we followed it and saw the boy. Some ran for the guards—they surrounded the horses to make the guards come. Others went for a cot, and the stronger men among us climbed into the pit to carry him up. I heard you calling and came out to find you."

The men stopped as the ambulance passed. No two parts of the camp were farther apart than the swimming pool and the hospital—an unbearable distance. They set off again, increasing their pace, cutting diagonally across the compound—past latrines, through sections of two-family dwellings, between the laundry and boiler house, and around regiments of tin Victory Huts. At last the hospital came into view.

They found Johan pacing outside. His trousers were still thick with dust from his fall, but he had put on a shirt. Otto thanked his Japanese companions, realizing only after they walked away that he had failed to ask their names, or the names of anyone who had rushed to help him. He turned to Johan.

"Is Nina inside?"

"She is at my house, with Liese. I thought it best, not knowing what she might see here."

"What do you know?"

"With Kurt—perhaps not so bad. I asked the driver what he heard. There is a cut on his head, not deep. The medic thinks a few cracked ribs, possibly broken, but nothing worse. Bruises, of course."

"And Gerhard?"

"I saw them take him from the ambulance." Johan looked at the ground. "Had I not seen the attack, I would not have known him."

A new weakness rocked Otto's balance. He flung a hand to Johan's shoulder. "Thank you for coming to me." He had meant only to stop himself from falling, but suddenly he was embracing Johan, near to weeping. "Thank you. Thank you, my friend."

"Yes, yes," Johan said, patting his back. "Yes, Otto. My friend. Go to them now. I will bring Nina."

People tried to stop him, but Otto shouldered his way down the hall and into a room where everyone was too busy to bother with him. Women, dressed as nurses, scurried in answer to the calls of two men—one German, one Japanese—who were bent side by side over a gurney Otto could not quite see. He stopped a woman, gave his name, and said he was looking for his sons who had been badly beaten. She pointed, and Otto found himself at the foot of the gurney where the doctors worked.

What he saw was monstrous.

Gerhard, naked, lay on his back. A sheet was draped over his lower half, exposing only his calves, bruised, slashed and bleeding, both his ankles knocked at impossible angles. Above the sheet, on his chest, more slashes and whorls of rising bruises, suggesting fists and cudgels. A swollen and painful curve between wrist and elbow told of a complete break in his right arm.

But the greatest shock was his son's face—so lumpish, oozing, and bloody, Otto understood why Johan would not have recognized him.

It was here the doctors focused their urgent attention. One held a pitcher, pouring a thin, steady stream of water over Gerhard's left cheek, while the other peered through a magnifying glass at the pulsing burn. Even now, Otto could see the sharp, deliberate outline of a triangle.

The beasts had branded his son.

He heard Nina's voice as she called out, "Otto! Kurt! Gerhard! Where are you?"

She must not see. She must not see. Otto reached the door in time to block her.

Sobbing, she struggled against his embrace, hit his shoulders with her fists. "Let me in! Let me in!"

He couldn't find a voice to say anything to her, so he held her, tighter and tighter, making himself a mountain she couldn't get round. At last she accepted the power of his arms and let him carry her down the hall and into a small sitting room.

When the wave of her sobs subsided, Otto told her what he knew, beginning with what Johan had said of Kurt. Of Gerhard, he told her about the pit, and of his bruises, long cuts and broken bones. He told her everything—except the burning. She would know of it soon enough, have to learn to look upon the wound, and then upon the scar Gerhard would carry in the open for the rest of his life.

There were three chairs in the sitting room. Otto pushed two together and centered the third one facing them. They sat down side by side, and Otto showed Nina how, if they leaned against each other, with their feet propped on the extra chair, they could rest more comfortably while they waited, perhaps even doze a little. From time to time throughout the night, someone—sometimes a doctor, usually a nurse—came to ask questions: how old was Kurt and had he ever had a head injury before; was Gerhard the same young man they had treated for pneumonia-scarred lungs; had he suffered a recent illness that might account for his having lost so much weight. Other times, they brought information: Kurt's injuries were not severe—some cracked ribs—so he could be released in a day or two, but couldn't do heavy work for several months; Gerhard's broken bones had been set, the cuts cleaned, the deepest of them stitched; he would be continuously sedated for three or four days, possibly more, in order to keep him still, and to spare him the worst of the pain from the breaks and the burn.

"Burn?" Nina's face went white. "He is burned? Where? How?"

Otto had to tell her then.

"First the ugly jokes," he said. "I have heard them mocking. And now, they mark him so all the world will judge him for what they think him to be." Nina fell against him and wept into his chest, but, now that he had begun, Otto could not stop talking. "They mean for him to have no life at all—a life of torture."

Nina put her hand over his mouth. "Stop, Otto. Listen to me." Her face was wet and splotched red from all her crying, but she looked into his eyes. "Listen, and hear me. As to the mark, it does not alter who Gerhard is—a boy who loves, with no evil in any of his love." She slid her hand to his cheek. "Do you understand? Do you understand that his grief for Hugh is what mine would be for you?" She choked on a sob. "Perhaps even greater—for they have not had their lives together as we have. Otto, tell me you understand what I say."

He had a strange vision, of Nina's words shaping themselves into a key—a key that fit the lock of a trunk he hadn't known existed, but that held all the thoughts that had drifted through his mind ungrasped. "I understand," he said. "And I am ashamed."

"Ashamed of Gerhard?"

"No!" He held her tightly. "Ashamed of myself, for not realizing. If I had seen, I could have done more. I could have protected him." He rubbed away his tears until they were too many, and these he let roll down, spilling into Nina's hair.

Her cheek still pressed against his breastbone, Nina said, "To have his life—Hugh's, too—was always going to be a great struggle. But because of this mark, so much more difficult. He cannot go with us to Germany. Impossible."

What was to be done?

"Mr. and Mrs. Aust?" The nurse who had become most familiar to them—a young Japanese woman with softly styled black hair and gentle brown eyes—stood in the doorway. "Your son—Gerhard." She said his name slowly, taking care to pronounce it correctly. "He's deeply asleep now, breathing easily, so he won't be feeling any pain at all."

Nina wiped her face, stood up, and smoothed her dress. "I should like to sit with him."

The nurse hesitated. "He won't know you're there."

"I will know," Nina said. "I promise I will make no disturbance." She pressed away a few more tears. "Not a sound."

"Please," said Otto. "Let her come." He looked at the nurse. "Perhaps I should go back to the cottage to collect Kurt's clothes—our elder son."

"It's long after curfew," the nurse said. "I could get you a pass, but it would be better for you to wait until morning."

"In front of the hospital, then. To stretch my legs."

The nurse nodded. "That should be okay. But only in front. The guards make it hard for even the staff to get in and out for night shifts."

"Just wait here, Otto."

He grasped Nina's hand and lifted it to his lips. "You have promised our friend the nurse you will make no disturbance. I have promised her I will not go far. Are we not people of our word?"

When he stepped outside, Otto looked up, trying to see through the floodlights to the black sky—perhaps two hours before dawn. The infinite darkness above intensified the light, which was absorbed and reflected by the yellow ground, glowing like a plain of fool's gold.

There was an eeriness in looking across the camp, knowing that if the electricity were cut, the whole of Crystal City would be swallowed into the black. It was eerie, too, knowing that, from the towers, dozens of eyes watched him turn his head, take a few steps east, push back his hair, retrace his steps west—eyes that had the power to decide, in the second it took to lift and cock a rifle, whether that little man, exposed as he paced through the surreal light, deserved to die. So many guards to watch him, to evaluate his slightest movement—but last night, none to help him and Kurt but other German prisoners, and none to help Gerhard until the Japanese had taken it on themselves.

From Johan and Kurt, when he was well enough to talk, he would learn the identities of the attackers. But he would also ask Kurt if he could remember the name or the face of the man who had cared for him before the ambulance came. And when he found that man, he would ask about the others. Then, in the Japanese section, he would go door to door until he found everyone who had helped despite the risk.

He looked up to the nearest tower, feeling a fresh surge of hatred toward the guards, who, for once, might have used their weapons for good, to keep an innocent boy from being beaten nearly to death by foul creatures who had no right to claim the name of *men*.

He went back inside. The hospital seemed quieter, all the patients asleep, the doctors and nurses going about their business in restful, well-deserved silence. He'd been in the sitting room only a moment when the young nurse returned.

"My wife? My son?"

"That's all fine," she said. "Your older son—Kurt—he wants to talk to you. He's been asking for you since he got here. I told him you were here and that he could see you tomorrow, after he'd had some sleep, but he won't quiet. I can get him into a wheelchair and bring him to you here."

"What is it? What troubles him?"

The nurse shrugged. "I'll go get him."

His broad-shouldered son looked strangely small and frail in the wheelchair. His head was wound with layers of gauze, so low on his forehead his eyes seemed sunken in the darkly bruised sockets. The strength of his chest and arms was lost in the large and shapeless hospital shirt. Because of his fractured ribs, he held himself stiff against the back of the chair—a great effort, Otto could see, and every breath cost him more.

The nurse wheeled him into the room. "Bring him back to Ward 6 when you're ready," she said to Otto, then slipped out, closing the door behind her.

Not twelve hours ago, Otto had stopped his work and waited for Kurt near the road, where the dressing rooms would be built when the swimming pool was finished. They had talked easily all the way home—about what, he could not now remember—but he had taken notice of the ease as it happened, because it was the first time he had felt it since Nina told them Hugh was lost. He had known the ease would fail again when they got back to the house, but even so, he had been glad for it—a first sign that they would, in time, find their way through their grief. Now, he could not think how to begin.

With a sharp breath, Kurt said, "Gerhard?"

"He is here."

Kurt nodded, showing he had been told this. He took another sharp breath, held it, and let his words rush out with it. "Nurse says he's worse than I am—but he'll be okay?"

Otto returned a quiet, "Yes. There is good hope for that." Several hours ago, the German doctor had come to the sitting room and said if they could prevent infection from taking hold, Gerhard would likely recover, though his knitted bones might trouble him for years and his body would bear many scars. It was clear Kurt did not yet know of the brand seared onto his brother's face. There was no good in telling him now.

"*Vati!*"

The deep misery of Kurt's cry shocked him.

"I'm sorry. Sorry. Sorry." Each word was its own cry. "It's my fault. All my fault."

Otto put his hand over Kurt's. "You could not have known Nazi brutes were hiding, waiting for a chance. It could have been anyone at the showers. How could you have known?" As he said the words, he was stung by doubt—a doubt that shocked him.

Earlier, while he and Nina talked of the attack, trying to discover a reason, she told him that not long ago she had seen Kurt return a Nazi salute to Kuhn and his followers. "He did not want to do it. I believe this," Nina said. "They were shouting his name, demanding he attend them—and he resisted. Perhaps he was afraid for me. I don't know. He did not explain."

There were too many things Kurt had not explained. Except for the daily counts, Gerhard had not been out of the house in nearly a month—and yet the Nazis had set upon him with such ferocity it seemed deliberate. Was it because he was so clearly the weaker of the two young men? Or because they recognized Gerhard as particular prey? Otto thought of the brand again—a tool someone had taken time to shape, a fire at the ready.

"Kurt, did you know? Or suspect?"

"You think I'd lead my brother into a trap?"

"Of course not." Otto pressed his head between his hands. He could not believe such a thing of his son—but neither could he believe all had been coincidence. "I want to understand what happened. How it happened. Even when I found you hurt, when the man came with the sheet to cover you, you said you were to blame. What is it you believe to be your fault?"

"I knew they were watching him—for a long time." There was a ratcheting sound to Kurt's breathing, as if to take a moderate breath he had to take several tiny ones, holding each while he leapt across the pain to the next. "I didn't know they were watching *for* him."

"You should have told me," Otto said, "so I too could have watched them. But still, I should have seen. You cannot carry all the blame."

Kurt shook his head. His face grew red in his struggle to draw an adequate breath. "My fault all of you are here."

"No, Kurt. We have talked of this before. In early days, we each believed the same—that something we had done had brought trouble on the family."

"I don't mean at the beginning." He lifted himself straighter, wincing at the pain. Tears clung to his lashes. "At Fort Lincoln. That day McCoy called me in. Remember?"

Otto had never forgotten—the fogged look in his son's eyes, his sudden obsessive need to imagine the camp where Gerhard was held and believe it to be warmer and greener than Fort Lincoln. After that, he had abandoned Johan's woodshop for the seamen's barracks and, with their help, transformed himself into a corrupted American Mephistopheles.

"Kurt…what happened that day?"

"McCoy, two guys in suits. Looked like FBI agents. They said they weren't." The sentences cost Kurt great energy, so he rested for a moment. "They named some other office. I said it sounded made up. One showed a gun. The other told me to shut up." He paused for another breath. "Said they'd heard about my proficiency with dialects. Said I looked so much the perfect Aryan they could put me in an SS uniform, drop me anywhere in Germany, and no one would ever suspect I was a spy."

Otto sat back in his chair, remembering how McCoy had enjoyed his game of cat-and-mouse, opening his desk and throwing down the small map. He could easily imagine that smug look, tripled, turned on Kurt.

Kurt struggled on. "I told them they were crazy. The way I walk, move my hands. What I notice, what I talk about, even my inflections—everything would give me away. I'd be no good to them, dead inside a week. They said they'd take that chance—and make it worth it to me."

"How?"

"They promised you and Gerhard would be released the minute I was on the ground in Germany. Full pardons—no chance of rearrest." He gripped the wheelchair's armrests. "I said there was nothing to pardon you for—that whoever had ordered us all locked up were the ones in need of pardons. They didn't like that."

"Your refusal—was that not an end to it?"

Kurt shook his head. "Only the start. They said they'd see to it you and *Mutti* got the restaurant back, or give you enough cash to set up somewhere else."

Otto looked out the room's single window. The eerie yellow from the floodlights was slowly dissipating, overtaken by the dawn.

"I told them, do all that first," Kurt gasped, "and I'll be your spy. They laughed—said if they did that, there'd be no incentive for me to follow through. I said I had the same problem." Tears ran down his face. "I would have done it, *Vati*, if I could have believed they'd let you go. But how could I believe them?"

Otto could be quiet no longer. "You are not to blame. Never would we want you to sell yourself in such a way. I would say you must forgive yourself—but there is nothing to forgive."

"There is. I made it worse." Kurt tried again to sit straighter. "When they let me go, they said if I told anyone about the meeting, they'd get the FBI to pick up *Mutti* right away. And they'd see to it that evidence we were planning sabotage got in among the things taken from the restaurant."

Otto felt the strings of all his nerves pulling tight, forcing the air out of his chest. On every side, his family was trapped in a thicket of lies. Where was there an opening they could struggle through?

"But still, I made it worse. I should have walked away, shouldn't have let them get to me. That stupid play—I handed them an excuse to arrest me. One nobody would question." He shook so hard the wheelchair rattled. "They came again when I was in the stockade. And once at Kenedy. Same story, different men. I almost agreed." He curled his hands into fists, opened them to stretch his fingers. "But I knew they were lying—and I told them so. That's when they said I'd be going back to Germany one way or another, so why not take easy way and do what they wanted. I didn't even answer that time. A few days after, I got the deportation notice. So that was one threat they made good on."

"Enough to keep you quiet," Otto said.

"Enough. Because what if the rest was true? Maybe they'd already planted something. Maybe they were waiting for my doubts to drive me crazy." Kurt's voice seemed strangled. He lifted a hand to his throat, massaged it gently. "If I'd said yes, maybe they would have let you go, saved the restaurant. Maybe Gerhard would have been home for his graduation—and he would never have been here." Tears poured down his cheeks as heavily as the blood had. "If I'd said yes, maybe Hugh wouldn't have enlisted—and wouldn't be dead."

"It is too much, Kurt," said Otto. "You are not to blame." The words were true, but far from enough. Otto could see his son would have willingly paid his life for the rest of them—but even that willingness might not be enough to quiet his doubts, to stop him from tormenting himself with the thought that a yes instead of a no might have prevented so much suffering.

"Enough, son." Otto rose and gripped the back of the wheelchair. When they reached Ward 6, he helped Kurt into the bed.

"Sleep now," Otto urged, laying his hand softly over his son's heart. He held it there until his boy had fallen asleep.

It was time, now, for him to act.

In the hall, he saw the Japanese nurse who had been so kind, and he asked after Gerhard. She waved for him to follow. When she came to another door, she put a finger to her lips and pointed inside. It was a small ward with four beds, only one of them occupied. Nina had drawn her chair as close to the bed as possible, and she was asleep now, her head fallen to the side, just touching the edge of Gerhard's pillow.

Otto moved away from the door and, his voice as soft as he could make it, said to the nurse, "When she wakes, tell her I will not be away long."

When he reached the hut, Otto realized he'd never been alone there before. It seemed even smaller without his family in it. A darker patch of floor around the icebox told him that all the ice had melted, overflowing the drip pan. Most of the water had seeped into the concrete, but he got the mop anyway, trying to tidy as Nina would have done. Inside the icebox he found a half bottle of milk, still cool to the touch, so he drank it. Beneath Gerhard's bed, he found a small crate with a pen and some blank letter forms. He took two, along with the pen, and carried them out to the table.

Paper was hard to come by in the camp—even the government-issued sheets designed for their twenty-four-line letters—so after placing one form in front of him and writing neatly at the top *To Commander O'Rourke*, he sat for a long time, sifting through sentences in his head.

He filled the first five lines with his family's brief history in the camp—their names, their identification numbers, his place among the original builders, Nina's status as a voluntary internee, Kurt's and Gerhard's ages, and the jobs they had held in Crystal City. In the remaining lines, he described the attack on his sons and the reasons for his suspicion that the men responsible were followers of the Nazi Fritz Kuhn. "There are matters most urgent," he wrote, "which I hope we can settle between us. I will wait at the gatehouse until you agree to speak with me." He signed and dated the note. If he'd had a clock, he would have added the hour and minute.

It took only a few minutes to write his letter to Egon Merkel. When it was done, he took it to his room and laid it under his good white shirt folded on the shelf of the pegboard Kurt had made. While he was shaving, the morning siren sounded. He finished quickly and was still buttoning his clean work shirt when he took his place in front of C-15.

As Otto knew he would, the guard stopped his horse and dismounted. When the guard demanded an accounting of the missing persons, Otto explained that his wife was at the hospital, waiting for news of their sons, both of whom had been so badly beaten last night that they might have died, had not many other German and Japanese prisoners risked their own safety to help. Otto looked directly into the guard's eyes as he said this, meaning to press the point that none of his kind had moved to break up the attack or pursue the criminals.

The moment the release siren blared, Otto was on his way to the gate, where he presented his sealed note to the guard and said, "Please deliver this to the commander now. I will not leave until I have spoken to him."

It wasn't long before the guard returned for him and Otto was led through the gate, into the administration building, and to the door of Mr. O'Rourke's office.

O'Rourke stood when Otto entered, and, with formal politeness, offered his hand and invited Otto to sit down. He asked only a few questions, gathering more detail about Gerhard's injuries before he gave Otto permission to make his proposal.

Within twenty or thirty minutes, an operator had connected a call to Mr. Charles Griffin in Newman, Indiana. "The limit is three minutes," O'Rourke said when he handed Otto the receiver. "The operator will give you a fifteen-second warning."

Having already written the note, Otto found he could explain to Mr. Griffin what had happened, clearly and concisely, without being overcome again by the horror of it. Even so, he could feel less than a minute remaining, so he said, "You must fight for his release, sir. Gerhard cannot remain here much longer, and he cannot go into Germany. Either will mean his death." Otto's mouth had gone dry. "Gerhard is a man—as Hugh was."

"I understand," said Mr. Griffin.

"Fifteen seconds," said the operator.

"I'll start this morning," said Mr. Griffin. "I'll send you a telegram—whatever happens."

"Nina must not know, unless the release is granted." Otto heard a small click as he gave his thanks, so he didn't know if the lawyer had heard him say, "Someday, we will find a way to repay your goodness." He would write that.

When the call was done, Otto restated his promise to Mr. O'Rourke and went back to the hut to retrieve the letter he had written to Egon, explaining his plan and asking if Nina and Gerhard might come to Wyoming without him. On the way back to the hospital, he dropped it off at the post office.

Three days after Christmas, while Otto was at work, troweling smooth a section of freshly poured concrete, a guard came to tell him he had a telegram. He finished his task, asked his supervisor for an hour's leave, and headed toward the gatehouse, taking the long way round the community building in case Kurt, teaching the mathematics class in the German school, might happen to glance out the window and see him passing.

When the gatehouse guard handed him the telegram, he stood for a moment, looking around him for a place where he might open it—a place where he could hide himself for a few moments while he absorbed the news. If it was not as he wished, his family would never know of it, and the secret, in all its layers, would be his burden only.

The carpentry shop was just there—where, almost a year ago, he had waited, watching for the bus that would deliver Nina into his arms again. Soon, he might be the one on a bus, being carried away from her, not to hold her again for years, if ever.

The few men who were working in the shop paid him no mind when he took a seat on the bench, just inside the door. He didn't know them—they were new to Crystal City—and he felt no need to know their names, where they had come from, or how.

He breathed in the sweetness of the sawdust, letting it carry him, briefly, to some of the few sweet memories of this fenced life: Kurt sanding smooth the inlay of Bess's name on the writing box; laughing when Johan tripped over the bubbling words as they sang the Champagne song from *Die Fledermaus* while they hammered boards for the stage floor; the clean pop when his saw broke through the first beam he cut in Crystal City, knowing his sons were on their way to him.

Two of the men in the shop had stopped their work to watch him, but he looked through them, pretending not to see. He opened the telegram.

Gerhard Aust cleared. Release set mid-February 1944. More details by mail. C. Griffin.

He took another deep breath, letting the wood smell saturate him. First, he would return to the gatehouse, and they would take him again to the commander's office, where he would keep the promise he had made in exchange for the phone call to Charlie Griffin. O'Rourke would watch him sign his name to the voluntary repatriation form, and Otto would watch the commander add his name to the transport list, beside Kurt's, for a ship called *Gripsholm*.

When that was done, he would fold the telegram into his pocket and return to finish the day's work.

1944

THOSE LAST DAYS, NINA WOULD remember as still photographs, taped haphazardly in a scrapbook she never wanted anyone else to see. Liese Cappelmann pointing to Otto's name on the first page of the notice for repatriation; herself, tearing the page from the board; herself, shaking the notice in Otto's face; Otto and Kurt massed with others in the warehouse, hundreds of hands plunged deep into piles of castoff clothes, desperate to snatch up winter boots, heavy coats, anything wool; she and Gerhard standing with Kurt and Otto for hours, in a line of over four hundred outside the community building, everyone there believing they had come only to deliver the repatriates' luggage for search and storage before the voyage; the four of them, reaching the head of that line, being ordered by FBI agents to make hasty goodbyes; Gerhard and Kurt, hugging each other so tightly one of them was sure to break.

In that same still photo, her sons in half the frame, she could see herself clinging to Otto, pressing into the safe little valley of his breastbone, where her cheek just fit. She could look upon that invisible photograph and see Otto folding around her like a mountain cleaving to its own center—but she could not feel his heat, or hear his heart, or smell his particular scent of juniper bark, fallen oak leaves, and spring wheat. For six days, she had been trying to conjure those living, breathing senses—but they had been consumed by the shouting guards, the siren, the scorched dust, the hot tar huts of Crystal City.

For those six days, Otto and Kurt were locked up with the other repatriates in buildings no more than a quarter mile outside the fence—but for all she could see them or even feel their presence, they might already have been on a ship in the middle of the ocean. She had known they were to be loaded onto a bus in the small hours of yesterday morning, long before the first siren, and she had believed she would wake at that moment, that she would open the door and stand in the road, her body turned toward where they were kept, and feel them being pulled away. But she had not.

In the two weeks between the notice and the leaving, the Austs' hours had been full of talk. Otto and Nina told stories from their childhoods in Koblenz, and of their crossing to America; the early months on Franz's farm; the opening day of the restaurant, which had been empty of customers until they went to all nearby stores and offices that were closing for the night to invite the employees as their dinner guests. Kurt shared stories the farmers at Fort Lincoln had told him—stories of Germany in the 1880s, and decades further back, to their parents' and grandparents' youth; stories of their first glimpse of America, then stories of clearing the land, finding a wife and having children, telling him that even after twenty, thirty, forty hard years, they had not yet learned the full range of capricious American weather. Gerhard called himself the Great Spider Hunter and made them laugh over his first clumsy efforts to trap black widows that heavy rain had sent paddling in ditches. He spoke warmly of the imprisoned German doctor who made the antivenin, telling of their long talks which, he could see now, had been valuable medical lessons to help him understand how his body was working to heal itself. Otto recalled as much as he could of what Egon Merkel had told him about life in Wheatland, Wyoming, especially proud when he remembered the name of the childless couple—Talbot—who had sold their farm to open a feed store, which had become the social center of the town.

They never talked about music, and they never talked about Bess or Hugh, cutting wide arcs around the twelve years they would all have counted their happiest.

Despite all this talking, Nina found those hours, too, had fixed in her mind as still photographs—widened eyes here, a pensive look there, a smirk, a laugh, a loving smile—each captioned with the story being told.

The only words she still heard, as if they were perpetually being sung softly into her ear, were Otto's—said to her when she had finally stopped weeping and raging at him, demanding to know what had driven him to put his name on the repatriation list without hers, why he had done it without asking or telling, why he had left her to learn the truth when it was too late to change it.

They were outside, in the shadow of the tower that threatened the little house. Otto had pulled her out the back door to keep the worst of their argument from Kurt and Gerhard. He stroked the last tears from her cheeks and took her hands in his.

"Our work is not yet finished," he said. "The worlds our sons must go into now are strange and dangerous. We cannot leave them to find their way alone. So you must go with one; I, the other. And when we have helped to set their feet firmly on new ground—when they are steady and we know their legs are strong enough to carry them forward—then you and I will find each other again. Perhaps in America. Perhaps in Germany. Perhaps in still another new land. But for now, we must give ourselves to our sons."

Though she and Gerhard were leaving this afternoon, they had not yet packed. There wasn't much. The larger bags had gone with Otto and Kurt. Nina had kept back one suitcase, which she and Gerhard could easily share if they carried their coats. They'd spread their essential papers on the table—Gerhard's release, the rescindment of Nina's voluntary internment, their identity cards, and their train tickets to Wheatland, Wyoming, with a stopover in Newman, where they would stay the night in the little room behind Mr. Griffin's office, collect their meager treasures from his safe, and do their inadequate best to thank him for his dogged generosity and faith.

There was no one else to meet in Newman, so a day would be enough. Without waiting to sell either the house or the business, the Beales had gone to Fort Wayne. Iris couldn't bear to see the streets Hugh and Gerhard had loved to walk.

Gerhard had gone to the post office to make one last check for mail, hoping another misrouted letter from Hugh would turn up, like the one that had come in December, a St. Nikolas Day blessing.

Nina carried the broom to the bedroom and swept the suitcase for scorpions, tipping it over and scooting it along the floor in case one might be clinging to the bottom. Satisfied, she grasped the handle and carried the case to Gerhard's room. He had already laid out on his bed the few things he wanted to take: his underclothes, two shirts, two pairs of trousers—all clean, none of them worth keeping, but all he had. There was a bundle of Hugh's letters—the ones Otto had saved—tied with string, and, in a box, the fragments of torn letters she and Kurt had collected from the floor. His notebook was there, too, with the poems. She had been afraid he wouldn't want them, the letters or the poems—afraid he would believe now that he wouldn't want them ever. She put them in the case first, followed by Hugh's banner, now stitched with a gold star. Liese had cut it from the lining of a sequined evening purse that she, in anxious haste, had tossed into her bag the day she was arrested. In the days when Nina waited in the hospital, like Mrs. Kimura before her, Liese had come to give her the star—perfectly cut, its edges already finished—saying, "That silly purse has finally come to some good."

After the letters, the notebook, and the banner, she placed Gerhard's clothes, then her own, and finally the Kimuras' exquisite goldfinch, spreading its magnificent black-bordered wings in flight. The packing was done.

She heard the front door and carried out the suitcase to set it by the table. Gerhard was there, leaning hard on his cane, sweatier and dustier than would be comfortable for him on the long journey to Newman, but there wasn't time to wash and dry what he was wearing. The patch covering the burn scar was beginning to come loose, so Nina said, "I've left the fresh bandages in the washroom. You can change the dressing now and put a few extra in my handbag. I don't know if we will be allowed our suitcase inside the train."

He held out an envelope. "It's from Wyoming. Addressed to *Vati*."

Nina took the letter, opened it. "Egon Merkel is dead." She handed the letter to Gerhard. "It is his daughter who writes." She moved to the table and looked at their train tickets. "I'm grateful your father does not know."

Gerhard came to stand beside her, placing the letter on the table. "She says we're still welcome—that we can stay at the farm until it's sold, or come on to Casper instead. Her husband's willing to help us find jobs."

"They are very kind," Nina said. "It is a confusion to think of how people we had known for many years, and thought our friends, could turn away so easily, when strangers offer so much."

"Should we go? We can send a telegram when we stop. Maybe even make a call."

"We can talk about it while we travel. Perhaps it would help to have Mr. Griffin's opinion."

At the gatehouse, they had to sign a paper swearing they would never speak or write to anyone about Crystal City or any other internment camp or detention facility where they had been held. If that guard could have reached into their skulls to scrub their minds, Nina thought, he would have done it. On the other side of the fence, another guard searched their suitcase, pushing things around with little interest until he found the notebook. He held it tightly, turning its pages slowly enough to read. Quickly, Nina said, "They are poems my son, Gerhard, has written—about my third son." She reached into the suitcase and pulled out the banner. "Killed in the war."

The guard looked at the banner for a moment, then said loudly enough for other guards to hear, "This is fine," and casually tossed the notebook back into the case.

Because they were the only two leaving Crystal City, they were driven to the train station in a jeep. On the first train, the other passengers were locals who seemed to realize instantly she and Gerhard were from the camp, so they kept their distance. Most of them got off in San Antonio, and others, including several soldiers, got on, but they too sat as far away as possible, occasionally eyeing her and Gerhard from beneath hat brims or over hands cupped around cigarette lighters. Perhaps the others recognized in them some kind of prisoners' taint, besides their shabby clothes. Or maybe they were disturbed by the nineteen-year old boy with the bandaged face who hobbled down the aisle but didn't wear a uniform.

Nina could think of little but the decision before them—whether to go on to Wyoming, or to study the map in the Newman train station until they chose some other place. A place chosen because they liked the name, or because they thought it might be a city large enough to get lost in. She suspected the same was true of Gerhard. They didn't talk about it. Gerhard slept, or seemed to sleep, much of the time. Though he never complained, Nina knew that all the walking and standing in the heat before they left Crystal City, the hard bumping in the jeep, more standing on the station platform, and the constant jostling of the train had deepened the ache in his just-knitted bones. From time to time, she saw his fingers twitch, and once or twice he raised his hand toward the bandage, but he had trained himself, even in his sleep, not to scratch at the forming scar. In time, the doctor in Crystal City had said, a surgeon might be able to modify the scar, blurring its edges, making it appear to be a birthmark.

They reached Newman at 10:15 a.m.—right on time, the conductor crowed—two and a half days since they had left behind the miserable hut, the towers, the fence, the Nazis, and a few good friends. It was raining—a familiar February storm, with rain that was heavy and cold, but carried in on warm winds that teased of spring. Nina and Gerhard stood, but none of the other passengers getting off showed any sign of giving way to the crippled boy and his mother, so they waited, brushing wrinkles from their clothes and helping each other into their coats.

Nina went first, unsure if there would be a porter to help Gerhard down the steps, but there was. The man's tipped hat—his "Let me help you there, son. Hold on to me, now"—were the first kindnesses they'd had since they bid the Cappelmanns goodbye. Nina reached for the clasp on her purse, flushing when she remembered she had nothing to give the porter, but he waved his hand. "No, no. Pleasure, ma'am. Pleasure to help the young man." He stayed with them until they reached the covered part of the platform, carrying their bag with one hand while keeping the other lightly on Gerhard's arm, ready to catch him if he stumbled.

"Thank you," Nina said. "Thank you." Tears rose in her eyes as she recalled the police officer who, long ago, had taken her arm so gently and put her on the bus back to her family. "Thank you," she said again, as if the porter had somehow become all the strangers who had been briefly, but so importantly, kind.

He tipped his hat and disappeared in the crowd.

Nina took Gerhard's arm. "I had forgotten you cannot recognize Mr. Griffin, but he will looking for us." She leaned right and left, trying to see past the crowd. She stood on her toes, stretching her neck as high as she could. "I think he is there," she said, pointing, but someone walked into her view.

A moment later, she had another glimpse. Though it was hard to see through the gray rain, thick as fog, she was almost sure that was Mr. Griffin, near the soldiers huddling around the coffee kiosk. He stood under the awning in front of a life-sized poster of Uncle Sam. She squinted. Beside Mr. Griffin, there was a slender, white-haired man, and beside him, a small woman, her arm linked in his. They were all looking about at the people getting off the train.

"Is it Iris?" Nina said.

Though her words could not have been heard across the station, the little woman turned her face, as if to Nina's voice. The woman's arm shot up. She waved.

It *was* Iris.

Nina waved back, and the men waved, too—Everett and Mr. Griffin. Gerhard lifted his cane and swirled it in the air.

"Nina!" she could hear someone calling. "*Tante* Nina!"

A bolt of blue shot from the huddle at the kiosk. A girl in a bright blue coat, cornflower blue.

Bess. Running. Her arms open.

HISTORICAL CONTEXT FOR
IN OUR MIDST

ACCORDING TO EARL G. HARRISON, former Commissioner of the Immigration and Naturalization Service, more than 1,000 civilians, nearly 90% of them German-Americans, had been arrested by the FBI in thirty-five states before the end of the day on December 8, 1941. In testimony before a U.S. Senate committee in 1981, former Assistant Attorney General James Rowe, Jr., said, "We picked up right after Pearl Harbor about 60,000 enemy aliens—I think mostly German, a large number of Italians and a large number of Japanese."

Such an extensive and rapid roundup was possible because FBI Director J. Edgar Hoover, had, for as long as five years, been preparing a secret Custodial Detention Index (CDI), cataloging the names, addresses, professions, and social affiliations of thousands of people of German, Italian, and Japanese ancestry residing in the United States. In a memo regarding the CDI, dated December 2, 1939, Hoover described the index as a list of people "to be apprehended and interned immediately upon the outbreak of hostilities." Thousands more were included in the CDI as persons "who should be watched carefully."

Scholars disagree on how much President Franklin D. Roosevelt knew about Hoover's index—or how long he might have known it—but most agree on its illegality. Regardless of the extent of Roosevelt's prior knowledge, he authorized the FBI to arrest hundreds from the CDI rolls in the hours following the attack on Pearl Harbor, without waiting even to sign a Presidential Proclamation that would allow official warrants of arrest to be issued from the attorney general's office.

In his memoir, *In Brief Authority*, former Attorney General Francis Biddle writes that on December 8, 1941, he went to the White House to present Roosevelt with drafts of Presidential Proclamations 2526 and 2527, which would authorize the arrest of German and Italian aliens "deemed dangerous to the security of the United States"—a process Biddle says he did not know Hoover had already begun. According to Biddle, President Roosevelt, after signing the proclamations, asked about the number of German and Italian aliens living in the United States, with a view toward interning them all. When Biddle indicated such a plan would encompass millions of people, the president told him, "I don't care so much about the Italians. They're a lot of opera singers. But the Germans are different; they may be dangerous."

Originally, the CDI catalogued German-Americans whose names appeared on membership rolls for organizations known to be in sympathy with Nazis, such as the German-American Bund, but it quickly expanded to include people who participated in German social organizations, who subscribed to German-language newspapers, or who maintained ties with relatives in Germany. Hearsay evidence of disloyalty to America, its principles, or its government was also included in individuals' files—evidence the FBI rarely made reasonable effort to corroborate. According to scholar Arnold Krammer in *Undue Process: The Untold Story of America's German Alien Internees*, a memo written by J. Edgar Hoover, dated August 21, 1940, indicates the FBI "fielded some 78,000 accusations" related to the CDI "in 1939 alone."

Between December 7, 1941 and late 1944, tens of thousands of German-Americans were detained by the FBI and held for questioning for several hours up to several months. Many were released without facing hearing boards, only to be picked up again weeks or months later for further questioning. Those who were taken from detention facilities to stand before one of more than ninety hastily organized three-member hearing boards were not permitted legal counsel. While the guidelines established for the hearing boards allowed detainees to bring a witness to speak on their behalf, very few knew of this right before their hearings, and many never knew it at all.

More than 11,000 German-Americans were ordered interned by the Attorney General following these hearings. When voluntary internees—spouses and minor children—are added, that number nearly doubles. Under pressure from the United States government, more than 8000 people of German descent residing in Latin American countries were arrested—men, women, and children. Half that number were shipped, against their will, to the United States (along with Latin Americans of Japanese and Italian descent), stripped of their passports, and charged with illegal entry into the United States, making them subject to deportation. Because most internees passed through as many as four or five detention facilities and internment camps, absolute numbers have not yet been settled, and likely never will be, but scholarly estimates of the total number of people of German descent imprisoned as enemy aliens in U.S. internment camps ranges from 25,000 to 31,000. Some remained in U.S. internment facilities as late as 1948, with parole for many stretching well into the 1950s.

Not a single German internee was ever convicted of a war-related crime against the United States.

Upon being released from the camps, those internees permitted to remain in the United States were required to sign an oath of secrecy, which threatened them with deportation if they ever spoke of their arrest or internment. Camp employees were also expected to sign similar oaths, which accounts for how this episode in American history was so quickly and almost entirely erased from living memory.

My research for *In Our Midst*—which began at least a year before I had written a word and continued up to the day I wrote the final page—led me to hundreds of books, articles, and websites, ranging from general histories of World War II to German literature and music, but the sources related specifically to the interment of German-Americans that I relied upon most heavily and consulted most often are as follows:

- The Freedom of Information Times website, www.foitimes.com

- The German American Internee Coalition website, http://gaic. info/

- *Fear Itself: Inside the FBI Roundup of German Americans During World War II* by Stephen Fox, 2005. (Originally published as *America's Invisible Gulag: A Biography of German-American Internment & Exclusion in World War II*, Stephen Fox, 2000.)

- *Undue Process: The Untold Story of America's German Alien Internees*, by Arnold Krammer, 1997.

- *Enemies: World War II Alien Internment*, by John Christgau, 1985, republished with a new afterword by the author, 2009.

- *Schools Behind Barbed Wire: The Untold Story of Wartime Internment and the Children of Arrested Enemy Aliens*, by Karen L. Riley, 2002.